Jessica Gilmore's magical duet

The Life Swap

Embracing a new life...discovering a new love!

Meet Maddison Carter, New York socialite,
and Hope McKenzie, English homebody.
These two women couldn't be more different,
but for six months they will be swapping jobs,
swapping homes and swapping lives!
And in doing so they'll meet two men
who will turn their worlds upside down...

Read Maddison's story in

In the Boss's Castle

and Hope's story in

Unveiling the Bridesmaid

Both available now!

UNVEILING THE BRIDESMAID

BY
JESSICA GILMORE

&MILLS
BOON

First Published in Great Britain 2016
By Mills & Boon, an imprint of HarperCollins*Publishers*
1 London Bridge Street, London, SE1 9GF

© 2016 Jessica Gilmore

ISBN: 978-0-263-92016-1

23-0916

Our policy is to use papers that are natural, renewable and recyclable products and made from wood grown in sustainable forests. The logging and manufacturing processes conform to the legal environmental regulations of the country of origin.

Printed and bound in Spain
by CPI, Barcelona

A former au pair, bookseller, marketing manager and seafront trader, **Jessica Gilmore** now works for an environmental charity in York, England. Married with one daughter, one fluffy dog and two dog-loathing cats, she spends her time avoiding housework and can usually be found with her nose in a book. Jessica writes emotional romance with a hint of humour, a splash of sunshine and a great deal of delicious food—and equally delicious heroes!

For Kristy, roommate, cocktail enabler
and partner in crime extraordinaire.

Here's to many more RWA conferences—
and another evening in the rum bar some day. xxx

CHAPTER ONE

BEEP, BEEP, *BEEEEEP*.

Hope McKenzie muttered and rolled over, reaching out blindly to mute her alarm, her hand scrabbling to find the 'off' button, the 'pause' button, the *'Please make it stop right now'* button. Only... Hang on a second... She didn't *have* an alarm clock here in New York; she used her phone on the rare occasions when the sun, traffic and humidity didn't wake her first. So what was that noise? And why wouldn't it *stop*?

Beeeeeep.

Whatever it was, it was getting more and more insistent, and louder by the second. Hope pushed herself up, every drowsy limb fighting back as she swung her legs over the metal frame of the narrow daybed and staggered to her feet, glancing at the watch on her wrist. Five-thirty a.m. She blinked, the small room swimming into dim focus, still grey with predawn stillness, the gloom broken only by the glow of the street light, a full floor below her sole window.

Beeeeeep.

It wasn't a fire alarm or a smoke alarm. There were no footsteps pounding down the stairs of the apartment building, no sirens screeching outside, just the high insistent beep coming from the small round table in the window bay. No, coming from her still-open laptop on the small round table in the window bay.

'What the...?' Hope stumbled the few short steps to the table and turned the laptop around to face her. The screen blared into life, bright colour dazzling her still-half-closed eyes, letters jumbling together as she blinked again, rubbing her eyes with one sleepy hand until the words swam into focus.

Faith calling. Accept?

Faith? At this time? Was she in trouble? Hurt? Wait, where was she? Had she left Europe yet? Maybe she'd been framed for drug smuggling? Maybe she had been robbed and lost all her money? Why had Hope left her to travel alone? Why had she swanned off to New York for six months while her baby sister was out there by herself alone and vulnerable? With a trembling hand Hope pressed the enter key to accept the call, pushing her hair out of her eyes, scanning the screen anxiously and pulling up the low neckline of the old, once-white vest top she slept in.

'Faith?' Hope took a deep breath, relief replacing the blind panic of the last few seconds as her sister's tanned, happy face filled the screen. 'Is everything okay?'

'Everything is fab! Oh, did I wake you? Hang on, did I get the time wrong? I thought it would be evening in New York.'

'No, it's morning, we're behind not ahead. But don't worry about that,' she added as her sister's face fell. 'It's lovely to hear from you, to *see* you. Where are you?' Still in Europe somewhere, she thought, doing a quick date calculation. Despite Faith's promises to call and write often, contact with her little sister had been limited since Faith had boarded the Eurostar, just over three months ago, to start her grand tour. She was spending the summer Interrailing around Europe before flying to Australia to begin the global part of her adventures but, unlike her big sister, Faith preferred to go with the flow rather than follow a meticulously thought-out plan. Which meant she could be anywhere.

Hope grinned at her sister, the early hour forgotten. It was okay that Faith had been a little quiet; she was busy exploring and having fun. The last thing she wanted to do was call her fusspot of a big sister who would only nag her about budgets and eating well.

'I'm in Prague.' Faith pulled back from the screen a little to show the room—and view—behind her. She was in some kind of loft, sitting in front of French windows, which led out to a stone balcony. Hope could just make out what must be dazzling views of the river and castle behind. Wow, youth hostels were a lot fancier than she had imagined.

'I thought you arrived in Prague six weeks ago?' Faith hadn't intended spending more than a few days in any one place and Hope was pretty sure her sister had texted her from Prague at the beginning of July.

'I did. I never left. Oh, Hope, it's like a fairy tale here. You would love it.'

'I'm sure I would.' Not that she had been to Prague—or to Paris or to Barcelona or Copenhagen or Rome or any of the other European cities so tantalisingly in reach of London. Their parents had been fans of the great British seaside holiday, rain and all—and since their deaths there had been little money for any kind of holiday. 'But why did you stay in Prague? I thought you wanted to see everything, go everywhere!'

'I did but…well…oh, Hope. I met someone. Someone wonderful and…' Hope peered at the computer screen. Was Faith blushing? Her sister's eyes were soft and her skin glowing in a way that owed nothing to the laptop's HD screen. 'I want you to be happy for me, okay? Because I am. Blissfully. Hope, I'm getting married!'

'Married?' She couldn't be hearing correctly. Her little sister was only nineteen. She hadn't been to university yet, hadn't finished travelling. Heck, she'd barely *started* travelling! More to the point Faith still couldn't handle her own bills, change a fuse or cook anything more complicated than pasta and pesto—and she burnt that two times out of three. How could such a child be getting married? She could only think of one question. 'Who to?'

Her sister didn't answer, turning her head as Hope heard a door bang off-screen. 'Hunter! I got the times wrong. It's still early morning in New York.'

'I know it is, honey. It's not even dawn yet. Did you wake your sister?'

'Oh, she doesn't mind. Come and say hi to her. Hope, this is Hunter, my fiancé.' The pride in Faith's voice, the sweetness in her eyes as she raised them to the tall figure who came to stand next to her, made Hope's throat swell. Her sister had been deprived of a real family at such a young age. No wonder she wanted to strike out and find one of her own. Hope had done her best but she was all too aware what a poor substitute she had been, younger than Faith was now when she took over the reins. Maybe this boy could offer the stability and opportunities she had tried so hard to provide.

And if he couldn't she would be there, making sure he stepped up. She forced a smile, hoping her fierce thoughts weren't showing on her face. 'Hi, Hunter.'

'Hi, it's great to meet you at last. I've heard so much about you.' She summed him up quickly. American. Blond, blue-eyed, clean-cut with an engaging smile. Young. Not quite as young as Faith but barely into his twenties.

'So, how did you two meet?' Hope forced back the words she wanted to say. *Married? You barely know each other! You're just children!* She had promised herself nine years ago she would do whatever it took to make sure Faith was happy—and she had never seen her sister look happier.

'Hunter's an artist.' Pride laced every one of Faith's words. 'He was doing portraits on the Charles Bridge and when I walked past he offered to draw me for free.'

'You had the most beautiful face I'd ever seen,' Hunter said. 'How could I charge you when all I wanted to do was look at you?'

'So I insisted on buying him a drink as a thank you and that was that.' Faith's dark eyes were dreamy, a soft smile playing on her lips. 'Within an hour I knew. We've been inseparable ever since.'

A street artist. Hope's heart sank. However talented he was, that didn't sound too promising as far as setting up a home was concerned and Faith had no career or any idea what she wanted to do after this year was up. She forced another smile. 'How romantic. I can't wait to see the portrait—and meet Hunter in person rather than through a screen.'

'You will! In just over two weeks. That's when we're getting married! In New York and…' Faith adopted a pleading expression Hope knew only too well. 'I was really hoping you'd take care of some of the details for me.'

Hope froze. She knew what 'taking care of some of the details' meant in Faith speak. It meant do everything. And usually she did, happily. Only this was her first time away from her responsibilities in nine years. It was meant to be Hope Getting A Life Time.

Admittedly she hadn't actually got very far yet. Oh, she'd rushed out her first week here in New York and splashed out on a new wardrobe full of bright and striking clothes, had her hair cut and styled. But she couldn't rid herself of feeling like the same old boring Hope. Still, there were three months of her job swap left. She still had every opportunity to do something new and exciting. She just needed to get started.

'Details?' she said cautiously.

'Hunter and I want a small, intimate wedding in New York—just close family and a few friends. His mother will host a big reception party a couple of days later and Hunter says she'll go all out so I think the wedding day should be very simple. Just the ceremony, dinner and maybe some entertainment? You can handle that, can't you? I won't be there until a couple of days before the wedding. Hunter hasn't finished his course and I don't want to leave him alone. Besides, you are so good at organising you'll do a much better job than I ever could. You make everything special.'

Hope's heart softened at the last sentence; she'd

worked so hard to give Faith a perfect childhood. 'Faith, honey, I'm more than happy to help but why so very soon? Why not have it later on and plan it yourself? Travel first, like you arranged.' *Give yourself more time to get to know each other*, she added silently.

'Because we love each other and want to be together as soon as possible. I'm still going travelling—only with Hunter on our honeymoon. Australia and Bali and New Zealand and Thailand. It's going to be the longest and most romantic honeymoon ever. Thank you, Hope, I knew I could rely on you. I'm going to send you some ideas, okay? My measurements for dresses, flowers, colours, you know the kind of thing. But you know my taste. I know whatever you pick will be perfect.'

'Great. That will be really good.' Hope tried to keep her voice enthusiastic but inside she was panicking. How on earth could she work the twelve-hour days her whole office took for granted and plan a wedding in just two weeks? 'Thing is I do have to work, you know, sweetie. My time is limited and I still don't know New York all that well. Are you sure I'm the best person for the job?' She knew the route between her apartment and the office. She knew a nice walk around Central Park. She knew her favourite bookstore and where to buy the perfect coffee. She wasn't sure any of that would be much use in this situation.

Faith didn't seem to notice any of her sister's subtext, ploughing on in breathless excitement. 'There's no budget, Hope, whatever you think is most suitable. Don't worry how much it costs.'

Hope swallowed. 'No budget?' Although she and Faith had never been poor exactly, money had been tight for years. Her parents had been reasonably well insured and the mortgage on their Victorian terrace in north London had been paid off after they died, but after that tax had swallowed up most of their inheritance. She had had to raise Faith on her wages—and at eighteen with little work experience those wages had been pretty meagre. 'Faith, I know that you have your nest egg from Mum and Dad but I don't think it'll stretch to an extravagant wedding.' Was Faith expecting Hope to contribute? She would love to buy her sister her wedding dress, but the words 'no budget' sent chills down her spine.

'Oh, Faith doesn't need to touch her money—I'm taking care of everything,' Hunter said, reappearing behind Faith. 'I've arranged for a credit card to be sent to you.' Hope's eyes flew open at this casual sentence. 'For expenses and deposits and things. Anything you need.'

'For anything I need?' Hope repeated unable to take the words in. 'But…'

'Only the best,' Hunter continued as if she hadn't spoken. 'Anyone gives you any trouble just mention my name—or my mother's, Misty Carlyle. They should fall into line pretty quickly.'

'Mention your name. Okay.' She seemed incapable of doing anything other than parroting his words but the whole situation had just jumped from bizarre to surreal. How did a street artist in Prague have the power to send credit cards for a budget-free wedding shopping spree across the ocean without batting an eyelid? Just who was Faith marrying? A Kennedy?

'Actually, the best person to speak to will be my stepbrother Gael. Gael O'Connor. He only lives a few blocks away from you and he knows everyone. Here,

I'll email you the address and his number and let him know to expect you.' He beamed as if it was all sorted. For Faith and him it was, she supposed. They could carry on being in love in their gorgeous attic room staring out at the medieval castle while Hope battled New York humidity to organise them the perfect wedding.

Well, she would, with the help of Hunter's unexpected largesse. She would make it perfect for her sister if it killed her. Only she wasn't going to do it alone. She was all for equality and there was nothing to say wedding planning had to be the sole preserve of the bride's family after all. As soon as it was a respectable hour she would visit Mr Gael O'Connor and enlist his help. Or press-gang him. She really didn't mind which it was, as long as Faith ended up with the wedding of her dreams.

Gael O'Connor glanced at his watch and tried not to sigh. Sighing hadn't helped last time he checked, nor had pacing, nor had swearing. But when you hired a professional you expected professional behaviour. Not tardiness. Not an entire twenty minutes' worth of tardiness.

He swivelled round to stare out of the floor-to-ceiling windows that lined one whole side of his studio. Usually looking out over Manhattan soothed him or inspired him, whatever he needed. Reminded him that he had earned this view, this space. Reminded him that he mattered. But today all it told him was that he was taking a huge gamble with his career and his reputation.

Twenty-five minutes late. He had to keep busy, not waste another second. Turning, he assessed once again the way the summer morning light fell on the red velvet chaise longue so carefully positioned in the middle of the room, the only piece of furniture in the large studio. His bed and clothes were up on the mezzanine, the kitchen and bathroom were tucked away behind a discreet door at the end of the apartment. He liked to keep this main space clutter-free. He needed to be able to concentrate.

Only right now there was nothing to concentrate on except the seconds ticking away.

Gael resumed pacing. Five minutes, he would give her five more minutes and if she hadn't arrived by then he would make sure she never worked in this city again. Hang on. Was that the buzzer? It had never been more welcome. He crossed the room swiftly. 'Yes?'

'There's a young lady to see you, sir. Name of...'

'Send her up.' At last. Gael walked back over to the windows and breathed in the view: the skyscrapers dominating the iconic skyline, the new, glittering towers shooting up around him as New York indulged in a frenzied orgy of building, the reassuring permanence of the old, traditional Upper East Side blocks maintaining their dignified stance on the other side of his tree-lined street. He shifted from foot to foot. He needed to use this restless energy while it coursed through him—not waste it in frustration.

The creak of the elevator alerted him to his visitor's imminent arrival. No lobby, not when you had the penthouse; the elevator opened right into the studio.

And he did have the penthouse. Not as a gift, not as a family heirloom but because he had worked for it and bought it. Not one of his friends would ever understand the freedom that gave him.

The doors opened with an audible swish and heels

tapped tentatively onto the wooden floor. 'Er…hello?' English. He hadn't expected that. Not that he cared what she sounded like; he wasn't interested in having a conversation with her.

'You're late.' Gael didn't bother turning round. Usually he made time to greet the women, put them at their ease before they got started but he was too impatient for the niceties today. 'There's a robe on the chaise. You can change in the bathroom.'

'Excuse me?'

'The bathroom.' He nodded to the end of the room. 'There's a hanger for your clothes. Go and strip. You can keep the robe on until I've positioned you properly if you prefer.' Some did, others were quite happy to wander nude from the bathroom across the floor to the chaise. He didn't mind either way.

'My clothes? You want me to take them off?'

'Well, yes. That's why you're here, isn't it?'

He moved around to face her at the exact same moment she let out a scandalised-sounding, 'No! Of course not. Why would you think that?'

Who on earth was this? Dark-haired, dark-eyed, petite with a look of outraged horror. She was pretty enough, beautiful even—if you liked the 'big dark eyes in a pale face' look. But he was expecting an Amazonian redhead with a knowing smile and whatever and whoever this girl was she certainly wasn't that.

'Because I was expecting someone who was supposed to be doing exactly that,' Gael said drily. 'But you are not what I ordered. Too short for a start, although you do have an interesting mouth.'

'Ordered?' Her cheeks reddened as the outrage visibly ratcheted up several notches. 'I'm sorry that I'm not your takeout from Call Girls Are Us but I think you should check before you start asking complete strangers to strip.'

'I'm not the one who has gatecrashed their way past the doorman. Who are you? Did Sonia send you?'

'Sonia? I don't know any Sonia. There's clearly been some kind of mix-up. You *are* Gael O'Connor, aren't you?' She sounded doubtful, taking a cautious step back as if he might pounce any second.

He ignored her question. 'If you don't know Sonia then why are you here?'

She took a deep breath. 'My sister is getting married and...'

'Great. Congratulations. Look, I don't do weddings. I don't care how much you offer. Now, I'm more than a little busy so if you'll excuse me I have to make a call. I'm sure you can find your own way out. You seemed to have no trouble finding your way in.'

The dark-haired woman stared at him, incredulity all over her face as he pulled his phone out of his pocket. Ignoring his unwanted visitor, Gael scrolled through what felt like an endless stream of emails, notifications and alerts. His mouth compressed. Nothing from the agency. With a huff of impatience he found their name and pressed call. They had better have a good explanation. The phone rang once, twice—he tapped his foot with impatient rhythm—three times before a voice sang out, 'Unique Models, how may I help?'

'Gael O'Connor here. It's now...' He glanced up at the digital clock on the otherwise stark grey walls. 'It's nine a.m. and the model I booked for eight-thirty has yet to show up.'

'Gael, lovely to speak to you. I am so sorry, I meant to call you before but I literally haven't had time. It's been crazy, you wouldn't believe.'

'Try me.'

'Sonia was booked yesterday for a huge ad campaign—only it was a last-minute replacement so she had to literally pack and fly. I saw her onto the plane myself last night. International perfume ad, what an opportunity. Especially for a model who is...' the booker's voice lowered conspiratorially '...outsize. So we are going to have to reschedule your booking I am so sorry. Or could I send someone else? We have some lovely redheads if that's what you require or was it the curvier figure you were looking for?'

With some difficulty Gael managed not to swear. Send someone else? An image of the missing Sonia flashed through his mind: the knowing expression in her green catlike eyes, the perfect amount of confident come-hitherness he needed for the centrepiece of his first solo exhibition. 'No. I can't simply replace her, nor can I rebook. I've put the time aside right now.'

After all, the exhibition *was* in just five weeks.

'Sonia will be back in just a couple of days. All I can do is apologise for the delay but...'

It would help, he thought bitterly, if the booker sounded even remotely sorry. She would be—he would never use a Unique model again. He hung up on her bored pretence for an apology. Once Sonia was back she would be of no use to him. Unlike his photographs Gael didn't want the subjects of his paintings to be known faces. Their anonymity was part of the point. He spent too much time documenting the bright and the beautiful. For this he wanted real and unknown.

His hand curled into a fist as he faced the bitter facts. He still had to paint the most important piece for his very first exhibition and he had no model lined up. He mentally ran through his contacts but no one obvious came to mind. Most of the models he knew were angular, perfect for photography, utterly useless for this.

Damn.

'Mr O'Connor.'

Palming his phone, Gael directed a frustrated glance over at his unwanted intruder. 'I thought you'd left,' he said curtly. She was standing stiffly by the elevator, leaning towards it as if she longed to flee—although nobody was stopping her, quite the contrary. Gael allowed his gaze to travel down her, assessing her suitability. Before he had only looked at what she lacked compared to the model he was expecting to see; she was much shorter, slight without the dramatic curves, ice to Sonia's fire. She wore her bright clothing like a costume, her dark hair waving neatly around her shoulders like a cloak. Her eyes were huge and dark but the wariness in them seemed engrained.

She took another step back. 'Do you mind?'

'It is my studio…' he drawled. That was better; indignation brought some more colour into her cheeks, red into her lips.

'I am not some painting that you can just look at in that way. As if…as if…' She faltered.

But he knew exactly what she had been going to say and finished off her sentence. 'As if you were naked.'

He had lit the fuse and she didn't disappoint; her eyes filled with fire, her cheeks now dusky pink. She would make a very different centrepiece from the one he had envisioned but he could work with those eyes, with that innocent sensuality, with the curve of her full mouth.

He nodded at her. 'Come over here. I want to show you something.'

Gael didn't wait to see if she would follow; he knew that she would. He strode to the end of the studio and turned over the four unframed canvases leaning against the brick wall. There would be twenty pictures in total. Ten had been framed and were stored at the gallery, another five were with the framers. These four, the most recent, were waiting their turn.

He heard a sharp intake of breath from close behind him. He took a step back to stand beside her and looked at the paintings, trying to look at them with fresh eyes, to see what she saw even though he knew each and every brush stroke intimately.

'Why are all the women lying in the same position?'

Gael glanced over at the red chaise standing alone in the middle of the studio, knowing her eyes had followed his, that she too could see each of the women lying supine, their hair pulled back, clad only in jewellery, their faces challenging, confident, aware and revelling in their own sensual power.

'Do you know *Olympia*?'

Her forehead creased. 'Home of the Greek gods?'

'No, it's a painting by Manet.'

She shook her head. 'I don't think so.'

'It was reviled at the time. The model posed naked, in the same position as each of these,' he waved a hand at his canvases, at the acres of flesh: pink, cream, coffee, ebony. 'What shocked nineteenth-century France wasn't her nudity, it was her sexuality. She wasn't some kind of goddess, she was portraying a prostitute. Nudes at that time were soft, allegorical, not real sensual beings. *Olympia* changed all that. I have one more painting to produce before my exhibition begins in just over a month.' His mouth twisted at the thought. 'But as you must have heard my model has gone AWOL and I can't afford to lose any more time. I want you to pose for me. Will you?'

Her eyes were huge, luminous with surprise and, he noticed uncomfortably, a lurking fear. 'Me? You want *me* to pose? For you? On that couch? Without my clothes? Absolutely not!'

CHAPTER TWO

HE WANTED HER to *what*? Hope stepped back and then again, eyeing Gael O'Connor nervously. But he lost interest the second she uttered her emphatic refusal, turning away from her with no attempt to persuade her. Hope could see her very presence fading from his mind as he began to scroll through his phone again, muttering names speculatively as he did so.

Maybe she should just go, try and arrange this wedding by herself. She looked around, eyes narrowing as she took on the vast if largely empty room, the huge windows, the high ceiling, the view... This much space, on the Upper East Side? Hope did some rapid calculations and came up with seven figures. At the very least. Her own studio would fit comfortably in one corner of the room and the occupant probably wouldn't even notice she was there. Hunter had said that his stepbrother could get her into all the right places and this address, this room, Gael's utter certainty that he commanded the world indicated that her brother-in-law-to-be hadn't been lying.

Hope cleared her throat but her voice still squeaked with nerves. 'Hi, I think we got off on the wrong foot. I'm Hope McKenzie and I'm here because your brother—stepbrother—is engaged to my sister.'

He didn't look up from his phone. 'Which one?'

'Which what?'

'Stepbrother. I have…' he paused, the blue eyes screwed up in thought '…five. Although two of those are technically half-brothers, I suppose, and too young to be engaged anyway.'

'Hunter. Hunter Carlyle. He met my sister, Faith, in Prague and…'

'Hunter isn't my stepbrother. He *was*,' Gael clarified. 'But his mother divorced my father a decade ago, which makes him nothing at all to me.'

'But he said…'

'He would, he clings to the idea of family. He's like his mother that way. It's almost sweet.'

Hope took a deep breath, feeling like Alice wrestling with Wonderland logic. 'As I said, he's engaged to my sister and I was wondering…'

'I wouldn't worry. I know he's young. How old is your sister?'

Was she ever going to say what she had come here to say? It had been a long time since she had felt so wrong-footed at every turn—although being asked to strip by a strange man at nine a.m. would wrong-foot anyone. 'Nineteen, but…'

He nodded. 'Starter marriages rarely last. There will be a prenup, of course, but don't worry, the Carlyles are very generous to their exes. Just ask my dad.' Bitterness ran through his voice like a swirl of the darkest chocolate.

'Starter marriages?' This was getting worse. Was

she going to be able to formulate a whole sentence any time soon?

He raised an eyebrow. 'That's why you're here, isn't it? To ask me to stop the wedding? I wouldn't worry. Hunter's a good kid and, like I said, the prenups are generous. Your sister will come out of this a wealthy woman.'

Hope's lips compressed. 'My sister is marrying Hunter because she loves him.' She pushed the part of her brain whispering that Faith had only known Hunter for six weeks ruthlessly aside. 'And I am sure he loves her.' Based on a two-minute conversation through a computer screen but she wasn't going to give Gael O'Connor the satisfaction of seeing her voice any doubts. 'They want to get married, here in New York, two weeks on Thursday and they asked me to organise the wedding.'

Gael's mouth pursed into a soundless whistle. 'I wonder what Misty will say to that. She prides herself on her hostessing skills.'

'I believe she is holding a party on Long Island shortly after. A small and intimate wedding, that's what Faith's asked for and that's what I am going to give her. But it's going to be the best small and intimate wedding any bride ever had. Hunter thought you would be able to help me but it's very clear that you are far too busy to get involved in anything as trivial as a starter marriage. I won't bother you any more. Good day.'

Head up, shoulders straight and she was going to walk right out of here. So she might not have Gael O'Connor's connections; she had a good head on her shoulders and determination. That should do it.

'Hope, wait.' There was a teasing note in his voice

that sent warning shivers through her. Hope was pretty sure that whatever he wanted she wasn't going to like it.

'Pose for me and I'll help you give your sister the perfect wedding. I can, you know,' he added as she gaped at him. 'My little black book…' he held up his phone '…is filled with everyone and anyone you need from designers to restaurateurs. You do this and your sister will have the wedding of her dreams. And that's a promise.' His gaze swept over her assessingly, that same lazy exploration that made her feel stripped to the skin. She shivered, her heart thumping madly as each nerve responded to his insolence.

Mad, bad, definitely dangerous to know. She was horribly out of her depth. 'I…look, this isn't something you can just throw at someone. It's a big deal.'

A small smile curved his mouth. It didn't reach his eyes; she had a sense it seldom did. 'Hope, life modelling is a perfectly respectable thing to do. Men and women of all ages and body shapes do it day in, day out.'

She cast a quick glance at the canvases still facing out, at the exposed flesh and the satisfied, confident gazes. 'But these aren't men and women of all ages and shapes,' she pointed out. 'They are all women and they are all beautiful, all sexy.'

'That's because of the theme of the show. If Olympia had been a middle-aged man then we wouldn't be having this conversation. It'll be quite intensive. I'll need a week or so of your time, first a few sketches and then the actual painting. The first session is the most important—I need to know that you're comfortable with the pose, with the jewellery you choose and its symbolism. The tricky bit is finding the right mood.

The other models have spent some time thinking about their past, about their sexuality and what it means to them; the original Olympia saw sex as business and that comes across in her portrait. She is in control of her body, what it offers.'

Which meant, she supposed, that he thought she could portray sexuality. Awareness quivered through her at the idea. Awareness of his height, of the lines of his mouth, the steeliness in his eyes. It was an attractive combination, the dark hair, such a dark chocolate it was almost black, and warm olive skin with the blue-grey eyes.

Eyes fastened solely on her. Hope swallowed. It had been a long time since anyone had intimated that they found her sexy. Attractive, useful, nice. But not sexy. It was a seductive idea. Hope stared at the red couch and tried to imagine it: her hair piled up, pulling at the nape of her neck, the coolness of a pendant heavy on her naked breast, the way the rubbed velvet would feel against the tender skin on her thighs and buttocks, against her back.

How it would feel to have that steely gaze directed intently on her, to have him focus on every hair, every dimple, every curve—Hope sucked in her stomach almost without realising it—every scar.

Hope's cheeks flamed. How could she even be having this conversation? She didn't wear a bikini, for goodness' sake, let alone nothing at all. If she could shower in her clothes she would. As for tapping into her sexuality…she swallowed painfully. How could you tap into something that didn't actually exist? Even if she had the time and the inclination to lie there exposed she didn't have the tools.

'You're talking to the wrong woman.' Her voice was cold and clipped, her arms crossed as if she could shield herself from his speculative sight. 'Even if I wanted to model for you—which I don't—I don't have the time. I have a job to do, a job which takes up twelve hours of every day and often my weekend as well. I have no idea how I am going to sort out a wedding in less than three weeks and still keep Brenda Masterson happy but, well, that's my problem. I will manage somehow. I don't need or want your help. Goodbye, Mr O'Connor. As you don't consider Hunter to be part of your family I doubt we'll meet again.'

Hope swivelled and turned, heading for the door, glad of the heels, glad of the well-cut, summery clothes and the extra confidence they gave her. She was new Hope now, new Hope in New York City. She had time to invest in her career, a little money to invest in herself and the way she looked. Any day now she would try her hand at salsa or Zumba or running, join a book club and go to interesting lectures. So she had missed out on being a young adult? It wasn't too late to become the person she once dreamed of being.

But first she would organise her sister's wedding. And not by taking off her clothes and posing for some artist no matter how much she liked the way his eyes dwelled on her. Eyes she could feel follow her as she crossed the room, and pushed the button to summon the lift. Eyes that seemed to strip her bare and see straight through the thin veneer of confidence she had plastered on.

If he did paint her she knew it wouldn't just be her body that would be bared for the world to see. It would be her soul as well. And that was a risk she would never be able to take.

'Did you say you work for Brenda Masterson?'

She paused. One minute he was dismissing her, the next making her an outrageous proposal—and now small talk? She turned and glared at him, hoping he took her impatient message on board. 'Yes, I work at DL Media. I'm in New York on a job swap as Brenda's assistant.' Brenda's very late assistant. She was probably focussing that famously icy glare right at Hope's vacant desk right this moment.

Gael kept her gaze as he pressed his phone to his ear, a mocking smile playing on his well-cut lips. 'Brenda? Is that you?'

What? He knew Brenda? He had said he knew everybody but she didn't think he meant her boss.

'Hi. It's Gael. Yes, I'm good, how about you? I've been having a think about that retrospective. Uh-huh. It's a good offer you made me but there's some work I need to do first, going through the old blogs, through the old photos.' He paused as Brenda spoke at some length, her words indiscernible to Hope.

She shifted from foot to foot, wishing she had worn less strappy heels in this heat—and that she had catlike hearing. This job was her chance to be noticed, to stop being Kit Buchanan's loyal and mousy assistant and to be someone with prospects and a real career—if Gael O'Connor messed this up for her she would knock him out with one of his own paintings...

'As it happens,' Gael continued smoothly, 'I have your assistant here. Yes, very cute. Love the accent.' He winked at Hope and she clenched her jaw. 'It would be great if you could spare her for a couple of weeks to help me with the archiving and labelling, maybe start to put together some copy. Yeah. Absolutely. You're a doll, Brenda. Thanks.'

A what? Hope was pretty sure nobody had ever called Brenda Masterson a doll before and lived through the experience. Gael clicked his phone off and smiled over at Hope. 'Good news. You're mine for the next couple of weeks.'

She *what*? In his dreams. And she was going to tell him so just as soon as she had the perfect withering put-down—and when she had answered the call vibrating insistently through her phone. Hope pulled the phone out of her pocket and the words hovering on her lips dried up when she saw Brenda's name flashing on the screen. She didn't need to take a course in fortune telling to predict what this call would be about. With a withering look in Gael's direction, which promised that this conversation was totally not over, Hope answered the call, tension twisting in her stomach.

'Brenda, hi. Sorry, I'm on my way in.' Damn, why had she apologised? She hadn't realised just how much she said 'sorry' or 'excuse me' until she moved to New York where no one else seemed to spend their time apologising for occupying space or wanting to get by or just existing. Every time she said sorry to Brenda she felt her stock fall a little further.

'Absolutely not. Stay right where you are. I didn't realise you knew Gael O'Connor.' Was that admiration in Brenda's voice? Great, three months into her time here and she had finally made her boss sit up and take notice—not through her hard work, initiative or talent but because of some guy she'd only met this morning.

'My sister is engaged to his stepbrother. Ex-stepbrother.'

She couldn't have this conversation in front of him, not as he leaned against the wall, arms folded and an annoying *Gotcha* smirk on his admittedly handsome face. Hope walked past him, heading for the door she'd seen at the other end of the apartment. It might lead to his red room of pain or whatever but she'd take the risk. Actually it led to a rather nice kitchen—an oddity in a city where nobody seemed to have space to cook. It was a little overdone on the stainless-steel front for Hope's tastes and ranked highly on the 'terrifying appliances I don't know how to use and can't even guess what they're for' scale but it was still rather impressive. And very clean. Maybe having a kitchen was a status thing, the using of it optional.

She shut the door firmly behind her. 'I don't know Gael O'Connor exactly. I only met him today to discuss wedding plans.'

'You've obviously impressed him. Let's keep it that way. I'm seconding you to work with him over the next two weeks. I want regular updates and I want him kept sweet. If you can do that then I can promise that all the right people will know how helpful you've been, Hope. It wouldn't surprise me if you got your pick of roles at the end of this secondment here or back in London. After all, as you've probably heard by now, Kit Buchanan's resigned from the London office inconveniently taking my assistant with him. Maybe we could arrange for you to stay here, if you wanted to, that is…'

Hope's breath caught in her throat. *Keep him sweet?* Did Brenda know just what he wanted her to do? Was she suggesting that nude modelling was part of her job description? Because Hope was pretty sure she'd missed that clause unless it fell somewhere under 'any other business.'

But Brenda had also tapped into a worry that Hope had been trying very hard not to think about. Her role in London had been working as a PA for the undoubtedly brilliant if often frustrating Kit Buchanan. Yet in less than three months he had fallen in love with Maddison Carter, her job-swap partner and owner of the tiny if convenient Upper East Side studio Hope was currently living in. And that had changed everything. She hadn't expected to feel so *lost* when she'd heard the news, almost grief stricken. It wasn't that she was jealous exactly. She wasn't in love with Kit. She didn't really have a crush on him either, although he had a nice Scottish accent, was handsome in an 'absent-minded professor' kind of way and, crucially, was the only single man under thirty she spent any time with. But Kit's resignation meant that in three months she would be returning to a new manager—and possibly a different, less fulfilling role.

It was a long time since Hope had dreamed of archaeology; she'd pushed those dreams and any thought of university aside after her parents died, starting instead as an office junior at a firm of solicitors close to her Stoke Newington home. But when she had moved to DL Media three years ago Kit had been quick to see potential in his PA and ensured there had been a certain amount of editorial training and events work in her duties. There was no guarantee a new manager would feel the same way. But if Brenda was impressed with her then who knew what opportunities would open up? Hope took a deep breath and tried to clear her head.

'Why does Gael need an assistant from DL Media?' *And why me?* she silently added.

'Because Gael O'Connor is planning a retrospective of his photographs and the blog that catapulted him into the public eye and I want to make sure that he chooses DL Media as his partner when he does so. I've been courting him and his agent for nearly a year and got nowhere. They say that his archive is incredible, that he could bring down careers, end marriages with his photos,' Brenda's voice was full of longing. 'I can smell the sales now. This could be huge, Hope, and you could be part of it straight from the start. I want you to get me those photos and the anecdotes that accompany them. Help him sort out his archive and make sure that at the end he is so impressed he signs on the dotted line of the very generous contract we offered him. Take as long as you need, do whatever you have to do but get that signature for me. You have an in. He asked for you, your sister is marrying someone he's close to. Anyone would kill for that kind of connection. Exploit it. If you do then I guarantee you a nice promotion and a secure future here at DL Media…'

Hope didn't need to ask what would happen if she failed—or if she refused. Back to England in ignominy and coffee-making, minute-taking and contract-typing-up for the rest of her days. If she was lucky. But if she agreed then she was not only getting a huge boost up the career ladder but she would also be away from the office, out from under Brenda's eye and could grab the time to sort out Faith's wedding. Damn Gael O'Connor, he had her exactly where he wanted her.

'Okay,' she said, injecting as much confidence into

her voice as she could manage. 'I'll do it. You don't have to worry, Brenda. I won't let you down.'

Gael couldn't hear Hope's conversation with her boss but he didn't need to. Hope was as good as his. He'd met Brenda Masterson several times and he knew her type; her eyes were fixed firmly on the prize and she wasn't going to let anything or anyone get in her way.

The kitchen door opened and Hope stalked through, her colour high but her eyes bright with determination. 'I suppose you think you are very clever,' she said. 'Of course some might call it blackmail...'

'Call what blackmail? Your boss wants my archive and I need help organising it. Seems like a fair trade to me.' But Gael couldn't stop the smile playing around his lips. 'You should thank me. I'm much less of a clock watcher than Brenda. You might even get some wedding organising done while you're here. In fact you can have today to get started. Consider it my wedding gift to the happy couple.'

'Is there even an archive or is this just some kind of ruse to keep me here?'

Gael stilled. He was so used to people knowing who he was, what he was, that the scorn in her all too candid eyes took him back. Back to the days before *Expose*. The days when he was nothing. 'I see. You think this is a ploy to get you to pose? Get real, princess. I may have asked you to sit for me but I don't beg and I certainly don't coerce. Every one of those women over there...' He nodded over at the canvases. 'They came to me freely.'

Her forehead creased. 'So why did you ask Brenda if I could work for you?'

'Because I was planning on saying yes to Brenda's offer anyway and this saves me the hassle of finding an assistant. Because I won't mind how you organise your time as long as the archiving work gets done so this way you can pop out to look at venues or cakes or whatever else you need to do. Not to force you into anything. Nobody is keeping you here against your will, Rapunzel, there's no escape ladder needed. You can leave at any time.'

Hope looked over at the chaise, a frown still creasing her forehead. 'I'm sorry, I just thought...you said you wouldn't help me with the wedding and then this all happened so fast.'

'I'm *not* helping you. I'm giving you time but that's all you'll get out of me. I have a model to find and paint, an exhibition to put on and an archive to explain to you and oversee. The wedding's your problem, not mine. Unless you change your mind about the picture, in which case I'll keep my end of the bargain and help you but, like I said, your decision. It's not part of your duties here. I have no interest in a reluctant subject.'

She took a visible deep breath, her eyes clouded, her forehead still wrinkled with thought. She was close to a decision but whether that decision was changing her mind and posing or walking out and telling him to go to hell he had no idea.

It was intriguing, this unpredictability.

'If I said yes...' She stopped, her eyes wary again.

He should be feeling triumphant. He almost had her, he could tell. But Hope McKenzie wasn't like his usual subjects. They were all eager for him to tell their stories with his paintbrush—she was all secrets and disguises. 'Before we go any further, I need you to know exactly what you're getting into.'

'I lie there and you paint me. Right?' The words were belligerent but her eyes dark with fear.

'It's not easy being a life model. It's a skill. You have to keep the same pose for hours. No complaining about being cold, or achy or hungry.'

'Okay.'

'I asked each model to wear some jewellery that meant something to them. Something very personal.' He pointed over at one canvas. 'That girl there, Anna? She's wearing pins in her hair she wore on her wedding day. This lady, Ameena, she's wearing gold necklaces and bangles gifted to her by her parents when she emigrated to the US.'

'And they have to be naked. I mean, I would have to be. Totally. I couldn't, instead of jewellery have a scarf or something. It's just…'

'Sorry.' And he was. It wasn't easy for even the most seasoned model to lie there so exposed to him and even though his other models had been enthusiastic about the project they had still found posing difficult, embarrassment covered in a multitude of ways, by jokes, by attempted seduction, by detachment.

'That's okay.'

It didn't seem okay; her hands were twisting together in an attempt to hide a slight shake.

'The last thing is probably the most important. If you model then I need you to think about sex. What it means to you, good and bad. I need you to think about that the whole time I paint you. I know that's an odd request but it's the theme of the paintings and it needs to show in your eyes, on your face. If it helps I can play any music you want, audiobooks, relaxation tapes—whatever makes you comfortable.'

It was odd, he'd had this conversation many times before and he had never felt so like some kind of libertine before. Every other model had known exactly why she was there, had volunteered for this. It was business, not personal.

But this time it felt horribly personal and he had no idea why.

'Think about sex?'

'Is that a problem?'

'It might be.' Her colour was even higher, rivalling the red of the chaise. 'You see, I haven't actually... I don't... I'm not...what I'm trying to say is...' she swallowed '... I'm a virgin. So I don't think I can lie there and think about something I know nothing about. Do you?'

CHAPTER THREE

'THANK YOU. No, I see. Yes. Absolutely. Thank you.'
Hope clicked her phone off and resisted the urge to
throw it off the fire escape and let it smash into smith-
ereens. Another hotel she could cross off her 'possibles'
list. Three hours of calling and emailing and she still
hadn't made one appointment.

She scanned the list she'd made the second she'd arrived home. It had all seemed so simple then.

1. Find a dress
2. Sort out flowers
3. Ceremony—where????
4. Read through Brenda's six zillion emails
*5. Try and show Gael O'Connor that you're com-
petent and professional and not a complete bas-
ket case...*

Hope resisted the urge to bang her head on the
wrought-iron railing she was propped up against. She
might have managed to steal one day of wedding planning from Gael O'Connor's manipulative hands but
where had it got her? Every venue she had phoned had
either laughed at her incredulously or sounded vaguely

scandalised. 'A wedding? In two weeks? Ma'am, this isn't Vegas. I suggest you try City Hall.' And as for a dress…you would think she had asked them to spin straw into gold, not supply one white dress, US size four.

And yes, she could try City Hall. And she could pop into any one of a dozen shops and pull a dress off the racks and it would do. And she could book a table in a five-star restaurant and the food would be great. But it wouldn't be special. It wouldn't show Faith just how much Hope loved her. It wouldn't make up for the fact that Faith would have no proud father walking her down the aisle, no mother in a preposterous hat wiping away tears and beaming proudly. Faith deserved the best and Hope had vowed nine years ago that she would have it. This wedding wasn't going to beat her, no, not if it killed her. Her baby sister would have the finest and most romantic whirlwind wedding New York had ever seen. She just needed to work out how and where.

Hope took a sip of coffee and stared at her laptop, balancing precariously on her open window ledge, hoping it would give her some much-needed inspiration. Maybe if she had spent a little more time actually in the city itself and less time either in the office or here, sunning herself on the fire escape outside her apartment window, she might actually have some unique and doable ideas. Okay. She was in the greatest city in the world, how could her mind be so blank? 'New York,' she muttered. 'New York.'

A ping from her laptop broke her half-hearted reverie and Hope looked across at it, sighing when she saw yet another email from Brenda flashing on her screen. What was going on? She had never seen her famously ice-cool boss this het up over anyone. Hunter had said that Gael knew everybody and what was it Brenda had whispered? He had the power to finish careers and destroy marriages? Remembering the mocking smile and the coldness in the blue-grey eyes, Hope didn't doubt it.

Setting her coffee cup to one side, she scrambled onto her knees and pulled up her internet browser. 'Who exactly are you, Gael O'Connor?' With a guilty look around, as if the starling on the rail above could see her snooping, Hope pressed Enter and waited. She wasn't sure what to expect but it wasn't the lines and lines of links that immediately filled her screen. Headlines, photos, articles—and a comprehensive Wikipedia entry.

Gael O'Connor. Photographer. Blogger. Society darling. It looked as if he didn't just *know* the New York scene—he dictated it, moving through it, camera at the ready, creating instant stars.

Nowhere would say no to him. Nowhere would tell him that two weeks was impossible. No one would suggest that Gael O'Connor tried City Hall…

Damn.

Her choice was stark. Either she compromised on the wedding or she agreed to Gael's demands and posed for him. If he still wanted her, that was, after her moment of hysterical oversharing. Hope groaned, slumping back again against the sun-hot railing. It was going to be bad enough facing him the next day in a working capacity, how on earth could she bring up the whole naked posing thing? Maybe she should run away instead. Somewhere no one would ever find her—she'd bet Alaska was nice and anonymous and a nice bracing contrast to this never-ending humidity.

At that moment her phone rang. She didn't recognise the number and answered it cautiously. After this morning's 'blurting out secret personal information to a stranger' debacle she'd probably tell the telemarketer about the time she wet herself in playgroup or when she shoplifted a chocolate bar when she was five —and how her mother made her take it back with a note of apology. 'Hope speaking.'

'How's the wedding planning coming along?' A gravelly voice, like the darkest chocolate mixed with espresso.

Hope glared at her laptop. How had Gael known she was thinking of contacting him? Maybe he had sold his soul to the devil and just thinking about him summoned him? 'Great!' Just a little lie.

'That's good. I was worried that two weeks' notice might be too tight for any of the really good venues.'

'How sweet of you to worry but actually I have it all under control.' Another little lie. Any moment her nose was going to start growing.

'Excellent. So you'll be here nice and early tomorrow to start work?'

'I can't wait.' Yes, she'd better hope that long noses were going to be fashionable this year because the way she was going hers was going to be longer than her outstretched arm.

'All you need is your laptop and a lot of patience. I do hope you like cataloguing.'

'I love it. I'd hate to get in your way though, while you're painting. I could work from the office or from mine if that's more convenient.' *Please let it be more convenient.*

'There's nothing to get in the way of. I haven't found

a model yet.' The mockery slipped from Gael's voice, his frustration clear.

'Oh.'

It was a sign. A big neon sign. He still needed a model and she, like it or not, needed his help. Hope took a deep breath. 'Look, Gael. I hate to deprive you of the joy of wedding planning and it looks like we're going to be spending some time together anyway so...' It was even harder to say the words than she'd antici-pated.

'So?'

He knew, she could tell, but was no doubt taking some unholy satisfaction from making her spell it out.

'So I can pose. For your picture. If you still want me after, well, if you still want me...' She wasn't going to own up to her virgin status again. She still couldn't believe she had mentioned it at all, said it out loud. To a complete stranger. A state of affairs she had barely acknowledged over the last few years, pushing the thought away as soon as it occurred. Her own secret shame. Hope McKenzie, old before her time, with-ered, sexless.

'An intriguing offer.'

She tried not to grind her teeth. 'Not really,' she said as breezily as she could. 'I didn't exactly give you an answer, if you remember.' No, she had backed away, muttered something about needing to get things sorted, said, 'Thank you for the offer to take today to start planning and see you tomorrow, thank you very much...' and scarpered as fast as her feet could carry her, out of the studio and back to the safety of her own apartment.

'I thought your mad dash out of the studio was answer enough. Why the sudden change of heart?'

Hope never admitted to needing anyone; she didn't intend to start now. 'You need someone to start straight away and spend the next two weeks at your beck and call. Well, whether I like it or not I am already at your beck and call. It makes sense.'

'How very giving of you. So you're offering because it's convenient?'

Her fingers curled into a fist. *He'd asked her*—why on earth was she the one working to convince him? 'And although I am more than capable of sorting this wedding alone it would be foolish of me not to use all the resources available. I barely know the city but you live here, your input could save me a lot of wasted effort—and this is the only way you'll help. I'm big enough to admit that if I want Faith to have the best wedding possible then I need to involve you.'

'Another altruistic motive.' Hope's cheeks heated at the sardonic note in Gael's voice. 'And very laudable but you've seen the other portraits. Sacrificial victim isn't the look I'm going for. It's not enough for you to agree to pose. I need you to want it. Tell me, Hope. Do you want it?' His voice had lowered to a decadent pitch, intimately dark. Hope swallowed.

Did she want to pose for him? Lie on that chaise, his eyes on every exposed inch of skin?

Hope stared out through the black iron railings. She knew the view by heart. The buildings opposite, the tops of the trees. This was where she hung out with a coffee and a book or her laptop, too scared to venture out of the comfort zone she'd carved for herself. She didn't mean to speak but somehow the words came spilling out. Another sad confession. 'I meant to shake things up when I moved here. New York was my chance to reinvent myself. I started, I bought new clothes and chopped off some of my hair and thought that would be enough. But I'm still the same. I don't know how to talk to people any more, not when it doesn't involve work or superficial stuff. I don't...' She hesitated. 'I don't know how to make friends, how to have fun. Maybe this will help me loosen up. It'll be a talking point if nothing else.'

'You want me to help you loosen up?' Her pulse quickened at the velvet in his voice.

'Yes. No! Not you exactly. What I mean is that I need to try something different, to be different. Posing for you will be new, unexpected.'

'Okay. Let's try this.'

She hadn't known how tightly she was wound waiting for his answer, how the world had fallen away until it was just the two of them, sharing an intimate space even though they were half a mile apart, until he agreed.

'Great.' She inhaled a shaky breath. 'So what now? Do you want me to come over and...?' Her voice trailed off. How was she going to do it if she couldn't even say it?

The laughter in his voice confirmed he was probably thinking the same thing. 'Not today. I think we need to warm up a little first. You, Hope McKenzie, have just admitted you need me to help you discover new things.'

That wasn't what she had said. Was it? Certainly not in the way she thought he was implying. 'And you think you can do that for me, do you?'

'Maybe.'

She didn't have to see him to know that he was smiling. Anger rose, sharp, hot and a welcome antidote to the sudden intimacy—but she wasn't entirely sure if she was more angry with Gael for his presumption or herself for laying herself open like that. 'How very altruistic of you, and what's in it for you? A better painting or the virtuous glow of helping poor, virginal Hope McKenzie? Sprinkle a little of your privileged, glamorous Upper East Side fairy dust on me and watch me transform? Well, Professor Higgins, this little flower girl doesn't need your patronage, thank you very much.'

'Are you sure about that?' Before she could respond Gael continued smoothly. 'In that case why don't we get started on planning this whirlwind wedding? Any venues you want to see?'

Hope glared at the laptop as if it were to blame for her lack of possibilities. There was no way she wanted to admit she didn't have one idea as yet. 'Yes. Meet me…meet me on top of the Empire State Building in an hour and a half.' Did they do weddings? It almost didn't matter. It was iconic and it was a start.

'On top of the Empire State Building? How romantic. What a shame it isn't Valentine's Day. Am I Cary Grant or Tom Hanks in this scenario?'

'Neither, you're not the hero. You're the wisecracking friend who ends up handcuffed to a stripper on the stag night.'

'I must have missed that scene. Oh, well, there are worse things to be handcuffed to.' And he hung up leaving Hope with a disturbing image involving Gael O'Connor, handcuffs and the red chaise longue. What was more disturbing was the swirl of excitement in her stomach at the very thought...

It was predictably busy at the top of the Empire State Building, the sun and the wind combining to make the walkway uncomfortable in the early afternoon heat, but none of the tourists seemed to be complaining, too busy taking selfies and pointing out landmarks to notice the conditions.

And they would all be tourists. No self-respecting New Yorker would be up here at this time, during the height of the sightseeing buzz. In fact Gael couldn't remember the last time he had set foot up here. It had probably been for a photo shoot—that was why he visited most tourist locations.

Which was a shame because, even hardened local that he was, he had to admit the view was pretty spectacular, the blue of the ocean merging with the blue of the sky and the city rising from the ocean's depths like some mythological Atlantis.

Gael walked around three sides of the viewing platform before he spotted Hope, bright in the same red dress she'd been wearing earlier. She was standing half turned away from him, leaning on the railing staring out over the city, the dark strands of her hair whipping in the wind. It was odd, he'd only met her this morning but her image was indelibly printed on him—probably because most women didn't gatecrash his studio, demand he help them with a wedding and then blurt out their sexual history—or lack of—before nine a.m.

A smile tugged at his lips. He hadn't seen that one coming and at this stage in the game he could have sworn he'd seen it all. Dammit, he had to admit he was intrigued. How old was Hope? He looked at her assessingly. Somewhere in her mid to late twenties, he'd guess. Which meant she had to be either holding out for true love or had a considerable amount of baggage and neither of those things appealed to him. Not that he was interested in Hope in that way. He just needed a model.

She shifted and her full profile came into view. Nice straight nose and a really good mouth—full bottom lip and a lovely shape to the top one. Almost biteable. Almost... 'So, is this it? The perfect spot?'

She jumped as he joined her at the barrier, her cheeks flushing as she threw a stilted smile his way. 'I don't know. It looks a bit busy for a wedding.'

'Which is a good thing because it turns out you can only get married up here on Valentine's Day and only then if you win a competition. I checked...' he added as she raised an enquiring eyebrow. 'They could marry elsewhere and then come up here for photos but to be honest with you Hunter isn't that keen on heights.'

'He isn't?'

'Turns green on the Brooklyn Bridge,' Gael confirmed.

'Why didn't you tell me any of this before I arranged to meet you here?' She turned and glared, hands on her slim hips in what was clearly meant to be an admonishing way. She looked more like a cute pixie.

'And ruin your Deborah Kerr moment? Or are you Meg Ryan? Isn't it every girl's dream to arrange a meeting on the top of the Empire State Building?'

'I already told you, your role is the wisecracking best friend, not the hero.'

'What about your role, Hope? Who are you?' No

woman he knew was content to play the supporting role in their own lives.

'Me? I'm the wedding planner.' She stared out over Manhattan, her face softening. 'Isn't it breathtaking? I can't believe I haven't been up here yet.'

'Seriously? I thought this was the first destination on every tourist's wish list.'

'I'm not exactly a tourist. I live here. Well, for three more months I do. I mean to do the tourist trail at some point but I haven't had a chance yet.' Her voice was wistful.

Not the heroine of her own story, neither a tourist nor a native. If he didn't have a pose in mind he'd paint Hope as something insubstantial, some kind of wandering spirit. 'Why are you here, Hope?'

She turned, blinking in surprise. 'To meet you and make a start on the wedding, why?'

'No, why are you in New York at all? Here you are in the greatest city on earth but you're barely living in it, not experiencing it.'

'"I'm planning to.' But her words lacked any real commitment and she looked away. 'But I want a real career, to make something of my life that's about me. All this…' She waved her hand over Manhattan. 'This can wait. It will still be here in ten years' time. I'm here because for the first time in nine years I don't have to worry about anyone but myself. I can put my career and my choices first.'

'Is that what this is? Putting yourself first? Because from where I'm standing you've agreed to all kinds of things you don't want to do for other people. For Brenda, your sister…'

'Brenda's my boss, of course I'm going to do what

she asks me to do. As for Faith, it's complicated. Our
parents died when I was eighteen and Faith was only
ten. I've raised her. I can't turn my back on her now,
not when she needs me, wants me. Besides, she's marrying Hunter in two weeks. She won't be my responsibility any more. This is the last thing I can do for her
and I want it to be perfect.' Her mouth wobbled and
she swallowed. 'It will be perfect.'

She'd raised her sister? That explained a lot. 'Of
course it will. I've agreed to help. Besides, as soon as
you mention the Carlyle name any door in the city you
want opening will swing open.'

'There's no budget for the wedding at all. Hunter's
sending a card. But seriously, what does that even mean?
Everyone has some kind of budget.'

Gael couldn't help his grin. It was so long since
he'd spoken to someone who didn't live in the rarefied
Upper East Side bubble. 'No, not the Carlyles. You've
heard people say money's no object?' She nodded, dark
eyes fixed on him. 'The Carlyles take that to a whole
new level. I have no idea how rich they are but filthy
doesn't even begin to cover it.'

'Wow.' She looked slightly stunned. 'And I was worrying that Faith was marrying a street artist with no
prospects. I think I was worrying about all the wrong
things. I don't think Faith and I are going to fit in with
people like that. We're very ordinary.' She hesitated
and then turned to him, laying her hand on his fore-
arm. 'Will she be okay? They won't look down on her,
will they?'

He might be standing on a platform hundreds of feet
up in the air but the air had suddenly got very close.
All Gael could feel was that area of skin where Hope's

hand lay, all he could smell was the citrus notes of her perfume. He tried to drag his concentration back to the conversation. 'Misty doesn't think like that. She's the least snobby person I've ever met and, believe me, living where I live and doing what I do I have met a *lot* of snobs.' A thought struck him. 'She'll be delighted I'm helping with the wedding. In her head Hunter and I will always be brothers even though he was an annoying three-year-old brat when I moved into their house and we've never hung out in the same circles.' Truth was Hunter had always idolised him. He'd even decided to follow in his footsteps and study art rather than the business degree Misty Carlyle had picked out for her only son.

'She sounds nice, Misty. If she was such a good stepmother then maybe she'll be good for Faith.' Hope's mouth trembled into a poor attempt at a smile. 'Poor Faith has only had me for so long, she deserves a real mother.'

Gael suspected that Misty would be delighted to have a young and pliable daughter-in-law. She still introduced herself as *his* mother even though she'd divorced his dad ten years ago. Still, that was more than his own mother did. 'She is nice,' he conceded. 'By far the best of my parents.'

Hope blinked. 'How many do you have?'

'Are we counting discarded steps? Misty is my father's second ex-wife. My mother was his first. His current wife is number four. We all try and forget about number three.'

Her eyes widened. 'That's a lot of wives.'

'Misty's just divorced husband number five and my mother is on her third marriage.' He shrugged. 'No one in my family takes the whole "as long as you both shall live" part very seriously.'

'My parents met at university, married as soon as they graduated and that was that. I used to think they were really boring. Old before their time, you know? Now I envy them that. That certainty.'

'Oh, my parents are certain every time. I'm not sure if it's more endearing or infuriating, that eternal optimism. They were dancers, Broadway chorus dancers, when they met.'

'No way.'

'Oh, yes,' he said wryly. 'It was very *Forty-Second Street.* Right up to the minute my twenty-year-old dad knocked up my nineteen-year-old mom and carried her back to Long Harbor to the family bar.' His poor young mother, a streetwise Hispanic girl with stars in her eyes, wasn't content with a life serving drinks to the moneyed masses who flocked to the Long Island resort in the summer. 'I don't remember much about that time, but I do remember a lot of yelling. She's Cuban and my dad's Irish so when they fought crockery flew. Literally. Just before my fifth birthday she packed her bags and walked out. Never came back.'

He hadn't realised that he was clenching his fist until Hope's hand covered his, a warm unwanted comfort. He'd shed the last tear he would ever shed on his mother's behalf on his fifth birthday when she'd failed to turn up to her own son's birthday party. 'I'm so sorry. Do you see her now?'

'Occasionally, if I'm near Vegas. She has a dance troupe there, she's doing well but the last thing she needs is a six-foot, twenty-nine-year-old son reminding her that she's nearer fifty than thirty.'

'So you were raised by your dad?'

'And my grandparents, aunts, uncles—anyone else who wanted to tame the wild O'Connor boy. Not that there was much time to run wild, not with a family business like the Harbor Bar—there's always a surface to clean, a table to clear, an errand to run if you're stupid enough to get caught. And Dad wasn't broken-hearted for long. It seemed like there was a whole line of women just dying to become my stepmom. But they all were swept away when Misty decided she was interested. She was fifteen years older than my dad and it was like she was from a different planet. So calm, so together. So one minute I'm that poor motherless O'Connor boy living on top of a bar with a huge extended family, the next I'm rattling around a huge mansion with a monthly allowance bigger than my dad's old salary. It was insane.'

'It sounds like a fairy tale. Like *Cinderella* or something.'

'Fairy tales are strictly a girl thing. It's okay for Cinderella to marry the prince, not so okay for an Irish bartender to marry his way into the upper echelons of society. The more polite people called him a toy boy, but they all wore identical sneers—like they knew exactly what Misty saw in him and didn't think it should be allowed in public. And as for me? Breeding counts, money counts and I had neither. When Dad became Misty Carlyle's third ex-husband then I should have returned to the gutter where I came from.'

By unspoken accord they moved away from the railing and began to walk back to the elevator lobby. 'What happened?

'Misty. She insisted on paying for college, per-

suaded my dad to let me spend my holidays with her,
Christmas skiing, spring break in New York, the sum-
mers in Europe. Of course everyone at school knew I
was there on charity—not even her stepson any more.'
It was hard looking back remembering just how alone
he had been, how isolated. They hadn't bullied him; he
was too strong for that—and no one wanted to incur
Misty's wrath. They had just ignored him. Shown him
he was nothing. Until he'd started *Expose* and made
them need him.

'That must have been tough.' Her dark eyes were
limpid with a sympathy he hadn't asked for and certainly didn't want.

'Expensive education, great allowance and a suite of
rooms in one of the oldest and grandest houses in the
Hamptons? Yeah, I suffered.' But Gael didn't know if
his words fooled Hope. He certainly never managed
to fool himself. He greeted the elevator with relief.
'Come on, I'll buy you a coffee and fill you in on everything you need to know about life with the Carlyles.
I'll warn you, you may need to take notes. There's a
lot to learn.' For Gael as well as Hope. He wasn't entirely sure why he'd decided to go all *This is Your Life*
with her but one thing he did know. He wouldn't let
his guard down again.

CHAPTER FOUR

'IT'S ALL SET UP and ready to go. Where do you want me to start?' Hope was perched on one achingly trendy and even more achingly uncomfortable high stool, her laptop set up on the kitchen counter, her bright yellow skirt and dotted cream blouse feeling incongruously feminine and delicate set against the stainless steel and matt black cupboards and worktops.

To one side was Gael's own laptop and several backup drives plus a whole box of printed photos, most of which had names and dates pencilled on the back. Hope had spent the morning looking through the box and scanning through a couple of the hard drives before setting up the spreadsheets and database she was planning to use.

Gael strolled into the kitchen carrying yet another box, which he set next to the first. Great. Even more photos. 'I think you are best off starting with the old blog posts. They're all archived and filed.' He pushed one of the hard drives towards her and Hope plugged it into the side of her laptop.

'Okay. So what do you want? Names obviously so we can cross reference them, dates—what else?'

'Any references made to the subjects in *Expose*.

Once we've finished with that we'll move on to the photos I either didn't use or were taken after the blog closed down. We'll only need names and dates unless they were used professionally in which case the magazine will need referencing as well. Most are saved with all the relevant information but any that aren't put aside into a separate folder and I'll go through them with you at the end of each day.'

She was scribbling fast, taking notes. 'Got it. I don't think it'll take too long. You've kept good notes and everything seems to be labelled…' She hesitated and he looked at her. Really looked at her for the first time since they had left the Empire State Building yesterday afternoon. Oh, she'd spent time with him. Had coffee, learned some tips on handling her new in-laws-to-be, drawn up a list of possible venues for her sister's wedding, but he had retreated behind a shield of courtesy and efficiency. She barely knew him and yet that sudden withdrawal left her feeling lonelier than she had for a long time.

'Everything okay?'

'Yes, it's just… Obviously I know that you're a photographer.'

'Were,' he corrected her. 'Hence the retrospective. I'm a struggling unknown artist now.'

Hope looked around at the kitchen full of gleaming appliances, each worth the same amount as a small car, and repressed a smile. There were few signs of struggling in the studio. '*Were* a photographer. And you do—did—a lot of society shoots and fashion magazines and stuff…'

'And?'

'Where does the blog fit in? If I'm going to cata-

logue properly I need to know what I'm dealing with.'
Somehow Brenda had failed to make this clear in any
one of her excitable emails, most of which just reminded Hope how important this assignment was.

Gael leaned on the counter close beside her. He was
casually clad in dark blue jeans and a loose, short-
sleeved linen shirt. Hope could see every sharply defined muscle in his arms, every dark hair on the olive
skin. '*Expose* was a blog I set up when I was at prep
school. My plan, not surprisingly given the name, was
to expose people. The people I went to school with to
be more precise. I took photos chronicling the misad-
venture of New York's gilded youth. It just skated the
legal side of libellous.' His mouth curved into a provocative smile. 'After all, there was no proof that the
senator's son was *going* to snort that line, that couple
on the table weren't necessarily going to have sex, but
it was implied.' The smile widened. 'Implied because
generally it was true.'

Hope thought back to the hundreds of black and
white photos she had already seen today, stored on hard
drives, in the box, some framed and hung on Gael's
studio walls, the attractive, entitled faces staring out
without a fear in the world. What must it be like to have
that sort of confidence ingrained in you? 'And they let
you just take photos, even when they were misbehaving?' She cursed her choice of word. Misbehaving! She
was living her own stereotype. She'd get out a parasol
next and poke Gael with it, saying, 'Fie! Fie!' like some
twenty-first-century Charlotte Bartlett.

He laughed, a short bitter sound. 'They didn't even
notice. I was invisible at school, which was handy because nobody suspected it was me. They simply didn't

see me.' How was that possible? Surely at sixteen or
seventeen he would still have been tall, still imposing,
still filling all the space with his sheer presence? 'By
the time I was outed as the photographer the blog had
become mythic—as had its subjects. To be posted, or
even better named and the subject of a post? Guaranteed social success. The papers and gossip magazines
began to take an interest in the Upper East Side youth
not seen for decades—and it was thanks to me. Instead
of being the social pariah I expected to be I found myself the official chronicler of the wannabe young and
the damned. That was the end of *Expose*, of course. It
limped on through my first years at college but it lost
its way when people started *trying* to be in it. I became
a society photographer instead as you said, portraits,
fashion, big events; lucrative, soulless.'

'But why? Why set it up in the first place? Why run
the risk of being caught?' She could understand taking
photographs as a way of expressing his loneliness—
after all, she had been known to pen the odd angsty
poem in her teens. But that was a private thing—thank
goodness. She shivered at the very thought of anybody
actually *reading* them.

Gael straightened, grey-blue eyes fixed on Hope
as if he saw every secret thought and desire. No wonder he'd been so successful if his camera's eye was
as shrewd as his own piercing gaze. She swallowed,
staring defiantly back as if she were the one painting
him, taking him in. But she already knew as much as
she was comfortable with. She knew that his hair was
cut short but there were hints of a wild, untamed curl,
that his eyes were an unexpected grey-blue in the dark,
sharply defined face. She knew that he could look at

a girl as if he could see inside her. She didn't want to know any more.

'Because I could. Like I say, I was invisible. The people at the schools I went to cared about nothing except your name, your contacts and your trust fund. I had none of the above, ergo I was nothing.' His mouth twisted. 'The arrogance of youth. I wanted to bring them down, show the world how shallow and pathetic the New York aristocracy were. It backfired horribly. The world saw and the world loved them even more. Only now I was part of it for better or for worse. Still am, I suppose. Still, at least it should guarantee interest in the show. Let's just hope the paintings are as successful as the photographs were.'

'But why change? You're obviously really successful at what you do.'

'Fame and fortune have their perks,' he admitted. 'The studio, the invitations, the parties, the money...' the women. He didn't need to say it; the words hung in the humid New York summer air, shimmering in the heat haze. She'd seen the photos: pictures by him, pictures of him—with heiresses, actresses, It Girls and models.

Hope didn't even try to suppress her smirk. 'It must have been very difficult for you.'

'I'm not saying my lifestyle doesn't have its benefits. But it wasn't the way I thought I'd live, the way I wanted to earn a living. *Expose* was just a silly blog, that was all. I thought anyone who saw it would be horrified by the excess, by the sheer waste, but I was wrong.' He shrugged. 'My plan was always art school and then to paint. Somehow I was sidetracked.'

'So this is you getting back on track?'

'Hence the retrospective. Goodbye to that side of my life neatly summed up in an A4 hardback with witty captions. Right, lunch was a little on the meagre side so I'm going to go out and get ice cream. What do you want?'

'Oh.' She looked up, unexpectedly flustered. 'I don't mind.'

He shot her an incredulous look. 'Of course you mind. What if I bought you caramel swirl but really you wanted lemon sorbet? The two are completely different.'

'We usually have cookie dough at home. It's Faith's favourite.' Hope's mind was completely blank. How could she not know which flavour she preferred?

'Great, when I buy Faith an ice cream I'll know what to get. What about you?'

'No, seriously. Whatever you're having. It's fine.' She didn't want this attention, this insistence on a decision, stupid as she knew that made her look. Truth was she had spent so long putting Faith's needs, wants and likes before her own it was a slow and not always comfortable process trying to figure out where her sister ended and she began. 'Thank you.'

Gael didn't answer her smile with one of his own; instead he gave her a hard, assessing look, which seemed to strip her bare, and then turned and left leaving Hope feeling as if she'd failed some kind of test she hadn't even known she was meant to study for.

'Any more? I don't think you tried the double chocolate peanut and popcorn.'

Hope pushed the spoon away and moaned. 'No more, in fact I don't think I can ever eat ice cream again.' She stared at the open tubs, some much less full than others. 'And even after eating all this I don't know which my favourite flavour is.'

'Mint choc,' Gael said. 'That one has nearly gone. Impressive ice-cream-eating skills, Miss McKenzie.'

'If I ever need a reference I'll call you.' She paused and watched Gael as he placed the lids back onto the cartons and stacked them deftly before carrying them to the industrial-sized freezer. She hadn't known what to say, what to think when he'd returned to the studio carrying not one or two but ten different flavours of ice cream.

'You wouldn't pick,' he'd said in explanation as he'd lined the pots up in front of her. A bubble of happiness lodged in her chest. Nobody had ever done anything so thoughtful for her. Maybe she could do this. Work with this man, pose with him, because there were moments when she crossed from wariness to liking.

After all it would be rude not to like someone who bought you several gallons of Italian ice cream.

The pictures on the computer screen blurred in front of her eyes. 'I feel sleepy I ate so much.'

'Then it's a good thing you're about to get some fresh air. There's no time to slack, not with your schedule.'

'Fresh air?'

'Central Park. I spoke to a couple of contacts yesterday and they might just be able to accommodate your sister.'

Central Park! Of course. One of the few iconic New York landmarks she had actually visited and spent time in. Hope obediently slid off her stool, pressing one hand to her full stomach as she did so. She couldn't remember the last time she'd indulged so much. The last time she'd felt free to indulge, not set a good example or worry about what people thought.

Central Park was barely a ten-minute stroll from Gael's studio. Hope had spent several hours wandering around the vast city park but it felt very different walking there with Gael. He clearly knew it intimately, taking her straight to a couple of locations that had availability on Thursday in two weeks' time.

'What do you think?' he asked as they reached the lake. 'Romantic enough or did you prefer the Conservatory Garden?'

'The garden is lovely,' she agreed. 'It's a shame the floral arch is already booked. I think Faith would love it. But with such short notice she'll just have to be grateful we found her anywhere at all.'

'Why on earth is it such short notice? Is it a religious thing? Is that why your sister wants to marry Hunter on six weeks' acquaintance? Why you are still a virgin? You're waiting for marriage? For true love?' She could hear the mockery inherent in the last phrase.

The small bubble of happiness she'd carried since the moment she'd seen the bags heaped with ice cream burst with a short, sharp prick. He thought she was odd, a funny curiosity. 'I don't see that it is any of your business.'

'Hope, tomorrow, or the day after or the day after that, the moment I think you are ready, that you can handle it, you are going to pose for me for a painting which is supposed to symbolise sex. If this is going to work I need to understand why you have made the choices you have. I'm not going to judge you—your body, your decisions. But I need to understand.'

Hope stopped and stared out over the lake, watching a couple in a boat kissing unabashedly, as if they wanted to consume each other. Her stomach tightened. 'Honestly? Is it that unbelievable that a twenty-seven-year-old woman hasn't had sex yet? Does there have to be some big reason?'

'In this day and age, looking like you do? You have to admit it's unusual.' Happiness shivered through her at his casual words. *Looking like you do.* It was hard sometimes to remember a time when she had felt like someone desirable, bursting with promise and confidence, confident in her teeny shorts and tight tops as only an eighteen-year-old girl could be.

'It's no big mystery. It's not like I have been saving myself for my knight in shining armour.' She didn't believe in him for one thing. 'It just happened.' Hope turned away from the lake, dragging her eyes away from the oblivious, still-snogging couple with difficulty. For the first time in a really long time she allowed herself to wish it were her. Oblivious to everything but the sun on her back, the gentle splash of the water, his smell, his taste, the feel of his back under her hands. She had no idea who 'he' was but she ached for him nonetheless.

'I told you I raised Faith after our parents died. My aunt offered to help. She had a couple of kids Faith's age and would have been happy to have had her. But I wanted her to grow up where I grew up, in the family house, stay at her school with her friends.' She twisted her hands together. It all sounded so reasonable when she said it but there had been nothing reasonable about her decision at the time. Just high emotion, bitter grief and desperate guilt.

'So you put everything on hold?' He sounded disbelieving and she couldn't blame him; it sounded crazy said so bluntly. But she had had no real choice— not that she wanted to tell him that. To let him know she was responsible for it all. She had to take care of Faith—if it wasn't for Hope she would have had her family intact.

She swallowed, the old and familiar guilt bitter on her tongue. 'I didn't mind. But it meant my life was so different from my friends' new worlds—they were worrying about boyfriends and exams and going out and I was worrying about paying bills and childcare. It was no wonder we drifted apart. My boyfriend went to university just a few weeks after the funeral and I knew it would be best to end it then, that I wouldn't be able to put anyone else first for a long time.' It had seemed like the logical thing to do but she had hoped that he would fight for her, just a little.

But he had disappeared off without a word. He was getting married in just a few short weeks, his life moving on seamlessly from grungy teen to pretentious student to a man with responsibilities, just the way it was supposed to. Just as hers was supposed to have done.

Gael was like a dog with a bone. 'Let me get this straight: you didn't date at all? Since you were eighteen you have been single?'

How could she explain it? It all sounded so drab and dreary—and in many ways it had been. Those first few years when she earned so little, the long nights in alone while Faith slept, studying for her Open University degree, the ever-widening chasm between herself and her school friends until the day she realised she had no one to confide in. Too young for the mums at the school gates and the other secretaries at her law firm, too old at heart and shackled by responsibilities for the few girls around her age she managed to meet.

And then there was the rest: the lack of money or time to take care of herself and the slow dawning realisation she had lost any sense of style or joy in clothes and hair. It was hard when she had no budget to indulge herself and little time or talent to make the most of what she could afford. But there had been other things that compensated—watching Faith star in her school play, taking her ice skating at Somerset House, organising sleepovers and pamper evenings and homemade pizza parties for her sister and her friends and seeing her sister shine with happiness. Surely that was worth any sacrifice?

'No, I dated. A little. But I didn't like to stay out late, even when Faith was older and no one could stay over, it didn't seem right. And so the few relationships I had never really went anywhere. It's really no big deal.'

'Okay,' but she could hear the scepticism. Hope didn't blame him. How could she fool him when she had forgotten how to fool herself? 'Come on.'

Gael took her arm and turned her down a path on their left, his walk determined and his eyes gleaming with a devilish glint she instinctively both distrusted and yearned for. 'Where are we going?'

He stopped in front of a red and yellow brick hexagon and grinned at her. 'When's the last time you rode on a carousel, Hope?'

Was he mad? He *must* be mad. Hope stared over at the huge carousel. It was like a step back in time, wooden horses, their mouths fixed open, heads always thrown up in ecstasy, their painted manes blowing in a non-existent breeze as the circular structure turned to the sound of a stately polka. 'I don't know when I last rode on one,' she said and that was true. She couldn't pinpoint the date but she knew it was before Faith was born. Before she had elected to opt out of family life. She vividly remembered standing by the side of a carousel in the park as her parents took her laughing baby sister on one. She had refused to accompany them, had said it was too babyish. Instead she had stood by the side feeling left out and unloved, hating them for respecting her word and not forcing her to ride.

'You'll always be able to answer that question from now on. The eighteenth of August, you can say confidently. In New York, around...' He squinted at his wrist. 'Around two-forty in the afternoon.'

'No, I can say the eighteenth of August is the day some crazy person tried to persuade me to go on one and I walked away.' She swivelled, ready to turn away, only to be arrested by a hand closing gently around her wrist. She glared at Gael scornfully. 'What, you're going to force me to go on?'

'No, of course not.' He sounded bemused and who could blame him? She was acting crazy. But she could still see them, the two forty-somethings cradling their precious toddler tight while their oldest child stood forgotten by the exit.

Only she hadn't been forgotten. They had waved every time they passed by, every time. No matter that she hadn't waved back once. Hope swallowed, the lump in her throat as painful as it was sudden. Why hadn't she waved?

Gael leaned in close, his fingers still loose around her wrist. His breath was faint on her neck but she could sense every nerve where it touched her, each one shocking her into awareness. 'Doesn't it look like fun?'

Maybe, maybe not. 'I'll look ridiculous.'

'Will you? Do they? Look at them, Hope.'

Hope raised her eyes, her skin still tingling from his nearness, a traitorous urge to lean back into him gripping her. *Stop it*, she scolded herself. *You've known him for what? Two days? And he's already persuaded you to pose nude, holds your career in his rather nicely shaped hands and is trying to make a fool of you. There's no need to help him by swooning into him.*

But now he was so close she could smell him, a slight scent of linseed and citrus, not unpleasant but unusual. It was the same scent she had picked up in his studio. A working scent. He might be immaculately dressed in light grey trousers and a white linen shirt but the scent told her that this was a man who used his hands, a physical being. The knowledge shivered through her, heating as it travelled through her veins.

'Hope?'

'Yes, I'm looking at them.' She wasn't lying, she was managing somehow to push all thoughts about Gael O'Connor's hands out of her mind and focus on the carousel, on the people riding it. Families, of course. The old pain pierced her heart at the sight; time never seemed to dull it, to ease it.

But it wasn't just families riding; there were groups of older children, laughing hysterically, a couple of teens revelling in the irony of their childish behaviour. Couples, including a white-haired man, stately on his golden steed, smiling at the silver-haired woman next to him. 'No,' she admitted. 'They don't look ridiculous. They look like they are having fun.'

'Well, then,' and before she could formulate any further response or process what was happening she was at the entrance of the building and Gael was handing over money in crisp dollar bills.

'Go on, pick one,' he urged and she complied, choosing a magnificent-looking bay with a black mane and a delicate high step. Gael swung himself onto the white horse next to hers while Hope self-consciously pulled her skirt down and held on to the pole tightly. He looked so at ease, as if he came here and did this every day, one hand carelessly looped round the pole, the other holding a small camera he had dug out of his jeans pocket.

'Smile!'

'What are you doing?'

He raised an eyebrow. 'Practising my trade. Watch out, it's about to go. Hold on tight!'

The organ music swelled around them as the carousel began to rotate and the horses moved, slowly at first, before picking up speed until it was whirling around and around. At first Hope clung on tightly, afraid she might fall as the world spun giddily past, but once she settled into the rhythm she relaxed her grip. Gael was right, it was fun. More than that, it was exhilarating, the breeze a welcome change on the hot, sticky day. Above the organ music she could hear laughter, children, adults and teens, all forgetting their cares for one brief whirl out of time. She risked a glance at Gael. He was leaning back, nonchalant and relaxed, like a cowboy in total control of his body; his balance, his hand was steady as he focussed the camera and snapped again and again, watching the world through a lens.

And then all too soon it was slowing, the walls

slowly coming back into focus, the horse no longer galloping but walking staidly along as the music died down. She looked over at Gael and smiled shakily, unable to find the words to thank him. For a moment then she had been free. No one's sister, no one's PA, no expectations. Free.

'Another go?'

'No, thank you, one was enough. But it *was* fun. You were right.'

'Remember that over the next two weeks and we'll be fine.' Gael dismounted in one graceful leap, holding a hand out so that Hope could try and slide down without her skirt riding up too far. 'Come on, let's have a drink at the Tavern on the Green and you can decide if you like it enough to shortlist it for the wedding drinks.'

'Good idea.' Damn, why hadn't she thought of that? Celebrating her sister's wedding in such an iconic venue would certainly be memorable.

Hope stopped, suddenly shy, trying to find the right words to frame the question that had been dogging her thoughts since their conversation at the lake. 'Gael, when will I be ready? To be painted?'

It wasn't that she felt ready; she wasn't sure she ever would be. But knowing that at some point it would happen, at some point she would have to keep her word, made it almost possible for her to relax.

Gael didn't answer for a moment, just stared at her with that intense, soul-stripping look that left her feeling as if she had nowhere left to hide.

'When you start living,' he said and turned and walked away. Hope stood still, gaping at him.

'I am ready,' she wanted to yell. Or, 'Then you'll be waiting a long time.' Because the truth was she was scared. Scared of what would happen, scared of who she was, scared of what might be unleashed if she ever dared to let go.

CHAPTER FIVE

HOPE STOOD IN her walk-in wardrobe and stared at the rack of carefully ironed clothes, fighting back almost overwhelming panic. Panic and, she had to admit, a tinge of anticipation. Every day for the last nine years had followed its own dreary predictable pattern and even here, in the vibrant Upper East Side, she had managed to re-establish a set routine before she'd worked out the best place to buy milk.

But not today. She had no idea what Gael had in store for her. He'd told her to be ready at ten a.m. and that he would call for her. Nothing else.

He'd mentioned risks. Allowing herself to live. Unlocking herself. Hope swallowed. She liked the sound of that, she really did. She just wasn't sure whether it was possible, that if she stripped away the layers of self-sufficiency and efficiency and busyness there would be very much left.

'Okay,' she said aloud, the words steadying her. 'What's the worst that could happen?'

Oh. She shouldn't have even thought that because now, now she had opened up the floodgates, it turned out she could think of *lots* of worst things. Maybe he was going to suggest skydiving or bungee jumping off the Brooklyn Bridge—illegal but even Hope had heard the rumours and she bet Gael O'Connor didn't give two figs for legality anyway. Or climbing up some skyscraper—or walking a tightrope between them. She inhaled shakily. No, she was pretty sure she could strike the last one off her list.

Or maybe when he said he wanted her to loosen up he was talking about her V card. He might be a member of one of those exclusive clubs where expensive call girls and even more expensive cigars and whisky were shared by men in ten-thousand-dollar suits. Possibly. She'd seen a TV show once where the detective went undercover in exactly that kind of club right here in New York City...

Or maybe he would want her to explore her own sexuality in a burlesque class or pole dancing or actually perform in some kind of club or...or no. Ten minutes would be nine minutes and fifty nine seconds longer than she needed to convince any stage manager that she most definitely didn't have what it took. After all, how many four-year-olds were asked to leave baby ballet?

'Stop thinking.' Hope grabbed a pair of high-waisted orange shorts and a cream *broderie-anglaise* blouse and marched out of the wardrobe, throwing them onto the daybed, which doubled as a sofa and place to sleep. Living in a studio so compact it practically redefined the word had meant she needed to find new levels of neatness and organisation or resign herself to living surrounded by everything she had brought with her in disordered chaos. And that, obviously, would be intolerable.

Dressed, her hair brushed and tied back into a high ponytail, and her feet encased in a comfortable pair of cream and tan summer loafers, she should, she reflected, have felt better. That was what her new, eye-wateringly expensive wardrobe was supposed to do. Make her feel ready for anything. Make her feel like someone. Instead she felt all too often like a little girl playing dress up in the bold colours, designs and cuts. Maybe she should get changed…

Right on cue, as if Gael knew the exact moment she was feeling the most insecure, the buzzer went. No doorman here, no lift or fancy hallway. Just a buzzer and several flights of stairs.

Not that the four flights of stairs seemed to faze him. He was annoyingly cool when she opened the door, his breathing regular, not a damp patch to be seen on the grey short-sleeved shirt he'd teamed with a pair of well-cut black jeans. His clothes gave no clue to the day's activities although she could probably rule out the gentleman's club. Her eyes met his and, as she took in the lurking laughter, all the calm, welcoming words she had prepared and practised fell away.

'Do you want to get going?'

He took a step forward until he was standing just inside her threshold. 'Are you in a hurry? It's usually considered polite to invite a guest in. Or is there something you don't want me to see?'

As if. Her life was an open book. A very dull book, which had been left to gather dust on the library shelf, a little like her. 'Not at all. I just thought you might want to get started. Ah, come in. Although you are. In.'

How had he done that? Eased himself in through the door and past her so smoothly she had barely noticed. She should add magician to his list of talents.

Come on, Hope, get some control. 'Tea?' When in doubt revert to a good national stereotype.

'Iced?'

'No, the normal kind. I have Earl Grey, normal, Darjeeling and peppermint.'

His mouth quirked. 'Seriously?'

'Er…yes. I found this little shop which sells imported British goods and I stocked up…' *Stop talking right now, Hope.* But her mouth didn't get the message. 'Tea and pickle, sandwich pickle, not gherkins. And real chocolate, no offence. There's many things the US does better, like coffee and cheesecake, but I would give my firstborn for a really mature cheddar cheese and pickle sandwich followed by a proper chocolate bar.'

Just in case he had any doubt she was socially awkward she was spelling it out for him loud and clear. She hadn't always been this way; if only she could turn the clocks back nine years—although if it was a choice between getting her confidence back or her parents there was no contest. She'd happily be awkward for ever.

Mercifully Gael didn't pursue the conversation. He stood in the middle of the room, dominating all the space in the tiny studio. 'Nice address.'

'Location is everything. Apparently it makes up for the lack of actual space—at least that's what Maddison says. It's her apartment,' she explained as his eyebrows shot up in query. 'We swapped homes when we swapped jobs.' Not that Maddison was currently occupying either Hope's home or her job; instead she was cosied up in the home of Hope's old boss, Kit Buchanan, planning a future together. Hope had worked with Kit for three years and he had never stepped even a centimetre over the professional line but barely a couple of months with Maddison and he had given up his job and was planning a whole new life with the American. Hope couldn't help wondering how the job swap had turned Maddison's life so radically upside down while hers was left untouched.

And look at Faith. Less than three months into her travels and she was engaged to the heir to a multimillion-dollar fortune, which was an awful lot more than most people managed on a gap year. What had Hope done in the city that never slept? Tried a few new bagel flavours and experimented with her coffee order. Hold the front page.

Maybe today wasn't going to be so horrendous after all. Whatever Gael had planned at least it would be *new*. Maybe this was all for the best—what was the point in bemoaning the dullness of her life if she didn't grasp this chance to shake things up a little?

Gael strolled over to the window in just four long strides. 'I like it. Nice light.' The apartment didn't compare with his, of course, but thanks to the gorgeous bay window the light did flood in, bathing the white room with an amber glow. The window opened far enough for Hope to climb out onto the fire escape so she could perch on the iron staircase, cup of tea in one hand, book in the other, soaking up the sunshine.

'It does for me. I don't need much space.' Which was a good thing. A tiny table and solitary chair sat in the bay of the window, the daybed occupied the one spare wall lying opposite the beautiful and incongruously large fireplace. The kitchen area—two cupboards and a two-ring stove—took up the corner by the apartment door and a second door to its right led into the

walk-in closet equipped with rails and drawers, which
opened directly into the diminutive but surprisingly
well appointed bathroom. Two people in the studio
would be cosy, three a crowd, but this was the first time
Hope had shared the space with anyone else. Unless
she counted the Skype conversations with her sister.

Loneliness slammed into her, almost knocking the
breath out of her.

Gael's mouth quirked into a knowing smile. 'I'm
sure you don't. More used to accommodating others
than demanding space, aren't you?'

'There's nothing wrong with being able to live simply. What do I need? For today? A coat? Different
shoes?' She wasn't going to ask what they were doing,
show any curiosity, but she wasn't above digging for
a clue.

Gael turned and looked her over slowly and deliberately. It was an objective look, similar to the way
he'd looked at her when he asked to paint her, as if she
were an object, not a living, breathing person and certainly not as if she was a woman or in any way desirable. And yet her nerves smouldered under his gaze
as if the long-buried embers remembered what it felt
like to blaze free.

'You'll do as you are.' That was a fat lot of help.

'Great.' Hope grabbed her bag. 'Lead on, then. The
sooner we get this over with, the sooner I can get on
with some wedding planning for Faith. Don't think I'm
here for any other reason.'

But even as she said the words Hope knew she
wasn't being entirely honest, not with him, not with
herself. She could tell herself as much as she liked that
she was only spending time with Gael for her sister,

for her job. But the truth was she needed a way out of the rigid constraints and fears she had built around her. And whatever happened over the next two weeks or so Hope knew that she would be changed in some way. And that had to be a good thing, didn't it? Because this life swap had shown her that it wasn't her old job, or raising Faith or living in her childhood house that had imprisoned her. It was Hope herself. Which meant there was no handsome prince or fairy godmother waiting in the wings to transform her life, to transform her.

This was her chance and she was going to grab it.

'So, where exactly are we going? Do we need to get a cab?' Hope was trying to sound nonchalant but Gael could tell that she was eaten up with curiosity. What had she been imagining? Probably the worst—after all, hadn't he told her that he wanted her to take some risks? To start living? She'd probably put those remarks together with the paintings and come up with some seduction scenario straight out of a nineteen-seventies porn movie.

But it wasn't her body he needed to start exploring, no, not even in those shorts, which hugged her compact body perfectly, lengthening her legs and rounding nicely over what was a very nice bottom. He had never deflowered a virgin, not even in his school days, and had no intention of starting now. Inexperience physically meant inexperience emotionally and Gael had no intention of dealing with crushes or infatuation or anything else equally messy. No matter how enticing the package.

Hang on—when had Hope gone from convenient minion and model to enticing? He'd been so busy with the exhibition he'd been living like a monk for the last few months—which was more than a little ironic, considering how much naked female flesh had been on display in his studio. It wasn't *her* per se. No, Hope was just the first woman he had spent any time with in a social capacity in a while. Obviously boundaries would blur a little.

Not that this was really social. Sort out the wedding, crack open that shell she'd erected around herself and she'd be ready for him to paint. That was why he was here, why he'd spent yesterday afternoon wandering around Central Park encouraging her to forget her dignity and enjoy the carousel ride. At the end of the day it was all business.

And he refused to dwell on just how enjoyable the business had ended up being... 'No cab needed. It's just a few blocks.'

'Okay.'

She still sounded apprehensive and Gael's conscience gave him a small but definite nudge. His skill, talent aside, had always been to put people at their ease, so much so that they almost forgot he was there. That was how he managed to take so many fly-on-the-wall photos; no paparazzi tricks for him. No, just the ability to blend in, to become part of the furniture. But something about Hope McKenzie had him rubbed up all the wrong way; he liked seeing her bristle a little too much, couldn't resist winding her up. But a brittle, wary subject wasn't going to give him the kind of picture he needed. It was time to turn up the charm. 'We're going to the Metropolitan Museum of Art. I want you to look at an original Manet and some portraits to get an idea of what I want from you—and then we can look at the roof terrace. It's beautiful up there and you might want to consider it for the reception. They don't usually hire it out but I might be able to pull some strings.'

'That sounds great.'

Gael repressed a grin as Hope exhaled a very audible sigh of relief. 'What, did you think I was going to send you on some kind of Seduction 101 course? Starting with the dance of the seven veils and ending up in some discreet bordello?'

'Of course not,' but the colour in her cheeks belied her words. Interesting, her imagination had definitely been at play. Had he figured in it at all? The seducer, the cad, the lover? The architect, leading her through her seductive education? Gael tore his mind back to the matter at hand, refusing to allow it to dwell on the interesting scenes so effortlessly conjured up.

He stopped as Hope halted at a snack stand to pick up a bottle of water and an apple. She turned, the apple in one hand, like Eve tempting him to fall. 'Would you like anything?'

'No, thanks.' He'd forgotten that girls, that women, did that. Bought their own water, a normal bottle of water from a normal silver metal snack stand just outside Central Park. The women he dated demanded fancy delis and even fancier water imported from remote places with prices to match.

And they never paid their way. Hope hadn't even sent him a hopeful sideways look; instead she'd offered to treat him. To water and a piece of fruit, but still. It was a novel experience—and not a displeasing one.

'So.' She had sunk her teeth into the apple, juice on her lips. He tried not to stare, not to be too fascinated by the glistening sweetness, but his eyes were drawn back to the tempting plumpness. The serpent knew what it was doing when it selected an apple; Adam had never stood a chance. 'Do we have to go into special rooms to look at the paintings or are they respectable nudes?'

'It's all perfectly respectable,' he promised as they turned the corner and walked towards the steps leading up to the arched entrances of the museum. As usual the steps were crowded: groups of girls gossiping while sipping from huge coffee cups, lone people scrolling through phones, sketching or reading battered paperbacks, couples entwined and picnicking families. The usual sense of coming home washed over him. The museum had been a sanctuary when he had lived in Misty's town house, the place he had come to on exeats from school. The only place where he had felt that he knew who he was. Where his anonymity wasn't a curse but a blessing as he moved through the galleries, just another tourist.

Hope tossed her apple core into a trash can and wiped her hands on a tissue before lobbing that in after her apple. 'I pass this every day on my way to work,' she said as they began to climb the stairs. 'I always meant to come in.'

'What stopped you? It's open late and at weekends.'

Hope shrugged. 'I don't know, the usual, I suppose.'

'Which is?'

'That because I haven't before I don't know how to. And before you say anything, yes, I know it's stupid. But even though we lived in London my parents weren't really museum people or theatre people—they were far more likely to take us for a walk. They liked nothing better than driving out to a hill somewhere so we could walk up it and eat sandwiches in the drizzle. It was always drizzling!'

'My parents didn't take me to museums either— Misty's interest only runs to showing off her philanthropy and my dad only stepped foot inside when it was the annual ball and only then under duress. I think that's why I loved it so much; it's somewhere I discovered for myself. What did you do as a teenager?'

'Hung out with friends, the usual.' But her voice was constrained and she had turned a little away from him, a clear sign she didn't want to talk about it.

They reached the doors and entered the magnificent Great Hall with its huge ceilings and sweeping arches. Gael palmed his pass, steering Hope past the queues waiting patiently to check their bags in and pay for admittance until he reached the membership desk.

The neatly dressed woman behind the desk smiled, barely looking at his pass. 'Good morning, Mr O'Connor. Is this young lady your guest?'

'Good morning, Jenny. How's the degree going? Yes, Hope's with me.'

'First-name terms with the staff?' Hope murmured as he led her down the corridor, expertly winding his way around tour groups and puzzled clumps of map-wielding visitors.

'I may come here fairly regularly.' Plus he was a patron—and Misty sat on the prestigious Board of Trustees but Hope didn't need to know that. He didn't want to dazzle her with his connections; he'd learned long ago that women impressed with those were only after one thing—influence. He'd vowed long ago never to be used again. He might be enjoying Hope's company but, just like every other woman, she was with him because of what he could do for her. It was a lesson he was unlikely to forget.

Hope sank onto the couch with a grateful cry. 'I wore my most comfortable shoes and *still* my feet ache. We must have walked miles and miles and miles without ever going outside. And my eyes ache just as much as my feet.'

Gael suppressed a smile. 'It's not easy compressing two thousand plus years of art history into a four-hour tour.'

'Five hours and only a twenty-minute coffee stop,' Hope said bitterly. 'I almost fainted away right in front of the Renoir—or was it Degas?'

'Better get it right or you'll fail the written test later. I've ordered a cheese plate, water and a glass of wine. Do you think that will fortify you?'

'Only if I don't have to move again. Ever.'

'Not for the next half hour,' Gael promised. 'But then we have a private tour of the roof garden and the Terrace Room. Your sister can't get married here but she can certainly have the reception. Do you know how many you're organising it for yet?'

Hope rubbed her temples. 'Not exactly but because Misty is planning such a lavish party and a blessing two days later the wedding day itself is to be kept small and intimate. Last email she said that she would like to keep it down to me, you, Hunter's mother of course. His father—will that be awkward in such a small group?'

'I don't think so. Misty and he still move in all the same circles. I told you yesterday, she specialises in civilised divorces.'

'Then a couple of the groom's friends and apparently they are paying for two of Faith's school friends and our aunt and her family to fly over. So that will be...' she totted up the amount on her fingers '...fifteen.'

'Hmm, we might rattle around a bit in the Terrace Room. Let's have a look and see what you think.'

'Faith emailed yesterday to say she would definitely like to have two dresses, which is great because finding just one isn't proving to be at all awkward. Something subtle for the wedding because it's so small, but I think she wants to go all out for the party, especially as they will be repeating their vows.' Hope bit her lip. 'It's such a responsibility. The couple of places I spoke to yesterday seemed to imply that it was easier to learn to do heart surgery in a fortnight than it is to buy and fit a wedding dress. And it's not just the dress. There's a veil, tiara, jewellery. Underwear. And she wants me to sort out bridesmaids' dresses for just me for the ceremony but for both friends and our cousin for the party as well.'

Gael got that Hope felt responsible for her sister, that she had raised her. But this amount of stress all for someone else? He couldn't imagine a single member of his family—including all the exes and steps—putting themselves out for someone else. He had them all on the list for his exhibition's opening-night party and knew Misty would be there if she possibly could. His father if there was nothing better to do. But his mother? She hadn't made his graduation from school or college, he doubted she'd make the effort for a mere party. Funny how, much as he told himself he didn't care, her casual desertion still stung after all these years—only he was so used to it that it was more of a pinprick than anything really wounding.

He didn't know if it was better or worse that she adored his two half-brothers so much, every occasional email a glowing testimonial to their unique specialness. No, he might still have two living, breathing parents but Faith was luckier than he was. What would it be like to have someone like Hope on your side? Someone you could count on? 'You could say no. Ask her to come and organise it herself.'

But she was already shaking her head. 'No. I promised her that I would take care of everything. If things were different she'd have a mother to help her. Well, she doesn't, she only has me. I won't let her down.' There was a telltale glimmer in her eyes and her words caught as she spoke. She looked away, swallowing convulsively as the waitress brought their food and drink over.

Gael sat back, smiling his thanks as the waitress placed their drinks and the cheese platter onto the table. Hope swallowed again and he gave her a moment to compose herself, glad that it was so quiet in the members' only lounge he had brought her to. 'What about you, Hope? Who takes care of you?'

She stared at him, her eyes wide in her pale face. 'I take care of me. I always have.'

'And you're doing just fine, is that what you're saying? You don't know how to step out of your limited comfort zone. You pour all your energy into work and looking after your sister and you're lonely. But you don't need anyone. Sure. You keep telling yourself that.'

What was he saying? He was all about the self-sufficiency himself. But it was different for him. He was toughened whereas Hope was like a toasted marsh-mallow—a superficial hardened edge hiding an utter mess on the inside. He'd only known her for less than three days but he'd diagnosed that within the first day. And it was a shame. She was a trier...that was evident. She cared, maybe a little too much. A girl like that should have someone to look out for her.

'Thanks for the diagnosis, Doc.' Hope picked up her wine glass and held it up to him in a toast. 'I'll make sure I come to you every time I need relationship advice. Especially as I spent a lot of time yesterday looking through photos at your place and do you know what I didn't see? I didn't see a single photo of you having fun. Oh, yes...' as he tried to interrupt. 'There are pictures of you posing next to women. Sometimes you have your arm around their waist. But you never look like you're enjoying yourself, you never look relaxed. You're as alone as I am—more so. I have Faith. Hunter said you were his brother but you were very quick to deny any relationship with him at all.'

Touché. Gael clinked her glass with his own. 'But I prefer to be by myself. It's my choice. Is it yours, or are you just too afraid to let anyone in? Either way, here's to Hunter and Faith, getting their wedding and this painting out of the way and returning to our solitary lives. Cheers.'

CHAPTER SIX

WHAT WAS IT about Gael O'Connor that made her bristle like an outraged cat? Hope usually hid her feelings so well sometimes it seemed, even to her, that she didn't have any. Slights, slurs and digs passed her by. It didn't rankle when the girls at work went out without her, when they chatted about nights out in front of her as if she weren't even there. She barely noticed when photos of school reunions she hadn't been invited to showed up on her social-media pages or when wedding photos were circulated and she wasn't amongst the guests. Hope had chosen to remove herself from the human race, had chosen to devote herself and her life to Faith; she wasn't going to complain now her job was almost done.

Why would she when she had raised a happy, confident, bright girl who had her whole future before her? She could never fully make things up to her little sister but she had done as much as was humanly possible—and if she had sacrificed her own life for that, well, that felt like a fair trade. She was at peace with her decision.

At peace until Gael opened his mouth, that was. As soon as that mocking note hit his voice her hackles rose and she responded every single time. Was it because he didn't care for the official 'Hope is wonderful to give everything up for Faith' line, instead making her sound like a pathetic martyr living life vicariously instead of in reality? She didn't need it pointed out. She knew she wasn't wonderful or selfless but she didn't feel like a martyr. Usually.

Still, she couldn't complain too much when in one afternoon he had managed to sort out the wedding venues and in such smooth style. It helped that they were looking at a Thursday afternoon wedding and not the weekend but Gael had known all the right people to talk to, to ensure the tight timescales weren't a problem. After consulting with the blissful and all too absent couple they had decided to hold the ceremony in Central Park itself, at a beautiful little leafy spot by the lake, followed by cocktails at the Tavern on the Green. The Met's Roof Garden closed to the public at four-thirty p.m. and wasn't usually available for private hire, but Gael had managed to sweet talk the event coordinator into letting them in after hours for drinks and dinner. So all Hope needed to do was organise afternoon entertainment, evening entertainment, flowers and clothes. She still had just over ten days. Easy.

Now all she wanted to do was fling herself onto the surprisingly comfortable daybed and sleep for at least twelve hours. Her feet still throbbed from the whistle-stop tour through the history of art and her head was even worse. But sleep was a long, long way away. Instead she had less than an hour to shower and get ready. 'I'll pick you up at eight,' Gael had said brusquely as they'd finalised the details with first the event organiser at the Met and then with the Central Park authorities. 'It might be worth eating first.'

Okay. This wasn't a date. Obviously. It was part work, part family business but still. Hope would bet her half of her overpriced London home that not one of the beauties she had seen hanging off Gael's arm in photos had ever taken less than three hours to get ready—and he would have always bought them dinner.

She crammed the rest of her Pop-Tart into her mouth and grabbed a banana reasoning that the addition of fruit turned her snack into a balanced meal.

Thirty minutes later she was showered with freshly washed and dried hair and dressed in one of her new dresses. She hadn't dared wear it before, much as she liked the delicate coffee-coloured silk edged with black lace; it was just so short, almost more of a tunic than a dress... She fingered a pair of thick black tights; surely they would make the dress more respectable? But it was still so hot and humid and her own legs were the brownest they had ever been thanks to weekends spent reading on her fire escape. Hope stared down at what seemed like endless naked flesh before cramming her feet into a pair of black and cream sandals she'd bought on sale but not yet worn because she wasn't entirely sure she could walk in them.

Hope steeled herself to look in the mirror. It was like looking at a stranger: a girl with huge eyes, emphasised with liquid liner and mascara, hair swept back into a low, messy bun, tendrils hanging around her face. This girl looked as if she belonged on the Upper East Side; she looked ready for anything. This girl was an imposter but maybe, just maybe, she could exist for a night or two.

The sound of the buzzer brought her back to the room, to the evening ahead, and Hope blinked a couple of times, getting her bearings back, returning to reality. Rather than buzz Gael up she grabbed her bag and slowly, teetering slightly as she adjusted to the height of the shoes, made her way out of the studio and down the stairs into the evening heat.

Gael took one look at her feet and hailed a cab, much to Hope's relief. She breathed a deep sigh of satisfaction as she sank into the back seat and swapped the evening humidity for the bliss of air conditioning. She had spent twenty-seven years in London considering air conditioning a seldom-needed luxury—less than a day in the New York summer and she'd changed her tune for ever.

She didn't recognise the address Gael gave the cab driver and so sat back, none the wiser about her destination, watching the streets of Manhattan slide slowly past. They were heading west and down, towards the busy tourist hotspots of Times Square and Broadway. She lived barely half an hour's walk from the lively theatre district and yet had only visited once, quickly defeated by the crowds and the heat. Hope stared out of the cab window at the crowded streets thronged with an eclectic mix of tourists, locals and hustlers—the busiest district of New York City by far.

The cab made its slow progression along Fifty-First Street until just after the road intersected with Broadway and then pulled up outside a small, dingy-looking theatre. Hope hadn't been entirely sure what to expect but it wasn't this down-at-heel-looking place. She pulled the dress down as she got out of the cab, wishing she had worn the black tights, feeling both overexposed and overdressed. Gael took her arm. 'This way.' They were the first words he had said to her all evening.

He ushered her through the wooden swing door into the lobby. It was a study in faded glory: old wooden panelling ornately carved and in need of a good dust, the red carpet faded and threadbare in places. It was the last place she had expected Gael to bring her. He was smart in a pale grey suit, his hair sleeked down, as incongruous a contrast to the tatty surroundings as she was. He handed two tickets to a woman dressed like a nineteen-forties usherette and then led Hope down the corridor into the theatre.

It was like stepping into another world. The huge chandeliers hanging from the high ceiling gave out a warm, dim glow, bathing the gold-leafed auditorium in flattering lowlights. The seats had been removed from the stalls and instead it was set up cabaret style with round tables for two, four or six taking up the floor space instead. Many tables were full already, their laughing, chattering occupants wearing anything from jeans to cocktail dresses.

The stage was set up with a microphone and a comfortable-looking leather chair. Nothing else. Steps led up from the floor to the stage.

Gael led her to a small table with just two chairs near the front, pulling a chair out for her with exaggerated courtesy. 'Two glasses of Pinot Noir, please,' he said to the hovering waitress, who was also dressed in nineteen-forties garb. Hope opened her mouth to change the order, she preferred white wine to red, especially on a hot night like this, but she closed it again as the waitress walked away, not caring enough to call the woman back.

'What is this?' she asked as she took her seat. 'Are you thinking this will be suitable entertainment for after the wedding meal?'

'What? Oh, no. We're looking into that later. Right now, this is all about you.' The wolfish look in his eyes did nothing to reassure her and she took the glass the waitress handed her with a mechanical smile. This wasn't some kind of comedy improvisation place, was it? Oh, no, what if it was audience participation? She would rather dance in public than try and tell jokes. And she'd probably prefer to strip naked rather than dance. Maybe that was the point.

Just as she tried to formulate her next question the lights dimmed and one lone spotlight lit up the chair and the microphone. The buzz of conversation quietened as, with an audible scrape and squeak, all chairs turned to face the stage. It remained empty for what was probably less than a minute but felt longer as the anticipation built, the air thick with it. Hope clasped her glass, her stomach knotted. She doubted she was here to see an avant-garde staging of Shakespeare or some minimalist musical.

Finally, a low drum roll reverberated throughout the room, the low rumble thrumming in her chest as if it were part of her heartbeat, and a woman stepped out onto the stage. She was tall, strikingly dressed in a floor-length black dress, a top hat incongruously perched on her head.

'Good evening, ladies and gentlemen, I am delighted to welcome you to the Hall of Truth tonight. As you know the entertainment is you and the stage is yours. This is where you are able to free yourselves of an unwanted burden. You are welcome to share anything—a secret, something humorous, a sad tale, a confession, a rant, a declaration, anything you like. Here are the rules: what's said in the Hall of Truth stays in the Hall of Truth unless it's illegal—there's no confessor's bond here, people.' A nervous laugh at this as people turned in their seats as if searching out any potential villain.

The blonde Master of Ceremonies smiled as the laugh faded away. 'No slander, no judgement and—most importantly—no lies. And no singing or dancing. There are no directors here searching out their next star! Oh, and please switch your cell phones off. Anyone caught recording or videoing will be prosecuted and, besides, it's bad manners. Okay. As is customary on these occasions I'll start. Anyone who would like to contribute please let a waitress know and you'll be added to tonight's set list.' She took in a deep breath, her rich tones captivating the audience. 'Tonight I am going to share with you the story of my daughter's hamster and my parents' dog and I must warn you that I can't guarantee that no animals were harmed during the making of this tale.'

'You've brought me to a place that tells pet snuff tales? Shame on you,' Hope whispered and a gleam of amusement flickered on Gael's face.

'Compared to some of the stories I've heard here this is practically fluffy and warm.'

'I bet that's what the dog said.' But Hope's mind was whirling. He'd come here before? More than once. Did he sit here and listen, just as he'd sat to the side and taken photos when he was younger? Or did he join in? What did he have to confess? She couldn't imagine him telling a funny story.

'Have you done this?' she whispered as the first audience participant stumbled up onto the stage, pale and visibly nervous as he launched into a tale of wreaking revenge at a school reunion on the bullies who had made his school life a misery. Gael leaned in, his mouth so close to her ear she could feel the warmth of his breath on her bare shoulder. Hope shivered.

'I can't tell you that, I'm afraid. You heard her. What's said in the Hall of Truth stays in the Hall of Truth.' He leaned back and the spot on her shoulder tingled, heat spreading down to the pit of her stomach. Hope drew in a shuddering breath, glancing sideways at Gael. He was concentrating on the stage, his eyes shuttered. Why did he come here to hear strangers speak? And more importantly why had he brought her?

Hope wouldn't have thought it possible that so many people would be prepared to stand up and bare their souls to a room of strangers but, as the first hour ticked by, there was no shortage of willing volunteers. There was a pattern, she noticed. Most ascended the steps nervously, even the ones with confident grins showed telltale signs, the way they tugged at their hands or pulled at their hem. But they all, even the woman who confessed to crashing her husband's car and blaming it on their teenage son, bribing him to take the fall, descended the steps with an air of a weight having been removed from their shoulders, a burden lessened. It was an appealing thought.

The red wine was heavier than she cared for and yet the first glass was finished before she noticed and replaced with a second, which also disappeared all too easily. Gael motioned the waitress over to get their glasses topped up again and a wild idea seized Hope. Maybe she too could lessen some of her burdens. True, she didn't deserve to. But she'd been carrying the guilt around for nine long, long years. Would it hurt to share it? To let this crowd of strangers be her judge and jury.

Her breath caught in her throat, the very thought of speaking the words she'd buried for so long out loud almost choking her. But as the man on stage finished relating a very funny tale of neighbourhood rivalry taken to extremes her mind was made up and when the waitress came over in response to Gael's gesture Hope handed her the slip, slumping back in her chair as the waitress nodded.

What have I done? Her chest was tighter than ever, nausea swirling in her stomach as her throat swelled— her whole body conspiring to make sure she didn't say anything. She glanced at Gael and saw his eyes were fixed on her. Was that approval she saw in their blue-grey depths? He'd brought her here for this, she realised. Wanted her to expose herself emotionally before she did so physically. He was probably right—posing would be a doddle after this.

If she went through with it.

She barely took in the next speaker, her hands clammy and her breath shallow. She swigged the wine as carelessly as if it had been water, needing Dutch courage in the absence of actual courage. She didn't have to do this; she could get up and walk away. She *should* get up and walk away. What was stopping her? After all, her sister's wedding was almost sorted—and if this was the price she had to pay for her career then maybe she needed to reassess her options.

True, Gael wasn't making her do this. Just as he wasn't making her pose for him and yet somehow she was agreeing to do both. He was her puppet master and she was allowing him to pull her strings.

Her head was buzzing, the noise nearly drowning out every other sound and she barely heard her name called. Just her first name, anonymity guaranteed. *She didn't have to do this*...and yet she was stumbling to her feet and heading towards the steps and somehow walking up them, even in the heels from hell, and heading towards the microphone. She grasped it as if it were the only thing keeping her anchored and took in a deep breath.

The spotlight bathed her in warmth and a golden light and had the added bonus of slightly dazzling her so that she couldn't make out any faces on the floor below, just an indistinguishable dark grey mass. If she closed her ears to the coughing, throat clearing, shuffling and odd whispers she might be alone.

'Hi. I'm Hope.' She took a swig of the water someone had thrust in her hand as she had stepped onto the stage, glad of the lubrication on her dry throat. 'I just want to start by saying that I don't usually wear heels this high so if I stagger or fall it's not because I'm drunk but because I have a really bad sense of balance.' Actually after three glasses of Pinot Noir following a dinner comprising of two Pop-Tarts and a banana she *was* a little buzzed but, confessional or not, she didn't see the need to share *that* with the crowd.

Hope took another long slow breath and surveyed the grey mass of people. It was now or never. 'My parents loved to tell me that they named me Hope because I *gave* them hope. They planned a big family, only things didn't work out that way until, after four years of disappointment and several miscarriages, I was born.

They thought that I was a sign, that I was the beginning of a long line of babies. But I wasn't.' She squeezed her eyes shut for a long moment, remembering the desperation and overwhelming need in their voices when they recounted the story of her name to her.

'My childhood was great in many ways. I was loved, we had a nice house in a nice area of London but I knew, I always knew I wasn't enough. They needed more than me. More children. And so my earliest memories are of my mother crying as she lost another baby. Of tests and hospital appointments and another baby lost. I hated it. I wanted them to stop. No more tears, no more hospitals, no brothers or sisters. Just the three of us but happier. But when I was eight they finally gave me the sister I didn't want. They called her Faith…' was that her voice breaking? '…because they'd always had faith that she would be born. And although they still didn't have the long line of children they had dreamed of, now Faith was here they could stop trying. She was enough. She completed them in a way I hadn't been able to.'

The room was absolutely still. It was like speaking out into a large void. 'Looking back, I know it wasn't that simple. They didn't love her more than they loved me. But back then all I knew was that she wasn't told to run along because Mummy was sad or sick or in hospital, her childhood wasn't spent tiptoeing around grief. She had everything and I… I hated her for it. So I pulled away. Emotionally and physically, spending as much time at friends' houses as I could. I pushed my parents away again and again when all I really wanted was for them to tell me I mattered—but they had no idea how to deal with me and the longer they gave me space, the angrier I got and the wider the chasm became. Once I hit my mid-teens it was almost irreparable.

'I wasn't a very good teen. I drank and stayed out late. I wore clothes I knew they'd hate and got piercings they disapproved of. Hung out with people they thought trouble and went to places they forbade me to go. But I wasn't a fool, I knew my best shot at independence was a good education and I worked hard, my sights set on university in Scotland, a day's travel away. And still they said nothing, even when I left prospectuses for Aberdeen lying around. I thought they didn't care.' She took another sip of water, her throat raw with suppressed tears.

'The summer before I was due to go away they booked a weekend away for my mother's fiftieth birthday and asked me to look after Faith. You have no idea how much I whinged, finally extorting a huge fee for babysitting my own sister. I was supposed to have her from the Friday till the Monday morning but on the Sunday I called them and told them they had to come home because I had plans.'

This was the hard bit. True, she had never told anyone what a brat she'd been, how miserable she'd made her family—and herself—but that was small stuff. This, now, was her crime. Her eternal shame. 'I'd been seeing someone, a boy from school, and his parents had made last-minute plans to spend the Sunday night away. I thought I might be in love with him and I didn't want to go to university a virgin, and this seemed like the perfect opportunity to finally sleep together—in his house, in a bed with total privacy.

'I called my parents and told them they needed to

finish their weekend early. That I would be leaving the house at four and if they weren't back then Faith would be on her own. It was their choice, I told them, they were responsible for her, not me. And I put the phone down knowing that I had won. I had. Right that moment they were packing their things, their weekend ruined by their own daughter.' She swallowed, remembering the exact way she had felt at that moment. 'I knew even then that I was being unfair, I didn't feel victory or anticipation, just bitterness. At myself for being such a selfish idiot—and at them for allowing me to be. I hadn't left them much time to get home so I think they were distracted, hurrying. They weren't speeding and my dad was a really good driver. But somehow he didn't react in time to the truck that pulled out right in front of him. It was instant, the police said. They probably didn't feel a thing. Probably.'

Utter silence.

'I didn't lose my virginity that night but I did become a grown-up. I had deprived my sister of her parents and so I took on that role. I gave up my dreams of university, gave up any thought of carving out my own life and dedicated myself to raising my sister.' Hope couldn't stop the proud smile curving her lips. 'I think I've done okay. I spoiled her a little but she's a lovely, warm-hearted, sweet girl. And she loves me. But I've never told her what I did. And I don't know if I ever will. Thank you for listening.'

He only had himself to blame. He'd wanted to know what she was hiding, had wanted her to open up and now she had.

He should be pleased, Hope had shed a layer of armour, allowed her vulnerability to peek through just as he had planned. It would make her picture all the rawer. So why did he feel manipulative? Voyeuristic in a way he hadn't felt even as a teen taking secret photos to expose his classmates?

Because now he knew it all. He knew why she was still a virgin, why she would put her whole life on hold to plan her sister's wedding, why she put herself last, didn't allow herself the luxury of living. And Gael didn't know whether he wanted to hug her and make it better—or pull her to him and kiss her until all she could do was feel.

The way she looked on that stage was terrifying enough: endless legs, huge eyes, provocative mouth. But the worst part was it wasn't the way she looked that had him all churned up inside. It was what she said. Who she was. He had never met anyone like her before.

For the first time in a long time he wasn't sure he was in control—and hadn't he sworn that he'd never hand over control to a woman, to another human being ever again? Because in the end they always, always let you down.

Hope slid into the seat next to him, shaking slightly as the adrenaline faded away. He remembered the feeling well, the relief, the euphoria, the fear. 'Can we go?' she asked.

'Sure. Let me just pay.'

'Great, I'll wait for you in the lobby.' And just like that she was gone, walking tall and proud even in the heels she could barely balance in. His chest clenched painfully. He'd never met anyone like her before. Brave and determined and doing her best to cover up how lost she actually was. He'd spent so long with society queens obsessed with image, with money, with power that he had forgotten that there were women out there who played by a whole different set of rules.

It didn't take long for him to settle up and join her. Hope was standing absolutely still, lost in a world of her own, her dark eyes fixed on something he couldn't see. Guilt twinged his conscience. 'That was a brave thing you did in there.'

'Was it?' She looked at him pensively. 'I don't know. Letting go would be brave. Telling a room full of strangers? I don't know if that's enough.'

'Who else could you tell?'

'Sometimes I wonder if I should let Faith know the truth. If she should know just what kind of person I really am, not worthy of her love and respect.'

'Punish yourself more, you mean? What would that accomplish? Look at me, Hope.' He took her chin gently in one hand, forcing it up so her eyes met his gaze. They were so sad, filled with a grief and regret he couldn't imagine and all he wanted was to wipe the sadness out of them. 'What matters is what you have done in the last nine years and that makes you more than worthy of her love and respect. Don't make her feel that she wasn't a responsibility you accepted joyfully but a burden that you took on through guilt. Think that she's the reason you've spent the last nine years locked away from any kind of normal life. Honesty isn't always the best policy, Hope.'

'You think I should keep lying?'

'Do you love her?'

'Of course I do!'

'Would you sacrifice everything for her?'

'Yes!'

'Then that's your truth. How you got to this point is just history. Goddammit, Hope, the girl lost one set of parents. Don't threaten the bond she has with you as well.' He knew all too well what it felt like to have that bond tossed aside as if it—and he—had meant nothing. 'Come on, I'll take you home.'

But she didn't move. 'I thought we were going out afterwards. You said you knew the perfect place we could go to after the wedding dinner and we should try it out tonight.'

'Haven't you had enough excitement for one night?' He knew he had. He wanted to get back to his studio and draw until all these inconvenient feelings disappeared. This sense of responsibility, of kinship. This stirring of attraction he was trying his damnedest to ignore. So her legs went on for ever, so a man could get lost in her eyes, so he never quite knew what she would say or do next, one minute opinionated and bossy and the next strikingly vulnerable. So he wanted to make everything that had ever gone wrong in her life better. None of this meant anything. Once he'd painted her all these unwanted thoughts and feeling and desires would disappear, poured into the painting where they belonged.

Irritation flashed in her eyes. 'Don't tell me what I have or haven't had, Gael O'Connor. You may have orchestrated tonight but I've been looking after myself for a long, long time. You promised me that I would loosen up and have some fun—well, right now I'm more tense that I think I've ever been so what I need is for you to keep your word and for you to show me a good time.'

Her words were belligerent but the look in her eyes was anything but. She wanted to forget; he understood that all too well. He weighed up the consequences. He should put her in a cab and go somewhere where he could drink until every word she had said on stage was no longer scared into his brain. But common sense seemed less than desirable, everything seemed less than desirable while she stood there in a dress that barely skimmed her thighs, need radiating from her like a beacon. He swore under his breath. He was a fool—but at least he was aware of it. 'Come on, then, what are you waiting for?'

CHAPTER SEVEN

IT WAS A short walk to their destination but, after a swift assessing look at her feet, Gael flagged down a cab, tipping the driver well in advance to make up for the swift journey. It took less than five minutes before the car pulled up and Hope blinked as she took in their surroundings, unable to keep the surprise off her face as she looked around at the massive hotel they'd been dropped off by. As she turned she could see the bright lights of Times Square flashing brashly just a few metres away. 'Every time you take me somewhere you surprise me,' she said. 'Art museums, funny little theatres and now a hotel?'

'We're not going into the hotel proper,' he assured her and steered her past the darkened windows of the hotel to the bar tucked into the ground floor. 'Just into here.'

'Okay,' but she wasn't convinced as he opened the anonymous-looking door and stood aside to allow her to precede him inside. 'It's just this is a hotel bar and it's not really the kind of thing I think Faith is wanting...' She stopped as abruptly as if her volume had been turned down, her mouth still open as she slowly turned and surveyed the room. It was perfect.

Wood panelled and lit with discreet low lights, the piano bar evoked a long-gone era. Hope half expected to see sharp-suited men propping up the bar, their fedoras pulled low and ravishing molls, all red lipsticks and bobs, on their arms.

The long wooden bar took up most of the back wall, a dazzling array of drinks displayed on the beautifully carved shelves behind. A line of red-leather-topped stools invited weary drinkers to sit down and unload their cares into the ever open ears of the expert bartenders. Gael nodded towards a table, discreetly situated in the corner. 'Cocktail?'

Hope weighed up the consequences. A cocktail on top of all that wine? But the five minutes she had spent on stage had sobered her up more effectively than an ice-cold shower and she needed something to alleviate the buzz in her veins. 'Yes. Please. I don't mind what. I know, I'll try one of the house specialities.'

She took a seat, watching Gael as he ordered their drinks. He fitted in here, sleek and handsome with an edge that was undeniably attractive, probably because it was unknown, slightly dangerous. She looked away quickly, hoping he hadn't caught her staring, as he joined her. 'This place is awesome. It's like the New York I hoped to find but haven't yet, if that makes sense.'

'It's exactly like a film set,' he agreed. 'Piano and all. They'll have a jazz band playing on the night of your sister's wedding...'

'So we can come here after the dinner? Oh, Gael, thank you. What a brilliant idea. Faith is going to be so happy. The only thing is it's not that big and there will be fifteen of us. Can we reserve a table?'

He nodded. 'They don't usually but I should be able to…'

'Pull a few strings? I've noticed that. Hunter was right. You know everyone.'

'That's why he sent you to me.'

'Yes. I could never have done this on my own, thank you.'

'I'm not helping you out of the goodness of my heart,' he reminded her.

'Oh, I know, I owe you a debt.' She did but she couldn't begrudge him that, not now. Hope had seen a lot of weddings recently, mostly vicariously through photos shared on social media, far too cut off from her old social group to merit an invitation. They all varied in location, in expense, but the trend seemed to be for huge, extravagant, glitzy events. This small but very sweet wedding she and Gael were putting together in record time made the rest seem tawdry and cheap. It was, she realised with a jolt, the kind of wedding she would want for herself.

The realisation slammed into her and she gripped the table. Would she ever have the opportunity to do this for herself? She wasn't sure she'd know how to date any more, let alone fall in love—and suddenly it was dawning on her just how much she wanted to. Spending the last three days with another human being, a very male human being, had been eye opening. She wasn't entirely sure she always liked Gael; she certainly wasn't comfortable around him. But he challenged her, pushed her, helped her. Attracted her.

Yes. Attracted. Was that so wrong? She was twenty-seven, single, presumably with working parts. Attraction was normal. Only she was a beginner and she was pretty sure he was at super-advanced level. Far too much to handle for her first real crush in a decade. She should start slow. With a man who wore tweed and liked fossils.

Thank goodness, here was her cocktail and it was time to stop thinking. With relief Hope took an incautious sip, eyes watering as the alcohol hit her throat. 'Strong,' she gasped.

'They're not known for their half measures. How are you?'

'Choking on neat gin?'

He raised an eyebrow and she sighed. 'I feel like I've been for a ten-kilometre run or something. It's exhausting baring your soul to complete strangers.'

'I know.'

It was obvious that he did. Either the alcohol or the knowledge he truly had seen everything she was emboldened her to push deeper. 'What did you say? When you went up? You did go up, didn't you? That's how you know it's what I needed.' It had been, she realised. She'd needed to drain some of the poison from her soul.

Gael didn't answer at first, fingering the rim of his glass as he stared into the distance. Hope watched his capable-looking fingers as they caressed the glass in sure strokes and something sweet and dark clenched low inside her.

'I first went there because I was looking for inspiration. My photos felt stale, uninspired. I had just been asked to shoot a series for *Fabled* about the next generation of Upper East Side, all unimaginatively dressed up as Gatsby and co. There they were, ten years younger than my friends and just as entitled, just as arrogant, nothing had changed. I came to the Truth night looking for hope. I didn't expect to be getting up on stage and bearing my soul.' His mouth twisted. 'It could have been professional suicide. I know it's supposed to be confidential but if a journalist had heard me confess how much I hated my work they could have destroyed me.'

'Is that what you said?'

'It's not what I meant to say but near the end it hit me. I was miserable. I needed to change, get back to what I'd originally planned to do—paint.'

'So what did you say?'

'I don't know why but I wanted to tell them about the first time I went to Paris, about the effect the whole city had on me. I'd spent days in the Louvre and so when I went to the Musée d'Orsay I was a little punch-drunk.'

'I can relate to that after this afternoon.'

He grinned. 'Not so punch-drunk that I mixed up Renoir and Degas.' Hope pulled a face at him, absurdly pleased when he laughed. 'Then I saw her, Olympia. I don't know why she struck me the way she did. It wasn't that I found the painting particularly sexy or shocking or anything. But her honesty hit me. I didn't know that relationships could be that honest.'

Hope set her drink down and stared. 'But isn't she a courtesan?'

He nodded. 'And she's upfront about it. There's no coyness, no pretence. "Here I am," she says. "Take me or leave me but if you take there's a price." Everyone knows where they stand, no hard feelings.'

Hope tried to put his words into a context she understood. 'But a relationship, a real one, a lasting one, that's based on honesty, surely.'

'Is that what you believe?'

Was it? She was doubting herself now. 'It's what I'd like to believe.' That much she knew.

'Exactly! You've been sold the fairy tale and you want to believe it's true, but you and me, we live in the real world, we know how rare true honesty is.'

'Hey, don't drag me into your cynical gang of two! What happened to make you so anti love?'

He smiled at that, slow and serious and dangerously sweet. 'Oh, I believe in love. First love, love at first sight, passion, need. I just don't believe in happy-ever-after. Or that love has anything to do with marriage. The marriages I see are based on something entirely different.'

'What's that?'

'Power. Either one person holds all the power and the other is happy to concede it—that's how the whole trophy-wife—or husband, in my father's case, it can be equal opportunity—business works. One half pays, the other obeys. Once they stop being obedient, or they live past their shelf life, then they get replaced.'

'In your crazy world of wife bonuses and prenups maybe, not in the real world.'

'In every world. It may not be as obvious or under-stood but it's there.'

'But if that was the case then all marriages would fail eventually,' she objected. 'And they don't. Some, sure. But not all.'

Gael shrugged. 'Some people are happy with the imbalance. Or they have equal power and can balance each other out, but that's rare. Now my dad, he keeps marrying women with money. In the beginning they like that he's younger, they think he's handsome, it gives him status—he holds the power. But once they are used to his looks and the lust dies down and they realise their friends aren't so much jealous as amused by their marriage then the power shifts. That's where he is right now. Again.'

'Does he love them? The women he marries?'

'He loves the lifestyle. He loves that they don't demand anything from him. My mom, she held the power because he was absolutely besotted. He tried everything to make her happy. That's her trick. Only in her case she always stays on top. She leaves them when a better deal comes along. Although she's been with Tony for ten years and they have two kids so who knows? Maybe this one she'll stick out.'

'Not all marriages are like that. Your parents were so young when they married.'

'Like Hunter and Faith?'

'Yes.' She wanted to say things would be different for them but how could she when they were still such strangers? But her sister's marriage was hers, to succeed and fail as it would. Hope would help where she could but in this her sister, for the first time in her life, was on her own. 'But they are hardly typical either. Look, you have spent your whole life watching these absurdly rich, absurdly spoilt people play at marriage, play at love, grabbing what they want and walking away the second it gets tough. The real world isn't like that. My parents survived seven miscarriages— seven—IVF. Me,' she finished sadly. She was all too aware just what a strain her behaviour had been on her parents. She would give anything to go back and do it all over again. Yes to Saturday night pizza and films, yes to Sunday walks in the country, yes to that damn carousel ride.

She tried again. 'Look, I might have little real-time experience of love or relationships. I've obviously never been married. But I know something about living up to expectations. If you go around believing everyone is looking to shaft everyone else then that's what you'll find. I don't believe that. I won't.'

His eyes narrowed. 'Look at that, Hope McKenzie all fired up. I like it.'

And she was. She was on fire, living, completely in the moment for the first time in nine years. Her chains loosened, her self-hatred relieved. 'In that case,' she said slowly, scarcely believing the words coming out of her mouth, 'I believe we have a painting to start working on.'

Time stilled as Gael studied her, his eyes still narrowed to intense slits, his focus purely on her. Hope made every muscle still, made herself meet that challenging stare as coolly as she could. If they didn't start this now she wasn't sure she'd ever have the guts to go through with it. But right here, right now, she was ready.

He pushed his stool back and stood up in one graceful, almost predatory movement. 'Yes, it's time,' he said and a shiver ran through her at his words. 'Let's get this painting started.'

The scene was set. He'd planned it all out the day he met her and it was the work of seconds to pull the chaise round to exactly the right angle and to set up the spotlights he used for his photographs to simulate the sun. 'Here,' he said, throwing a clean robe over to her. 'Go and get changed. Can you screw your hair up into a high knot?'

Hope nodded. She had barely said a word since they had left the bar, since her unexpected challenge. But she'd lost that wide-eyed wariness that had both attracted and repelled him. Tonight she was filled with some other emotion, an anticipation that pulled him in. She was ready, ripe for the unveiling.

Gael swallowed. She wasn't the only one full of anticipation. His hands weren't quite steady as he threw a white sheet over the chaise, adding a huge pillow and a rumpled flowery shawl. The other models had brought in their own jewellery, pillows, throws to lie on, things that had significance to them, but he was painting Hope in almost identical colours and attitude to the original. The virgin posing as the courtesan.

'Wait, take this as well.' He handed her a bag.

Hope took it, opening it and peering at its contents. A thick gold bracelet, a pair of pearl earrings and a black ribbon to tie around her neck. Mule slippers. An orchid for her hair. 'Okay. What about make-up?'

'You don't need any. You have perfect skin.'

A blush crept up her cheeks at his words and she threw him a quick smile before heading off to the small bathroom he had directed her to just three days ago. Was that all it was? He'd lost count but what he did know was that it felt like weeks, months since he had met her and he didn't want to analyse why that might be.

It didn't take him too long to set up his tools: paints, palette, brushes, linseed oil, rags. They evoked a fire deep inside that his camera and lenses never could; the messy, unpredictable elements appealed even as he tried to impose order on his emotions. Gael ran a hand through his hair as he took stock one last time. The setting was perfect, all he needed was his model.

'Hi.' She appeared at the door as if summoned by his thoughts, the white robe clasped tightly around her waist, the mule slippers on her feet. She'd fastened her hair up as directed, the orchid set above one ear, the vibrant pink contrasting with the paleness of her face. Two pearls dangled from her lobes.

'Hi.'

'So where do you want me?' She grimaced. 'Stupid question.'

She walked over to the chaise, slow, small steps, obviously steeling herself as she neared the middle of the room. She halted as she reached the chaise and looked at him enquiringly. 'Do I just...?'

Gael nodded. 'You can drop your robe behind the chaise or hand it to me, whichever.'

'I don't expect it makes much difference. I'm going to end up the same way whichever I do.' But she didn't loosen the robe although her hands were knotted around the tie.

'I could put on some music? If that helps?'

'I don't think so, thank you. Not tonight anyway. Do you need silence while you work or could we talk?'

'I don't mind either way unless I'm focussing on your face. Your mouth will want to stay in one position then but that won't be for a few days.' He usually left conversation up to the models. Some liked to chat away, almost as if they were in a therapy session, others preferred silence, lost in a world of their own. Gael didn't care as long as he got the pose and expression he needed.

Hope walked around the chaise and stared down at the sheet, the pillow, the rumpled shawl. 'Looks comfy.'

'Okay, you've seen the painting. You're propped up on the pillow, your head slightly raised and looking directly at me. One leg casually over the other with the slipper half on, half off—but I can adjust that for you. The arm nearest me bent and relaxed, the other resting on your thigh.' Although she would be fully nude the pose preserved a little bit of modesty, a nod to the Renaissance nudes that had inspired the original pose.

'Got it.' With a visible—and audible—intake of breath Hope untied the robe and slipped it off, handing it to him as she did so. Gael turned away to place it on the floor behind him, deliberately not looking as she lay on the chaise and positioned herself. He had done this exact thing nineteen times before and not once had he had this dizzy sensation, as if the world were falling apart and rearranging itself right here in front of him. Not once had he been both so eager and so reticent to turn around and examine his model.

It's just another model, another painting. But he knew this girl, knew her secrets and her hopes. Had coaxed them out of her so that he could capture her in oils and hang her up, exposed, for all the world to see. Only right now he didn't want the world to see, he wanted to keep this unveiling for himself, her secrets to himself. It was his turn to take a deep breath, to push the troubling, unwelcome thoughts out of his mind and turn, the most professional expression he could muster on his face.

She was magnificent. Almost perfect, as pale as the original except for her legs, tanned to a warm golden brown. Petite and curvy with surprising large breasts proudly jutting out and the sexy curve of her small belly. Every woman Gael had dated boasted prominent ribs and a concave stomach; they looked fantastic in the skimpy designer clothes they favoured but felt insubstantial, as if the real joys in life eluded them. Not surprising when they considered dressing on a salad a treat and cheese the invention of the devil.

She was almost perfect, in a way he hadn't even considered, conditioned as he was by the gym-going gazelles he had been surrounded by for the last fifteen years. Her only flaw was the silver scars crisscrossing the very top of her thighs. There were more lines than he could count, covering the whole thigh from the side round to the fleshy inner thigh. They stopped just where a pair of shorts would end. Where the dress she was wearing tonight had ended, hidden from the world.

She stiffened as his gaze lingered there and when he looked back into her eyes all he could see was shame mingled with hurt pride and something that might be a plea for understanding. 'It hurt when my parents died. It hurt giving up my dreams. It hurt how much I blamed myself. Sometimes it hurt so much I couldn't stand it.'

'You don't have to explain anything to me.' He picked up the yellow ochre and squeezed an amount onto his palette before adding in some cadmium red light, the titanium white close at hand ready to lighten the blend to the exact shade of Hope's upper half.

'Every time I swore it was the last but then the pressure would get too much and the only thing that let it out was blood. For that second, when the blade sliced, I had peace. But then the blood would start to well up and I would feel sick again, hated myself, knew I was so weak. Faith used to ask why I wore old-fashioned swimsuits, you know, with skirts and I pretended it was because I liked the vintage look. In reality I couldn't bear for anyone to see my thighs.' She stopped. 'They will though, won't they? They'll see them on this.'

'I can't exclude them. It would be like editing you. Not quite real.'

'I knew that's what you'd say.'

'When did you stop?'

'When I'd accepted the situation. When it became my reality and not this horrible nightmare with no escape. When I put my old self and my old dreams away and devoted myself to Faith. Then I could cope.'

'Or you exchanged one mechanism for another? How long have you been locked in that box, Hope? How long have you suppressed who you are, what you want, what you need?' His voice had deepened and he wasn't even pretending to mix colours any more, the palette lying in his lap, the brush held casually in his hand as his eyes bore into hers.

'I don't any more. I'm at peace with who I've become.' *Liar*, a little voice inside her whispered.

'That teen rebel who kept a clear head on her shoulders while she did just what she wanted? The girl who had her future planned out down to where she wanted to study and when she was going to sleep with her boyfriend. The girl with dreams which took her away from the family home, away from London. Has she really gone?' His words sent an ache reverberating through her for the lost dreams and hopes she barely even acknowledged any more.

'I am away from London.'

'Still anchored to your family home. To your sister. Still doing the sensible thing.'

'This isn't that sensible,' she whispered.

His eyes pinned her to the pillow; she couldn't have moved if she'd wanted to. 'No.'

Hope had a sense she was playing with fire and yet she couldn't, wouldn't retreat. 'I'm bored of being sensible. So very, very bored.'

'Your hand,' he said hoarsely. 'I just need to position it.'

Hope's mouth was so dry she couldn't speak, couldn't do more than nod in agreement as Gael put the palette down and walked towards her. He had changed into old, battered, paint-splattered jeans and a white, equally disreputable shirt, buttons undone at the neck. She could see the movement of his muscles, a smattering of hair at the vee of the low neck and something primal clenched low down inside her.

She had never been so aware of her own body before, not as a teenager, her mouth glued to her boyfriend's as she fended off his hands, not as she'd stood in the bathroom, razor blade in hand. Every nerve was pulsing, jumping to the increasingly rapid beat of her heart. She could sense Gael over the ever shortening distance, sense him physically as if she were connected to him on some astral plane.

'This hand.' His voice was now so hoarse it was almost a rasp. 'I need it here.'

The second he touched her she gasped, unable to bear the pressure building up so slowly inside her any longer. His fingers on hers, the coolness against the heat of her skin, the sight of those deep olive tones on her own pale hand, the gentle strength inherent in his touch as he moved her. It was as if she had been craving his touch without even knowing it and that one movement opened up a deep hunger inside her.

But she had no doubt, no hesitation. She might be inexperienced but she instinctively knew what to do. She half closed her eyes, watching him through her lashes. 'Here?' She slid her hand a little way along her thigh and, with feminine satisfaction, watched him swallow. 'Or here?' She slid it slightly further so the tips of her fingers met his and, almost of their own volition, caressed the roughened tips.

'Hope…' She didn't know if he was uttering a warning, an entreaty or both but she was past caring. The last few days this man had laid her bare, exposed her deepest secrets and made her confront them. She was tired of confronting, tired of hiding, she just wanted to feel something good—and if her nerves were tingling like this from the mere touch of hand on hand then she had the suspicion this could get really good really soon.

'I think here, don't you?' Her fingers travelled up his hand to explore the delicate skin at his wrist. Gael closed his eyes and Hope thrilled at the knowledge that one simple touch could have such a potent effect, only to draw in a breath of her own as he captured her hand in his, his thumb sliding down to return the favour. One digit, one tiny area of skin but her whole body was lit up like Piccadilly Circus and she knew she couldn't, wouldn't walk away.

She should feel shame or embarrassment lying here wearing nothing but a flower in her hair, a ribbon round her neck while he was still dressed but she didn't feel either of those things. She felt powerful as she tugged at his hand, powerful as in answer to her command he sat at the side of the chaise, powerful as she raised her hand to his face and allowed herself the luxury of learning the sharp cheekbones, the dimple by the side of his mouth, the exquisitely cut lips.

'Hope,' he said again, capturing her hand once again, this time holding it still while he looked deep into her eyes. She saw concern and chafed at it. She saw need and fire and thrilled to it. 'This isn't right. It's been an emotional evening. I can't take advantage of you...'

'Right now I feel like I'm taking advantage of you.'

A primal fire flashed in his eyes and her whole body liquefied as his mouth pulled into a wolfish grin. 'You believe that if you want, sweetheart.'

'Would you be pulling back if I was any other woman?'

'I wouldn't be here if you were any other woman.' The admission was low, as if it had been dragged from him.

Oh.

'That's not what I meant and you know it. If I wasn't a virgin, if you knew I'd been swinging from the chandeliers with a whole regiment of lovers, then would you be pulling away?'

'No,' he admitted. 'But you are and the first time, Hope, it should be special. With someone you love. I don't do love, I don't do long term and I don't want to hurt you. You deserve better.'

'How very teen drama of you. I'm twenty-seven, Gael. I don't know how to flirt or date or *be* in that way. The way things are going I'll be a thirty-eight-year-old virgin and you holding my hand will be the single most erotic thing that's ever happened to me and it would be most unfair of you to condemn me to that. I'm not holding out for a knight on a white charger, you know that. If things were different I'd have lost it to Tom Featherstone nine years ago, in his parents' bed with a White Musk candle to create the mood and James Blunt on the speakers telling me how beautiful I was. I liked Tom. I liked him a lot. I wanted to sleep with him, but I didn't love him and I promise not to fall in love with you. I know you think you're good but you can't be *that* good.'

His mouth curved into a reluctant smile. 'That sounds like fighting talk.'

'It was supposed to be seductive talk.'

The virgin seducing the playboy. It was completely the wrong way round but it turned out that this playboy had scruples. Hope respected them, she just wanted him to get over them already and respect *her* choice.

Gael studied her for a second longer and Hope stared back more brazenly than she ever had, allowing all her need and want and desire to spill out until, with a smothered groan, he leant in, arms either side of her head, his face close to her, mouth within kissing distance, almost.

Hope moistened her lips.

'Let's get this straight,' he said. 'If there's going to be any seducing tonight then I'll be the one who's doing it.'

Her body liquefied again, every bone melting so she felt as if she could simply slide off the chaise to lie in a puddle on the floor—and he wasn't even touching her.

Only then he was, one hand tilting her chin up before he claimed her mouth with his and the last coherent thought Hope knew was that when it came to seduction Gael was right: he was definitely the one in control.

CHAPTER EIGHT

IT WAS ALMOST like a relationship. Almost. The door-man let her straight up without even buzzing first, she had a bag with hot bagels and two coffees in one hand and a Bloomingdale's bag in the other, her toothbrush and a change of underwear in the handbag slung over her shoulder, just in case.

But it wasn't a relationship. When the lift doors opened and she walked into the studio Gael looked up and smiled—which was an improvement on his old non-greeting—but he made no move to come over and kiss her. They didn't kiss, or hold hands, or feed each other titbits or cuddle. They had sex. Every night for the last week and a couple of times in the day as well—after all, she was spending most of the day naked—but they weren't affectionate.

It was as if life was in two halves: the normal half filled with wedding planning, painting, archive sorting and anything else that needed doing—and the secret half. The half when Gael's eyes darkened to a steely blue and just the look in them made her stomach swirl and her pulse speed up. And the two halves were to-tally disconnected.

That very first night, afterwards, he had asked if

she was okay. Probably still worried that she was going to transfer twenty-seven years of singledom into one giant, all-encompassing *'thank you for the first orgasm I didn't sort out on my own'*, wholly inappropriate crush. Obviously all the serotonin and oxytocin had been a little overwhelming; she'd wanted to be completely absorbed in and by and round him while her heartbeat returned to its normal pace and her breathing slowed. Hope completely understood, for the first time, how knee-weakening, chest-tightening, dry-mouthed lust could be mistaken for love.

But she'd spent the last nine years ignoring her wants and wasn't going to let a little bit of—okay, a lot of—sex change the carefully ingrained habits. A wide-eyed, 'So that's what all the fuss is about,' followed by, 'I can't believe it's taken me so long,' wrapped up with a 'thank you' was all that she allowed before wrapping the handy robe around herself and disappearing into the bathroom.

And so she'd reassured him—and herself—that she was more than okay, that she understood exactly what this was. Temporary, fun, no strings, no expectations. Hope guessed that this was what was meant by friends with benefits. Not that they were exactly friends either. Soon to be kind of in-laws with benefits?

Gael threw a pointed look at the industrial clock on the wall. 'Got lost? I thought you were heading back to yours for a change of clothes. Last time I looked your apartment was a ten-minute walk from here.'

Hope felt a slight twinge of guilt. She *was* supposed to be cataloguing again this morning. 'I know I took longer than expected, but I did bring coffee and bagels because, honestly, it is far quicker to go and buy coffee than it is to work that fiendish machine of yours.'

'Coffee from Bloomingdale's?' He nodded at the huge bag in her hand.

'Well, no. I just popped in while I was passing...'

'Passing? Your apartment is straight north from here. How were you passing Third Avenue?'

'Okay, I took a little detour. I know we have an appointment at the bridal shop this afternoon...yes. *We*,' she added firmly as he pulled an all too expressive face. 'I am not going on my own. But Faith needs two gowns and it's stressful enough getting one made up on time, so as the New York dress can be a lot less formal I thought I'd look elsewhere. Besides, I haven't really had a chance to flex the credit card Hunter gave me yet. Shopping with an unlimited budget is a lot more fun than bargain hunting, let me tell you. This might not be an actual wedding dress but it cost more than most entire weddings. I seriously thought they'd added an extra digit by mistake.'

She placed the bag carefully on the floor and opened it. 'What do you think? It was the last in her size so I bought it straight away but now I'm worrying I didn't look at enough options.' She pulled out a delicate cream dress with a lace overlay on the short bodice and cap sleeves, the silk almost sheer around the high waist before cascading into a long pleated skirt. 'I wanted something floaty and unstructured which will be comfortable to wear. After all, she's moving around a lot on the wedding day—Central Park, then to the boat for the afternoon cruise.'

Hope had been unsure what to do with the fifteen guests in the four hours between the cocktails at the

Tavern on the Green and dinner at the Roof Garden. They were such an odd selection of people from Hunter's multimillionaire socialite mother to her aunt and uncle who lived in a small village in Dorset and hated big cities. Luckily inspiration had led her to a small business that chartered boats out and she had booked an old-fashioned sailboat for the afternoon to take the guests on a cruise around Manhattan. It would probably be a little unsophisticated for Misty, who actually owned her own yacht, but Faith and her UK guests would love it.

'Then she's at the Met and finally the piano bar. It's a busy day and she wants white for the party and blessing so I wanted to make sure there was a contrast. It's such a beautiful shimmery cream as well. I got a gorgeous cashmere wrap in a soft gold and both flat shoes and heels so she can swap. What do you think?'

Gael didn't just nod and say, 'Very nice, dear,' as her father used to do. She guessed that was the advantage of wedding planning with an artist and former society photographer. Instead he took the hanger from her and hung the dress from a hook on the wall, standing back, brow creased in concentration.

'Gold accessories?'

Hope felt a little as if she were taking a test. 'Soft gold, not metallic. Because of the thread in the lace.'

'So Hunter and I will need ties in that colour. His dad too probably.'

Hope stared at him, horrified. Suits? She hadn't even thought about suits. Dear God, she wasn't expected to sort the rings out as well, was she?

To her relief Gael carried on. 'My tailor has already started on the suits for the party. A light grey with white linen shirts. You can work with that? We'll order the ties once you have chosen the bridesmaids' dresses. I think we'll want a darker, almost charcoal suit for the wedding, to go with the soft gold accents in the cream of the dress. And a lightweight fabric.' He pulled his phone out and started tapping. How could it be that simple?

Easy, she reminded herself, he had connections. Besides, dress number one had been pretty easy for her thanks to the limitless budget. She'd met up with a personal shopper and this dress was the second she'd seen. She'd fallen for it instantly—more importantly she knew Faith would love it.

Gael looked up from his phone. 'What about you? Have you sorted a dress out yet?'

'No, not yet but I still have a few days. Besides, I don't have a limitless budget so an hour with a personal shopper isn't going to cut it for me. I thought I'd head downtown tomorrow and see what I can find in a soft gold. It's Faith's day anyway so as long as I complement her in the photos it's all good.'

'Hope, just use Hunter's card. He'll be expecting you to use it.' He threw her a shrewd glance. 'But sure, hide away in the background as usual.'

'I'm not! It's her wedding. Some sister I would be if I tried to overshadow her.' Besides, that huge canvas right there? She was in the foreground there. Enough in the foreground to last her a lifetime. 'I'll find something, I promise. Besides, Hunter wants me to put the bridesmaids' dresses for the party on the limitless card so this afternoon I'll spend big. You won't recognise me, my dress will be so attention seeking.'

'I'd know you anywhere,' he said softly and her heart trembled. *No*, she scolded herself. *No reading meanings into words. No thinking this is more than it is. You escaped awkward if sweet fumblings with Tom Featherstone for toe-curling, out-of-body-type sex. How many people go straight to advanced levels, huh? It's just your emotions are still stuck on beginner level. Give them a chance to catch up.*

Besides. She wasn't that stupid. She trusted Gael with her body but there was no way she would trust him with her heart. She was pretty sure he couldn't handle his own, let alone somebody else's. No, she would enjoy this for what it was and when it was over take the confidence and belief she was gaining day by day and go out and make herself a happy life. One day she might even feel that she deserved to.

'We're due at the shop in four hours. Do you need me to pose?' Airily said but each time she still needed to take a deep breath before she let the robe slip. Habits of a lifetime were hard to escape and after years of keeping in the background being under such intense scrutiny was hard. More than hard.

'No, there's not really enough time. I'm doing some work on the background so I don't need you. Why don't you get on with the archive?'

And there she was. Relegated from lover to muse to wedding planner to assistant in four easy steps. *Know your place*, she told herself sternly as Gael snagged the brown bag to take out his coffee—black, two shots—and bagel—pumpkin seed with cream cheese and smoked salmon. Both a stern contrast to her own more adventurous orders but she was a tourist, it was her duty to experiment. She grabbed her own food and headed off into the kitchen where her workstation was set up. She enjoyed the work but this time away from the office was making her face some uncomfortable truths. She'd hoped this job swap, working with Brenda, would give her the time she needed to work on her career—but instead it was becoming increasingly clear that although she was good at office work and ran events smoothly and meticulously she was bored. In fact she had been bored for a long time if she was honest with herself—something was missing and she couldn't put her finger on exactly what that was.

Hope had fallen into a rhythm over the last week. Gael kept good records and she was beginning to recognise many of the faces so she barely had to put any aside for future clarification. She had already worked her way through his junior year at school and made a good start on senior. The photos were all taken anonymously up to this point but there was a step change the second he was outed: less candid, more posed, less scandalous.

And more of Gael himself. Set-up group shots, time delays. He didn't look at ease, didn't pose, a faraway look on his face as if he was dreaming of being safely back behind the camera.

It wasn't just Gael who made more of an appearance. Time after time the camera lingered lovingly on a willowy blonde girl. She had possibly the most photogenic face Hope had ever seen, the sharp angles and exaggerated features made for the lens. It wasn't just the camera who loved her, judging by the close-ups. The photographer had too.

Hope checked the face against the records she was building up. The girl had been in the junior year pictures as well, only in the background, watching the main players as yearningly as the camera. At some point, like Gael, she had come out of the shadows to shine on centre stage. Tamara Larson.

With half an eye on Gael through the open door, Hope brought up her internet browser and typed in the name. In less than a second it presented her with thousands of possibilities. She pressed randomly on one link. She almost knew what she'd see before the picture loaded: Gael looking down at Tamara, almost unrecognisable. It wasn't just that he was more than a decade younger, slim to the point of skinny, still wearing the gangliness of a very young man. It was the softness in his face, the light in his eyes, the warmth in his smile that made him so alien. Hope had never seen him look that way, not even in their most intimate, unguarded moments.

'I believe in love,' he had said. The proof was right here. He had loved. Adored.

Hope's breath caught in her throat and her fingers curled into fists. It wasn't that she was *jealous*—well, she conceded, maybe just a teensy weensy bit in a totally irrational way but no, in the main it wasn't jealousy consuming her, it was curiosity. Something had happened to wipe that softness out so complexly replacing it with cynicism. What was it?

She clicked back and scrolled onwards until a headline caught her eye. '*Expose* photographer and muse to wed' it screamed in bold type over a picture of a beaming Tamara Larson showing a gigantic—and tacky, Hope sniffed—ring, Gael standing proudly behind her, his hands possessively on her shoulders.

Engaged! He must have still been a baby, younger even than Hunter.

What had happened? There was definitely no socialite living here in the loft. Of course Gael had no obligation to tell her if he was divorced, none at all.

Hurt flickered inside her. Small but scalding. He knew everything about her from the scars on her thighs to the scars on her heart and yet he had shared nothing that wasn't already public knowledge. No, this definitely wasn't anything like a relationship. For him she was a convenience; a convenient model, a convenient assistant, a convenient lover.

Which was *absolutely* no problem. She just needed to remember, remember exactly what this was—and exactly what it wasn't.

'Researching?' How had she not heard him come into the kitchen? Hope jumped guiltily. 'How very keen.'

'I didn't know you were engaged.' There was no point in prevaricating; she'd been caught red-handed.

His mouth twisted. 'Briefly. It was a long time ago.'

'What happened?' She saw the shutters come down and pressed on. 'You're going to have to tell me at some point. She's going to feature heavily in the retrospective; half your pictures from that time are of her.'

'Tale as old as time: boy meets girl, girl sees opportunity, boy falls for girl, it ends tragically. The end.' The mocking tone was back but this time it was entirely self-directed. That was worse in some ways than when he employed it against her.

She tried for a smile, wanting to lighten the suddenly sombre mood. 'Fairy tales have darkened since my day.'

'Oh, this is no fairy tale. It's an old-fashioned morality tale of lust, hubris and greed.' He hooked a stool out and sat down opposite her, leaning on the steel countertop, eyes burning with sardonic amusement. 'They rarely have a happy ending.'

Hope was right. He couldn't have a retrospective and not include his own secrets and shame. What would be the point in that? Besides, Tamara was no secret. Their relationship was well documented as the long list of web links on the laptop attested.

Gael spun the laptop round and stared at the photo. All he felt, all he wanted to feel was pity for the poor fool. Standing there looking as if he had won life's lottery, as if the right honeyed words from the right girl were all he needed to count in this world. 'It's really no big deal. It wouldn't be worth a footnote in the retrospective if I hadn't been stupid enough to think I was old enough to get married.'

'But you did get engaged?'

'Does it count as an engagement if the blushing bride-to-be had no intention of going through with the wedding?' He didn't wait for an answer. 'It's not that exciting, Hope. No big romance. Tamara was in the year behind me at school. She was...' he paused, searching for the right word '...she was ambitious. She felt that she belonged at the very top of the social strata; she was beautiful, smart, athletic, rich—but our school was full of beautiful and smart rich girls and somehow she couldn't even get into the inner circle, let alone rule it. She was left out on the fringes.'

'Like you.'

Like him but so much more ambitious. 'Like me. But I knew my place and had no desire to move upwards. I think she knew who I was before I was outed. Sometimes I think she was the one who outed me, because a couple of months before it happened, a few months into my senior year, she started to make a very subtle and clever play for me. Of course I, sap that I was, had no idea. I thought it was the other way round and couldn't believe that this gorgeous girl would ever consider a commoner like me. But the more I noticed her—and she made sure I did—the more I photographed her, the more she made it into *Expose* and the more she featured on the blog the higher her status grew.'

'She might not have planned it. You make her sound like Machiavelli.'

Proof Hope didn't belong on the Upper East Side; the boys and girls he'd gone to school with had studied Machiavelli at preschool. 'Oh, she planned it. She played me like a pro—like father, like son. Suckers for a poor little rich girl every time. No one can make you feel as special as a society goddess, like Aphrodite seducing a mere mortal. We started dating spring break that year and right through my first year at college. I asked her to marry me when she graduated from high school. Can you even imagine?' He couldn't. He couldn't begin to imagine that kind of wild-eyed optimism any more. You'd think his own parents would have taught him just how foolish marrying the first person you fell for was. Turned out it was a lesson he needed to learn for himself.

'She said yes?'

He nodded. 'Oh, she wasn't finished with me yet, and such a youthful engagement ensured she was in the headlines, just where she wanted to be. She dropped out of college to play at being a fashion intern, did some modelling and dumped me for the heir to a hotel empire. I don't think she has any regrets. Her penthouse apartment, properties in Aspen, Bermuda, Paris and the Hamptons more than make up for any lingering feelings she may have had.' He ran into Tamara every now and then. She usually tried to give him some kind of limpid look, an attempt at a connection. He always ignored her.

'You were much better off finding out what she was like before you got married.'

'That's what Misty said. She sent me to Paris for my sophomore year as a consolation prize and that's when I really fell in love.'

'With Olympia?'

He smiled then. 'Olympia and all her sisters.'

'You're lucky.'

'Lucky? Interesting interpretation of the word. Foolish, I would have said.'

'Not for Tamara, for Misty. To have someone who cares. Okay, you lost out a little in the parent lottery. They were too young, too self-absorbed to know how to raise you.'

'Were?' Neither of them had ever grown up, at least where he was concerned.

'But it sounds to me like Misty has always been there for you. Not everyone has that.'

Interesting interpretation. But there was a kernel of truth there that niggled at him uncomfortably. He'd never asked why Misty had kept him after she divorced his father; he'd been more focussed on the fact both biological parents had walked away rather than appreciating the non-biological one who'd stayed. But she *had* kept him. Supported him, still expected him to come and stay every Christmas, Thanksgiving, every summer. She'd have bought him the studio, made him an allowance if he weren't so damned independent. Her words.

He'd always thought that somehow he was fundamentally flawed, unlovable; that was why his parents didn't stay, why Tamara could discard him without a qualm. That was why he only dated women with short-term agendas that matched his, never allowed himself to open up. But maybe he wasn't the one who was flawed after all.

Because it wasn't just Misty who believed in him. He might have bribed Hope into posing, manipulated her into helping him, but she'd responded with an openness that floored him. The painting was almost taking on a life of its own, rawer and more honest than he had thought possible. And then there was the sex…

He'd be lying if he said that was unexpected. There had been a spark between them from the first moment and although he'd been reluctant to take her virginity in the end he'd been powerless when confronted by the desire in her eyes. She was a grown woman and she had made it clear she knew exactly what she was doing.

What was unexpected was how calmly she accepted the situation. No expectations for anything beyond his limited offer. He should be relieved. He wasn't sure what it meant that he wasn't. He was very sure that he didn't want to know.

CHAPTER NINE

LUCKY. SEVERAL HOURS later Hope's words were still reverberating around Gael's head. He'd been called lucky before—when his father married Misty and he stopped being one of 'us', a local, and became one of 'them', the privileged summer visitors. Lucky when he started seeing Tamara, lucky as his career progressed. It had been said with envy, with laughter, with amusement but never before with that heart-deep wistfulness.

He'd never been able to think about that time with anything but regret and humiliation. Tamara's manipulation had been the final confirmation of everything he had suspected since the day his mother had walked out, her next lover already lined up. His subsequent relationships hadn't done much to change his mind, a series of models, socialites and actresses whose beautiful eyes were all solely focussed on what he, his camera and his influence could do for them. The only thing in their favour was that they knew the score, were only interested in the superficial and the temporary and made no demands on his heart or future.

Of course he had never dated outside that narrow world. Never searched for or wanted anything more meaningful. Why would he when so many easy op-

portunities presented themselves with such monoto-
nous regularity?

Until Hope. She broke the mould, that was for sure.
The first woman he had met who seemed to want nothing for herself—he didn't know whether he admired
her or wanted to shake her and shout at her to be more
selfish, dammit. To *live*. It would be so easy to take
advantage of her, to hurt her. Every day he told himself that they should end their affair. And yet here they
still were.

Maybe he wasn't the one with the power here after
all; in his own way he was as bad as she was, living
safely, ensuring his emotions were never stirred, that
he remained safe.

Gael scowled, pushing the unwanted thought out of
his mind. He *was* challenging himself, opening himself
up to potential ridicule with his change of direction. In
a few weeks his paintings would be exhibited at one
of the most influential galleries in town, exposing his
heart and soul in a way that his photos never had. Besides, look at him now. Wedding planning, ordering
suits, playing happy families so that his pain of a little
brother could have the perfect wedding.

Little brother? He was usually so quick to disassoci-
ate himself from any close relationship with Hunter by
a judicious 'ex' and 'step'. Just as he always added the
'half' qualifier onto his mother's two children.

Gael shifted, uncomfortable on the overstuffed velvet seat. A few phone calls had led Hope and he here
to the exclusive bridal salon popularised on the TV
show *Upper East Side Bride*. Women from all over
the States—and further afield—travelled here, prepared to pay exorbitant prices for their one-of-a-kind

designs, hoping for a sprinkle of rarefied fairy dust to cast a sparkle over their big day.

'I have your sister's measurements and her choices from our available stock,' the terrifyingly elegant saleswoman had said, eyeing Hope as if she were a prize heifer. 'You're a couple of inches too short and a little larger around the bust but I think it's best if you try on the dresses I have selected. That way you'll know how they feel, how your sister will feel when she puts it on.'

Hope had gaped at her, looking even more terrified than when Gael had first asked her to model. 'Me?' she had spluttered but had been whisked away before she could formulate a complete sentence. That had been half an hour ago and Gael had been left in splendid isolation with nothing to occupy him except several copies of *Bridal World* and a glass of sparkling water.

Tamara had never tried on a wedding dress. They hadn't even discussed the guest list. In fact, looking back, she'd shown no interest in anything but the ring— the largest he could ill afford and one she hadn't offered to return.

'Don't laugh.' Hope's fierce whisper brought him back to the here and now. Finally. He'd begun to wonder if this was some form of purgatory where he would be left to ponder every wrong move he had ever made.

Hope teetered into the large room, swaying as if it was hard to get her balance. The private showroom was brightly lit by several sparkling chandeliers and a whole host of high and low lights, each reflecting off the gold gilt and mirrors in a headache-inducing, dazzling display. The walls were mirrored floor to ceiling so he couldn't escape his scowling reflection whichever way he turned. The whole room was decorated in soft golds and ivory from the carpet to the gilt edging on every piece of furniture. A low podium stood before him, awaiting its bride.

Or in this case a bridesmaid masquerading as the bride. A pink-faced, swaying bridesmaid.

'Because Faith's two inches taller they've made me wear five-inch heels,' she complained as she gingerly stepped onto the podium. 'I'm a size bigger as well but they have these clever expanding things so hopefully we'll get an idea but bear in mind that Faith won't spill out the way I am.'

Of course he was going to stare at her cleavage the second she said that—he was only flesh and blood after all—and she was looking rather magnificent if not very bridal, creamy flesh rising above the low neckline of the gown.

The huge, ornate, sparkling gown. It looked more like a little girl's idea of a wedding gown than something a grown woman would wear.

But what did he know? Gael understood colour, he understood texture, he understood structure. Thanks to the work he had done for many fashion magazines he knew if an outfit worked or not. But in this world he was helpless. The second they'd sat down he'd been ambushed with a dizzying array of words: lace, silk, organza, sweetheart necklines, trails, mermaids—mermaids? Really? People got married in the sea?—ball gowns, A-line, princess, crystals. This was beyond anything he knew or understood or wanted to understand, more akin to some fantasy French court of opulent exaggeration than the real world. Marriage as an elaborate white masquerade.

'Say something!'

Hope looked most unbridal, hands on hips and a scowl on her face as she glared at him.

'It's…' It wasn't often that Gael was at a loss for words but he instinctively knew that he had to tread very carefully here. His actual opinion didn't matter; he had to gauge exactly what his response should be. What if this was Faith's dream dress—or, worse, Hope's? He swallowed. Surely not Hope's. Her body language was more like a child forced into her best dress for church than that of a woman in the perfect dress, shoulders slumped and a definite pout on her face.

Gael blinked, trying to focus on the dress rather than the wearer, taking in every detail. There were just so *many* details. A neckline he privately considered more bordello than bridal? Check. Enough crystals to gladden the heart of a rhinestone cowgirl? Check. Flounces? Oh, yes. A definite check. Tiers upon tiers of them spilling out from her knees. It seemed an odd place for flounces to spill from but what did Gael know?

'It doesn't look that comfortable.' That was an under-exaggeration if ever he'd made one; skintight from the strapless and low bust, it clung unforgivingly all the way down her torso until it reached her knees, where it flowed out like a tulle waterfall. If Gael had to design a torture garment it would probably resemble this.

'It's not comfortable.' She was almost growling. 'Worse, I look hideous.'

'You could never look hideous.' But she didn't look like Hope, all trussed up, tucked in and glittering.

Hope pulled a face. 'Now you start complimenting me? Don't worry, Gael, I don't need your flattery.'

Was that what she thought? 'I don't do flattery. But

if you want honesty then I have to say that dress doesn't suit you. But you're not looking for you and I don't know your sister at all.'

She studied herself in the mirror. 'She did short-list it but I don't think she'd like it. I can't imagine her picking it in a million years but who knows? Even the sanest of women, women who think a clean jumper constitutes dressing up, get carried away when it comes to wedding dresses. This was designed for a reason. Someone somewhere must think it's worth more than a car. But no, I don't think Faith would. Still, it's not up to us. Take a photo and email it to her.'

The next dress was no better unless Faith dreamed of dressing up as Cinderella on steroids. The bead-encrusted heart-shaped bodice wasn't too bad by itself—if copious amounts of crystals were your thing—but it was entirely dwarfed by the massive skirt, which exploded out from Hope's waist like a massive marshmallow. A massive marshmallow covered in glitter. Gael didn't even have to speak a word—the expression on his face must have said it all because Hope took one look at his open mouth and raised eyebrows and retreated, muttering words he was pretty sure no nicely brought-up Cinderella should know.

He very much approved of dress number three. Very much so, not that it was at all suitable unless Faith was planning a private party for two. Cream silk slithered provocatively over Hope's curves, flattering, reveal-ing, promising. Oh, yes. He approved. So much so he wanted to tear it right off her, which probably wasn't the response a bride was looking for. Regretfully he shook his head. 'Buy it anyway, I'll paint you in it…' he murmured and watched her eyes heat up at the promise in his voice as she backed out of the room.

'I like this but I think it's too simple. She's already wearing one flowy dress, I think she wants something a bit more showy for the party.'

Gael looked up, not sure his eyes could take much more tulle or dazzle, only to blink as Hope shyly stepped onto the podium. 'I like that,' he said—or at least he tried to say. His voice seemed to have dried up along with his throat.

He coughed, taking a sip of water as he tried to re-gather himself. Brought to his knees—metaphorically anyway—by a wedding dress? Get a grip. Although Hope did look seriously...well, not hot. That wasn't the right word, although she was. Nor sexy nor any of the other adjectives he usually applied to women. She looked ethereally beautiful, regal. She looked just like a bride should look from the stars in her dark eyes to the blush on her cheek.

Looked just like a bride should? Where had that thought come from? He'd attended a lot of weddings, many of them his parents', but right up to this moment Gael was pretty sure he'd never had any opinion on how a woman looked on her wedding day. It was this waiting room, infecting him with its gaudiness, its dazzle, its femininity.

But Hope did look gorgeous. The dress was decep-tively simple with wide lace shoulder straps, which showed provocative hints of her creamy shoulders, and a lace bodice, which cupped her breasts demurely. The sweetheart neckline was neither too low nor too high and the skirt fell from the high waist in graceful folds of silk. She was the very model of propriety until she turned and he saw how low the back of the dress swooped, almost to her waist, her back almost fully exposed except for a band of the same lace following the lines of her back.

'I've seen statues of Greek goddesses who look like you in that dress.'

'I look okay, then?' But she knew she did. Look at the soft smile curving her mouth, the way she glowed. Not only did she look incredible, she obviously felt it too.

'Is this the one, then?' An unexpected pang hit him as he asked the question. Not at the thought of the day's purgatory finally ending, but because Hope should buy that dress for herself, not for someone else. It was hers. It couldn't be more hers if it had been designed and made for her. But here she was, ready to give up the perfect dress to her sister, just as she had given up everything for Faith every day for the whole of her adult life.

'I don't know.' Hope was obviously torn. 'I really, really love it. It's utterly perfect. But is it right? She asked for a showstopper for the party and this is too simple, I think. Take a photo and send it but I'm not sure she'll pick it.'

Gael disagreed. His show had been well and truly stopped the second Hope appeared in the dress. 'Whatever that dress is it isn't simple.'

'It *is* the most gorgeous dress I have ever seen. I can't imagine finding anything more beautiful. But I'm not sure it's what Faith has in mind.'

'There is a whole salon of showstopping dresses you haven't tried on yet,' Gael said, heroically reconciling himself to another several hours of dazzling white confections. 'Let's fulfil the brief and get your sister what she wants. But, Hope, you look absolutely spectacular in that dress. You should know that.'

She looked at him, surprise clear on her face. Surprise and a simple pleasure, a joy in the compliment. 'Thank you. I feel it, for once in my life I really do.'

Gael stood back and surveyed the painting before looking over at Hope, lying on the chaise in exactly the same position she had assumed every day for the last eleven days. She had complained that she was so acclimatised to it she was sleeping in the same position now. 'I think we're done.'

'Really done? Finished and done? Can I see?' Gael hadn't allowed her to take as much as a peep at her portrait yet and he knew she was desperate to take a look. 'I need to, to make sure you haven't switched to a Picasso theme and turned me blue and into cubes. Actually, that might be easier to look at. I vote Picasso.'

'No to the blue cubes, possibly to taking a look and no, not finished, but I don't need you for the second pass, that's refinement and detail. I have photos and sketches to help me for that. But I am absolutely finished for now. I'm going to let it dry for a few days and then work on it some more.'

Hope was manoeuvring herself off the couch, as always reaching straight for the white robe, visibly relaxing as she tied it around herself. 'It's good timing. Faith gets here in what, three hours? We've got a fitting almost straight away. Tomorrow I am going to walk her through the whole wedding day and then we have afternoon tea with Misty. I hope Faith's happy with the decisions we made. Not that she has much choice at this late hour.'

'If she isn't then just point out that rather than frolic in Prague she could have sorted it all out herself.'

Hope ignored him. 'Wednesday is the hen do all day—that's a spa day, afternoon tea, Broadway show followed by dinner and cocktails and then Thursday is the actual wedding. Friday we recover while the happy couple love it up in the Waldorf Astoria and then it's the blessing and party on Saturday. So it's a good thing you don't need me. I don't have any time to pose this week. I've just about finished the archiving as well. Brenda has a designer and a copywriter ready to start working with you the second that contract is signed.'

Which meant they were done. He didn't need her to cross-reference any more photos or pose and the wedding was planned. So where did that leave them? Funny how they had been heading to this point for nearly two weeks and yet now they were here he felt totally unprepared.

Because he *was* unprepared. The wedding was the end date; they both knew it. He'd finish his paintings and prepare for his show, she'd go back to DL Media and complete her time here in New York before heading back to London. Yet he felt as if something wasn't finished. As if *they* weren't finished.

Gael swallowed. It had been a long time since he'd cared whether a relationship was over or not. And this wasn't even a relationship, was it?

It wasn't meant to be... His chest tightened. Of course, it most definitely wasn't. He didn't do relationships, remember? Because that way he didn't get hurt. Nobody got hurt. And he'd told her that right from the start.

So why was he feeling suddenly bereft?

Hope kicked off the mule, stretching out her leg. 'Thank goodness that's over with. Do you know how uncomfortable it is holding your leg in that one position for hours at a time? So, may I see?' Hope nodded at the easel and gave Gael her most appealing smile. 'I know nothing about art anyway, so you know my opinion isn't worth anything.'

He narrowed his eyes. 'Why do you do that?'

'Do what?'

'Put yourself down. Your opinion is worth a lot more than most of those so-called critics who will make or break me in three weeks' time. Because it's genuine. Because somewhere hidden deep inside you have heart and passion and life if you'd just let yourself see that. But you never will, will you? Far easier to wallow and self-deprecate and hide than put yourself out there, risk falling or heartbreak again.'

He wanted to recall the words as soon as he'd said them as she physically recoiled, staring at him, her face stricken. 'I put myself out there. Good God, in this last two weeks all I've done is try new things.'

He could apologise. He *should* apologise but he kept going, dimly aware he wasn't so much angry with Hope as he was with himself. Angry because at some point he'd broken his own rules and started caring—and he hadn't even noticed. Angry because yet another person was about to walk away out of his life and not look back—and he had no idea how to stop her. 'You've let me lead you into new things. You followed. That's not quite the same thing.'

She straightened, her colour high and her eyes bright with anger. She looked magnificent. 'Oh, excuse me for not walking in here and stripping off and begging you to paint me. Of course, where I come from that behaviour can get a girl arrested but why should that have stopped me?'

'You never tell me that no, you don't want steak you want Thai, you never say no, I don't want red wine I'd like white even though I *know* you prefer white. You don't tell me what ice cream you prefer so I end up buying out the whole store. You don't tell me when your legs have cramps and the pose hurts. You don't tell your sister that organising a wedding in two weeks is impossible.'

'Because those things don't matter to me. I wanted to help Faith. I genuinely don't care what wine I drink. Why are you saying this?'

Gael stood back from the easel, his eyes fixed on her, expression inscrutable. 'Tell me this, Hope. Tell me what you want to happen next. Tell me what we do tomorrow when you no longer have to come here. What we say to your sister, to Hunter. Tell me how it ends.'

Tell me how it ends. There was no point telling him anything because no matter what he said there was no real choice. It would end. Today, Sunday, when she went back to the UK—only the date was in doubt.

She had to focus on that because if she thought about everything else he had said she would collapse. Was that how he saw her? She always thought of herself as so strong, as doing what was needed no matter what the personal cost. But Gael didn't see a strong woman. He saw a coward.

I know you prefer white.

She did. Why hadn't she said so? Because she was so used to putting other people's needs, their feelings first at some point it had become second nature. Well, no more.

'It has ended. It ended when you put that paintbrush down. We no longer have anything to offer each other.'

'So that's what you want,' he said softly.

Yes! No! All she knew was that it wasn't a choice because if he could make her feel like this, this lost, this hurt, this needy, after less than two weeks then she had to walk away with her heart and pride intact. Or at least her pride because it felt as if something in her heart were cracking open right now. It shouldn't be possible. She knew who he was and what he was and she had kept her guard up the whole time and yet, without even trying, he had slipped through her shields.

Without even trying. How pathetic was she? He didn't need to do anything and she had just fallen in front of him, like her aunt's dog, begging for scraps. The only consolation was that he would never know.

'You knew I preferred white and bought red anyway?'

The look he shot her was such a complicated mixture of affection, humour and contempt she couldn't even begin to unravel it. 'All you had to do was say.'

Affecting a bravado she didn't feel, she walked forward until she was standing next to him then turned and looked at the painting.

It was at once so familiar and yet so foreign. The pose, the setting so similar to the painting she had now seen so many copies of she could probably reproduce it blindfolded—but this was magnified. No dog, no servant, no backdrop, the attention all zoomed in on Hope. Her eyes travelled along her torso, from the so casually positioned slipper along her legs. She winced as she took in the scars, each one traced in silvery detail, an all too public unveiling.

The actual nudity wasn't as bad as she'd feared, not compared to the scars. She was curvier, paler, sexier than she had expected; she looked like a woman, not like the girl she felt inside. Her breasts full and round, even the slight roundness of her stomach suggested a sensual ease.

But her face... Hope swallowed. 'Do I really look that sad?'

Unlike Olympia she wasn't staring out at the viewer with poise and confidence. She wasn't in control of her sensuality. She looked wary, frightened, lost. She looked deeply sad.

Gael was watching her. 'Most of the time, yes. I paint what I see, Hope. I tried to find something else, thought if you confronted some of your sadness I could reach a new emotion but that's all there was.'

All there was. She wasn't just a coward, she was a miserable one.

'Between the scars and my emotions you have exposed everything, haven't you?' Hope whispered.

'I didn't expose anything, Hope, it was all right there.'

But it wasn't, it hadn't been, she'd hidden it all under efficiency, under plans, under busyness, until even she had no idea how she felt any more. It had taken his eye to see it and strip her bare until she couldn't hide any more. 'I hope you're satisfied, Gael. I hope this painting brings you fame and fortune. I hope it's worth it. But at the end of the day that's all you'll have. You tell me I'm a coward? I'm not the one recreating pictures of an idealised woman. I'm not the one cold-shouldering the family who love him, who care for him, who have done nothing but support him even when they no longer had any legal link. I'm too afraid to go for what I want? I'm not the only one. You'd rather photograph life, paint life than live it.'

Hope would have given anything to make a dramatic exit but unless she wanted to walk through the grand marble foyer, past Gael's doorman and out into the streets in a white robe that was never going to happen. She changed as quickly as she could, gathering all her belongings and stuffing them into a bag. It didn't take long. She'd practically lived here for the past eleven days, heading back to her own tiny apartment every couple of days to get a change of clothes, but she had left no residue of herself. Her bag didn't even look full and it was as if she had never stepped foot inside— apart from the painting, that was.

She walked back through the vast studio. At what point had the picture-covered brick walls, the cavernous empty space, the mezzanine bedroom begun to feel like home? Hope took one last look around; nothing would induce her to return.

Gael certainly wasn't going to make the effort. He was leaning by the window, a beer in one hand, looking out at the skyline. He barely turned as she walked by.

'I guess I'll see you at the wedding,' Hope said finally, glad that her voice didn't wobble despite the treacherous tears threatening to break through the wall she was erecting brick by painful brick.

'I guess.'

She pressed the lift button, praying it wouldn't take too long. 'Bye, then.'

He looked up then. 'Hope?'

Her namesake flared up then, bright and foolish. 'Yes?'

'You deserve more. You should go and find it. Believe it.'

She nodded slowly as the flare died down as if it had never been, leaving only a bitter taste of ashes in her mouth. 'You're right, Gael. I do deserve better. See you around.'

CHAPTER TEN

'Do I look okay?'

Gael turned to see Hunter pull at his tie, trying to fix it so it was perfectly aligned, pulling at the knot with nervous fingers until it tightened into a small, crumpled heap. Otherwise he looked like a young man on the cusp of a life-changing moment, shoulders broad in the perfectly cut suit, eyes bright and excited and a new maturity in his boyish face.

'Here,' Gael said gruffly, trying to hide the pride in his voice. 'Let me.'

He had taught Hunter how to tie a tie in the first place, how to ride a bike, how to swim. He'd bought him his first beer and listened through his first infatuations. And now his little brother was moving on without him, going forward, past Gael into a whole new life. 'There you go.' He stood back and surveyed him. 'I don't know what Faith sees in you but you'll do.'

Hunter still looked pale but he managed a smile. 'She's wonderful, isn't she? I don't know what I did to deserve her. I'm the luckiest man alive.'

He really believed it too; there was sincerity in every syllable. All credit to Misty for bringing up such a decent young man. Gael had known plenty of men with lesser looks, lesser pedigrees and lesser fortunes who prowled the earth believing themselves young gods. Hunter genuinely didn't believe his face, name or income made him any better than anyone else—it just made him work harder to prove he deserved his privilege. Gael had only met Faith once briefly, two days ago after her afternoon with her new mother-in-law, but had quickly decided that either she was the world's best actress or as genuinely besotted by Hunter as he was with her.

He had hoped to see Hope, to try and make some kind of amends so that the next few days wouldn't be too awkward, but Hope hadn't been with her sister. He hadn't seen her since she'd walked away without a backwards glance. Not since he'd allowed her to. It was better for them to be apart; they both knew it. So why that bitter twist of disappointment when Faith had announced that her sister had gone shopping—and why this even more twisty and unwelcome anticipation as he savoured the knowledge that in just an hour's time she would be by his side?

They were both adults. They had spent two enjoyable weeks together. She had inspired him to create one of the best paintings he had ever done, even if it wasn't exactly what he'd set out to paint; he was thinking of calling it Atlas—because she looked as if she were carrying all the cares in the world on her slim shoulders. They could meet to celebrate this wedding as friends, surely? But when he thought of her in that wedding dress, glowing, when he thought of her lying on the chaise, posed and perfect, when he thought of her in his bed, then 'as friends' seemed a cold and meagre ambition.

But what was the alternative? Ask her out properly? They had said everything that needed to be said; he knew her more intimately than some men knew their wives of fifty years. How could he go from that to the kind of dating he did? The kind of dating he was capable of? Premieres, dinners in places to be seen, superficial and short-lived. He couldn't but he knew no other way.

He didn't *want* to know any other way. Because his way couldn't go wrong. It ended without tears, without acrimony, without devastation. It was safe. There was nothing safe about Hope and the way he was with her—harsh, unyielding, pushy. He wanted too much from her and she let him demand it. But, oh, how he liked it when he surprised her; her face when he had laid out all the different tubs of ice cream. Like a small child set loose in a toy store. She almost made him believe he could be the kind of man who lived a different way. Almost.

He pushed the thought away. Today wasn't about him and, despite his attempts to deny kinship, he was proud that Hunter had asked him to stand by his side. 'You ready?'

Hunter nodded. 'I was ready the first day,' he said simply. 'I saw her walking towards me and I just knew.'

Gael's mind instantly flashed back to the moment he had first seen Hope. What had he known? Surprise that she wasn't the woman he was expecting, yes. Annoyance at the delay in his plans? Absolutely. Recognition? He would like to deny it but something had made him keep her there, manipulate the situation so she stayed with him. He didn't want to dwell too much on what his reasons might have been. He attempted humour instead. 'Knew she was hot?'

'Knew she was the one for me. I was prepared to learn Czech or German or French, whatever I had to do to talk to the girl with eyes like stars—you can imagine my relief when I discovered she was English! Not that it would have made any difference whatever nationality she was. We would have found a way to communicate.'

'Hunter, you've known her what, two months? And it's not like your mom has had the best track record with the whole happy-ever-after thing. Are you sure you're not rushing into things?'

'Man, I am totally rushing into marrying Faith. Full pelt. I just know that she's the one for me and I'm the one for her and I can't wait to get started on our adventures together. As for Mom? She'd be the first to say she never listened to her heart. She didn't trust it not to lead her astray so she married strategically, for fun, for friendship—and then ended up divorced anyway.'

When had Hunter got so wise? Gael straightened his own tie, unable to look the younger man in the eye. 'I don't know what a good marriage is. What makes a relationship worth fighting for.' The confession felt wrought out of him and he turned slightly so that Hunter wouldn't be able to see his expression.

'I think it's when you trust someone completely and their happiness means more to you than your own—and when you know that they feel exactly the same way. You balance each other out, make the other person safe.'

Balance. What had he said to Hope? That marriage was about power? Hunter was saying the same thing only he saw it as a positive thing. That allowing someone else the power just made you stronger. Gael was almost light-headed as he tried to work it out. But looking at Hunter, so happy and so *confident*, he couldn't help but wonder if he possessed a knowledge Gael just couldn't—or wouldn't—understand.

He didn't have much time to dwell on his stepbrother's words as the next hour was a flurry of activity, first meeting up with Hunter's father and the two friends the groom had invited to this small, intimate celebration, and then they had to make their way to Central Park and the little lakeside glade where Hunter and Faith would be making their vows. Hunter didn't seem at all nervous, laughing and joking with his friends and patiently listening to all his father's last minute advice—and who knew? Maybe Hunter's father did know what he was talking about because not only had he stayed good friends with Misty but he had clocked up fifteen years with his current wife, a record amongst all the parental figures in Hunter's and Gael's lives.

In no time at all they were at the lake, which had been made ready according to Hope's detailed instructions; a few chairs had been arranged in a semicircle either side of the little rustic shelter under which Hunter and Faith would make their vows. White flowers were entwined in the shelter and yellow and white rose petals were scattered on the floor. All against Central Park's stringent regulations but the Carlyle name had persuaded the officials that an exception could be made.

Gael looked up at the cloudless sky and smiled; somehow Hope had even persuaded the weather to comply and the rain and wind which sometimes heralded the beginning of September had stayed away. Hunter's father and friends took their places while Gael stood beside his brother at the entrance to the pavilion, making polite conversation with the official who was conducting the short service. But what he said he hardly knew. In just a few minutes he would see her—and the spell her absence had cast would be broken. She'd walked away before he had decided it was time. That was all this sense something was amiss was. Nothing more.

He turned as he heard feminine voices, his heart giving a sudden lurch, but it wasn't Hope, merely a group of hot-looking women dressed in bright, formal clothes, fanning themselves and giggling as they took their seats. They were accompanied by one harried-looking elderly gentleman who breathed a sigh of relief as he took in the other men. Hope's uncle must have felt fairly overwhelmed by all the womenfolk he had spent the last three days escorting around the city.

He took a brief headcount as Misty wafted in, looking as elegant and cool as ever. The five men in Hunter's party, Misty, the bride's uncle and aunt and four young women who must be her two cousins and two friends. They were all here except for the bride herself—and her bridesmaid. He took a deep breath and steeled himself. It had been a brief fling, that was all. He bumped into old flames all the time and didn't usually turn a hair. There should be nothing different this time.

Shouldn't be and yet there was.

And then the string quartet, placed just out of sight around the curve in the path, struck up and the small congregation rose to their feet and turned as one. Every mouth smiled, every eye widened, many dampening as Faith floated towards them in the ethereal designer dress Hope had chosen for her beloved sister. Her hair was twisted into loose knots with curls falling onto her shoulders, she carried a small posy of yellow and white roses and her eyes were fixed adoringly on her groom. But Gael barely took any of it in, all his attention on the shorter woman by her side. Faith had asked her sister, the person who had raised her, to walk her down the aisle both today and for the blessing in two days' time.

Gael was the only person there who knew how much this gesture cost Hope. How touched she was but also how full of grief that their father wasn't there to do it—and that she would be symbolically relinquishing the last of her immediate family to someone else. That the moment she stepped back she truly would be alone.

His chest swelled with empathic grief because although her full mouth was curved in a proud smile and her carriage straight her eyes were full of tears and the hand holding a matching posy was shaking slightly.

Hope's hair was also tied up in a loose knot with a cream ribbon looped around, contrasting with the darkness of the silky tresses. She wore a knee-length twenties-style dress in a slightly darker shade than her sister's soft golden cream; she was utterly beautiful, utterly desirable. Damn. That wasn't the reaction he had been hoping for at all.

Hope looked up as if she could feel the weight of his gaze. Her lips quivered before her eyelashes fell again. *Look at me*, Gael urged her silently. *Let me work out what's happening here.* But his silent plea fell flat and although she smiled around at the gathered audience she didn't look at him directly again, not once.

* * *

The day was at once eternal and yet it passed in a flash. One moment Hope was kissing her sister's cheek, knowing that this was the last time she would be her next of kin, her first confidante, her rock, the next she was listening as Hunter promised to take care of Faith for ever.

She believed him. They were absurdly young but there was a determination and clearness amidst the starry-eyed infatuation that made her think that maybe they had a shot at making it work. Faith had grown up so much it was impossible to take in that the sisters had only been apart for three and a half months.

They moved seamlessly from ceremony to drinks, from drinks to the boat, which dreamily sailed around Manhattan in a gentle ripple of sparkling waters and blue skies before the cars took them to the now shut Met for a VIP tour followed by dinner. Now, at the end of the day, they were back at the speakeasy, reserved exclusively for the wedding party until midnight; there had been a last-minute panic when Hope realised that Faith's age meant she would be unable to enter the premises if it was open to the public. The bar didn't usually do private parties but a quiet word from Gael had ensured their cooperation; she wouldn't have been able to organise half of the day without him. He knew exactly who to speak to, how to get the kind of favours Hope McKenzie from Stoke Newington wouldn't have had a cat in hell's chance of landing. She should say thank you.

She should say *something*. They had been in the same small group of people for ten hours and somehow avoided exchanging even one word. She should tell him that he was wrong about her, that when it mattered she would always stand up for herself; she should tell him that, uncomfortable as his painting made her, she still recognised what a privilege it was to be immortalised that way. She should thank him for all his help with the wedding. She should tell him that two weeks with him had changed her life.

But she didn't know where to begin. She was just so aware of him. They could blindfold her and she would still reach unerringly for him. She knew how he tasted, she knew how his skin felt against hers. She knew what it felt like to have every iota of his concentration focussed on her. How did people do it? Carry this intimate knowledge of another human being around with them? She hadn't expected this bond, not without love.

Because of course she didn't love him. That would be foolish and Hope McKenzie didn't do foolishness. She wasn't like her sister; she couldn't just entrust her heart and happiness to somebody else. Especially somebody who didn't want either and wouldn't know what to do with them even if he did.

The sound of a spoon tapping on a glass recalled her thoughts to the here and now and, as the room hushed, she looked up to see Faith balancing precariously on a chair, her cheeks flushed.

'Attention,' her sister called as the group clapped and whistled. 'Bride speaking.'

Hope slid her glance over to Gael and, as she met his eyes, quickly looked away, her chest constricting with the burden of just that brief contact.

'I know we're doing speeches on Saturday,' Faith said when she had managed to quieten the room. 'So you'll be glad to hear this isn't a speech. Not a long one anyway. I just wanted to say thank you to my big sister.'

Hope started as everyone turned their attention from Faith to her. She shifted awkwardly from foot to foot, cursing her sister as she met the many smiles with a forced one of her own. Faith knew how much she hated attention.

'There are so many thank-yous I owe her that I could keep you here all night and not finish. Most of you know that Hope raised me after our parents died. You might not know that she gave up her place at university to do it, that she planned to study archaeology and travel the world, instead she became a PA and worried about bills and balanced meals and cooking cakes for the PTA bake sale. She refused to touch the money our parents left us, raising me on her salary— and I never did without. It was only recently that I realised that while *I* didn't go without, Hope often did. But she never made me feel like a burden. She always made me feel loved and secure and like I could be or do anything.' Faith's voice broke as she finished that sentence and Hope felt an answering lump in her own throat, a telltale heat burning in her eyes.

She heard a gulp of a sob from her aunt and a murmur from Misty but her eyes were fixed on her sister. The two of them against the world one last time.

'She gave me this amazing day, the best wedding day a girl could have asked for, with only two weeks' notice. She has always, always put me first. Now it's time she put herself first and I am so happy that she's decided to quit her job and go travelling.'

'What?' Hope wasn't sure if anyone else heard Gael's muffled exclamation as the room erupted into applause. 'I know she can afford to do it by herself but, Hope, I hope you will accept this from Hunter and me.' Faith held out an envelope. 'It's a round-the-world ticket and an account with a concierge who will organise all the visas and accommodation you need. It doesn't even begin to pay you back for all you've done and all you are but I just want you to know how much I love you—and when Hunter and I start a family I just hope I can be half the mother you were to me.' Faith was clambering off the chair as she spoke and the next minute the two girls were in each other's arms, tears mingling as they held each other as if they would never let each other go. Only Hope knew as she kissed her sister's hair that this was them letting go, this was where they truly moved on.

'Thank you,' she said as she reluctantly and finally moved back. 'You absolutely didn't have to...'

'I wanted to. So did Hunter. It gives you three months to explore the US and South America before taking you to Australia, then New Zealand and from there to Japan and across Asia. You choose when and where—as long as you turn up in Sydney in three months' time because that's when we'll be there and I hope you'll join us for that leg.'

'You can count on it.' She knew this was the right thing for her to do, to start living some of the dreams she'd relinquished all those years ago. The world might seem larger, scarier—lonelier—than it had back then, but she was a big girl now. She'd cope. But as she glanced over at Gael's profile a sense of something missing, something precious and lost shivered through her. She couldn't leave without making sure things were mended between them. It wouldn't be the same, not after the things they had said, but she wasn't sure she would have had the courage to move on without him. He should know that. Because she knew he was broken too.

CHAPTER ELEVEN

It was nearly midnight. A car was waiting outside to whisk Hunter and Faith back to the Waldorf Astoria where they had a luxury suite booked for two nights. Hope would see Faith in less than forty-eight hours at the blessing and party in Long Island but as she hugged her new brother-in-law and kissed her sister goodbye it was as if she was saying goodbye to a whole portion of her life.

The bride and groom departed in a flurry of kisses and congratulations and the party began to disperse as the bar staff efficiently began to set the room back up ready to reopen to the public. Hope's aunt and uncle were taking their daughters and Faith's friends back to the apartment Hope had booked for them, a day of non-wedding-related sightseeing waiting for them the next day. Hope had excused herself from joining them with the excuse that she still had some arrangements to finish for the Saturday—but in reality all she wanted to do was lie in her apartment and work out the rest of her life. She fingered the envelope her sister had given her. She had a year's hiatus at least.

'Congratulations on the travel plans. It seems a little sudden though.' She shivered as Gael came up beside her, not touching and yet so close she could feel every line of his body as if they were joined by an invisible thread. Her body ached for him; she wanted to step back and lean into him and let him absorb her. Typical, first time she tried for a light-hearted fling and she was having to go full cold turkey, knowing one touch would drag her back in.

Okay, deep breath and light chit-chat. She could do this. 'Sudden or really overdue. I was always going to go travelling after university. I had my route planned out. Lots and lots of ruins. Machu Picchu, the Bandelier national monument, Angkor Wat…' Her voice trailed off as she imagined setting foot in the ancient places she had dreamed about studying.

'What about Brenda, the job you wanted so much?'

'I phoned her yesterday and handed in my notice. I know it seems that I'm just jumping into it but I'm not. It turns out there's plenty of time to think at a spa day. I lay there on a massage table covered in God knows what, baking like a Christmas turkey, and your words echoed round and round.'

He caught her wrist and pulled her round to face him. The nerves in her wrist jumped to attention, shooting excited signals up her arm.

'I was out of line.'

'You were right,' she said flatly. 'I let life happen to me—I only did the job swap because Kit told me to apply. If he hadn't I would still be in Stoke Newington, missing Faith, wearing baggy tunics with my hair four inches too long because regular haircuts feel like an extravagance, getting the same bus to work, eating the same sandwich on the same bench every lunchtime and not even allowing myself to dream of anything better. Thinking I didn't deserve anything better.'

They moved aside with a muttered apology as a waiter pulled another table into place and a waitress pulled chairs across the floor, their legs screeching as they dragged on the wood. Gael winced. 'Let's get out of here. We're going the same way, at least let's share a cab.'

A cab pulled up almost the second they hit the pavement and Gael opened the door. 'Will you come back to mine?' he asked as she climbed in. 'I have a bottle of white in the fridge. I would really like to clear the air before the party. We're almost related now, after all.'

He'd bought a bottle of white wine. It was too little too late but it was something. 'Okay.' They did need to clear the air. The last thing she wanted was for Faith to know that they had been involved; it was all too messy.

They didn't speak again until they reached his studio. It was only three days since she had last walked through the lobby, greeted the night porter and taken the exclusive lift that led up to Gael's penthouse studio but she felt as if she had been away for months, suddenly unsure of her place in this world.

'Wine?' Gael asked as they stepped into the studio and Hope nodded. He'd bought it for her after all, a peace offering, it would be rude to say no.

She kicked off the pretty, vintage-style Mary Jane shoes, uttering a sigh of relief as her feet were freed from the straps and three-inch heels. She looked around, unsure where to sit. The chaise held too many memories, there was no way she was heading up the winding staircase to the small mezzanine, which contained a bed and very little else—and there was no other furniture in the place. Hope placed her shoes on the floor and followed Gael through to the kitchen instead, perching herself on one of the high stools as he poured wine from a bottle with an obscure—and expensive-looking—label.

'To new adventures,' she said, taking the glass he slid over to her and raising it in a toast. 'My travels, your exhibition.'

'When are you off? A month's time?'

Hope took a sip of the wine. Oh, yes. Definitely expensive. You wouldn't get a bottle of this in a price promotion in her local corner shop. 'No. Next week.'

'Next week?' He set his glass down with an audible clink. 'Didn't you have to work out your notice?'

'No, thanks to you signing the contract I was so far in Brenda's good books that she's offered me a year's sabbatical. I don't know if I'll take it. Who knows what I'll want to do or where I'll want to be in a year's time but there is a job with DL Media if I need it, which is reassuring.' She grimaced. 'It's not easy being spontaneous all at once. Baby steps.'

'But next week! Don't you have to plan and pack and sort out an itinerary?'

Hope pulled the envelope Faith had given her out of her bag. 'No, thanks to Faith. These people will sort it all out. I tell them where I want to go and they make sure I do. They're already looking at converting my work visa here to a tourist one and sorting out everything I need for South America. I'll spend a couple of days shipping some things home and sorting out what I need and then I'll be ready to go. It's working out really well actually. Maddison is coming to New York to clear the rest of her things out of the studio. If I leave she can cancel her rent. I don't think she's planning on coming back to the city.'

It would be interesting to meet her life-swap partner, the woman who captured Kit Buchanan's heart. Funny how a six-month change of locations could alter things irrevocably. Maddison was engaged, moving countries, her whole world changing. Hope might be more alone than ever but at least she was no longer staying still.

'You have it all organised, as always.' There was a bleak tone in Gael's voice she didn't recognise but when she glanced at him his expression was bland.

'The plane ticket is first class as well. I can't believe they did this.'

'I can. Your sister loves you, Hope.'

'For the first time in nine years I feel unburdened. Free. I'll always miss my parents and I'll always regret the person I was but I'm ready to forgive myself.' She forced herself to hold his steady, steely gaze. 'Thanks to you, Gael. I'll always be grateful.'

'You won't be here for the opening night of the exhibition.'

'No.' She blinked, surprised at the sudden change of subject. 'I'm not sure I could have faced it anyway. People looking at me and then at the painting. It'd be a little like the nightmare when I'm walking down the street naked. Only it would be real.'

'That's a shame. I wanted you there.' He paused while Hope gaped at him, floored by the unexpected words. He wanted her at his big night? As a model—or to support him? 'Look. I wanted to let you know that I've decided not to show it, your painting.'

Time seemed to stand still, the blood rushing to her

ears as she tried to take in his words. 'But, you need it. The centrepiece. It's less than three weeks away.'

'I have nineteen pictures I am proud of. Nobody else knows I planned a larger twentieth. I'm not sure that I'll ever paint a better picture than the one I did of you but I don't need to show it. I'd rather not, knowing it makes you so uncomfortable.'

He was willing not to show the picture? After everything he had done to persuade her to pose? Even though he thought it was the best he had done? Hope had no idea how to respond, what to say. This graciousness and understanding was more than she had ever expected from anyone. She slid off the stool and walked to the door, pausing for a second as she took in the easel with the large canvas balanced perfectly on it dominating the empty space and then, with a fortifying breath, she went over to take a second look.

It wasn't such a shock this time. Her skin was as white, her body as nude, she still wished she'd done daily sit-ups so that her stomach was concave rather than curved but, she conceded, her breasts looked rather nice. Biting her lip until she tasted blood, Hope forced herself to step in and examine her scars, remembering the pain and the secrecy and the self-hatred that went into every one of the silvery lines.

She pulled her gaze away from her torso and looked into her own eyes. Sad, wary, lonely. That was who she was; there was no getting away from it, no hiding. She shouldn't blame Gael for painting what he saw. She could only blame herself. Well, no more.

'Show it,' she said. 'I want you to. It's real. Maybe one day you can paint me again and I'll be a different person, a happier one.'

'You can count on it.' He was leaning against the door, watching her, hunger in his eyes. She recognised the hunger because she felt it too. Had felt it all day, this yearning to touch him, for him to touch her. For the world to fall away, to know nothing but him and the way he could make her feel; sexy, adored, powerful. Wanted.

She was leaving in less than a week. What harm could it do, one last time?

'On Saturday we're the best man and the bridesmaid once more. We have busy, sensible roles to play.'

The hunger in his eyes didn't lessen; if anything it intensified. 'I know.'

'Sunday I'm helping Faith get ready to go off on her travels and then I need to spend a couple of days preparing for mine.'

Gael pushed away from the door frame and stalked a couple of steps closer. 'Hope, what are you saying?'

Deep breath. She could do this. 'I'm saying that this is the last time we can be ourselves, Hope and Gael. Painter and model. Carousel riders. Storytellers.' She moistened her lips nervously. 'Lovers.'

'Last time?'

She nodded.

He smiled then, the wolfish smile that sent jolts of heat into every atom in her body, the smile that made her toes curl, her knees tremble and her whole body become one yearning mass. 'Then we better make the most of it, hadn't we?'

The morning sun streamed in through the huge windows, bathing the bed in a warm, rosy glow. Gael had barely slept and now he rolled over to watch Hope slumber, the dawn light tinging her skin a light pink, picking out auburn lights in her dark hair.

He felt complete, that all was right in his world. Probably, he decided sleepily, because Hope and he had tidied up their brief relationship, ending it in a mutually agreeable and agreed manner. No more messy arguments or avoiding each other, no more hurt emotions or dramas. Instead a civilised discussion and one last night together before they went their separate ways. Neat, tidy and emotionless. Just how he liked it.

It was a shame she wouldn't be there for the opening night though; he would have liked to have seen her reaction when all the pictures were displayed together for the first time with her at the very heart of the show.

He trailed his finger over her shoulder, enjoying the silky feeling of her skin. She was right. Tomorrow they had their roles to play and those roles didn't involve making out on the dance floor. Probably for the best that they had agreed last night was to be the final time.

But right now, in dawn's early light, was in between times, neither last night nor today. They were out of time, which meant there were no rules if they didn't want there to be. And that meant he could press his lips here, and here, and here…

'Mmm…' Hope rolled over, smiling the sleepy yet sated smile he had come to know and enjoy. 'What time is it?'

'Early, very early, so there's no need to think about getting up yet,' he assured her, dropping a brief kiss onto her full mouth, shifting so his weight was over her. 'Can you think of any way to spend the time as we're awake?'

Her eyes, languorous and sleepy, twinkled up at

him, full of suggestion, but she put her hands onto his chest and firmly, if gently, pushed him off. 'Plenty, but none suitable for people who are just friends.'

'Ah.' That wasn't disappointment stabbing through his chest. He could walk away at any time, after all. 'We've reached the cut-off point, then.'

'I think it might be wise.' She sat up, the sheet modestly wound around her. The message was clear—*I'm no longer yours to look at or touch or kiss*. 'Besides, I could do with an early start. Your stepmother—ex-stepmother—has asked me to go to Long Harbor this evening and stay so that I'm there for the morning when the caterers and everyone arrives. I know this party is all her work but I think she'd appreciate some backup. You'll be with us Saturday before three p.m., won't you? That's when my family arrives, with the blessing ceremony due to start at four.'

They were back in wedding-planning mode, it seemed. Gael slumped back onto the pillows, curiously deflated. 'I'll be there.'

'Great. I'll see you then.' Hope slid off the bed, still wrapped in a sheet, and headed towards the stairs. She turned, curiously dignified despite her mussed-up hair, her bare feet, the sheet held up modestly, just her shoulders peeking out above its white folds. 'Thank you, Gael. For waking me up, for challenging me, for making me challenge myself. I'm not saying I'm exactly relaxed about giving up my job—even with a sabbatical as a safety net—and if I think too hard about travelling by myself I get palpitations here.' She pressed her hand to her stomach. 'But I know it's all really positive—and I don't think I would have got here on my own. So thank you.'

'You'd have got there,' he said softly. 'You just needed a push, that was all. You were ready to fly.' He wanted to say more but what could he say? He didn't have the words, didn't have the feelings—didn't allow himself to have the feelings—so he just lay there as she turned with one last smile and watched her walk down the stairs. And five minutes later, when he heard the elevator ping and knew that this time she really had walked out of his studio for the last time, he still hadn't moved. All he knew was that the complete feeling seemed to have disappeared, leaving him hollow.

Hollow, empty and with the sense that he might have just made the biggest mistake of his entire life.

Five hours later the feelings had intensified. Nothing pulled him out of his stupor, not working on the painting—that just made the feelings worse—not going over his speech for the next day, not proofing the catalogue for his show. The only thing that helped was keeping busy—but he couldn't keep his mind on anything. Finally, exasperated with the situation, with himself, Gael flung himself out of the apartment, deciding if he couldn't work off this strange mood he would have to run it off instead. He stuck his headphones on, selected the loudest, most guitar-filled music he could find and set off with no route in mind.

Almost inevitably his run took him through Central Park, past the carousel and down towards the lake. Every step, every thud of his heart, every beat an insistent reminder that last time he was here, the time before that and the time before that he wasn't alone.

Funny, he had never minded being alone before. Preferred it. Today was the first day for a long time that he felt incomplete.

It didn't help that everywhere he looked the park was full of couples; holding hands, kissing, really kissing in a way that was pretty inappropriate in public, jogging, sunbathing—was that a proposal? Judging by the squeal and the cheering it was. Were there no other single people in the whole of Central Park? With a grunt of annoyance Gael took a path out of the park, preferring to pound the pavements than be a bystander to someone else's love affair.

He. Preferred. Being. Alone. He repeated the words over and over as his feet took him away from the park and into the residential streets of the Upper East Side. The midday sun was burning down and the humidity levels high but he welcomed the discomfort. If you were okay on your own then no one could ever hurt you. If he hadn't loved his mother so much then her absence wouldn't have poisoned every day of his childhood. If he hadn't relied on his father so much then it wouldn't have been such a body blow when his father left him behind with Misty. If he hadn't fallen so hard for Tamara then her betrayal wouldn't have been so soul-guttingly humiliating.

You could only rely on yourself. He knew that all too well.

And yet he couldn't shake Hope's words. *You're lucky to have Misty, to have someone who cares.* Hunter had wanted—no, needed—him by his side yesterday. Misty hadn't just paid his school and college fees, she had given him a home, shielded him from his father's impulsive and destructive post-divorce lifestyle. In those tricky few days after his authorship of *Expose* became public knowledge she had stood by him. She insisted he came to her every Thanksgiving and Christmas even now.

Hope had seen that when he couldn't—or wouldn't. But then she knew all about being a mother figure, didn't she?

And now it was her time to shine. He wished he could see her as she finally visited the places she had always wanted to visit, could capture the look on her face as she finally reached Machu Picchu, in photographs, in pencil sketches, in oils. He could draw her for ever and never run out of things to say about the line of her mouth, the curve of her ear, that delicious hollow in her throat.

His steps slowed as he gulped for air, his discomfort nothing to do with the heat or his punishing pace. Somehow, when he hadn't even noticed it, Hope McKenzie had slid under his guard and he could walk away—leave her to walk away—and it would make no difference. She'd still be there. He'd still be alone but the difference would be now he'd feel it. He'd not just be alone—he'd be lonely.

He bent over, trying to get his breath back and re-order his thoughts, and as he straightened he saw a familiar sign, the shop they had visited so recently, the shop where Faith's wedding dress still hung, the last alterations completed, ready to be steamed and conveyed to Long Island in the morning. The shop where Hope had tried on a dress that, for one moment, had made him wish that he were a different man, that they had a different future. A dress that belonged to her.

Was this a sign or just a coincidence? It almost didn't matter. What mattered was what he chose to do next.

CHAPTER TWELVE

'YOU LOOK BEAUTIFUL.'

Hope smoothed down her dress and smiled at Gael, her heart giving a little twist as she did so. By tacit consent they had kept their distance from each other all day except when posing for photographs, but now the evening had drawn in and the event moved from celebration to party the rules they had set themselves didn't seem quite so rigid. They were aiming for friends, after all.

'It's all the dress. Lucky I had some expert help choosing it.' All the bridesmaids wore the same design, a halter-necked knee-length dress with a silk corsage at the neck, but while the other four bridesmaids' dresses were all a deep rose pink Hope, as maid of honour, wore a cream and pink flowered silk. 'If your show is a flop you could always turn your hand to wedding styling. You have quite the knack.'

'All I did was nod in the right places. I think you knew exactly what you were looking for.'

'Maybe. So that was a good speech you did back then.' She'd heard lots of people talking about it—and him. It was hard to keep a bland smile on her face when she kept overhearing beautiful, gazelle-like girls in dresses that cost more than her entire wardrobe discussing just how sexy they thought he was and speculating whether his net worth was high enough for a permanent relationship or whether he was just fling material.

They weren't lying about how sexy Gael looked today. Some men looked stilted or stuffy in a suit; Gael wore his with a casual elegance and a nonchalance that made a girl sit up and take notice. Even this girl. Especially this girl.

His tie was the same dark pink as the flowers on her dress. They looked as if they belonged together.

Funny how deceiving looks could be.

'Thank you. Hunter deserved something heartfelt and not too cruel. He's a good kid. Although now he's a married man I suppose I shouldn't call him a kid.'

'I suppose not.' Hope looked over at the dance floor where her sister swayed in her new husband's arms, the two of them oblivious to the two hundred or so guests Misty had invited. It was a beautiful party. Lanterns and fairy lights were entwined in the trees all around and in the several marquees that circled the dance floor, one acting as a bar, one a food tent, one a seating area and one a family-friendly place with games and a cinema screen for the younger guests.

The swing band that had accompanied the meal had been replaced by a jazz band crooning out soulful ballads as the evening fell. A sought-after wedding singer was due to come onto the purpose-built stage at nine to get the dancing really started and then a celebrated DJ would entertain the crowd into the early hours. The blessing had been beautifully staged and even though

Hope had seen her sister make similar vows just two days before she had still needed to borrow a hanky from her aunt when she welled up for the second time.

'Would you like to dance?'

The question took her by surprise. 'I don't know if that's wise. Maybe later when the music is less…'

'Less what?'

'Less sway-like. I hear the wedding singer does an excellent Beyoncé. I'll dance with you to that.'

'It's a deal.'

So they had made small talk and it wasn't too hard, made civilised plans for later. No one looking over at them would think that they were anything but the best man and the maid of honour relaxing after a long day of duties. Good job on both sides. It was probably time to drift away to opposite sides of the dance floor so Hope could resume sneaking peeks at him while pretending even to herself, especially to herself, that she wasn't.

The night after the wedding had been her gift to herself. A chance to be bold and brave. A way of ensuring that something sweet and special didn't turn sour, that her memories of Gael and her time with him were something to savour. A time for her to take control and show them both just what she could do, who she could be. And then she had walked away with her head held high. Chosen when, chosen how.

So why did her victory feel so hollow? She had a sinking feeling it was because things weren't finished between them, much as she tried to fool herself that they were. There had been a tenderness that night she hadn't felt before. A closeness that she wasn't sure she believed was real and not just a figment of her over-heated imagination. Truth was, Gael knew her better than anyone else in the entire world. How did she walk away from that?

But she didn't know what the alternative was or if she was brave enough to explore it. Hope turned away from the dance floor. Ahead of her, through the small scrub-like trees, was a private path that led directly to the beach. She'd been meaning to take a look at the ocean but hadn't had a chance to. 'I'm going to take a walk,' she said, kicking her shoes off, taking a couple of steps away. She didn't know if it was devilry or the moonlight that made her swivel back around and aim a smile in Gael's direction. 'Coming?'

He didn't answer but his movement was full of intent and she didn't demur as he took her hand, leading her through the trees with sure steps. The path through the trees was lit with tiny storm lanterns swaying in the slight breeze like an enchanted way.

All Hope knew was the salt on her lips, the sea breeze gentling ruffling her elaborately styled hair, the coolness of the sand between her toes and the firmness of Gael's grip. 'What was it like living here?'

He didn't answer until they cleared the trees and reached the top of the dunes. The beach spread out before them, dim in the pearl glow of the moon, behind them Hope could hear music and laughter, ahead the swish of the waves rippling onto shore.

'I didn't feel like I belonged,' he said finally. 'I was a scrubby kid who biked around Long Harbor getting into trouble, the kind of kid begging for a chance to go out on a boat, trying to find ways of earning a few dollars through running errands. Home was chaotic, living with my grandparents, I always fell asleep listening to the music in the bar downstairs. And then I came here. A driver to take me where I needed to go, money, more than I could spend, a boat that belonged to the family I could take out whenever I wanted complete with a crew. And when I fell asleep at night it was to total silence. I had a room, a study and a bath all to myself.'

'How did it feel?'

'Like I didn't know who I was.' His hand strengthened in hers. 'I still don't. Except...'

She wasn't sure she dared ask but did anyway. 'Except what?'

'These last couple of weeks I've had an inkling of who I could be, the kind of man I'd like to be.'

'Me too. Not the man part but the seeing a new way. It's not easy though, is it?'

Letting go of his hand, Hope sank down into the soft sand, not worrying about stains on her dress or if anyone was looking for her or if there were things she should be doing. All those things were undoubtedly true but she didn't have to take ownership of them. Gael folded himself down beside her with that innate grace she admired so much and Hope leaned into him, enjoying his solid strength, the scent of him. The illusion that he was hers.

'You've made a good start though. Travelling, carefree, no plans.'

'Hmm. On the surface maybe,' she conceded. 'I want to go, don't get me wrong, but there's still the little voice in my head telling me I don't deserve it. And another little voice shrieking at me to plan it all down to the final detail, account for every second because if it's planned it can't go wrong.'

'Sounds like it's getting crowded in your head.'

'Just a little. Planning makes me feel safe so trying to learn to be more spur of the moment is, well, it's a challenge. My real worry is…' She hesitated.

'Go on.'

'Being lonely,' she admitted. 'Even lonelier than I have been because I have always had Faith and a job, a routine. I'm not good at talking to people, Gael. I suck at making friends. A whole year of just me for company looms ahead and it terrifies me.'

'Oh, I don't know. It sounds pretty good to me.'

Surprise hit her *oomph* in the chest. In her heart. Not just the words but the way he said them. Low, serious and full of an emotion she couldn't identify. Her pulse began to hammer, the blood rushing in her ears, drowning out the sound of the sea. She'd always wanted to matter to someone, be worthy of someone, but at some point in the last two weeks her goalposts had shifted.

She wanted to matter to Gael.

Proud, cynical Gael. A man who gave no quarter and expected none. A man who knew what he wanted and pushed for it. A man who had made her confront all her secrets and sins and forgive herself.

A man who made her feel safe. Worth something.

'You could travel,' she said, looking down at her feet, at the way her toes squished into the sand. 'Do the whole Gauguin thing.'

'Been reading up on your history of art?'

'I remember some things from my whistle-stop tour.'

'I could. I could travel, stay here, move to Paris or

Florence or Tahiti. I'm not sure it would make much difference though. I'd still be hiding.'

'What from?'

'Myself. From emotion. From living. Do you know why that painting of you is the best thing I have ever done?'

She still couldn't look at him, shaking her head instead.

'Because I felt something when I painted it. Felt something for you. Complicated, messy, unwanted human emotions. Lust, of course. Exasperation because I could see you hiding all that you are, all that you could be. Frustration that you didn't see it. Annoyance because you kept pushing me, asking awkward questions and puncturing the bubble I had built around myself.'

Exasperation, annoyance. Frustration. At least she had made him feel something.

'And I liked you. A lot. I didn't want to. The last thing I needed was a dark-eyed nymph with a wary expression and a to-do list turning my carefully ordered world upside down.'

'Is that what I did?' She raised her head and looked directly at him, floored by the unexpected tenderness in his smile.

'I think you know you did. I have something to show you. Will you come?'

She nodded mutely.

Gael pulled Hope to her feet and led her back along the path to the house, skirting the party and the merry-making guests, neither of them ready or able to make small talk with Hunter's Uncle Maurice or Misty's drunken college room-mate. He took a circuitous route round the Italian garden and in through a side door that only he and Hunter had ever used as it led straight into a boot room perfect for dropping sandy surfboards and towels and swim trunks with a shower room leading right off it. It was empty today, no towels folded on the shelves, no boards hanging on the wall, no crabbing nets leaning in the corner. For the first time Gael felt a shiver of fond nostalgia for those carefree, summer days. He might not have ever admitted it but this huge nineteen-twenties mansion had at some point become his home—just as its mercurial, warm-hearted, extravagant owner had become his mother.

The boot room led into a back hallway, which ran behind the reception and living areas, avoiding the famous two-storey main hallway with its sweeping, curved staircase and ornate plasterwork. Instead Gael led the way up a narrow back stairway, once used solely by the army of servants who had waited on Misty's great-grandparents, the original owners of the mansion.

'I feel like I'm a teenager again, sneaking girls up to my room through the back stairs.'

'Was there a lot of that?'

'No, sadly not. I was too grand for the girls I grew up with and not grand enough for the girls Misty introduced me to. Besides, there wouldn't have been any sneaking. Misty would have offered us wine and condoms and sent us on our way. She was embarrassingly open-minded. Nothing more guaranteed to make a teen boy teetotal and celibate—even if he wasn't a social pariah!'

'I bet there were hundreds of girls just waiting for

you to look in their direction,' Hope said. 'I would have been.'

'Maybe,' he conceded. He had been so filled with his own angst he would never have noticed.

A discreet door led onto the main landing. Closed again, it blended into the wooden panelling. The house was riddled with hidden doors and passageways and he knew every single one of them.

'Don't think I'm not appreciating this behind-the-scenes tour of one of Long Island's finest houses but where are we going?'

'Here,' Gael said and, opening the door to his own suite of rooms, ushered her inside.

It hadn't changed much since he first took possession of the rooms as a boy. A sitting area complete with couch, a TV and a desk for studying. The computer console was long gone and the posters of bikini-clad girls replaced with paintings he admired by local artists, but the window seats still overlooked the beach and the Victorian desk was still piled with his paints and sketchbooks. A door by the window led into his bedroom.

'These are yours?'

'Misty apologised when she assigned them to me, said she hoped I wouldn't be too cramped but she thought I'd prefer not to be stuck out in one of the wings.'

Hope wandered into his bedroom, her eyes widening as she took in the king-size bed, the low couch by the window, and she opened the door to his bathroom complete with walk-in shower and a claw-foot bathtub. 'You poor thing, it must have been such a chore making do with just the two huge rooms and a bathroom fit for an emperor.'

'I managed somehow.'

Now she was here, now the moment was here, unexpected nerves twisted his stomach. What if he had got her, got them, got the situation wrong? For a moment he envied Hunter his certainty. He'd known, he'd said, the second he'd seen Faith. They had been together for just two months and there they were downstairs, husband and wife.

He'd known Hope for less than three weeks but he couldn't imagine knowing anyone any better after three years.

He looked over at her as she stared out of the window at the moon illuminating the sea. Her hair was still twisted up, held with a rose-pink ribbon, the dress exposing the fine lines of her neck and the fragile bones in her shoulders. Desire rippled through him, desire mixed with a protectiveness he had never experienced before, an overwhelming need to protect her from life's arrows. She'd already been pierced too many times. 'I got you something.'

She turned, a shy smile lighting up her face. 'You didn't have to.'

'I know. It's not a parting gift. It's an *I hope you come back* gift.'

Her mouth trembled. 'Really?'

Words failed him then, the speech he'd prepared during the sleepless night. Words telling her he wanted her to go, to experience, to live. But at the end of it all he hoped she'd choose to come back. To him. 'It's in the closet.'

With a puzzled frown wrinkling her forehead, Hope

opened the door to his walk-in closet. It was practically empty, the few essentials he kept here folded up and put away on shelves at the back. There was only one item hanging up.

Hope stood stock-still, one hand flying to cover her mouth. 'My dress.'

'I didn't think anyone else should have it.' It was hers. They had both known it the second she had put it on. Every line, every delicate twist of lace, every fold of silk belonged to her.

'But...it's a wedding dress.'

'I don't want to confine you, Hope. I don't want you to go away tied down. I want you to live and laugh and if you love then that's the way it's supposed to be.' He swallowed as he said the words, alternate words trembling on his tongue. *Stay with me.* 'This dress is a talisman, a pledge. That if you choose to come back to me then I'll be here. And if you don't, well. It's yours anyway. If you want it.'

Did she understand? Did she know what it meant that he had asked her to come back to him? He had never asked anyone before. Never exposed himself. Taken each desertion on the chin and then wrapped another layer of protectiveness around himself.

Hope couldn't take her eyes off the dress, perfect as it hung in the closet, every fold exactly where it should be. It did belong to her, he was right. Nothing had ever felt so right—nothing but being in Gael's arms. And he had bought it for her.

The dress had been exorbitant but she knew it wasn't the dollar price that made it special, utterly unique. It was the gesture behind the gift. It was opening himself up to rejection. It was allowing her the power to reject him. That was his real gift. He was giving her power. He trusted her with his heart just as she had trusted him with her body and soul.

'Come with me,' she said. 'Travelling. You can paint anywhere, can't you? Come with me.'

'But it's your big adventure.'

'And I want to share it with you.' That was what had been holding her back. Her dream travels seemed ash grey when she contemplated doing it alone. She wanted to share each discovery, each experience with Gael. She wanted him to tease her, to push her, to make her feel, to stretch herself. 'I have done since I booked it. I knew I should be excited but instead every time I thought about getting on that plane, flying away from you, I felt sick with dread.'

'You really want me along?'

'Always.' She put her hand on his shoulder and instantly knew she was home, that no matter where she was in the world if he was there she would be settled. 'When Faith told me she was marrying someone she barely knew I thought she was crazy. Well, people will tell me I'm crazy, that two weeks is nothing at all, but I have lived a lifetime in the last fortnight. A lifetime with you. It wasn't always easy or comfortable but for the first time in a long time I was alive. You brought me to life. I didn't think that I knew what love was, that I was capable of it, that I deserved it, but you have made me change my mind. I love you, Gael. I love you and I want to spend the rest of my life having adventures with you.'

His eyes had darkened to a midnight blue as he pulled her in close, caressing her with light scorching kisses along her brow, her cheeks, her mouth. Hope pressed herself as close as she could, her hands holding on tightly as if she would never, ever let go. And she wouldn't; this man was hers. She knew it with every fibre of her being and her body thrilled with ownership. He was hers and she was his.

'I love you,' he said, the words catching in his throat. 'I didn't want to, I fought against it but I think I loved you from the first moment you unleashed your outrage on me.'

'I'd barely said hello and you asked me to strip,' she protested. 'Gael, will you come with me? I don't want to be away from you, from us, but I don't want to walk away from a chance to do something new again. If I don't travel now I never will.'

'On one condition.' He smiled into her eyes. 'Monday you put on that dress and we go to City Hall and get married. I'll need to be in New York in three weeks for the exhibition launch party but otherwise I'm yours for the next year. For the rest of my life. What do you say?'

'I say you'd better ask me properly.'

She was only teasing but Gael stepped back, dropping to one knee, like a picture from a fairy tale. Hope's heart stuttered with longing and love as he took her hand in his. 'You'd better say yes now I'm down here.'

'Ask the question and then I'll be able to answer.'

'Hope McKenzie. Would you do me the honour— the very great honour of being my wife?'

She didn't answer straight away, taking a moment to take in the devilish glint in his eye mingling with the love and tenderness radiating from him. Hope dropped down to kneel in front of him, taking his face in her hands as she did so. 'Yes. Yes, I will. Always.' And as she leant in to kiss him she knew that her adventures were only just beginning and that she would never be lonely again, not while she had Gael by her side.

* * * * *

If you enjoyed this story, make sure you've read
Maddison and Kit's story
IN THE BOSS'S CASTLE
Available now!

"Anyway," he repeated, "now here we are…"

"Here we are," Livi echoed.

"And I thought maybe we should talk about… you know… where we go now."

He did meet her eyes then, and Livi responded with an acknowledging raise of her chin. But she didn't say anything because she had no idea where they should go now—especially factoring in that pregnancy test she had in that bag in the trunk of her cousin's car.

"How about we just put it behind us?" he suggested then. "Forget it happened. Start fresh…"

Easy for him to say.

"You want to help Greta," he went on, "and now she's kind of my job—her and the Tellers—so we'll be seeing each other. But Hawaii was… well…"

A one-night stand? A vacation fling? Pure stupidity on her part? Yes, what exactly should they call it?

As bad as the past two months had been for Livi, this was worse. This was excruciating. It felt like a brush-off. As if he was telling her that even though they'd slept together, he didn't want there to be anything more than that.

And while she certainly didn't, either, it was still a rejection. One she hadn't signed on for because she hadn't so much as entertained the idea of Hawaii going anywhere further.

* * *

The Camdens of Colorado:
They've made a fortune in business.
Can they make it in the game of love?

A CAMDEN'S
BABY SECRET

BY
VICTORIA PADE

MILLS & BOON

First Published in Great Britain 2016
By Mills & Boon, an imprint of HarperCollins*Publishers*
1 London Bridge Street, London, SE1 9GF

© 2016 Victoria Pade

ISBN: 978-0-263-92016-1

23-0916

Our policy is to use papers that are natural, renewable and recyclable products and made from wood grown in sustainable forests. The logging and manufacturing processes conform to the legal environmental regulations of the country of origin.

Printed and bound in Spain
by CPI, Barcelona

Victoria Pade is a *USA TODAY* bestselling author. A native of Colorado, she's lived there her entire life. She studied art before discovering her real passion was for writing, and even after more than eighty books, she still loves it. When she isn't writing she's baking and worrying about how to work off the calories. She has better luck with the baking than with the calories. Readers can contact her on her Facebook page.

Chapter One

Maybe I shouldn't have come today, Livi Camden thought as she leaned against the wall in one of the downstairs bathrooms of her grandmother's house.

For over a week now she'd been having slight waves of nausea—mostly in the mornings. But on this warm, sunshine-filled Sunday afternoon—the second week of October—it became much worse than a slight wave the minute she'd come in and cooking smells had greeted her.

The bathroom had a window to the backyard and she opened it so she could breathe in the outside air.

Better...

The wave began to pass.

That was good. She hated feeling nauseous and she also didn't want to have to go home. She loved Sunday dinner at her grandmother's house with all her family—

even if she wasn't sure she was going to be able to eat much today.

Family had been everything to her since she'd lost her parents as a child and, along with her siblings and cousins, had become the responsibility of her grandmother. It was her family that kept Livi going when loss struck four years ago with Patrick's death.

Plus, GiGi had called and said she wanted a few minutes alone with her today, and whatever request her grandmother made of her, Livi did her best to fulfill—especially if it meant helping with the family project of making amends to those wronged by the Camdens in the past.

The discovery of her great-grandfather H. J. Camden's journals had confirmed all the ugly talk that had haunted the family for decades. It was rumored that the Camdens had regularly practiced underhanded and deceitful tactics to build their highly profitable empire of superstores.

The current Camdens were determined to do whatever they could to make up for the past. Quietly, so as not to invite false claims on them, they were finding ways to help or compensate those who had genuinely been harmed.

It was a cause Livi believed in and she was ready, willing and able to do her part.

Actually, she *hoped* that was why her grandmother wanted to talk to her.

Maybe doing something good and positive for someone else might make her feel better about herself these days. And it might also give her something to think about other than the biggest mistake she'd ever made in her life, for which she couldn't seem to stop chastising herself.

Another wave of nausea hit her and again she took

some deep breaths of cool backyard air, trying to relax. She was sure that stress over her horrible choice two months ago was causing the nausea.

"Hey, Liv, are you okay? You've been in there a long time."

It was her sister Lindie's voice coming from the other side of the door.

"I'm good. I'll be right out," she answered, glancing at herself in the mirror.

Her color was fine—her usually fair skin wasn't sallow, the blue eyes that people called "those Camden blue eyes" were clear and not dull the way they got when she was genuinely under the weather. She looked tired, but not ill.

So it probably *was* stress, she told herself. That's all. She was upset about what she'd done and that was making her stomach upset. When she calmed down and managed to put Hawaii behind her, her stomach would settle.

Leaving the bathroom, she tried not to breathe in too deeply the cooking smells as she went to the kitchen. But even shallow breaths caused the queasiness again. So she opened the door to the patio, angling a shoulder through the gap so she was once again breathing outdoor air without being completely outside.

Her sister and her cousin Jani were in the kitchen, gathering dishes, napkins and silverware. They both paused to watch her.

"Are you still sick with that weird flu?" Lindie asked her.

A touch of the flu—that was the excuse she'd given the first few days that she'd been late getting to work while she'd waited out the nausea at home.

"It can't be the flu—that doesn't last as long as this has," Jani contributed.

The downside of being so close to her family—they sometimes knew too much.

"Okay, so it's not the flu," Lindie said. "But what is it? You've been all wound up ever since you got back from Hawaii."

"Travel can make a mess of my stomach," Livi hedged.

"But you've been back for weeks—plenty of time for your stomach to readjust."

"Her wedding anniversary was while she was there," Lindie pointed out to their cousin, as if she'd just hit on a clue. Then to Livi she said, "Was it bad this year? Did it set off something and put you back in a funk, stressing you out?"

Oh, the anniversary set off something, all right, Livi thought. But she couldn't say *that*.

"My anniversary is never a good day." And this year her response had been completely over-the-top and stupid. But again, she couldn't tell anyone, so instead she said, "I don't know. Maybe I've been a little tense since then. And that always gets to my stomach. I'm sure it'll pass, the way it always does," she added with confidence.

But those smells were getting to her again, so she opened the door a little farther and moved a few more inches over the threshold.

Her left hand hung on to the edge of the door. Her left *ringless* hand.

And just the way Lindie had before Livi went into the bathroom, Jani noticed.

"Am I seeing what I'm seeing?" she exclaimed. "You took off your wedding rings? That's probably it!"

"Oh, sure, I should have thought of that," Lindie concurred.

"Did you decide in Hawaii?" Jani asked. "That's a big deal, taking off your rings. No wonder you're all tied up in knots! Was it the anniversary that finally got you there? That *had* to be agonizing for you. And now you've done it… But that's good," her cousin added quickly. "That's great! Of course, it couldn't have been easy for you, and it's bothering you and causing the tummy trouble. But don't put them back on! This is the first step for you to really heal."

Livi felt like such a fraud. Along with the intermittent nausea, for some reason her fingers had swollen and she *couldn't* get her rings on. She had every intention of wearing them again when the swelling went down.

But since this assumption provided such a ready excuse to appease her sister and cousin, she let them think what they wanted.

Which might not have been the best course, because then Lindie said, "Maybe when she feels better we can even get her to go on a date."

"No," Livi interjected firmly, thinking that she couldn't let this go too far.

"You *need* to, Livi," her cousin added. "Usually people have their first love, get their heart broken—"

"Or break someone else's heart," Lindie interjected.

"Then do a lot of testing the waters with other people before they find Mr. Right," Jani finished. "But you—"

"Married my first love."

"And missed getting the experience of casual dating. And now you're just stuck in this limbo—Patrick is gone and you don't know how to do what the rest of us learned a long time ago. You need to get comfortable with the whole dating thing. Then maybe you'll be able to—"

Don't say move on again! Livi wanted to shout.

Instead she said, for what felt like the millionth time, "Patrick wasn't just my first love, he was also my *only* love, and you guys need to accept that. I have."

"People can have more than one love in a lifetime, Livi," Lindie persisted. "Look at GiGi—she has Jonah now."

"And I'm happy for her," Livi said. "But Patrick was *it* for me."

"So maybe you won't find another love-of-your-life," Jani reasoned. "Maybe you'll just find a close second. But that's still something. Don't you want companionship at least? Someone to have dinner with? Someone to go to the movies with? Someone to—"

"Have sex with?" Lindie said bluntly.

Oh, that made her *really* queasy!

"No," Livi said forcefully, meaning it. And unwilling to tell either her sister or her cousin just how clearly she now knew it was a mistake to veer off the course she'd set for herself since Patrick.

"I'm fine," she went on. "Honestly. I'm happy. I'm content. Sure, I wish things had turned out differently and Patrick and I had gotten to grow old together. But that wasn't in the cards and I've accepted it."

"What about kids?" Jani asked, resting a hand on her pregnant belly, round and solid now that she was entering her third trimester.

Livi shook her head. "I get to have all the fun with my nieces and nephews—more of them coming all the time these days—and none of the work. I'll spoil every one of them and be their favorite aunt and they'll like me better than their mean parents who have to discipline them. Then, when I'm old and gray in the nursing home, they'll all come to visit me just the way they do you guys."

Jani rolled her eyes. "It won't be the same."

"It'll be close enough."

"Close enough to what?" Georgianna Camden—the matriarch of the Camden family—asked as she came into the kitchen.

"Livi thinks that being an aunt is better than having kids of her own," Lindie answered.

The seventy-five-year-old grandmother they all called GiGi raised her chin in understanding but didn't comment.

"She took off her wedding rings, though," Jani said, her tone full of optimism.

"Oh, honey, I know how hard that is," GiGi commiserated. "Good for you!"

"Her stomach is bothering her because of it," Lindie explained.

"Well, sure. I'll make you dry toast for dinner—that always helps. But still, good for you," the elderly woman repeated like a cheering squad.

Livi was feeling guiltier by the minute. When this whole queasiness-swollen-fingers thing passed and she put her rings back on, she knew everyone would worry about her all over again.

But there was no way she could explain what was really going on. The true reason for her queasiness—the fact that she was so upset over what had happened in Hawaii—had to be her secret.

So she changed the subject and said to her grandmother, "I could use something to take my mind off everything, GiGi. I was hoping you wanted to talk to me today to tell me you have one of our projects for me."

"As a matter of fact, that *is* why I wanted to talk to you," she said, her tone more solemn. "Why don't we go sit outside and talk?"

Thinking that that was a fabulous idea, Livi wasted no time slipping out onto the back patio. Luckily, the beautiful Indian summer that Denver was enjoying made the weather warm yet.

Livi went as far from the house as she could to escape the cooking odors, and sat on the brick bench seat beside the outdoor kitchen they used for barbecues.

GiGi followed her, pulling one of the chairs away from a glass table nearby to sit and face her.

"This one makes *me* sick," her grandmother announced as a prelude. She then told the story of the Camden sons and Randall Walcott, who had been Howard and Mitchum Camden's best friend and so close to the entire family that GiGi herself—Howard and Mitchum's mother—had known him well.

As Livi listened her stomach finally did settle, allowing her to concentrate on what GiGi was telling her.

"Which brings us to today," GiGi said, when she'd given her the background. "I only read about what your grandfather and H.J. and my sons did a few weeks ago. I've been looking into it ever since to see how we could make some kind of restitution—I thought it would be to Randall's daughter. She and her husband and little girl live in Northbridge…"

"So you called Seth," Livi guessed. It was a reasonable conclusion given that her cousin and his family lived in the small Montana town on the family ranch, overseeing the Camden agriculture interests.

"I did," GiGi confirmed. "And he told me that two months ago, Randall's daughter and her husband were killed in a car accident. Thankfully, their little girl, Greta, wasn't with them."

"How old is she?" Livi's voice was full of the sympathy she felt, because she could identify with the childhood loss of parents.

"She's only nine."

"And does she have a GiGi?" Livi asked. It was her grandmother who had been the salvation of her and her siblings and cousins when their parents and grandfather had all died in that plane crash. If anyone had to suffer through what they all had, the best thing that could happen to them was to have a grandmother like they had.

"She only has the Tellers—the grandparents on the husband's side. But Seth said that Maeve Teller has health issues of some kind and apparently neither Maeve or her husband, John, are in a position to raise the little girl. There's some situation with a family friend who was granted guardianship of her in the parents' will. A single man—"

"They left a little girl with a single man? How is he handling that? Does Seth know him?"

"Seth wasn't able to get a name, though he heard that there's something about him that doesn't sit well with folks around there for some reason. But the parents must have trusted whoever this man is or they wouldn't have left him their child."

Livi hoped that was true.

"At any rate," GiGi went on, "I don't know what the financial situation is. The Tellers only have a small farm and Seth says it isn't doing well, so he doubts there's much money there, especially if Maeve has medical bills.

And regardless, the little girl can't be inheriting anything like what she would have if we'd treated her grandfather fairly."

"That's the ugly truth," Livi agreed.

"So what I want you to do is go to Northbridge and make sure this child has the care she needs now and anything she might need in the future. Let's make sure that whoever this family friend is wants her…"

"Hopefully, finding himself guardian of a nine-year-old girl didn't come as an unpleasant surprise," Livi muttered.

"Hopefully," GiGi agreed. "But let's make sure that he's capable of taking care of her, that he'll give her a good home. And maybe we can set up a trust fund for her, money for her college, whatever it takes to make sure she has the kind of life she would have had if…" GiGi's voice trailed off as if she was too disgusted, too disappointed, too ashamed of what her own husband and sons had done to repeat it.

"So I'll sort of be her GiGi," Livi said affectionately, not wanting her grandmother to go on feeling bad.

She was pleased when GiGi smiled in response. "Not necessarily a GiGi, but maybe the little girl could use a sort of big sister or a mentor—a woman in her life, too, even if everything is going well with the guardian. Or maybe she won't need anything but to be provided for financially. However, we won't know that until you check things out."

Livi nodded.

"Are you well enough?" the gray-haired woman asked.

"I'm fine. I feel better when I have a lot to do and don't think about…things. Like I said, I need a distraction."

"If you get tempted to put the rings back on, maybe

consider wearing them on your right hand. I still do that sometimes."

"I know," Livi said, fighting another surge of guilt at what she'd allowed her family to believe.

Once more wanting to skirt around it, she went back to what they'd been talking about. "I have some things I have to take care of this week that can't be put off. How about I go to Northbridge next Saturday and look up Greta and her grandparents and this guardian on Sunday?"

"The sooner the better, but I suppose another week won't make any difference," GiGi said. Then she stood. "Now let's go get you some dry toast for that stomach of yours."

Livi dreaded going back into the house and the smells that brought on the queasiness, so she said, "I'll be right there. I just want to sit here a minute."

And think about how nice it would be if her stomach stayed as settled as it was right then.

If her fingers returned to their normal size.

And if her period would start this month even though it never had last month.

Because if only it would, then she really could forget all about Hawaii.

And the man who had—for just one night—made her forget too many other things…

Chapter Two

"We knew there was some bad blood between Mandy's father and your family from a long time ago, but she never talked about it and, well…"

"Considering the way her father went out we never brought up anything about him, so all we know is that there *was* bad blood."

What sweet Maeve Teller had tried to say diplomatically, her blunt husband, John Sr., finished.

Livi had arrived in Montana on Saturday evening, to discover Seth had taken his wife and new baby to visit Lacey's father in Texas. He'd left the keys to his cars and trucks for Livi to use—as well as the directions to the Teller farm—and promised to be back Sunday night. Tonight.

Livi had actually been glad to have the Northbridge house to herself for a while. Along with the continuing bouts of nausea and the swollen fingers, she was so easily tired out these days that she'd been happy to go straight to bed.

Unsure what kind of reception she might receive, and not wanting to risk an outright refusal to be seen, she'd arrived at the Tellers' farm without warning at two o'clock. The door had been opened by a woman who looked to be her own age—Maeve's nurse. She hadn't even asked who Livi was. She'd merely said hi, and when Livi told her that she was there to see the Tellers, the woman had invited her in without any questions.

Small-town warmth and friendliness—it had made it easy for Livi to get to the living room, where an elderly couple was playing a board game with a little girl.

Livi had introduced herself and offered the condolences of the entire Camden family for the loss of Mandy and John Teller Jr. The Tellers had asked how her grandmother was—GiGi was a well-known native of Northbridge—and after briefly updating them about her, Livi had explained that Randall had grown up as the best friend of Livi's father and uncle, and that GiGi had thought of Randall as her third son. That having just heard about the accident that had cost Randall's daughter her life and orphaned his granddaughter, GiGi had requested that Livi make this visit on her behalf.

Though the Tellers admitted that they knew there was more to the story—that there had been, eventually, a very bitter parting of the ways between Randall and the Camdens—Livi's sympathies had been accepted with grace. What followed was an hour with the Tellers and Greta. And also with the home health care nurse, Kinsey Madison, who was looking after Maeve, who had broken her arm, shoulder and leg in a fall, leaving her in plaster casts and a wheelchair.

Livi learned that Maeve and John Sr. were both eighty years old. And while John Sr. didn't have any disabilities that Livi could discern, she'd seen enough to know that he moved slowly and very stiffly, barely lifting his feet. So even he was nowhere near as agile as seventy-five-year-old GiGi or her seventy-six-year-old new groom, Jonah. In fact, the attentive nurse seemed to be subtly caring for John Sr. almost as much as she was caring for Maeve, so Livi understood why Greta's parents had not left her guardianship to the elderly couple.

Livi didn't have any difficulty establishing rapport with the Tellers or with Greta, all of whom she liked instantly. And the more they all visited, the more Livi saw how much the Tellers doted on the little girl. They obviously loved her dearly.

For her part, Greta—an outgoing nine-year-old with long blond hair and big brown eyes—had quickly warmed to Livi and was clearly dazzled by her fashionable clothes and hairstyle. She was so enthralled that Livi had removed the scarf she'd used as a headband today and gifted it to Greta, who was now sitting on the floor at her feet so Livi could tie it around the girl's wavy locks the way she'd been wearing it herself.

Even while she was pampering Greta, Livi went on chatting with Maeve and Kinsey. John Sr. wasn't particularly talkative, but threw in a few comments from time to time.

All in all, Livi thought it was going smoothly, that she'd lucked out, that this particular restitution would be easily accomplished.

"You look beautiful, Greta," Kinsey declared when

Livi was finished and the nine-year-old looked to the nurse for approval.

"I wanna see," Greta announced, running from the room and bounding up the stairs to the second level of the old farmhouse, presumably to a mirror.

With the child out of earshot, it seemed like an opportunity for Livi to say, "I'm not sure what Greta's needs are, but we want to do whatever we can for her now and from here on."

"And you would be?" a deep male voice interrupted, coming from behind Livi.

Maeve and John Sr. were sitting across from Livi and they both looked beyond her to the man who had just come in.

Livi noted that John Sr. instantly scowled, while Maeve smiled and said, "This is Ms. Camden—"

"Oh, no, I'm just Livi."

"Camden," the man behind her repeated scornfully at the same time.

Undeterred, Maeve smiled at her and said, "Livi," to confirm that she would use her first name. Then she added, "Callan is an old friend of Mandy and John Jr.'s. He's Greta's godfather and now her guardian."

Livi froze.

Callan?

It wasn't a common name.

And it was the name of the man she'd spent the night with in Hawaii. The man she'd exchanged only first names with.

The man who had run out on her.

But it had to be a coincidence.

It *had* to be...

Then he came around into her line of vision.

And everything in her clenched into one big knot.

It was the same name because it was the same man.

Livi didn't know whether to slap his face or crawl away in shame.

"Livi?" he said when he got a look at her face, his voice full of shock. His expression almost instantly showed embarrassment before confusion sounded, too, as he said, "You're a *Camden*?"

"You two know each other?" John Sr. asked.

Neither of them answered immediately.

Then Callan said, "We've met."

"Once," Livi added, her gaze locked with his.

Actually, they knew hardly anything about each other. They'd talked about why they were in Hawaii—her for a sales convention, him for a business meeting. Beyond that?

They'd talked about the enormous sea turtle on the beach right in front of where Livi was sitting when he'd joined her without an invitation. About the weather. The hotel. The restaurants and food. The sites. About how beautiful the sunset they were watching together was.

But they hadn't talked about anything of any importance.

And she'd had a completely different impression of him—as the businessman she'd assumed he was. Right now, he looked more like a cowboy, in faded blue jeans and a soiled chambray shirt that still managed to accentuate his broad, broad shoulders.

The hair was the same, though—thick auburn, short on the sides and slightly longer on top, where it was carelessly mussed. Also the same was the model-handsome face, lean and sculpted, with a strong jaw shadowed with stubble around thin but hellishly sexy lips. His slightly longish nose was straight and narrow. His penetrating eyes as dark as black coffee, beneath brooding brows and a square forehead.

And tall—he was so tall. And muscular.

Nothing at all like her Patrick.

Which had been part of the reason for that night...

Livi swallowed with some difficulty, trying to manage so many emotions at once—the shame and humiliation, but also the attraction she wished she could repress. Because she couldn't help appreciating what an impressive, imposing specimen of a man he was.

"I didn't know you were a cowboy from Montana," she said weakly

"Cowboy?" John Sr. commented, breaking through Livi's shock. "He isn't really that."

"He is when he's getting his hands dirty doing our work around here," Maeve retorted. "And, yes, Livi is a Camden," the older woman confirmed to Callan. "She's Seth Camden's cousin, Georgianna Camden's granddaughter, and she came to offer sympathies and help with Greta."

Livi watched Callan's thick eyebrows dip together in a frown. "Help with Greta," he repeated without inflection. But the frown was enough to let her know that he wasn't as receptive to the idea as the Tellers had already seemed to be. "Why would a Camden want to do that?"

Suspicion. It was clear as day in his voice then.

So much for this going smoothly...

And despite what had happened in Hawaii and how monumental it was to her, Livi realized that their personal history was now on the back burner for him. That they'd veered into anti-Camden territory. John Sr. and Maeve hadn't seemed to know the details of the bad blood between the Camdens and Randall Walcott, but Livi was willing to bet Callan knew the whole story—and held a grudge.

"I know that once upon a time there was a falling out with the Camdens and Randall Walcott—"

"A *falling out*?" Callan repeated with an unpleasant huff. "You people played that guy for a sucker. You lured him in and then pulled the rug out from under him."

Livi took a deep breath, wishing she could deny any part of what he'd just laid at her family's doorstep, but knowing she couldn't. The harsh, often unethical behavior of the senior Camdens was the very reason she and her siblings and cousins were working so hard to make restitution.

"Until very recently none of the Camdens who are around today—me, my brothers and sister, my cousins and our grandmother—knew what went on all that time ago," she said. "My grandmother knew Randall Walcott as a boy her sons grew up with, worked with—"

"They *worked* him, all right," Callan continued with a sneer. "They had their old man give him advice on how to start his shoe business. Even gave him a loan so he could expand it. But about the time he had everything up and running they called in the loan, knowing he couldn't pay. Then they took over his company, stealing what he'd started and built up. You people still sell Walcott Shoes, if I'm not mistaken."

"You people" again…

"I was only two years old when it went down," Livi felt compelled to point out. "And no one alive today had anything to do with it. None of us would let something like that go on now and—"

But Callan seemed determined that the entire story be

told, because he interrupted her to go on. "Mandy's dad ended up with nothing! That poor bastard had to come here with his tail between his legs and move his family in with his in-laws. Mandy told me all about it. She was just a kid, but when you see your dad as upset and beaten down as he was, you remember it. She hated what had happened to him…especially with what happened next, when after two years of more failure here he ended up putting a gun to his own head—"

"Shh, shh, shh…" Maeve whispered suddenly, apparently spotting Greta just before she returned to the room, having changed clothes.

"I wanted to put on my dress that goes with the scarf," the little girl announced. Then, spotting Callan, she laid a small hand to the hair adornment and said, "Look, Uncle Callan—Livi gave me this and tied it like she had it. Isn't it pretty?"

"It is," he confirmed, but his voice was tight.

"Come on, Greta," Kinsey said in a hurry, as if she was looking for any reason to escape this scene herself. "Let's go see how many other things will match the scarf."

The nurse held out her hand to the little girl and Greta took it eagerly, chattering as if Kinsey was a girlfriend as they both left the room.

Not until they heard a door closing upstairs did anyone speak.

Then Callan broke the silence. "Any Camden is the last person on earth Mandy would want near her kid," he said flatly, as if that put an end to the discussion.

"But this girl didn't have nothin' to do with anything that happened all those years ago," John Sr. argued. "It's nothin' to do with Greta, neither, and far as I can see, it's nothin' to do with you no way, Tierney—"

His last name is Tierney?

The name meant nothing to Livi, but she tucked it away as information she might need.

"Least you could do," the elderly man went on, "is hear out Livi here. We hardly know Seth Camden, her—" he looked to Livi "—cousin, is it?"

"Yes," she said.

"We don't barely know him, but when word got around town about our troubles, he sent his crew over here to help out. Come pickin' time, they did our whole harvest. And when I asked what we owed them they said that they were on the Camden clock, that Seth Camden was just bein' neighborly and wantin' to help us out, and not to even mention it. Seems to me that's a sign of what this young lady is sayin'—the new breed isn't like the old one."

Livi took that endorsement as her cue. "We want to make up for what was done all those years ago. Greta is Randall Walcott's only living descendent and the only person we can compensate. We want to make sure she's looked after and has anything she needs. *Anything*—care and attention, a trust fund. A college fund, maybe—"

"She doesn't need your money," Callan said, as if financial matters were of no importance.

"But we want to take care of whatever she *does* need," Livi persisted.

Just then Greta came bounding back into the living room, running straight to Livi. "Look at this other scarf I found!"

"That's the sash to your Christmas dress, sweetheart," Maeve said.

"But it's *like* a scarf!" Greta insisted to her grand-mother, before honing in on Livi again. "Can you teach me how to tie it like you did? And could you paint my fin-gernails like yours, too? I think that would look nice with my outfit. Oh! You have pierced ears!" she exclaimed, apparently just noticing. "My mom's ears were pierced and she said I could have mine done, too. My friend Raina's mom pierced hers—can you do that?" the little girl asked eagerly.

"Greta, where did you go?" the nurse called from up-stairs. "Come back and see—I found something we can tie in your doll's hair like you wanted."

"I'll be right back!" Greta promised Livi, before charging out of the room again.

As she did, Maeve said, "She's attached to Kinsey. Follows her like a shadow. But what will happen when I'm better and don't need a nurse anymore? Then an old lady will be the only woman Greta has paying any kind of close attention to her. What she needs is a younger one, somebody who can give her what Mandy would have. And she seems to have taken to you, Livi…"

GiGi had suggested something similar—that Greta would need a woman in her life. And that had been some-thing Livi had thought she might be able to do, even if it was long distance. She could make frequent trips to Northbridge, she'd decided. And maybe Greta could oc-casionally come to Denver on long weekends or vacations from school, to give her guardian a break.

Only, now that Livi knew *who* Greta's guardian was, she couldn't say she was eager for any contact that might put her in the position she was in right now.

So she said, "I'd be happy to spend time with her, to act as a big sister. But I live in Denver. Seth might know of a woman here—between the two of us I'm sure we could find someone for her."

"Denver is where we're all headin'," John Sr. said under his breath, not sounding happy about it.

"That's where Callan lives," Maeve explained. "And he wants to look after us now that our John Jr. can't. We aren't doing so well on our own anymore."

Then I don't have an out? Livi was near panic at the idea of having to face Callan on a regular basis.

"I don't know about having her around Greta," Callan said, sounding frustrated at having his stance ignored. "She's come at us out of the blue. How do we know she doesn't have something up her sleeve, the way her family did with Greta's grandfather?"

"It isn't like you don't have some things to answer for in your own past," John Sr. grumbled to Callan. "And that was all you, not some long-gone relatives. Didn't keep Mandy and our John from lettin' you be around Greta."

Callan looked thunderous, which Maeve must have noticed, because she rushed to speak next. "I have good instincts about people and Livi seems like a nice person who's just wanting to make things right. Everybody makes mistakes. It's what they do to correct them that matters."

There was an underlying message in that, aimed at both John Sr. and Callan, but Livi had no idea what that message was. It kept both men quiet, though, while Maeve seemed to take the reins.

"I think it could be really good for Greta to have you be her big sister, Livi," the elderly lady said then. "To have a young woman's guidance so I don't have to worry that I'm not up-to-date enough for her. Today, meeting you, is the happiest I've seen her since we lost her momma and daddy. So if you're willing to take that little girl under your wing to atone for the past, I think we'd be lucky to have you."

It appeared that both men knew better than to argue with her

But with resignation in his almost-black eyes, Callan said to Livi, "Greta is my responsibility now and I'll be watching to make sure you're on the up-and-up with this."

He'd be *watching*? Did that mean that he was going to make sure he was around whenever she was with Greta?

Oh, great, that's all I need.

But what could Livi say? That he was the glaring reminder of her worst mistake and she didn't want to face him over and over again?

GiGi had given her the task of performing restitution to Greta It was her job to make sure Greta was well taken care of, that the little girl's needs were met—no matter what. Livi had to see it through. She didn't have a choice.

Maybe this is my punishment for Hawaii, she thought.

But without any way to back out now, she took a deep, bracing breath, plastered a smile on her face and said, "We just want to do something for Greta's good."

Regardless how difficult it might prove to be for Livi.

Because despite the way this had started out today, she was now afraid it was going to be very, very difficult...

"I'll go in and say hello to John, pay him directly."

"Yeah, sure," Callan said to the man whose truck he'd just loaded with hay bales.

There had been an edge of distrust in Gordon Bassett's voice, but Callan ignored it. Disdain and distrust for him in Northbridge was an old song Callan knew well. And apparently that was never going to change. It was the price he paid for being the kid from the other side of the tracks. A kid who had earned the reputation as a troublemaker.

But Callan had too many other things to think about at the moment to care about that. Actually, he wasn't even looking at the man he'd known all his life. He was watching the woman he now knew as Livi *Camden* drive away. And wondering what the hell was going on lately. Life was throwing him one curve ball after another.

Beginning in the middle of the night he'd spent with her.

If she'd told him her last name when they'd met at that beach bar in Hawaii, he might have left her sitting alone to watch the sea turtles and the sunset by herself.

Oh, who was he kidding? Even knowing what kind of people she came from, he probably would have stuck around.

She'd been too damn gorgeous sitting there in the fading sunlight with her long, bittersweet-chocolate-colored hair draping over her sexy bare shoulders. When she'd looked up at him with eyes that were a darker and more beautiful cobalt blue than the clear sky in the distance, eyes set in the face of an angel, he wouldn't have pulled away no matter what. Not with the mood he'd been in, having just accomplished a buyout he'd been working on for a year. He'd wanted to kick back and celebrate a little at day's end—so yeah, he'd have probably stuck around even if he had known she was a Camden.

He just wouldn't have ever told Mandy about it.

But the Livi of Hawaii *was* a Camden.

And now their paths had crossed again.

Two curve balls for the price of one…

He watched Livi's car get farther and farther away. He'd had every intention of going out to that car with her when she left so he could talk to her alone about Hawaii.

But then Bassett had showed up for his hay and Callan had had no choice but to head out to load the truck.

Now she was gone and he felt like an even bigger heel than he'd felt in the last two months whenever the thought of Hawaii came to mind.

As big a heel as she no doubt thought he was.

Not that they'd made any plans. Any promises. It had even been Livi who had dodged talk of what she'd called their "real lives."

But still, to take off without a word, without even thinking about her…

To be honest, in that moment he hadn't been thinking about anything but that middle-of-the-night phone call.

That lousy, freaking call that had caused his phone to vibrate enough to wake him without waking Livi, so he could take it into the living room of his suite and not disturb her.

That lousy, freaking call that had literally knocked the breath out of him, leaving him dazed and operating on autopilot, struggling to deal with the news that his two closest friends—Mandy and John Jr.—had been involved in a horrible car accident. That J.J. was barely holding on to life. That Mandy was already dead.

Callan had thrown on the clothes Livi had helped him discard hours before. Once he was dressed—taking nothing with him other than his wallet and cell phone—he'd rushed out of that suite, calling his pilot to arrange an emergency flight for his private jet, to get him to Montana immediately.

Calling the concierge to explain the situation and get the man to see to packing his bags, checking him out and sending the bags to him later.

Calling his assistant to get to Montana ahead of him and begin dealing with the nightmare.

By the time Callan was on his way to the airport, and finally remembered the woman he'd left in his bed, it was already too late.

He'd called his hotel room from the plane—no answer. He'd talked again to the concierge, who had gone to the suite while he was still on the line.

But Livi was gone, and there was no way for Callan to contact her when all he knew was her first name.

They'd gone from the beach to his suite, so he had no idea what room had been hers, no way of trying to get a belated message to her. No way of ever letting her know what had happened, and that he'd hoped and expected their time together to end much differently.

At the very least, it wouldn't have ended with him disappearing into thin air.

He felt rotten for how he'd treated Livi, even if he did have a reason for it. Under other circumstances, if they'd met again, he would have apologized, explained, maybe tried to make it up to her somehow.

But under these circumstances?

Nothing about these circumstances was normal.

She *was* a Camden. He knew how Mandy had felt about the Camdens—any generation of them. She would never have trusted them. And she would never have let any one of them near Greta.

And why *had* Livi come around?

Callan couldn't say that he trusted a Camden's motives, either. Not after what he knew they'd done to Mandy's dad.

Did Livi Camden have something up her sleeve?

She was the first Camden to make any contact since they'd got what they wanted all those years ago. It was something Mandy had always added when she'd told the story—that they'd never so much as said they were sorry, not even when her dad died...

And that was what they did to supposed *friends*.

Now Callan was being pressured to let one of them near Greta?

But just how hard-line could he be with her, after the way he'd abandoned her in Hawaii, even if there had been a good reason? Not to mention just how hard-line could he be going up against the Tellers, who had taken an instant liking to Livi and seemed willing and eager to have her mentor their granddaughter?

The Tellers, who he owed.

The Tellers, who he'd promised John Jr. on his death-bed he would take care of.

That promise was already hard enough to keep, given the way John Sr. refused to trust him. If Callan went against the man in this, it would just make the tensions between them that much worse.

It didn't seem like this was where to draw a line at all, except for Mandy's feelings about the Camdens...

Could he really let Livi into her daughter's life?

It felt wrong.

But apparently only to him.

By now, Livi Camden's car was out of sight. And with the weight of everything bearing down on him, Callan bent over, hands to knees, and stared at the dirt under his feet.

He'd had one hell of a lot to figure out even before he'd walked into the Tellers' farmhouse and found Livi-from-Hawaii sitting there.

Shortly, he'd be handing the farm over to the people he'd hired to look after it and taking the Tellers and Greta to Denver with him, and he had no idea what was going to happen then. Especially when it came to Greta. Raising a kid was so much more involved than anything he'd ever done before. He had to be her *father*. Her family along with the Tellers.

But what did he know about being part of a family? About having a family?

Nothing. Flat-out nothing.

At least nothing good, nothing he wanted to repeat.

And now it was on him to be that, to provide that for Greta.

"I need some help here, guys," he muttered to the memory of Mandy and John Jr.

More help than what his geriatric charges could give, he thought.

And the Tellers liked Livi.

Greta liked Livi.

Plus Maeve was probably right—Greta was going to need the influence and advice of a woman younger than eighty.

He didn't have a wife anymore—he'd already blown that. There was no one else on the docket to fill that bill and take over that duty.

And Livi Camden was applying for the job.

So he guessed that rather than buck the Tellers, rather than deny Greta something she should have and clearly wanted, he supposed he had to give in on this.

Sorry, Mandy, he said mentally to his lost friend. *But I swear I'll stick as close as I can every minute she's with Greta, to keep an eagle eye on her. No matter what, I won't let another Camden hurt somebody you care about.*

Even if it meant he had to take a hard line with Livi down the road, if he discovered she did have some kind of Camden ulterior motive.

Even if it meant he had to be a son of a bitch to her a second time.

He really hoped it didn't come to that. Not with the first woman he'd had the slightest inclination to approach since his divorce.

The woman he'd had on his mind a surprising amount during the last two months.

The woman who had—at first sight this afternoon—made his pulse kick up a notch. And not just out of guilt for how things had been left in Hawaii, but simply from setting eyes on her again.

He had to keep in perspective that that one night in Hawaii was nothing *but* one night. In Hawaii.

Because incredible blue eyes that made his pulse race or not, he couldn't deal with any more than he already was.

Chapter Three

The Camden ranch house was still empty when Livi got back after meeting Greta and the Tellers.

And Callan.

Callan from Hawaii.

She'd driven home in the same dull sense of disbelief that she'd been in since setting eyes on him again. She was glad her cousin Seth wasn't back yet because she needed some time for what had happened to sink in.

She dropped her purse in the foyer, took a sharp right to the living room and sank into one of the oversize leather easy chairs, slumping so low her head rested on the back cushion.

Her mind was spinning.

Callan.

The stranger on the beach in Hawaii was from Denver. With connections in Northbridge. Just like her.

And now they'd met again…

Was the universe toying with her or was she going to wake up and realize she was dreaming this whole thing?

She knew it was just wishful thinking that this was all some kind of nightmare that would fade away as soon as she woke up.

But still she pinched her eyes closed for a minute and then opened them wide.

No, she definitely wasn't dreaming.

And she wasn't nauseous.

That thought almost made her cry.

Because if the nausea was coming from stress, this was the time for it. She should have been miserably sick to her stomach, since the tension she was feeling was through the roof.

But she wasn't feeling queasy.

With the exception of the cooking smells at last week's Sunday dinner at GiGi's house, she was sick only in the mornings.

Morning sickness.

Her mind wasn't even letting her skirt around it now, as if seeing Callan again made everything more real. Even her memories of Hawaii…

That day had been the ninth anniversary of her wedding to Patrick. The fourth without him. It was still a bad day every year. A day she had to struggle through.

The first year she'd immersed herself in everything she'd had of Patrick's, everything that kept him alive for her. She'd set out every picture she had of him, worn one of his shirts, padded around in his bedroom slippers. She'd gone through everything and anything that reminded her of him. She'd wallowed in all she'd lost and her own misery.

That had been a terrible day.

So the next year she'd tried plunging herself into work, going into the office at six that morning, staying until the cleaning crew showed up that night, pretending it was just business as usual.

But the cleaners had found her sobbing at her desk, because work hadn't made anything better, either.

Last year she'd tried enlisting her family to distract her. And they had. They'd whisked her off to the mountains to go boating and water-skiing on Dillon Lake.

But all she'd been able to think about, to talk about, had been Patrick—how much Patrick had loved days like that with her family, how much he'd loved the water and how often he'd talked about retiring seaside somewhere, how much he'd loved barbecuing...

And by the end of the boating and barbecuing and s'mores, she'd still been a mess.

So this year, in Hawaii, she'd decided to deal with her anniversary by disengaging. By skipping the conference, not scheduling any meetings, any breakfasts, lunches or dinners. By not doing anything.

"Pamper yourself," her sister and Jani had urged, worried about her being so far away and alone on that day.

Taking their recommendation, Livi had slept until she couldn't sleep any more—until after noon, something she never did.

Then she'd gone to the hotel's luxury spa, where she'd had a massage in near silence, not inviting or welcoming any conversation from the masseuse, trying to keep her mind blank.

Afterward the massage therapist had advised her to sit in the sauna, to sweat out the toxins. *You'll feel like a new woman*, she had said.

Livi rarely used the sauna because she wasn't fond of heat like that, but on that day of all days she wanted to feel like a new woman, because feeling like the old one wasn't good. So she'd sat in the sauna, thinking only about how hot it was, about sweating away the old Livi and emerging a new one.

Which she'd actually sort of felt she'd accomplished by the time she'd finished. She'd been so calm and relaxed and…well, just different than she usually felt. Especially on her anniversary.

Different enough to decide to go with the flow of that feeling by moving on to the hotel's salon.

She hadn't had a haircut since Patrick's death. Four years without so much as a trim.

Patrick had liked her hair long and she just hadn't been able to have any of it cut.

But that day she'd actually felt like it. Nothing short, no huge change, nothing Patrick would have even noticed, just a little something…

Which was what she'd done—had a scant two inches cut off the length. But she'd also had the sides feathered, and then agreed to the highlights the stylist suggested.

It was funny how a small change could catapult her even further into feeling like a whole new woman.

And while she was at it, why not go all the way? The makeup artist had had a cancelation and offered Livi his services. Why not have her face done, too?

For Lindie's wedding, Livi had declined the opportunity for that and stuck with her usual subdued blush and mascara. But on that day in Hawaii she'd let the makeup artist go ahead with whatever he wanted to do—nothing dramatic, but different shades of the colors she liked, and slightly more of everything.

And while he'd worked, she'd also let the manicurist do a skin-softening waxing—feet and hands—for which she'd taken off her wedding rings.

By then she'd been all in with the idea of a New Livi for just one day, so she'd had her nails painted bright red and stenciled with white flowery designs—something more showy than she'd ever done before.

She honestly had felt like someone different when she'd left the salon, and she'd decided that maybe doing things she never did was the answer to getting through the anniversary. Certainly it had been helping to keep the sadness away more than anything had before.

And she'd definitely wanted to keep that going.

So she'd left her rings in her purse and splurged in the hotel's dress shop, changing into a halter sundress that exposed so much shoulder that it forced her to include her bra with the bag of clothes she'd had sent to her room.

She'd never been to a bar alone and she *had* chosen the table farthest out on the beach, away from the bar itself and the guests mingling around it, but it was still something the Old Livi would never have done.

And the New Livi had ordered a drink. And then a second one. Because, after all, the sun was low in the sky by then and she'd felt floaty and really, really nice. Really, really as if she were someone else. And that someone else wanted another drink...

It was that someone else who had looked up to find the oh-so-good-looking guy saying hello to her halfway through her second drink. That someone else who had said yes when he'd asked if he could sit with her. That someone else from then on.

Maybe it had been the liquor, but she'd found Callan as easy to talk to as Patrick had always been, and after a while she'd realized that she was having a good time with him. That she was feeling a connection—in the most superficial way, of course—with Callan. A connection she hadn't felt with any man she wasn't related to since Patrick.

And it helped that the only similarity between Callan and her Patrick was that she'd found them both easy to talk to. In every other way, Callan was very different.

Patrick hadn't been too tall—only five-eight. Patrick had not had an athlete's body—he'd been slight, weighing only twenty pounds more than she did.

Patrick's fair hair had been thin, his hairline receding, and he'd had unremarkable, boy-next-door good looks, with his ruddy cheeks and nondescript hazel eyes hidden behind the glasses he'd needed to wear.

It had been Patrick's winning personality that had gained him friends and jobs. And her.

So sitting at that beachside table—and, yes, hitting it off—with a tall, imposing guy with great hair and great eyes and great features, and a body that was not only athletic and hard, but also muscular and broad-shouldered and so, so masculine, had not been something Livi Camden-Walsh was experienced at.

And she most definitely wasn't experienced at not only chatting and laughing with the stranger, but flirting with him, too…

Yes, she'd been flirting with him.

And she'd never flirted with anyone but Patrick in her life.

But her Hawaiian alter ego had actually been good at it. Again, maybe because of the booze.

They'd sat there until late. Until the hula dancing was done. Until the live music ended. Until there were no more than a few people at the bar. She and Callan had sat there drinking and talking about nothing that meant anything.

Finally, Livi noticed that the moon was high, and decided it must be late and she should call it a night.

No, not yet—how about a walk on the beach? he'd said.

Any other time, any other man and she wouldn't have let him postpone her exit.

But that night, her Hawaiian alter ego had taken Callan's hand when he'd held it out to her to help her from her chair.

Then they'd walked on the beach side by side in the moonlight, laughing and flirting. And the farther up the beach they'd gone, the more removed she'd felt from everything but the beauty of that tropical paradise and that man who continued to bring her out of herself.

She was so much out-of-herself and so completely inhabiting her Hawaiian alter ego that when she stumbled and Callan caught her arm to keep her from falling, she hadn't minded.

And when that hand had stayed on her arm, when she'd looked up into that handsome face to make a joke about her clumsiness, she remembered well that he'd been looking down at her with a thoughtful smile and eyes that seemed too gentle for someone so big and manly.

She'd been lost in what she'd seen in those eyes, and when he'd kissed her, it wasn't as if he was kissing Livi Camden-Walsh, it was as if he was kissing someone else. And she was just getting to enjoy it.

And she *had* enjoyed it. He had a way about him, a technique, that was so…well, just so good that it drew her even further out of herself, forgetting about everything but that kissing that washed her mind of all other thoughts and carried her away.

She wasn't even surprised when she found herself kissing him back with just as much heat.

And from that moment on—until she woke up alone in his bed hours and hours later—she really, truly didn't feel that she was Livi Camden-Walsh. She was totally that someone else she'd set out to be after the sauna. That someone who got to forget herself and escape how much it hurt every time she thought about Patrick being gone.

That someone who had been sinking into a sated slumber when Callan had told her that the condom had broken *just a little*, so she hadn't worried about it…

She wished that that had woken her fully, bringing her back to herself…but it hadn't. She'd fallen asleep as that new person who didn't worry, didn't fuss, didn't grieve.

But she'd woken up as herself at four in the morning, horrified and ashamed.

At first she'd worried about how she was going to face Callan. Wherever he was—the bathroom maybe? As she'd dressed, she'd thought about the conversation she needed to have with him. She would explain that she hadn't been herself, that normally she was the last person to ever even consider having a vacation fling. And then she'd say that it would be best if they just went their separate ways. When she'd finished perfecting the words in her head, she'd walked over to tap on the bathroom door…but it had swung open under her touch, revealing that there was no one inside.

It was then that she'd started to realize that the whole place was too silent for anyone else to be in it.

She'd paused to actually look around, and discovered that Callan was gone.

It was four in the morning and he was gone. There was no note, no explanation. She tried to come up with excuses for him. Maybe he'd gone out for a cigarette, or to get some ice. But his teeth were too white for him to be a smoker, and the ice bucket was still on the bar. Nothing was open in the hotel at that hour, so he couldn't have gone to one of the restaurants or bars.

Still, she'd waited five minutes for him to get back from wherever he'd gone. Then ten. Then half an hour. By the time an hour had ticked by, she couldn't bear to wait any longer.

Livi had no experience with any of this, but she had friends who had talked about guys sneaking out once the deed was done, and she'd suddenly felt certain that that had to be what had gone on with Callan. She'd pictured him slinking out so as not to wake her and hiding somewhere. In the room of a friend, maybe? They hadn't talked about anything personal, so she had no idea if he was at the hotel alone or with other people. People he could take refuge with until she was gone.

All she'd wanted to do was get out of there, get to her own room, shower and call the airline to change her ticket so she could go home a day early.

Home, where she could write off that night to pure and utter insanity, and resolve never to think about it again.

As she'd left his suite she'd dug in her tiny purse for her wedding rings and put them back on with a vengeance. She'd just been grateful that what she'd done had happened far away from her loved ones, who would never need to know.

She'd also been grateful that she'd never have to see that guy again or be reminded of him in any way.

And she'd sworn to herself that she would never, ever, ever even wish to forget herself like that again.

Sitting in the big leather chair in the ranch's living room now, she groaned.

It had been such a good plan...

Until she'd missed her first period.

And now her second.

Until the nausea had started.

And her fingers had swelled too much to wear her rings.

It had been such a good plan, until she'd seen Callan again today...

The front door opened just then and her cousin Seth came in, calling her name.

"I'm right here," Livi answered, her voice weak as she opened her eyes once more.

But she couldn't let Seth think anything was wrong, so she got up from the chair and pasted on a smile.

"Hey there!" Seth greeted her, coming with open arms to hug her. "Sorry I had to be gone when you got here."

"You're here now," she said feebly, wishing he wasn't, that he had stayed in Texas, where she knew he'd left his wife and baby to visit longer with his father-in-law.

"I'm here, but kicking myself because I just remembered that I have a Cattlemen's Association dinner tonight and I'm gonna have to turn around and leave again."

There was some relief in hearing that. She had too much on her mind to socialize even with her cousin, who was like a brother to her.

"Don't worry about it. Do whatever you need to do. I'm fine on my own."

"There's plenty of food in the fridge, or if you want

to wait until I get back around eight I can bring you a pizza or something."

"I'll find something in the fridge. I was going to go to bed early, anyway."

"Tomorrow, then..."

Livi nodded, again not altogether tuned in to what was going on. "I promised to pick up my new charge, Greta Teller, after school tomorrow, and I was going to go to the store in town before that for a few things I didn't pack. But I'm free until about two or so."

"I meet with my ranch hands on Monday mornings to schedule out the week, but how about lunch?"

Which would give her time to stop being sick.

Unless she woke up tomorrow with her period and without the nausea, and everything was okay...

Apparently she still had a little denial left.

"Lunch would be good," she said.

With that settled, Seth dragged his suitcase in from the foyer and began to rummage in the side pockets. "So you must have found the Tellers' farm without me," he said.

"Yeah, I did. I just got back from there a few minutes ago."

"You met everyone? The Tellers and their granddaughter? The guardian?"

"Callan Tierney," she informed him.

That halted the search and Seth glanced up at her with arched eyebrows. "*Callan Tierney* is the girl's guardian? You know who he is, don't you?"

"Why would I know who he is?"

Seth went back to searching through his bag, but said, "I've never met him, but Callan Tierney is CT Software. *We* use his software and so do a slew of other businesses around the world. He's worth more than we are. I wonder how someone like him ended up the guardian of a kid in Northbridge?"

"I don't know," Livi said honestly.

"Ah, that's what I need for tonight!" Seth exclaimed, pulling a tablet out of the suitcase. Then, turning back to her, he said, "You'll have to fill me in when you find out."

"Sure. When I find out," she parroted.

Seth continued chatting with her, telling her about his time away. Livi did her best to keep up with that conversation. But she was still reeling inside and thinking more about the next day than anything he was saying.

The next day, when she would go into town before picking up Greta Teller.

When she would take the first step to putting denial to rest once and for all.

And buy a home pregnancy test.

After lunch with Seth on Monday, and a solo trip to the personal care section of Northbridge's general store that made Livi cringe inside, she picked up Greta from the local school.

The little girl was wearing the scarf Livi had given her the day before, and immediately asked her to tie it "better" because on the playground Jake Linman had pulled on it.

Livi obliged her as Greta launched into another outpouring of admiration for the ballet flats Livi was wearing today, the small leather cross-body purse she was using and the pin-tucked white blouse she had on over a pale blue tank top with navy blue slacks.

But Livi was only partially listening. Her mind was still on that pregnancy test and the results it might show when she took it.

"There you go," she said when the scarf was retied.

"Dumb Jake Linman," Greta grumbled. "He's always bothering me."

"Maybe he likes you. Sometimes that's how boys show it," Livi responded without much thought.

"That's what my gramma says," Greta said, as if she was hoping for something else from Livi. Then she added under her breath, "Doesn't matter. Tomorrow is my last day."

The last day for what? Livi wondered, before remembering that Greta was being made to move to Denver. That meant leaving her school, her friends, the town that was home to her.

And Livi had been thinking so much about her own problems that she hadn't recognized Greta's.

But that's the reason I'm here! she chastised herself.

She genuinely liked this little girl now that she'd met her, and not only had GiGi assigned her this make-amends project, Livi honestly wanted to help.

So regardless of what was going on in her own life, when she was with Greta, it had to be all about the girl, she realized. She had to take her own problems out of the picture. Greta had to be the center of things.

Which was exactly what Livi did for the remainder of the afternoon as she bought her ice cream and then a pair of new shoes and a matching purse that Greta admired in a shop window.

Apparently new shoes and a new purse had the same effect on little girls as big ones, because by the end of the afternoon Greta was in better spirits, and Livi felt as if she'd done some good.

It was after five when she drove up the dirt lane to

the Tellers' house, passing a truck loaded with bales of hay going in the opposite direction.

She could see Callan in the barn behind the house and that was when her vow to focus only on Greta hit a snag. One look at him and Livi stopped hearing what her young charge was saying.

He was rearranging hay bales, pivoting back and forth, facing her, then facing away.

She wasn't sure if Callan hadn't noticed her arrival or if he was merely ignoring it, but he didn't so much as look in her direction.

And that gave her the opportunity to watch him freely for a moment.

Like the day before, he was dressed in boots, jeans and a work shirt—this one plaid flannel. He looked every inch the cowboy, all rugged and strong. And watching him, she found it hard to think he was anything *but* a cowboy.

The weather was warm and he had the sleeves of his shirt rolled above his elbows, leaving a hint of biceps and impressive forearms bare to where suede gloves encased big hands. She could see the shift of muscles as he hoisted the bales. Muscles like nothing she'd ever seen in any other computer whiz.

Long legs braced the weight, with thick thighs testing the denim of his jeans. His shoulders were broad and straight and seemed more likely forged by backbreaking farm work than sitting behind a desk.

And that face that had so impressed her alter ego in Hawaii—clean-shaven that evening—was made only sexier with a scruff of day's beard shadowing his sharp jawline, making him look just gritty enough to be a turn-on.

Not that she was turned on. Livi was clear about that.

But still, there was no looking at Callan, watching him do what he was doing, without appreciating the undeniable appeal of a fit man's physique.

In a purely analytical way.

Until her traitorous brain zoomed somewhere else.

Back to Hawaii. To that night. She'd insisted on complete darkness, so she hadn't really seen him naked.

Something she suddenly regretted...

She realized belatedly that she'd completely missed whatever it was that Greta was talking about. She tuned back in as the child unfastened her seat belt and opened the car door, saying, "Let's go show Uncle Callan my new stuff!"

Oh.

Livi swallowed and got a grip on herself, coming totally into the present again.

What do I do now? she thought.

What was the protocol for two people in this situation? *Was* there a protocol?

Yesterday had been awkward, but there had been the Tellers and the nurse and Greta to serve as a buffer between her and Callan, plus so much going on that they'd both addressed only what was happening.

But now? If she followed Greta to the barn—as it seemed she should—then what?

Did they just go on acting like strangers?

Or did they, at some point, talk about Hawaii?

Did she tell him what a jerk she thought he was for ditching her in the middle of the night after sleeping with her?

Or was she supposed to act as if it hadn't fazed her? As if it was par for the course—sleep together, go your separate ways, it happened all the time...

Was that what he thought of her? That she slept around so much that it wouldn't be any big deal for a guy to slip out after the fact, without a word? That that *was* a common occurrence to her?

What an awful thought.

It made her want to shout that until him she'd slept with only one man in her life: Patrick. The man she'd loved and been devoted to. The man who had loved and been devoted to her. Her soul mate and the person she'd expected to spend her entire life with.

But if she did shout that she would just sound defensive, and Callan probably wouldn't even believe it.

What *did* people do in a situation like this?

For the second time in two days Livi just wanted to hide or run the other way.

But by then Greta had reached the barn and alerted Callan to the fact that they were there, and he was looking straight at Livi across the distance.

She took a deep breath and decided that, at any rate, she wasn't going to act as if she'd done something wrong.

Yes, she *felt* like she'd done something wrong—something terribly wrong—by sleeping with him, but in spite of that, people *did* hook up with someone they'd just met for one-night stands.

If anyone should be embarrassed, it should be him, for the way he'd treated her—slithering silently out like a snake.

If either of them needed to hang their head in shame, it was him!

So she got out of the car and followed Greta's path to the barn.

She had barely exchanged hellos with Callan when the little girl announced that she was going to show her grandparents her new shoes and purse. Thinking of that as a reprieve, Livi turned to follow.

Until Callan said, "Can you hang back, Livi?"

And off went Greta. Leaving Livi alone with this man she'd never wanted to see again as long as she lived.

"I wanted to talk to you yesterday, but then I had to come out and load that truck. John Sr. won't let me let anything slide…" Callan stopped short, as if to keep himself from saying more on that subject, and then started again. "And before I got back inside, you were gone. But we do need to talk."

"Okay," Livi said, with a note of challenge creeping into her tone. She was unwilling to give him any help.

"Hawaii…" he said. "I need to apologize to you for that."

For the night they'd spent together? Or for leaving?

She raised her chin and gazed at him.

"My phone was on vibrate, so it woke me but not you a couple of hours after we fell asleep."

Livi had thought yesterday was awkward, but this had it beat.

"I definitely didn't hear anything," she said with accusation in her voice, thinking that he was just making up some excuse.

"The call was to let me know that Greta's parents, J.J.—John Jr.—and Mandy, had been in a car accident here," he said, knocking some of the wind out of Livi's sails. "Mandy had died on impact. J.J. was still alive but in critical condition. No one was giving him much time…"

Callan's deep voice got more and more ragged as he spoke, and Livi could see that even now this was difficult for him.

And she'd thought that *she* was the one entitled to the emotions...

For the second time today she had to make an adjustment, suspend her own feelings and just listen.

"I had to get to J.J.," he went on. "I had to make sure everything that *could* be done for him *was* being done. I had to see him..."

Callan cleared his throat, and realizing how hard-hit he still was somehow made Livi feel guilty for all the nasty things she'd thought about him and his impromptu departure from that hotel room.

"Mandy, J.J. and I grew up here together," he explained. "We were close. And always stayed close. They were more family to me than my own..."

As if he needed a diversion, he looked down at his hands and pulled off his gloves, slapping them against his thigh.

And Livi hated that her brain was once again thinking about how glorious those hands and thighs were. What in the world was wrong with her?

"So when I got that call," he continued, "I was only thinking about getting to J.J. Everything went to that. I was in the air an hour later, and halfway here before I realized—"

That not even a thought of her had entered his mind? That fact still stung, even though he'd had a good reason to be otherwise occupied.

"—that I'd just rushed out on you without a word," he was saying. "By then, when I called the hotel, you were out of the room. And since I didn't even know your last name, I didn't have any way to track you down. I did try, I swear to you..." He paused, then added, "Anyway, I'm sorry."

Livi raised her chin a second time, accepting the apology that way because she couldn't *not* accept it when it came with that explanation.

But it wasn't easy to let go of the humiliation she'd felt at his vanishing without a trace. It was hard to move past thinking the worst of him.

Instead she chose to say quietly, "I'm sorry about your friends."

He nodded solemnly. "Yeah. Me, too. They were good people."

Again he didn't seem to want to make eye contact with her, instead turning to toss the gloves onto a hay bale. "Anyway," he repeated, "here we are."

"Here we are," Livi echoed.

"And I thought maybe we should talk about…you know…where we go now."

He did meet her eyes then and Livi didn't allow herself to look away. But she didn't say anything, because she had no idea where they *should* go now—especially factoring in that pregnancy test she had in that bag in the trunk of her cousin's car.

"How about we just put it behind us?" Callan suggested. "Forget it happened. Start fresh."

Easy for him to say.

"You want to help Greta," he went on, "and now she's kind of my job—her and the Tellers—so we'll be seeing each other. But Hawaii was…well…"

A one-night stand? A vacation fling? Pure stupidity on her part? Yes, what exactly should they call it?

As bad as the last two months had been for Livi, this was worse. This was excruciating. It felt like a brush-off. As if he was telling her that even though they'd slept together, he didn't want there to be anything more between them than that.

And while she certainly didn't, either, it was still a rejection. This made it seem as if she expected something from him that he was letting her know he wasn't on board for.

I belong to Patrick! she wanted to tell him in no uncertain terms.

But she resisted the urge. Instead, she tried to rise above what felt like an insult and said, "Hawaii is already forgotten."

Liar, liar, pants on fire...

"And we can just do..,whatever...for Greta and go on?" Callan asked.

"Sure."

"Not that Hawaii wasn't something damn memorable..." he said, as if giving credit where credit was due, his eyebrows raised in what looked like appreciation.

"But it's over and done with. Finished. On to a new chapter," she said curtly.

This time it was Callan who nodded in acknowledgment. "Yeah, I guess," he said, though now he sounded a little confused. And perhaps a little offended. "But maybe we should actually get to know each other...for Greta's sake."

Was that what he'd been trying to say? Livi didn't have any experience with any of this, and was running on high-octane emotions. Maybe he wasn't being a jerk—even if it still felt that way.

She took a deep breath and tried to look at things from a calmer, less sensitive perspective.

She'd been as responsible as he had been for them

spending the night together in Hawaii. And though he had left, he'd had a good reason.

Now here they were, but he'd inherited a nine-year-old—and apparently two geriatrics on top of it—and had his hands full. It stood to reason that romance was the last thing he needed at the moment. And yet he and Livi would still have to spend time together, for Greta's sake, so it made sense to settle things between them.

And it wasn't as if her own thinking was any different than it had been before she'd met him in Hawaii. Livi still couldn't imagine herself in a relationship with anyone other than Patrick.

Take away her newest worry, and Callan was right that they just needed to wrap up Hawaii and stuff it in a compartment. That they just needed to start over as nothing more than they actually were—two strangers brought together over the welfare of a little girl.

Thinking about it all like that helped Livi calm down.

"Hawaii is history," she decreed. "Let's wipe the slate clean and just move on."

Those words again. Only it was her saying them this time.

But in this instance she meant them. She just hoped that they *could* move on freely and with a genuinely clean slate. If they couldn't—if that pregnancy test came back positive… But she refused to think about that yet. She'd wait to deal with that hurdle when she'd actually taken the test and knew for sure what was going on.

There was certainly no need to tell Callan before then.

"So we're okay?" he asked, sounding sincere.

"We're okay," Livi confirmed, with more bravado than confidence.

"Good," he said, as if he was relieved.

"Good," she parroted, not relieved at all. Then she inclined her head toward the house, told him she needed to get going and wanted to say goodbye to Greta.

"Sure," Callan said, bending over to pick up those gloves, putting them on again.

Onto those hands that Livi suddenly recalled the feel of on her body.

Until she forced that memory out of her head, took a long pull of fresh air and turned to go to the farmhouse.

Chapter Four

It was positive.

Livi took the home pregnancy test first thing Tuesday morning and stared at the display on the stick until it showed the results.

But a positive reading didn't *necessarily* mean the test was right.

There were false positives, weren't there?

Or she could have done it wrong.

Dazed, feeling as if everything was spinning out of control, she reread the instructions.

Then she stared at the display again, willing it to show her something different.

And at the same time thinking that this would have been such happy news if Patrick was still alive.

They'd wanted children, had tried for them. She'd even had a plan for how to tell him.

But this?

She just couldn't face it happening like this.

So she wasn't going to, she decided.

She wasn't going to fully believe it until a doctor told her for sure.

Especially when she was hardly sick at all this morning.

She'd go to the doctor. The doctor would say this happened sometimes—an imbalance of hormones that was delaying her period and causing a false-positive test, but she wasn't pregnant.

She couldn't be pregnant.

The doctor would clear it all up.

The sooner the better.

So she called her gynecologist in Denver and made an appointment, trying desperately to stay in a state of denial.

Livi was surprised—and not particularly pleased—to find Callan at Greta's school when she went for Greta's going-away party that afternoon.

Greta had invited her the day before, but hadn't mentioned that Callan was coming, too. And Livi was in no shape to see him—the guy who wanted them both to just forget Hawaii and everything that had happened there.

How would she ever tell *him*?

But she couldn't think about it. She couldn't think about any of it. And she'd given herself permission not to until she saw her doctor, so she pushed any notion of pregnancy out of her mind.

What she couldn't push out of her mind, though, was Callan himself.

They were sitting on the side of the room, Callan

slightly ahead of her, just enough in her line of vision to distract her from what the teacher was saying about how much they would all miss Greta.

He was dressed more the way he'd been in Hawaii—in khakis and a navy blue polo shirt. But he couldn't have looked more uncomfortable, sitting like a giant in the too-small-for-him desk chair.

It wasn't only the chair, though. Even as the party got under way Livi could see how much of a fish out of water he was when it came to kids, Greta included.

The day before, when Greta had run to him in the barn, Livi had lagged behind, so she'd seen very little of the exchange between them. And on Sunday, when she'd witnessed his unenthusiastic response to Greta's delight in the scarf, Livi had thought that was due to his shock at seeing her.

But he wasn't any different at the going-away party. He was still wooden and overly formal, as if someone had set him down in a room full of aliens and he just didn't know how to relate.

It made Livi begin to wonder about him as the choice to raise Greta.

Or any child…

After the party Greta begged Livi to come back to the farm and stay for dinner with the family.

She didn't have the heart to say no, when saying good-bye to her friends had clearly left the little girl down in the dumps. The only thing that seemed to perk her up was the idea of Livi coming home with her so Greta could show her the mementos and going-away gifts her friends had given her.

So Livi accepted.

Over dinner she saw more of what she'd glimpsed only

a hint of on Sunday—a certain tension in the dynamic between Callan and John Sr.

Maeve Teller seemed to be fond of Callan. In fact, she doted on him the way she might have doted on a son. The thin, slight woman with the gaunt face and long, silver hair wound into a bun at her nape was warm and loving toward Callan.

John Sr. was another story. He was a big man—tall and boxy, with only a wreath of white hair remaining around a bald center, and a face that resembled a bulldog. There was nothing lighthearted about him in any way, but to Maeve and Greta he was gruffly loving. When it came to Callan, he was only gruff.

The two men didn't speak to each other unless it was necessary. Callan was strictly civil, but John Sr. bordered on rude, never looking at him without a scowl. Most of what he did say to Callan seemed to hint that he only expected the worst from him, that he didn't like or trust him.

It was understandable that Callan didn't appreciate it, and easy to see his negative feelings in response. But he tolerated John Sr.'s treatment of him without striking back, and Livi wasn't quite sure what to make of that. Certainly her impression of Callan was not as someone who would just accept such scorn and contempt.

After the meal there was a joint cleanup involving Livi, Callan, Greta and Kinsey, before Livi announced that she had to go. She was flying back to Denver before dawn in order to get to her doctor—though she only said she had an early flight, without giving the reason why.

Greta wanted her to stay, but Maeve and Callan both reminded the little girl that the next day was a travel day for them, too, and that she needed to get to bed.

Because the house had not even begun to be packed up, Livi was surprised to hear that they would be following so soon, but she assured the child that she would see her in Denver.

Then, although there was no need for it, Callan walked Livi out to her car.

"Do you have movers coming tomorrow?" Livi asked along the way to satisfy her own curiosity.

"The house is staying intact—I've hired a man and his wife to move in and take care of it and the farm for now, until the Tellers decide whether or not they want to sell. In Denver, they'll be living with me, too, so there's no reason to bring anything but what they need or want for themselves for now. My pilot flew in today and came out here to take what belongings the Tellers wanted with them to make their room feel like home, suitcases were mostly packed today to go out tomorrow with us, so we're all set."

"Oh," Livi muttered. She'd thought that she would have a little break from him, a little time to get her bearings at home before contending with everything. But she guessed not.

"Kinsey is driving in ahead of us tomorrow—her car is here, so she can't fly back with us," he was saying as they drew near Livi's borrowed sedan. "She'll be in Denver around noon and will go straight to my place to arrange accommodations for Maeve's wheelchair. Any chance you could meet her there and—I don't know— take a look at the room that will be Greta's? Maybe do a little something? A decorator handled everything, so it isn't all pink and frilly the way her room at home is, or even the way Maeve has her room here."

"Two things," Livi said in response to the request. "I

can't redecorate a room in a couple of hours. And I think it's a better idea to let Greta make the changes. It'll help it feel more like her room if she chooses the bedspread and curtains and anything that goes up on the walls. What I *can* do is maybe have some new stuffed animals and dolls waiting for her, so the space seems more welcoming. And once she's in town, I'd be happy to take her shopping for more things."

"Just the two of you…" he said, more to himself than to her. He seemed to consider that for a moment and then he let out an almost inaudible sigh that gave Livi the sense there were still reservations in his feelings about her being with Greta. But still he said, "Yeah, okay, I guess that would be good. Tomorrow—and the whole move—is going to be a big deal for all of them and I'm just trying to figure out how to make it easier."

When they reached Livi's car she opened the door but didn't get in. She was wondering about too many things from her afternoon and evening watching his interactions with all three Tellers. And since he'd wandered out here with her and the evening air was still warm—and he didn't seem to be in any hurry for her to leave—she thought she'd take the opportunity to do a little digging.

"You don't seem all that comfortable with…things," she ventured.

"Things?"

"Greta, being around kids…and John Sr., too. Did you know you were being named as Greta's guardian?" Livi asked, narrowing the scope of her inquiry to that for starters.

"Sure, I knew. Mandy and J.J. asked me if I'd do it. But you know, you never think anything is actually going to happen."

"And now that it has? Is it a job you really want?"

His brows drew down over those brooding, coffee-colored eyes, but he didn't hesitate to say, "I wouldn't have it any other way."

That surprised her. "It's just that you don't seem…" She struggled for a diplomatic way to express what she was thinking. "You aren't married anymore and don't have any kids of your own, if I'm remembering what you said in Hawaii—"

"Just before *you* said you weren't married—anymore—and didn't have any kids, either, and then told me you didn't want to talk about our real lives," he stated drily.

She needed fewer and fewer reminders of that night, as more and more details popped into her head every time she was with him.

But she stayed on track and said, "So you're a single guy without any experience with children, let alone a little girl. Yet they chose you as Greta's guardian."

"And you can't figure out why they would have," he surmised with a wry laugh and a hint of a smile that lifted one side of his mouth.

"I'm just wondering about it, is all."

"I grew up here," he said, nodding in the general direction of Northbridge. "On the wrong side of the tracks. My father's family had a good-sized working farm at one point, but when my old man inherited it he let everything go to seed, then sold it off acre by acre for booze money for him and my mother."

That was blunt and raised Livi's eyebrows. "Your parents had a drinking problem," she said, putting it in more polite terms.

"They didn't think it was a problem. For them, it was a way of life. They drank from the minute their feet hit the floor in the morning until they passed out. And when they came to, they drank more."

"Did they do that from when you were just a little kid?"

"I think they always drank, yeah—my mother even admitted that she drank some when she was pregnant with me. I can recall knowing as a little kid that there was my orange juice for breakfast and *grown-up* orange juice that I wasn't supposed to touch."

"You actually remember that?"

"I do," he said without question, before picking up where he'd left off. "But they held jobs until I was maybe seven or eight, so I guess they were initially what's considered 'functional alcoholics'—they'd just hit the bottle hardest after work. But they got less and less functional and kept losing their jobs. By the time I was about Greta's age, drinking was pretty much their occupation."

"But they still took care of you," Livi said, assuming that had to be true.

"In their way," he answered with a shrug. "The more they drank, the more I took care of them. But luckily, as that started to happen, I was old enough to do things for myself."

"Everything?" Livi asked, unable to imagine that a nine- or ten-year-old could take complete care of himself and his parents, too.

Callan looked embarrassed to admit it, but said, "I have a pretty high IQ and I guess that was to my advantage in more than my schoolwork. And this is the country—kids aren't pampered out here. They have to pitch in at an early age. For me, by the time I was in fifth grade, it wasn't feeding chickens or slopping hogs before school, it was fixing breakfast and getting my parents to eat, or dragging clothes to the Laundromat while they were buying liquor and cigarettes and groceries—"

"So they *did* buy groceries."

"Yeah, they did. I'd make a list for them—canned soup and beans, frozen dinners, bread, peanut butter. Stuff for meals I could manage myself, plus things like toilet paper and soap."

"Would they have only bought the liquor if you hadn't made them a list for the other stuff?"

"More than likely. They didn't really care about food. If I didn't make dinner, they didn't eat, just drank. I did the dishes—when there weren't any more clean ones. Brought cash to town to pay to keep our utilities on. Wrote my own notes for school and forged their signatures. I just kept things going—not great, but the best I could as a kid."

He didn't say that with any self-pity, his tone matter-of-fact.

"No one called Social Services?" Livi asked.

"It wasn't as if my parents ever physically hurt me, so there wasn't that to trigger anything. They loved me in their way. Booze was just their priority and I had to adapt."

Their priority over him.

That was so sad.

"Every year my father would sell off another acre or two of land and we'd live off that money. We had enough to get by, and I kept my mouth shut about what my home life was like."

"So no intervention?"

"No intervention. I guess I did just enough to dodge that bullet. But I wasn't the most popular person around," he said. "I was still the poor kid who lived out in a run-down trailer and wore secondhand clothes. That didn't put me on the guest list to many birthday parties. Most parents didn't want their kids around that kind of trash."

Was that something he'd heard said about himself? The thought made Livi feel even worse for him, for the little boy he'd been.

"But that didn't faze Mandy and J.J.," Callan concluded in a happier tone. "Don't ask me why, because I couldn't tell you, but Mandy and J.J. were friends to me in spite of what other kids and the rest of the town thought. From kindergarten on, we were stuck together like glue. The three of us."

Livi was leaning back against the car, listening raptly, and Callan moved forward to cross his arms over the top of the open door between them as he went on reminiscing. His striking face was relaxed now, his small smile at the memory of his friends not at all tight or forced.

"The three of us were together through elementary school, middle school, high school, even college—the University of Colorado. I finished my bachelor's degree in three years, then got my master's and graduated a little ahead of them. But the three of us shared a crummy apartment in Boulder—even after they discovered they liked each other as more than friends. I was best man at their wedding."

"You stayed living with newlyweds?" Livi asked.

"Sharing the space made the rent low enough that I could concentrate on developing software without worrying about anything else. So I could put every ounce of time and energy and everything I had into that, and then into the company I founded—CT Software. They just shuffled around me while I monopolized the computer we shared. Sometimes they had more faith in me than I had in myself."

That made Livi think of Patrick, who had seen more in her than she'd known she was capable of.

"Once things started to go my way and I launched the company," Callan went on, "there was no question that Mandy and J.J. should be in on it with me. I wanted them to be partners, but they wouldn't do that—not when I was funding it with the money I made from selling off the last acre of land that belonged to my family. But they let me make them my vice presidents and put them on the business side of things so we could work together every day. Which was great!" He said that with so much satisfaction.

"But when Greta came along, they wanted to raise her in Northbridge, where her grandparents were," he said then. "So we put a marketing and distribution center here for them to run."

"It must have been hard for you to lose them back to Northbridge."

"Yeah. But after they moved, a day never went by that we didn't talk or video chat or text."

"The Tellers said you're Greta's godfather," Livi murmured, beginning to understand the reasons behind J.J and Mandy's choice of guardian. It was more about their close-knit friendship than about Callan's relationship with their daughter.

"I am her godfather," he confirmed. "But because Mandy and J.J. were in Northbridge, I didn't spend a lot of time with Greta until now. Still, Mandy and J.J. had faith that I could and would step up to the plate for her, for them, if I needed to. And I will."

Livi could tell that he meant it, and she had to admire his determination and dedication to his friends.

She just had the impression that he wasn't quite sure how to "step up to the plate" when it came to Greta. But there wasn't anything more for Livi to say about that except, "So you'll work on it?"

He laughed—something she'd heard a lot that night in Hawaii. The sound made a wave of warmth wash through her.

"That's your way of saying I'm not doing well?" he asked.

"There's room for improvement."

He laughed again. "Okay. You want to be my mentor, too?"

A sweet sort of cockiness and a hint of challenge—there had been some of that in Hawaii, too, and Livi found herself smiling. "It's not like I'm an expert, but you—"

"Yeah, I know," he conceded. "I'm a computer nerd, not a kindergarten teacher."

There was absolutely nothing nerdy about him, but Livi didn't point that out. And she wished she wasn't so aware of just how not nerdy he was. In fact, maybe if he was more of a geek it would have kept her from falling under his spell. Which she felt a little like she was doing again, and was trying to fight.

What she did say was a goading, "You do know that Greta isn't in kindergarten, right?"

He laughed once more. "Yeah, I know that much. But it doesn't mean I know how to talk to her."

"How about just like you'd talk to anyone else? Like you're talking to me right now."

His expression revealed he wasn't sure he could do that.

"Just give it a try. Greta is a chatterbox. If you give her half a chance she'll do most of the work."

"She does kind of like to talk, doesn't she?"

It was Livi's turn to laugh. "She's a nine-year-old girl and has a lot to say. But I think you can keep up," she teased.

They'd been out here talking for a long time, so she knew she should say good-night. But Livi was still curious about the tension between Callan and John Sr.—who, according to Maeve, Callan wanted to "look after."

And now that she had him talking about these things, Livi hated to stop before she had the whole scoop.

So—not because she was enjoying standing here in the moonlight talking to him, but for legitimate other reasons, she assured herself—she said, "And the Tellers? Are you taking them with you to Denver to keep them close to Greta?"

"Let me guess—you saw that there was no love lost between me and John Sr., and you want to know about that, too."

Livi hadn't thought she was that transparent. But before she had the chance to respond, he warned, "It's another long story."

"I'd still like to know," she admitted.

He took a deep breath and sighed, seeming more reluctant to get into this one. "Mandy's folks have both passed, so the Tellers are the only grandparents Greta has left, and yeah, keeping them a part of her life the way Mandy and J.J. wanted them to be is a little of it."

"But not all."

"No," he confirmed. "By the time I got here from Hawaii, J.J. was at the end and he knew it…" Callan's voice cracked.

Livi understood all too well how hard it was to talk about people dearly loved and lost.

He cleared his throat. "J.J. was all Maeve and John Sr. had. He asked me to take over for him, to take care of them. I promised I would and I will. But there's more to it than that promise... I also owe them."

"You owe them?" Livi repeated.

"When my parents died—"

"When was that?"

"The end of my junior year in high school."

"Oh. I was thinking it was more recent, but you were just a kid," she said in surprise.

"I don't think I was ever much of a kid even before that. But I wasn't eighteen," he said ominously.

"They died together? Driving drunk?" she guessed.

He shook his head. "They *did* drive drunk—they did everything drunk. It's just lucky that around here it's mostly open country roads without a lot of other cars to get in the way. But no, they weren't in a car accident. They died in a trailer fire."

She hadn't expected that.

"Mandy and J.J. and I had stayed after school to work on a project," Callan said. "It was already too late when the fire department got there—in fact, that whole last acre around the trailer was on fire by then, because without any close neighbors it took somebody spotting the smoke in the distance to call it in. But investigators pinpointed the origin to inside the trailer, at the spot where my father's chair was. I figured my old man had probably passed out with a lit cigarette in his hand.

"And then...there was nothing," Callan concluded with a sad wryness. "I didn't have parents. I didn't have a place to live. All I had was an after-school job at the computer-repair shop. I didn't make enough to support myself."

"I'm so sorry…" Livi said, almost regretting that she'd gotten them into this now.

He didn't address her condolences, but went on matter-of-factly again. "I was seventeen. Going into the foster system would have just been weird at that point—I was mostly grown and I'd been taking care of myself and my parents for years. But I had no resources. All that was left of my family's land was the acre the trailer was on—but it was too charred from fire damage for farming or raising livestock, and would take years to be usable again. It looked like I was going to have to drop out and get full-time work, but then J.J.—and Maeve—went to bat for me. They pleaded with John Sr. to let me move in for that last year. He didn't want to do it—he'd never liked that J.J. was friends with me. And a couple of months before that I'd used J.J.'s computer to hack into the school's system to play a dumb prank that had wreaked a lot of havoc—"

"Uh-oh…"

"Yeah… I was a kid without any supervision—no curfew, no rules and a brain that was always working and not always on the right path," he acknowledged. "Anyway, the prank was traced back to J.J.'s computer and he got the blame. I set it right, even reversed what I'd done so I didn't get kicked out of school, but John Sr. had always been pretty down on me, and that had soured things more."

"With him, but not with Maeve?"

"She had a soft spot for me—something I was grateful for but never really understood. She teamed up with J.J. to lean on John Sr. and he finally gave in. Under the condition that I toe the line, keep my after-school job and still earn my keep working on the farm before school the way J.J. did."

"And you did."

"It wasn't something I could pass up. It was just for a year, and then I'd be headed to college—if I could get the scholarships lined up." He again nodded toward Northbridge, adding a heartfelt and desperate sounding, "And I wanted out of this town! So yeah, I did."

"Which let you finish high school and win the scholarship you needed."

"So I owe the Tellers."

"Even if you still haven't quite redeemed yourself in John Sr.'s eyes for some reason…" Livi said, hoping for an explanation of that.

But all she got was stoicism from Callan. "That's just how he is. And that's how I got here."

"So between the two things—your friend asking you to take care of his parents and you owing Maeve and John Sr.—you don't fight the way he treats you," Livi said.

"I won't let down J.J. and Mandy on anything. Not with Greta and not with John Sr.," Callan concluded with resignation.

Then he smiled, warmly enough to remind Livi of some of what had appealed to her in Hawaii, and said, "So, Hawaii is history—we're all the way into real life now, like it or not."

If only you knew…

The moon had gone high into the sky as they'd talked. The way its light caught the sharp lines of Callan's face made her think about their walk on the beach, when he'd first kissed her.

He was looking into her eyes just like he had been that

night. Uninvited and unwanted came a memory of that first kiss they'd shared—how instinctively she'd been drawn to it, how warm and gentle his lips had been.

She remembered thinking as she'd melted into the kiss that there was something indescribably good about the feel of that big body curving almost protectively down toward her in order to reach her mouth with his. About the pure size and power of the man himself—strong but reserved, silently inviting her in—that had added to the potency and made it impossible for her to resist drifting closer to him, to that kiss…

Then she realized what she was thinking about and how inappropriate it was.

And how she most surely shouldn't be having the absolutely insane urge to reexperience it!

She took a deep breath to clear her head and said, "I should go. Pack. Get ready to leave in the morning."

He didn't stop looking at her even as he nodded. "Yeah, tomorrow will be a full day. I'll have Kinsey text you when she gets in, and give you the address. Will I see you… I mean, will you be there when we get to my place, or will you just drop off whatever you buy for Greta? Which I'll reimburse you for, by the way."

"Whatever I get her can just be my welcome-to-Denver gift. And…I guess I did say I'd see her in Denver, but I don't know if it will be tomorrow."

Tomorrow, when *he* would get to see her—that was the way he'd put it at first, as if it wasn't about Greta at all.

Tomorrow, when Livi would get to see *him*—something she was thinking and trying not to.

"I guess it depends on how things go," she said. "When you get in. What I'm up to."

Whether or not the doctor rid her of her anxiety or confirmed it…

"But I'll try," she said. "For Greta's sake."

"Sure—for Greta's sake," he repeated.

Then he straightened and stepped back, opening the door wider for Livi to get in.

"Travel safe tomorrow," he said.

"You, too."

"And we'll take this show to Denver," he announced, sounding daunted, and making her laugh at him.

She started the engine and, taking his cue, Callan closed her door and turned back to the house.

Livi put her car into gear, but her eyes followed him, guiltily appreciating the sight.

There was just no denying that he was one of the finest-looking men she'd ever seen. Even from the back, where her gaze rode along for a while on that derriere-to-die-for.

But as he climbed the porch steps she reminded herself of all that was waiting for him inside that farmhouse. All that he had on his own plate.

A lot.

Too much.

That wildly hot man who had grown up dealing with more than any child should have had to, and was now determined to pay back what little help he'd been given.

What if she had to add to that burden? she asked herself as she tore her eyes off him and finally made the U-turn to drive away.

What if she told him he was going to be a father—how would he take it?

And why, even in the midst of all that she was fretting about, was a completely separate portion of her brain thinking once more about that Hawaiian kiss?

And yearning ever so slightly for him to do it again…

Chapter Five

Here we go, Callan thought as his private plane left the runway at a Montana airport, headed for Denver.

It was after four on Wednesday afternoon before they took off. Callan had been hoping to leave earlier, but it was tough to get the Tellers away. And hard on them to leave their home.

The last—and closest—of their friends and neighbors had begun to stream in to say goodbye at dawn, and the visits had gone on from there. Callan hadn't wanted to cut any of those goodbyes short. There was no love lost between himself and Northbridge or anyone in it, but for the Tellers it was a different story. They'd planned to live and die in the small town, surrounded by the people they'd shared the best and worst with for their entire lives.

So not until that stream had stopped had he texted his

pilot with a departure time, and finally loaded Maeve, John Sr. and Greta into the truck of the neighbor driving them to the airport.

It had been a long, silent drive during which Maeve—sitting across the truck's backseat with her leg braced on her husband's lap—had quietly cried. John Sr. had held her hand and patted her knee comfortingly, but his own jaw was clenched so tight that it seemed as if it might lock.

In the front seat, sitting between Callan and the driver, not even the chatty Greta had said a word. She'd just clutched her favorite doll and stared pensively ahead at the dashboard, not crying like her grandmother, but looking so sad it nearly broke Callan's heart.

He couldn't have felt worse for tearing three people from the only place any of them had ever called home. But he didn't know what comfort to give for a cut as deep as they were suffering, and he didn't know what else he could have done besides moving them all to Denver with him.

He'd assured them that he would get them back to Northbridge and the farm to visit often. But his business was in Denver and that's where he had to be. That's where he had to raise Greta. And while he'd offered to pay for continuous care and help for the Tellers to stay in Northbridge, they'd agreed that they wanted to be close to their granddaughter, and so had opted to go wherever she would be.

But it wasn't a good day for any of them, and as the flight got under way, Callan suggested a movie and started it for them.

Then he settled back and, for some reason, found himself instantly thinking that at the end of the dark tunnel that was today, at least there would be Livi Camden.

Kinsey would be there, too, he reminded himself. And that was good. He appreciated that—especially after having had to manage the Tellers without her today.

But still, it was Livi he was thinking of as the bright spot.

He tried to unseat her by thinking about Kinsey and Livi side by side. Because he recognized that the nurse was very attractive. If he was going to be unwillingly haunted by images of a woman, why Livi and not her?

No matter how hard he tried, however, it wasn't Kinsey who occupied his thoughts, it was Livi. The same way she'd been popping into his head almost constantly since they'd reconnected.

But why? Sure, at first maybe guilt for the way things had played out in Hawaii had caused it. But since they'd cleared the air about that? It was still happening and he couldn't figure it out.

He hadn't even thought this much about Elly, the woman he'd *married*. Of course, that had been part of the problem.

With all his energies focused on his business, he hadn't been there for Elly much. Instead, he'd delegated a lot of the "husband" responsibilities to his assistant. It had been up to Trent Baxter to pick out her anniversary presents, give her a lift when her car broke down, escort her to the society benefits Elly liked and Callan hated.

But somewhere during the course of that Trent had overstepped his bounds and taken Callan's place in bed with Elly, as well...

Lesson learned—marriage wasn't for him. And now, with the responsibility for Greta and the Tellers on his shoulders, he doubted he'd even have time for casual dating. So his preoccupation with Livi was a waste of time.

And yet he still couldn't get her off his mind.

What the hell was going on with him?

Maybe it was happening because when he was thinking about Livi he wasn't worrying about the change his life was taking. He wasn't fretting about how he was ever going to adapt to the whole family thing or meet everyone's needs. Every time he thought about *that* he felt as if he was rushing straight into another monumental failure like he'd had with Elly. Times three.

So maybe thinking about Livi was some kind of escape hatch

After all, he'd met her the first time in a tropical paradise. So now, when he needed a breather, maybe his mind just made some sort of connection—Livi equaled a getaway. And Lord knew he needed that, if only in his thoughts.

His divorce had been finalized just four months ago. Two months later he'd lost the people he'd been closest to, the friends he'd depended on, for most of his life. Since then he'd been running himself ragged, going back and forth between Northbridge and Denver. But the hardest part was dealing with the Tellers and Greta.

He had his marriage to prove what a colossal failure he was when it came to emotional relationships with anyone other than Mandy and J.J.—who, he knew, had done most of the heavy lifting to keep their friendship going.

And now here he was, dealing with not one, not two, but three people who weren't Mandy and J.J., and the relationships and everything else that came with them.

He was up to his neck in it and definitely needed some relief. So somewhere in the course of things, he'd apparently connected rest and relaxation with Livi, and surely that was why he couldn't stop thinking about her. Why she seemed like the light at the end of the tunnel. That's all it was.

That was why last night, standing out in the fresh country air alone with her, talking, Callan had felt more relaxed than he had in two months. But he certainly wasn't looking for a repeat of their affair.

Sure, that night in Hawaii had been great.

Sure, he felt something good wash through him the minute he caught sight of her now.

Sure, he'd lost track of time, talking to her last evening. And his willful brain had even drifted into thoughts of kissing her under the Montana moonlight the way he'd kissed her under the Hawaiian moon.

But none of that made any difference.

A vacation fling was one thing, but with Livi stepping into Greta's life, he was going to have to be around her on a regular basis. If he wanted to be with her, it would have to be a real relationship—and he knew better than to try for that. He'd bombed out so thoroughly with Elly that he was in no state of mind to try again anytime soon. Or maybe ever. But certainly not when his divorce was only four months old. Not when he'd lost his own support team in Mandy and J.J. Not when he had the Tellers and Greta, who all needed what he was already afraid he might not be able to give—time and attention and thought.

And not when Livi was a Camden. Greta needed a woman to turn to, and Livi might be able to fill that role for now. But with time, Callan hoped to be able to find someone else to take over, both because he knew Mandy wouldn't want a Camden in her daughter's life, and because he wasn't sure himself if he could trust her. He knew that that was where some of his own issues overlapped and made things worse. After his experiences with Elly, he was finding it a struggle to consider trusting any woman again.

And when the any-woman was a Camden?

As far as he was concerned, no one could be less trustworthy than a Camden...

"You're awfully pale. Are you feeling okay?" Kinsey Madison asked.

Livi had arrived late Wednesday afternoon at Callan's condominium, located in a stately building behind Denver's Cherry Creek Shopping Center. Kinsey was already there and had shown her around the expansive four-bedroom, four-bath place. Then Kinsey had helped her arrange the dolls and stuffed animals she'd brought for Greta, after which Livi had offered to help make Maeve's accommodations more comfortable. They'd been hard at work when the nurse made her observation.

"I'm fine," Livi answered. "Long day, is all. You drove all the way from Northbridge today, you must be feeling a bit weary yourself."

"I stopped at my apartment and took a nap before coming over here, so I'm not doing too badly," Kinsey said.

Livi had gone straight from the airport to her gynecologist and then home, too. But napping hadn't been possible. Being told by her doctor that she was definitely pregnant hadn't made for a restful homecoming.

"You're sure you aren't coming down with something?" Kinsey persisted.

I'm coming down with something, all right—a baby in seven months.

And between now and then she would have to face her family with the news and let them know how it had happened.

She had no idea how she was ever going to do that.

And then there was Callan.

She didn't know what she was going to do about him, either.

But of course she couldn't say any of that, so she shook her head and said to the nurse, "I'm just tired."

Tired and spent from the hours she'd passed alternately crying and staring into space until it finally, genuinely sank in—she was going to have a baby.

Without Patrick.

But it was still a baby.

Her baby.

Something she'd wanted once upon a time; something she'd grieved losing the possibility of, along with grieving Patrick. But something that she would now get to have.

Livi wasn't happy. But she'd reached some sort of acceptance and had begun to feel a tiny ember of something that, given time, might turn into excitement.

As long as she didn't think about Callan.

Which was remarkably difficult when there was also some part of herself she didn't recognize that *kept* thinking about him. And not only in terms of the baby.

She kept thinking about talking to him the night before and how, like in Hawaii, time had flown by and she'd been in no hurry to have it end. She kept remembering so many tiny details of the way he looked, and how she'd gotten lost in studying them. She even kept hearing the sound of his deep voice in her head and feeling some kind of strange ripple every time she did.

Livi realized belatedly that Kinsey was still talking to her.

"Your family is big, isn't it? I mean, if what I've read in newspapers and magazines is true," she was saying.

"It is big—and getting bigger and bigger," Livi answered as they moved some furniture around.

"There's your grandmother, right?" Kinsey continued. "And ten kids who came from just her two sons?"

"You really have read about us," Livi said with a laugh. Under other conditions the nurse's questions might have seemed nosy. But in the little while since they'd met, Livi had come to like Kinsey, who she guessed to be near her age. So this just seemed more like the beginning of a friendship. Besides, Livi had grown up in the public eye as a Camden and was used to people knowing about her family.

She confirmed that yes, all ten of the Camden grandchildren had come from only two sons, Mitchum and Howard.

"And which of them was your father?"

"Mitchum."

Since it seemed as if Kinsey was making friendly overtures, Livi thought she should, too, so she said, "What about your family? Big? Small?"

"My mom just died."

"I'm so sorry," Livi murmured.

"Thanks," Kinsey responded, before going on. "I've lived in Denver since leaving home for college, but Mom was the reason I was in Northbridge. My three brothers and I grew up there—on a farm about the size of the

Tellers' place, and not far away—with Mom and our adopted father."

"Were your parents divorced?"

Kinsey didn't answer that immediately. For some reason she hesitated, then said, "No. Our father died when Mom was pregnant with me. She married Hugh Madison when I was two. He died a year ago. Mom stayed on the farm, but she didn't do well after that. I quit my job in Denver to take care of her when she started to really fail."

"How about your brothers? Did they help, too?"

"They're marines—all three of them overseas in Afghanistan. They couldn't get here. One of them— Declan—was injured the same day Mom died."

"Ohh...is he all right?"

"He'll survive, but he was pretty badly hurt. He's had two surgeries at the naval hospital there, but now he's being transferred to a hospital in Germany for a third operation that might include amputating his leg. Our oldest brother, Conor, is a doctor, and he's with Declan. Conor can't treat him because he's family, but he's overseeing things. So neither of them could get back for Mom's funeral. Declan's twin, Liam, was on a special mission and couldn't be reached at all. He didn't know Mom had died or that Declan had been hurt until a few days ago. So I've been on my own with...well, everything."

Kinsey sounded as if she'd faced her own overwhelming situation. Sympathizing, Livi was inclined to say she was sorry again, but wasn't sure it was called for.

So instead she said, "You went back to Northbridge to take care of you mother and her affairs, but ended up working with the Tellers?"

"Maeve fell the day after my mom's funeral. The doctor in Northbridge put Callan in touch with me to take care of her. It was a good fit because I could start there, and then come back here when they made the move."

But that seemed to be as much as Kinsey wanted to say about herself, because she returned to asking Livi about her family—her siblings and cousins, her grandmother and especially her father.

And since it kept the conversation away from her current troubles, Livi just let that happen and answered Kinsey's questions.

But as she did, she began to think about how nice Kinsey was, how warm and personable. And how pretty, too; she had coloring like Livi's own—dark hair, fair skin and blue eyes.

Livi began to think that if any of her brothers or male cousins were still single she would have told them about the home health care practitioner and offered to set one of them up on a date. But none of them were single anymore.

Callan was, though...

Had he noticed Kinsey? Livi wondered all of a sudden.

How could he not have? Circumstances put them together a lot. And Kinsey had plenty of charms to attract a healthy single guy.

But why did it bother her to think that surely he *had* noticed the pretty nurse? That he could even be attracted to her?

Was that why he was so eager to put Hawaii behind them? So he could feel free to start something up with Kinsey?

"Are you sure you're okay?" the nurse asked, sounding alarmed. "I thought you were pale before, but the color just disappeared from your face altogether."

"Really, I'm just tired," Livi repeated in a clipped tone.

But what if there was something going on between Kinsey and Callan? she asked herself.

It shouldn't affect her. It shouldn't matter to her. She should be glad for everyone involved. After all, Greta and the Tellers were already fond of the nurse and she was good to them. Callan clearly needed help. If he and Kinsey got together the whole lot of them could be one big happy family.

And Livi hated the idea so much she was tempted to take the decorative geode from the wooden plank coffee table they were about to move and throw it at Kinsey.

Perfectly nice Kinsey, who was doing nothing but being friendly to everyone, including her.

Perfectly nice Kinsey, who Livi had not seen Callan take any special interest in at all.

Perfectly nice Kinsey, who only seemed peripherally aware of Callan and even then only as her employer.

But still the thought of the two of them together was so horrible to Livi that she didn't know what to do now that she'd had it.

She was aware that what she was feeling was ridiculous. And she reminded herself that she'd had Patrick. Patrick was her one-and-only. He couldn't be replaced. Whatever went on in any other man's life didn't matter to her.

But *why* did she have to remind herself of that? She'd never had to before. It had always been so deeply ingrained in her that she never lost sight of it.

"Maybe I better sit down for just a minute," she muttered, wilting onto the sofa once they had the coffee table centered in front of it.

"I'll get you a glass of water," Kinsey said, leaving her alone.

Livi took a few deep breaths, trying to calm herself. Trying to clear her head. Trying to understand.

Maybe this was because of hormones?

The doctor had said she was flooded with them now. So many that they were already making enough changes in her body for the ob-gyn not to need a blood test to confirm the pregnancy. That had to be what was wrong with her. Why else would she be so freaked out by the thought of Callan with Kinsey?

The nurse returned with a glass of water and handed it to her. Livi thanked her, then blurted, "So I'll bet you'll be glad to see Callan when he gets here."

No! She hadn't really said that, had she?

Kinsey laughed slightly. "So he can move his own furniture?" she guessed.

Livi forced a laugh of her own, gratefully seizing the excuse Kinsey was giving her, because she felt like an idiot for what she'd said. "This stuff is massive," she added with a nod toward the pieces, which were large enough to fill the room and substantial for even the two of them to have to push across the hardwood flooring, since they were too heavy to lift.

"We're doing okay. If being without my brothers has taught me anything it's that women can do whatever they have to do without men."

Oh, God, I hope so... Livi thought.

She was going to have this baby on her own. And maybe that's what had caused that strange burst of jealousy? Maybe it was a biological thing, to want her baby's father to be free to take care of her and the child?

But even if she and Callan were having a baby, that didn't mean they were anything else to each other. Or that he couldn't or wouldn't or shouldn't go on to find his own one-and-only. She should even be hoping that he would. Eventually.

Maybe just not today.

And maybe not Kinsey.

Livi finished the glass of water and got to her feet as if she had renewed energy. "Okay, ready to go again," she announced.

But as she and Kinsey got back to work she started thinking of what single men she did know.

And who she might be able to fix the nurse up with in a hurry.

"I never turn down help cleaning," Callan said to Livi several hours later.

He'd arrived home with his three charges at a little after seven o'clock. Then he'd left the Tellers to Kinsey, Greta to Livi, and gone back out to pick up the dinner they'd all agreed on, while Livi and Kinsey got everyone shown around the condo and moved in to their respective rooms.

They'd all eaten when he'd returned with the food, then left the mess so that Callan and John Sr. could rearrange the furniture in the room the elder Tellers would occupy, while Kinsey got Maeve ready for bed and Livi urged Greta in that direction, too.

Greta had fallen asleep almost the minute her head hit the pillow, and once the Tellers' room was in order Callan had left Kinsey to deal with the elderly couple.

Slipping out of Greta's room, Livi had found him tackling the dining room and kitchen, and asked if he wanted another pair of hands.

But she wasn't just trying to be helpful.

From the moment Callan had gotten there she'd been

watching him and Kinsey. Hating herself for it. Not understanding why she was so driven to do it, but doing it, anyway.

She hadn't seen a single indication that there was anything going on between them, but something in her wouldn't let her leave until she knew Kinsey was gone, too.

So she'd offered to help Callan clean up.

"A Camden doing the dishes—is this a first?" he asked jokingly.

"It is a first," she said teasingly. "As a Camden I've always had a whole staff to do everything for me—put the toothpaste on my toothbrush, cut my food, hold the cup with my morning coffee for me to sip out of, dab the corners of my mouth after every bite I'm fed by my feeder…"

He laughed. "I know it isn't like that, but you *are* a Camden."

"Clearly you've never met my grandmother. She was a farm girl from Northbridge—get her started and you hear stories about slopping pigs and milking cows and what it really means to get your hands dirty. And since she raised me—along with my five brothers and sisters and four cousins—from the time I was six years old, I can promise you that I have done more dishes than you've probably seen in your lifetime."

"That's a *lot* of brothers and sisters and cousins. Your grandmother raised you all after the plane crash?" he asked as they stacked take-out containers, gathered used napkins, plates, silverware and glasses. "I remember hearing about the crash when it happened, but I was just a kid myself. I never thought about there being kids left behind until now."

"Well, there were. A full ten of us. I'm just grateful we still had my grandmother—plus my great-grandfather, H. J. Camden. He's the one who started the whole Camden enterprise. The two of them had to stay home at the last minute because H.J. had hurt his back. They ended up being the only two left to take care of us."

"Or they would have been lost, too," Callan said with some astonishment. "It's weird. Until now I've only been on the other side of this. I have to admit, I wasn't heartbroken that the people who had stolen Mandy's dad's business didn't end up living long and prosperous lives themselves."

Livi didn't know what to say to that.

"Sorry, that was…" Callan paused, then said, "I have some mixed feelings going on here. On the one hand you're Livi. From Hawaii. And when that's all you are… well, I can't say I hate being around you."

That sounded like an understatement. Did it mean that he *liked* being with her?

"On the other hand," he continued, "you're a Camden. And one of my best friends hated Camdens so much I wouldn't have trusted her to be in the same room with one. So when that part comes up…I guess I go into Mandy-mode and…well, I'm sorry if I say something I shouldn't."

Livi nodded, distracted by his inadvertent admission that he liked being with her.

Then he seemed to make an effort to separate her from her family name, and said, "So tell me about being raised by your grandmother. Ten of you, huh?"

"Ten kids, yeah," she confirmed. "But only eight births, because I'm a triplet with my brother Lang and my sister, Lindie."

"I've never met a triplet before."

"You don't run into too many of us. Lang and Lindie and I, and our cousin Jani, are the youngest of the family—Jani is the same age we are."

"So she was six when the plane crash happened, too."

"Right. GiGi—that's what we call our grandmother—took over after that and raised us all. With some help from H.J., who had to come out of retirement at eighty-eight to run Camden Inc., and with Margaret and Louie Haliburton, who started out as staff but became just like family."

"They were the ones who put the toothpaste on your toothbrush?" Callan teased.

Livi laughed and appreciated that he'd lightened the tone. "I think they might have, actually. Once or twice when I was little. But the Camden name and coffers didn't mean a thing to GiGi. She raised us the way she'd been raised."

"You had pigs to slop and cows to milk?"

"No, but every one of us had chores, from the moment we went to live with GiGi until the day any one of us moved out—and even on vacations home from college. We all still pitch in there when something needs to be done."

"But you started doing chores when you were six?"

"I did. I learned to make my own bed, pick up after myself, and we all got together in the kitchen every single weeknight to lend a hand making dinner and then cleaning up."

"So *you* were the staff?" he joked again.

"We were just one big family. We worked together and played together and we're still a pretty tight-knit group."

"And it sounds like you like that."

"I did and do. There's always been company and support and help when any one of us needs it…" Things she knew she was going to need again now, facing pregnancy and single parenthood. Things she was counting on. "We still do what GiGi started all those years ago—we have movie nights at her house, dinner every Sunday. We share the responsibilities and run Camden Incorporated equally and keep up with each other's lives and babysit for one another and whatever."

"So basically your grandmother is an expert at doing the whole family thing."

"Well, yeah…" Livi said, hearing in his voice that the idea seemed foreign to him.

"And now that I'm doing what she did, taking over for Mandy and J.J., that puts me in her position? Does that mean I should do that kind of thing?" he asked, as if this was news to him.

"Should you assign chores so Greta learns responsibility? Cook dinner yourself every night and make sure the whole family is together for Sunday dinner every week? Should you have movie nights and arrange fun stuff for everyone to do together? I suppose you have to make it work for you and the Tellers and Greta, so there might be variations of all that, but sure. Were you not thinking about being Greta's family now? Because you are… Along with the Tellers, of course, but they won't be around forever. And you aren't just loaning rooms out in your house."

"I guess I didn't really think about any of that," he admitted, frowning as they began to take things from the formal dining room into Callan's ultracontemporary kitchen.

Neither of them said anything as they made a few trips

to clear the dining room. Livi had the impression that he was contemplating what seemed to have been a revelation to him. She left him to it as she packaged leftovers and he rinsed plates and put them in the dishwasher.

They'd just about finished when Kinsey came in to say that Maeve and John Sr. were in bed for the night and she was leaving, that she would be back the next morning.

Livi thought she should say good-night, too, and walk out with the nurse. But the kitchen wasn't completely clean. The dining room table needed to be washed off. And she *had* volunteered to help...

Oh, who was she kidding? She just wasn't eager to have her time there end yet.

Callan said only a perfunctory good-night to the nurse, without casting a glance in her direction, as he loaded the dishwasher.

He didn't seem to hear Kinsey say in a more casual, genial voice to Livi, "Get some rest tonight."

"You, too," Livi countered.

Then Kinsey said a general "See you all tomorrow" that only Livi answered, and left.

When she had, Callan's attention was solely on Livi again.

"Didn't you sleep well last night?" he asked.

No, she hadn't slept well. Not with that doctor's appointment this morning on her mind. But she didn't want to mention that, so she said, "I was up early to leave Northbridge—the same way Kinsey was. We were commiserating before you got here." It was Livi's turn to pause before she said, "She's nice..."

Callan shrugged. "Kinsey? Yeah, she is," he agreed vaguely. "I haven't had a whole lot of interaction with her—she keeps me updated, but she's just sort of... around, doing her job. But yeah, she's nice enough."

"She's pretty, too," Livi said, confused by why she had such a need to push this with him. But she did. "Is she single? I've never heard her mention anyone."

"Maeve says she is—I think it was some kind of hint that I should take a look or something." More ambiguity.

"But you didn't?"

"Nah," he said, as if he couldn't give it a second thought.

And yet Livi was still compelled to test. "I was thinking that I might fix her up. I know a few single men she might like..."

"Just don't get her all wrapped up in some new romance until I can spare her around here."

The fact that he was so focused on Kinsey's work—and nothing else about the pretty nurse—made Livi feel worlds better as she went into the dining room to wipe down the table.

When she returned to the kitchen, Callan had that finished, too, and after rinsing the sponge she'd used and handing it to him to put away, it occurred to her that there was nothing more holding her there.

"I should probably get going, too," she said.

"There's no rush..."

Because he wanted her to stay or because he was being polite?

It didn't matter, she told herself. She'd come to welcome Greta, she'd pitched in out of good manners and now it was time to go.

Like it or not...

"It's been a long day," she replied, repeating what she'd said earlier to Kinsey. "For you, too."

"I'm fine," he insisted.

So maybe he wasn't just being polite?

It was satisfying to think that he wanted her to stay—and tempting, too—but she thought better of it and didn't give in to the inclination to.

"I really should get going."

"I'll walk you down to your car then," he said. "The parking garage is pretty secure, but I'm still not crazy about the idea of a woman down there alone at night."

Livi didn't point out that he'd just let Kinsey leave alone, because she didn't want to admit to herself that she didn't hate the prospect of him escorting her to her car.

And she also didn't want to encourage him to start being more attentive to Kinsey.

So she just picked up her purse and put on her jacket.

Callan opened the door for her and they stepped across the hall to the elevator that brought them down to the basement level, where she'd been directed to park.

"The dolls and stuffed animals were a big hit. Thanks for doing that for Greta," Callan said along the way.

"I'm just glad she liked them all. I wasn't sure what she might already have, so I went into the toy department in our store on Colorado Boulevard and asked for the newest arrivals that sales figures indicate are trending for her age group."

"You had a plan," he said with a laugh. Livi flushed as she realized after the fact that her explanation was more detailed than it needed to be.

It was just that being alone with him, standing so close in the elevator, made her even more aware of him. How substantially built he was. How much she liked the cologne he wore.

They reached her car, but tonight Callan stopped short of going to her door. Instead he hitched a hip onto her rear fender and crossed his forearms over the thick thigh he raised.

Livi obliged him and came to a stop, too, facing him. And trying to ignore the fact that even dressed in casual navy blue twill slacks and a white polo shirt, he was something to see. Especially with that stubble shadowing his bad-boy good looks.

"So you're taking Greta shopping for things to redecorate her room tomorrow?" he said then.

Ah, so that was what he wanted to talk about. He was probably having misgivings about it again.

"If that's okay," Livi answered. "I know it was Maeve's suggestion at dinner, and you didn't say much. But I wasn't sure how long I'd be in Northbridge, so I took all this week off and I'm free..."

"I'd like to be there, but I've been gone for twelve days this time, to close up the farm and get everybody ready for this move. I have to go into work."

"And your favorite thing to do is shop for stuff to redecorate a room, and you don't want it done without you?"

He laughed again. "Actually, to me, that kind of shopping is punishment enough for a capital crime—I *hate* it. But..."

"You want to keep an eye on me when I'm with Greta in case I'm an evil Camden and not on the up-and-up," Livi said, paraphrasing his warning that first day at the farm and also recalling his reservations when they'd talked about this before.

He grinned sheepishly and confessed, "Something like that."

"So do you not want us to go tomorrow?"

He took a moment to think about it, not looking at her. Then he drew a deep breath and sighed. "Greta was really excited about it," he admitted. "She hardly said five words all day long, but when Maeve came up with that…" His eyebrows arched as if in concession.

"She's big enough for you to question when we get back, you know," Livi suggested. "You can keep tabs on things that way to monitor me."

She didn't know what about that made him flash a devilish little smile, before he said, "I s'pose. You've kind of got me over a barrel, having Maeve in your corner."

"I won't do it if you're uncomfortable with it," Livi said. "I'll even take the blame—I can call Greta in the morning and say something came up and I can't make it."

"That would make you the bad guy instead of me," he said, as if there was some appeal in that. But then he shook his head. "No, that would disappoint Greta. And I want her room to be what she wants. But I'm paying this time. Whatever she picks out, have the salesperson call me and I'll give my credit card number for it."

It was Livi's turn to laugh, because he'd said that as if it somehow justified him agreeing to let Greta be alone with her. "If that makes you feel better. And I swear I'll try not to corrupt her while we're picking out dust ruffles."

"I don't know what a dust ruffle is, but thanks," he said facetiously. He shook his head again. "I told you, this is all pretty mixed up for me."

Livi nodded. "I get it—it'll just take some time for you to see that I really only want to make up for what was done years ago."

"So you aren't a Camden Trojan horse."

"What exactly would I be infiltrating?" she challenged, a part of her realizing how much she liked these teasing exchanges.

"I don't know. I only know how Mandy felt about Camdens, and I'm trying to do right by her."

"I respect that," Livi admitted. "You're just being a good friend and looking out for her daughter."

And it was something about him and his character that she noted herself. Admiring it in him even if it did make him suspicious of her.

He was studying her face as if to reassure himself. Or maybe to resolve those two elements that he found at odds—her being whatever it was he'd thought of her in Hawaii with the fact that she was a Camden.

Then he pushed off her fender and stood in front of her. "It's also tough," he confided, "because Camden or not, you're a big help to me. And I need it all the way around. At least, while I'm trying to figure this whole thing out, Greta doesn't have to suffer for my incompetence as her guardian."

"So think of it as that—help to you that Greta benefits from."

"That sounded a little Trojan horsey—like you're trying to suck me in so I lower my guard," he said with one eyebrow arched.

But his voice was more playful than venomous. And the expression on his handsome face changed to something more intimate.

Then he reached a hand to her upper arm, squeezing it affectionately, as if that was a perfectly natural thing between them. "Anyway, thanks for what you did today and for sticking around tonight. Like I said, it put Greta in a better mood, and I think the Tellers were happy to see you, too." He paused a beat, squeezed her arm a second time, and added, "And I can't say I was *un*happy to see you…"

She liked hearing that more than she wanted to.

Then, when she wasn't expecting it at all, he leaned forward and kissed her forehead.

Livi froze, taken by surprise and knocked off balance by that contact.

But it was over the next moment when he let go of her arm to step back.

Nodding toward the driver's side of her car, he said, "Go on home and get some sleep."

Livi swallowed with some difficulty and could barely find her voice to say good-night before she did as he'd instructed.

But after an entire day of muddled emotions, as she drove home she felt even more confusion.

In her entire life she had never seen herself with anyone but Patrick.

In Hawaii she'd been outside of herself. But here she was now, with her feet firmly planted on home turf.

And while she wasn't actually seeing herself with Callan, something did seem to be happening.

Something she didn't understand, that had never happened before.

Something that left her arm still tingling where Callan had touched her.

Something that left her hungering for more than that platonic forehead kiss.

And thinking—for the first time, here and now, on home turf—that maybe Patrick *wasn't* the only man she could be with…

Chapter Six

"Good, you're still here! But everybody else—"

"Sound asleep. Kinsey left a few minutes ago, and I was just about to," Livi told Callan when he came in on Friday night. He'd caught her in the middle of putting on her short, black leather jacket over the white mock-turtleneck T-shirt topping her jeans and boots.

"Damn, I did it again?" he said.

Livi assumed he meant that he'd come home from work for the second day in a row too late for any of his charges to so much as set eyes on him. And according to Greta, he left for work before they woke in the morning, so none of them had seen him since Wednesday night.

Neither had Livi—something she was more aware of than she wanted to be.

On Thursday she'd taken Greta shopping, making sporadic contact with Callan along the way through texts, and thinking that she would see him that evening. Looking forward to seeing him, in spite of herself.

But a little before six he'd texted that he was held up and wouldn't be home for dinner. He'd asked if she could pick something up. So Livi and Greta had ordered takeout from an Italian bistro next to the mall and brought it home for everyone. Callan still hadn't shown up when Livi had put Greta to bed and Kinsey had done the same with Maeve.

This morning, Livi, Greta, Kinsey and John Sr., supervised by Maeve in her wheelchair, had started turning Greta's room into a nine-year-old girl's dream, a project that took them into the evening.

Still no sign of Callan.

And because during the last two days Greta's highs had been sprinkled with some very low lows, Livi hadn't wanted to just leave her. So she'd suggested the five of them have a pizza-and-movie night.

Which was what they'd done.

But even though Greta had stayed up past her bedtime, eager to show Callan all they'd done to her room, by ten o'clock Maeve insisted that her granddaughter get to bed, and the elder Tellers had followed suit.

Since the pizza and movie had been Livi's idea, along with popcorn, she'd stayed to clean up, sending Kinsey home once the nurse had finished getting Maeve situated for the night.

And even though Livi told herself she wasn't consciously stalling in hopes of seeing Callan, she knew she sort of was. But she'd run out of excuses to stay, and so she was about to leave when he came in.

"What time is it?" he asked, keeping his voice low as he took off his tan suit coat and striped tie.

"Not quite eleven," she informed him, going on to explain about the movie and cleanup and Greta trying to wait for him, certainly not letting him know that she had been, too. And trying hard not to feast on the sight of him as if she were starving for it.

"I brought doughnuts…" he said, as if they were consolation, raising the bakery box he was carrying.

"They can eat them for breakfast?" Livi proposed.

He nodded, but said, "I blew it, huh?"

She merely raised her eyebrows at him to confirm it.

"Can you hang around a little bit and bring me up to date? I know it's late, but…" He raised the box again and repeated temptingly, "I have doughnuts. And tonight is the first night the fire pits were lit in the courtyard downstairs. It's still a nice night. We could take the doughnuts down there and talk…"

It was late and pregnancy was sapping Livi's energy.

But it *was* Friday night, and there was nowhere she needed to be in the morning. Plus there were a few things she thought he should be updated on. Besides, there was nothing and no one waiting for her at home—just an empty house.

"I'm weak when it comes to doughnuts," she said.

He grinned as if she'd granted him something deeply important. "Give me five minutes to change clothes and I'll be right back," he said, handing her the pastry box.

This isn't because I feel any kind of attraction to him, she told herself while he was gone.

It couldn't be.

If she was genuinely attracted to him it would be another complication in an already overly complex situation. She needed to be able to think clearly in order to make sure she made the right choices now. Much, much better choices than she'd made in Hawaii.

So while she knew she needed to get to know Callan, what she didn't need was any kind of emotions clouding the situation.

Yet when he walked back into the entry a few minutes later, dressed in jeans that fitted him like an old friend and a gray hoodie that had somehow mussed his hair into looking even better than it had, coupled with that sexy stubble on his jaw Livi couldn't help appreciating the whole picture. Which made it difficult to go on believing that she wasn't attracted to him.

But still, she tried.

"Okay, let's go," he said, taking the doughnut box back and opening the door for her to step out ahead of him.

"You've been at work all this time?" she asked as they rode the elevator to the first floor.

"Before dawn yesterday until after midnight last night, and then in again before dawn today. We're launching new operating system software in another month and I've been gone to Northbridge so much that we're behind schedule. My people have been working overtime to make up for me not being there. Tempers are short and disputes had to be dealt with. And there were meetings I've been putting off, on top of work I'm behind on..." He stopped short. "You run a big business—you know how it is."

"I share responsibilities with nine other people, so the weight of everything doesn't fall on any one of us... So, no, we don't get as swamped as that."

"Lucky you," he said, as he guided her through the lobby and out a back door into a courtyard that made Livi feel as if she'd stepped into a forest retreat.

A flat, grassy meadow-like area was enclosed in moss-covered rocks and evergreen trees that blocked out any view or sounds of the city, and instead made it seem as if they were in the mountains.

But the setting was luxurious, too, with lushly cushioned outdoor furniture surrounding several fire pits. They were all lit, giving off enough heat to chase away any chill.

"Great—we have it all to ourselves," Callan said, motioning to the grouping not far from the door.

Each fire pit was centered amid four seats larger than easy chairs, providing more than enough room for one. Livi sat where he directed and he joined her, keeping it cozy. Especially when he rested his arm on top of the wrought-iron frame behind her. He wasn't touching her in any way, but it *was* cozy.

And nice.

Though again, she tried not to register that.

He opened the doughnut box and held it out to her.

There was a chocolate-glazed chocolate one with chocolate sprinkles; Livi didn't have to think twice.

"You're a chocolate girl," he observed.

"Through and through," she confessed, as he picked a plain glazed and set the box on the small table beside their chair.

"These will be even better dunked in coffee tomorrow morning," he said, just before they both took a bite.

Her mornings hadn't included coffee for a few weeks because the smell of it made her sicker. And anyway, she was watching her caffeine intake now that she knew she was pregnant.

But that wasn't a comment she was going to make,

so she just took another bite of her doughnut, enjoying it tonight while she could.

"So what's been going on?" he asked.

Livi filled him in on the time since he'd last been with her or anyone else in his household, then said, "Greta has had a few rough patches. When we were shopping there were a couple of times when she mentioned her mom—like she forgot for a minute that Mandy was gone. Twice she said she liked something but didn't know if her mom would, then she caught herself and got really quiet. At home she kept asking Maeve if her parents would have liked her choices—as if she was hoping Maeve could channel some approval. And she kind of disappeared into her room last night, and when I found her she was crying."

Callan sobered and frowned. "Is that normal?"

"I talked to her about what it was like for me when I lost my parents, when I had to move away from my house to live somewhere else. That brought up a lot of questions about if I thought or felt this or that, as if she's been worrying that she might be doing it wrong. I told her I'd thought and felt the same things, and it seemed like she got a little happier."

"So she's going through what you went through and it *is* normal?"

"I think so."

"But it was a tough couple of days that I wasn't around for."

"It has been tough," Livi confirmed, without condemning him. "This is even more upheaval for her than I went through. I went from my home to my grandmother's house, somewhere I was familiar with. It doesn't seem as if you and Greta are as close as I was to GiGi…"

"I'm pretty busy all the time," he admitted.

"For Greta, this is all new and unfamiliar," Livi continued. "Your place is beautiful, but it isn't what she's used to and she's worrying about what she should use, what she can and can't touch, where she can and can't go in the condo. And the same goes for the Tellers, I think. Maeve keeps fretting about things being too nice to use, not wanting to risk damaging this or that. She tells John Sr. to be careful constantly. Plus, for John Sr.—"

"I'm in trouble all the way around, huh?"

Livi didn't want to scold Callan, but he needed to know what was going on. "You have to take into consideration how big a change this is for all of them. I think they need you around reassuring them that it's their home now, too. Or setting some sort of parameters if there are things you *don't* want them to do."

"They can do whatever they want," he said, as if he genuinely wasn't concerned.

"But they need to be made to feel welcome and at home. By you—because, after all, it's your place. But you've kind of disappeared on them. Maeve keeps worrying, and John Sr. is chafing at things—"

"The old man *chafes* at everything. Especially when it comes to me."

Any mention of the elder male Teller always seemed to rub Callan the wrong way, and vice versa. Livi ignored his comment. "But I think he's feeling kind of stranded. Maeve is incapacitated and not up to anything but resting, but John Sr. isn't. I mean, I can see where he couldn't handle all the farm work on his own anymore, or provide all the nursing of Maeve needs, but he's said more than once in these last two days that if he was home he could get in his truck and go into town to get—"

"His sunflower seeds and jerky and beer!" Callan said with a grimace. "I forgot. He was going to bring his own supply and I told him I'd stock them as soon as we got here, and I didn't."

Livi didn't mention that she knew that because the elderly man had complained about it. "I did a grocery run this morning and got what he wanted. But I think it's more than that. I think he needs a car—or truck—so whenever he feels like it he can get out for a while on his own. He's feeling kind of penned in…"

"Sure, but he was in Northbridge before, not Cherry Creek, where there's traffic. You know driving around here is a lot different than the open country roads he's used to."

"You could take him out, show him some back ways to get around and how to avoid traffic so he could at least go to the grocery store or the mall or whatever. Enough so he has some independence left. He's a proud old guy and—"

"And you're saying that I've cut him off at the knees. But you know, the Tellers aren't as young as your parents or mine would have been if they were still alive," he argued.

"I know. Maeve told me how John Jr. was a surprise late-in-life baby, that she was forty-five when she had him. But their age is all the more reason why they need some independence. I can tell you from the way things are with my grandmother that even basically healthy people that age end up with a lot of back and forth to doctors and pharmacies just for maintenance. Right now Kinsey is taking care of all the meds and monitoring for both Maeve and John Sr., but when she's gone, they'll need to get in to a doctor's office and a pharmacy more than you can imagine. John Sr. can take them around for a few more years if you just get him comfortable driving in the city. In the long run that's to your benefit, too."

"True…" Callan said thoughtfully.

"Kinsey examined him, gave him reflex and vision tests. She said he's fine on that count," Livi added, to convince him.

"Maybe he could even take Greta back and forth to school," Callan mused.

It was something else Livi had planned to use to build her case. But now that it had occurred to him on his own she was a little afraid he might go too far. Yes, the Tellers could help out shuttling Greta back and forth, but as her guardian, Callan should really take on some of those responsibilities himself.

So she said, "But even though John Sr. can pitch in a little, it would still be good if you kept to some kind of schedule where they all could expect to see you every day. Just leaving them wondering if you'll be around or not—"

"Is bad," he said, as if it was a complaint he'd heard before. "I know I have to pay more attention to what's going on at home. I'm just used to staying at work until the work is done, no matter how long that takes. I grab something to eat when I get hungry, not because it's any particular time of day. And—" his tone turned guilty "—I barely remember there's anyone at home, waiting. And I know that's lousy for whoever *is* at home. But at least I haven't had my assistant filling in." Callan sounded proud of himself for a moment, then frowned and added, "Although I guess that's pretty much what you and Kinsey have been doing…"

He released a sigh of self-disgust and said, "I really haven't learned my lesson."

"You took on responsibility for another elderly couple and a nine-year-old girl once before and should have learned something from it?" Livi joked.

"No, but I *did* neglect my wife right into the arms of my assistant."

Livi wasn't quite sure what to say to that. It did make her curious, though.

"I have a history of dropping the ball when it comes to relationships," Callan explained.

After seeing what had gone on for the last two days, Livi didn't find that a surprise.

He chuckled mirthlessly and added, "Actually, that dates all the way back to the sixth grade, when Mandy had a crush on me."

"Not on John Jr.?"

"Nope, that didn't happen until we were older. In fact, I was so oblivious that I didn't even know she'd ever felt that way about me until she told me about it years later. We all laughed about it because it had just been a kid thing. But after that I sometimes had the feeling that I was on the outside looking in at what I might have had."

"Did you have those kinds of feelings for Mandy?" Livi asked.

"No, I never saw her as anything but a friend. But you know, it's the what-if—what if I'd gone through that door instead of walking right past it."

"Greta would have been yours," Livi said, testing for his reaction.

But he only laughed. "I'm sure I would have screwed things up long before that—I have with every other woman. Mandy was always sending me on blind dates, trying to find me someone. But even when I liked the person, eventually the way I work got in the way."

"So it's common for you to work as hard and long as you have the last two days?"

"The past few days have been extreme, since I had a lot of catching up to do, and the product launch is around the corner. But we have our share of crises and they usually mean I end up chained to my desk. In any case, Mandy said I was bad about letting anybody get too close, that I used my job to make sure they didn't."

"But you did get married," Livi reminded him. "Was that from one of Mandy's setups?"

"Actually, no. I married my secretary."

Livi laughed. "A relationship you could *combine* with work?"

He laughed, too. "At first, I guess. Mostly it was a relationship that got scheduled in when I wasn't really looking."

"How does that happen?"

"Elly was my first secretary when CT Software took off. And, don't get me wrong, she was cute and smart and I was aware of it—I'm not blind. But mostly she was just around. If I worked, she worked. I didn't ask that of her, but she said that was her job. And it was nice having her there whenever I needed something—dinner ordered in at eleven at night, paperwork when I remembered it at four in the morning. I thought it was just loyalty, but—"

"It was a way to spend time with you." Sort of what Livi was doing, sitting in that courtyard with him as the clock ticked toward midnight.

"Right. Things got more and more chummy and then flirty. Elly started to make comments about how I owed her a night on the town for all the nights she'd worked, and she just sort of eventually scheduled herself in."

"Because who better to know when you *would* have time to get away from work."

"Yep."

"And by the time you got to paying her back for all those long work nights, you must have been fairly close. *From* all of those long work nights."

"Also yep. We were married the year after Greta was born."

It didn't sound very romantic, but Livi didn't say that. "So, you got married eight years ago? Did Elly stay your secretary?"

"For about three years. But then we bought some land to build a house on and she decided she wanted to do everything herself so the place would be exactly right. She thought that should be her full-time job. And it wasn't as if we needed the money, so she quit."

"While you kept on working the way you had?"

"Uh...yeah," he admitted reluctantly. "But for a while she didn't complain *too* much."

"She knew better than anyone how you were about your job."

"Right. And she was swamped herself with designing the house and overseeing the building and then decorating it."

"And did you have a new secretary?" Livi asked leadingly, hoping this story didn't end with him having an affair. She wanted to think he wasn't that kind of man.

"I did. The same one I have now. Rose, who's old enough to be my mother, is devoted to her husband and works strictly from nine to five. But along the way I also gained an assistant..." Callan finished that in an ominous tone. "A man named Trent Baxter, because Elly didn't want it to be a woman."

That wasn't difficult to understand. Especially not for Livi as she sat there watching him and thinking that she couldn't imagine any woman not being a little awestruck by those good looks.

"How long was your wife occupied with building and decorating the new house?" she asked.

"Altogether? Almost three years. We moved in on our sixth anniversary—a day I remember too well, because on top of the move and the anniversary, we had a world-class fight."

"Seems like you should have been celebrating."

Looking embarrassed, he admitted, "I was at work for most of that day and it was my assistant filling in for me, overseeing the move. During the fight Elly said that I didn't have a mistress on the side, I had a wife on the side, and she called my assistant her 'proxy husband.'"

Livi flinched for him. "And how exactly was he your proxy?"

"Turned out, in all ways," Callan said under his breath. Then, more openly, he went on. "Besides being there for the move that day, Trent had taken on the job of buying my gifts for Elly, for birthdays and Christmas and all anniversaries and holidays and special occasions. Actually, too many times I didn't even give them to her— Trent ended up delivering them while I stayed working."

"Which you do a lot."

He nodded. "Trent took my place at social functions so Elly didn't have to go alone. I even sent him with medicine and chicken soup when she got sick, and to give her a lift when she had car trouble."

Livi could tell that he knew those were mistakes. "Did

you stop having your assistant be your proxy after the fight?"

"I'd like to say yes…"

"But you can't."

Apparently he couldn't. Instead he said, "Then Elly got pregnant unexpectedly, a little over a year ago."

His tone was more ominous still.

"I was happier about it than I expected to be," he said sadly.

"You didn't want kids before that?"

"I wasn't against the idea. But I was busy and…" He paused. "I know this will sound lazy or selfish or something, but it seemed like a wife was enough to keep up with."

"Even though it was really your assistant who was keeping up with her?"

"Yeah," he admitted ruefully. "But once I thought there was going to be a kid, I thought, okay, great, we'll have a family. Maybe we'll be like Mandy and J.J., after all. And I actually started to get kind of excited about it."

"So you didn't think your marriage was like your friends' marriage without kids?"

"It wasn't," he said categorically. "Not that I didn't love Elly. I did. And even though she sort of manipulated us into a relationship, I like to think that she loved me, too, that that's *why* she scheduled herself into my life. But did we have what Mandy and J.J. had? I can't explain why, but…we didn't. There was just something…I don't know…more superficial about the way we were together. I thought maybe it was just because Mandy and J.J. had history—hell, they had history even before they started dating. I thought maybe Elly and I just needed to put in more years together…"

"And that a baby would bring you closer?"

He shrugged. "I guessed that if we had a family, we'd seem more like a family—if that makes any sense. Coming from what I came from, it wasn't like I had a role model for being a husband and father. Yes, I lived with the Tellers for a year, but John Sr. never opened up to me, and there's only so much you can pick up by watching. I understood Mandy and J.J.'s relationship better, and what they had was great. I thought getting married would give me the same thing. But once I was in it, it didn't. Only I couldn't tell you what was lacking. Just that something was."

"And you think it was all you?" Livi guessed.

"I think I dropped the ball big-time and that if I had handled things differently, Elly would never have done what she did."

"Which was what?" Livi asked, admiring that he took responsibility for his own actions, but still wanting to know what part his wife had played.

"About six months into the pregnancy I got home one night to find Trent there waiting for me *with* Elly. So they could tell me together that they were pretty sure the baby was his and they wanted to get married. That *they* wanted to be a family."

Hearing the note of lingering shock in Callan's voice, Livi felt her heart go out to him. "Ouch," she said.

"Yeah. Believe it or not, it hit me hard. I never saw it coming—which I suppose makes me about the most oblivious person on earth after she'd already told me he was her 'proxy husband.'"

"And *was* the baby his?" Livi asked carefully.

"Yes—DNA tests proved it."

"A second punch," she sympathized.

"The whole thing was a jolt," Callan agreed with some sadness in his voice. "And, yes, it was rotten of Elly and Trent to hook up behind my back. But I'd handed them the opportunity on a platter—I neglected Elly. I neglected the relationship. I sent someone else in to do what I should have been doing."

He really was determined to take the blame. Livi could see that nothing she said would change his mind, so she opted for a different take.

"Okay, but now you have a chance to mend your wanton ways," she pointed out with some levity, trying to find something positive that might help with his current situation.

He smiled at her. "Was this a roundabout way of getting me to admit that I need to make it home for dinner every night?"

"Actually, I believe I sort of started out saying that," Livi stated.

"So I'm a slow learner, too?" he joked.

"Apparently not when it comes to computers, but maybe a little when it comes to people..."

"Okay, no denying it. If I promise to try harder would that make you feel better?"

"It would."

He smiled again and bowed slightly "Okay. I will try harder to remember there are people at home waiting for me, and to get there at regular intervals."

Livi laughed. "Well, it takes a little more than that, but that's a beginning, anyway."

"Lesson one. But you'd better leave it at that for now. You don't want to overwhelm a slow learner with too much at once."

"True. I think, seeing what I'm working with, patience is probably what it takes," she agreed, giving him a hard time.

He seemed to enjoy their back-and-forth, though, because the tension visible in his striking features when he'd been talking about his past was now gone. It was replaced by a little sparkle in those dark eyes that was not coming from the fire.

"Are you going to be around for any of the dinners I'm supposed to make sure I come home to?" he asked, with something else in his voice. Something enticing.

"I guess if I'm invited I might be," she said, more flirtatiously than she intended.

"How about I give you a blanket invitation here and now?"

"Forgetting that I'm a Camden and you aren't sure I should be around at all?" she challenged.

He grinned full-out then, drawing crinkles at the corners of his eyes. "Oh, yeah, I did forget about that. Again."

Maybe because he was looking into her eyes the same way he had two months ago in Hawaii, when they'd been just Livi and Callan.

And there on that comfy chair under the stars, bathed in the golden glow of the fire burning nearby, it felt as if they were again.

Callan's hand came from the back of the chair to her nape, so softly she barely felt it.

His eyes were still searching hers. And maybe it was due to the fact that it was so late and she was weary, or maybe it was being outdoors with him again, in the night air, but Livi didn't fight the feeling that took them back two months.

Instead, when he closed the distance between them,

she didn't draw away. She stayed where she was, letting him kiss her.

Not on the forehead tonight, however.

No, tonight he kissed her on the mouth, his lips warm and talented.

And without thinking about it, she found herself kissing him back, basking in sweetness that had a titillating bit of sensuality to it.

Then it was over and Callan was the one to draw away, taking a deep breath. "Yeah, just plain Livi tonight," he mused. "Without being plain at all… Could *you* fix *that*?" he teased.

Coming to her senses, Livi still couldn't help smiling at him. "You want me to wear a bag over my head?"

He grinned yet again. "No, I'd miss the sight of you. Even if it would make things easier on me."

She had to admit that it was nice to receive a little flattery. But she knew better than to let it go too far, so she took her own turn at a deep breath and stood up.

"It's late," she said. "And do you remember that tomorrow Greta is supposed to visit her new school?"

She could tell he hadn't. But he didn't own up to it. Instead he covered, saying, "I do seem to recall something about that. Even though it's Saturday, there's some kind of event, so the school will be open and the principal will be there. He'll have some free time on his hands and thought that would be a good opportunity to give her the tour."

"Right."

"And let me guess—Greta wants you there?" Callan said.

"But you need to be there, too," Livi warned.

He laughed, standing along with her and picking up

the bakery box with the remainder of the doughnuts. "You don't trust me to know that without prompting?" he challenged, as they headed back inside.

"After your disappearing act the last couple of days?"

"Okay, good point. Yes, I will be there, too."

Livi bypassed the elevator to the underground parking, explaining as she headed to the front entrance of the building, "Someone here was having a big party tonight and the visitor parking was reserved, so I'm out at the curb."

Callan set the doughnut box on the counter in the lobby and said to the uniformed security guard, "Help yourself," as he followed Livi.

"What time is Greta supposed to be there tomorrow?" he asked as they headed for the street.

Livi told him, thinking more about that kiss they'd just shared and wondering if she was in store for another when they reached her car.

But once they got there and she'd unlocked it, he opened the door wide and held it for her to get in. Which she did, to avoid a second kiss that she told herself shouldn't happen, anyway.

Even if she was wishing it would...

"I'll have to go into my office tomorrow before the school thing," Callan said as she started her engine. "So if I'm a little late getting back here, just wait for me, okay?"

Livi nodded. Then he closed her door, tapped the roof over her head as if to signal her to go and stepped back.

Something compelled her to look at him one more time, waving as if that was the purpose of the glance.

But in truth she just wanted one last glimpse of him, to cement in her mind that while he was not Patrick, it seemed possible that Callan could be starting to take up a small place in her thoughts.

A small place that was all his own…

Chapter Seven

"Pregnant?"

"Livi…"

"How did that happen?"

"The usual way," Livi answered Lindie's last question, suffering the embarrassment of having to admit it.

Lindie and Jani had dropped in on Saturday morning. It was unusual for any of them not to see or hear from each other for a week at a time. But because Livi had taken the week off to travel to Northbridge, and since then had been so enmeshed in her own problems, on top of what she was doing with Greta Teller, she hadn't done more than text everyone that she was back. So Lindie and Jani had taken it upon themselves to check in with her.

Right in the middle of her daily bout of morning sickness.

And because they were alarmed to find her so nauseous again—or still—they'd wanted to take her to the nearest urgent care. Of course, Livi couldn't let that happen. And she'd felt too bad to keep up the facade any longer. Besides, she was well aware that she was going to have to tell her family eventually—sooner rather than later. It might as well be now.

So she'd told her sister and her cousin. Since they were also her best friends, it was where she would have started, anyway.

Their first response, after outright shock, was to hug her, tell her how happy they were with the prospect of a baby, then make her comfortable on her large, overstuffed white sofa with pillows and a blanket. They also made her weak, decaffeinated tea and brought her soda crackers.

Once all that was done, Jani and Lindie sat in front of her on the large oak coffee table and settled in to talk.

"Have you been seeing someone and keeping it quiet?" her sister asked.

"No."

"Then who? How? When?" Lindie demanded gently.

"It's complicated…" Livi said, before she explained the whole thing, including that the man in Hawaii had turned out to be Callan Tierney—Greta's guardian.

"Fantastic!" her sister exclaimed, when she was finished.

"It is?" a confused Livi muttered.

"It is," Jani confirmed, apparently on the same wavelength with Lindie. "It's such a relief!"

"Did you guys hear me right? I don't have Patrick, I'm pregnant, the father is someone I had a one-night stand with in Hawaii and—"

"It's been four years since we lost Patrick," Lindie

said, cutting her off. "We all loved Patrick, Livi. We all miss him and will never forget him. But we've been so afraid that you were just going to let your life be over, too."

"We couldn't stand it," Jani added bluntly. "Worrying that you would go on all by yourself forever, without anyone but us. This is fate telling you no, and thank God for that!"

"Or thank GiGi," Lindie proposed. "Sometimes I think she's psychic or has magic powers or something. We all keep ending up with someone we come into contact with through these little projects of hers."

"I'm not *ending up* with Callan Tierney," Livi insisted. "I'm not even sure I'm going to tell him that the baby is his."

"Why would you not tell him?" her sister asked.

"We aren't involved with each other…like that," she said, pushing the memory of the kiss in the courtyard the night before out of her mind.

Which was not an easy thing to do when she'd been awake half the night thinking about it.

Okay, and reliving it, too.

And craving more of it. More of a lot of things she had no business craving. Or even thinking about.

"We've put Hawaii behind us," she insisted, dodging her own train of thought. "I'm writing it off to tropical fever or something. Something that caused an insane, irrational act that we've agreed to forget."

"How are you going to forget how you got this baby?" Jani reasoned. "Especially when the daddy is the guardian of this little girl you've taken under your wing? Your paths will keep crossing—what do you think he'll say when he sees you getting bigger and bigger?"

"I can always say that I had artificial insemination. Right after Hawaii. I know enough about that from when you were considering it, Jani, before you met Gideon."

"This Callan guy is king of the software business. You think he isn't bright enough to put two and two together and come up with four?" her sister said facetiously.

Livi rolled her eyes. "Of course he's *bright*, but I don't think he'll *want* to put two and two together and come up with four. I think he might be relieved with a lie that gets him off the hook on this."

Or would he? He *had* told her last night that he'd liked the idea of having a family when his wife had turned up pregnant.

But that was before he'd lost his friends, before he'd had to take over raising Greta and caring for the Tellers. Now he *did* have a family—maybe not in the traditional way, but he did—and he wasn't doing all that well with any of them. He also wasn't particularly thrilled with the situation and the demands it made on him. He was clearly uncomfortable in the role of dad, of family man. And none of it spoke in favor of adding more to his roster.

"You think he'd rather *not* know he's going to be a father?" Lindie reiterated. "If so, then he's a jerk—because I think any man who wouldn't want to know he'd fathered a baby, who would be happy to be *let off the hook* rather than have a relationship with his own child, is a jerk. At the very least."

Livi shook her head. "He's not," she said firmly. "But he *is* obsessed with his work. And he grew up hard and doesn't really relate well to a lot of people because of it. He has no concept of what it is to have a family. And he's uncomfortable with it and already juggling more than he may be able to handle. He's trying, and I think he genuinely wants to meet the obligations, but I'm not sure he can. And I'm really not sure I should pile on more. Or that I want to."

"You aren't going to try to think of this baby as Patrick's, are you?" Jani said fearfully.

Actually, it was slightly unnerving how much Patrick seemed to be fading from her thoughts, Livi realized. Not that she was forgetting him. It was just that he was somehow receding into a compartment that was separate from the present. She hadn't realized how much she'd been living in the past until the pregnancy had forced her to focus on the here and now.

But regardless of what was causing her to begin to slide Patrick off center stage, she knew it was probably for the best.

So she could honestly answer her cousin's question by saying, "No, I'm not. That would be crazy. I'm trying to think of it as *mine* and maybe mine alone."

"Don't you like this guy?" Lindie asked. "Is he just really, really gorgeous, with an irresistible body, so you let go for once, but it was only physical?"

Even her sister's general description brought the image of Callan to mind in all his glory. Yes, he was definitely gorgeous. But it wasn't only the way he looked. There was more to it. Like there had been in Hawaii, when she'd felt comfortable with him. He'd been funny, charming. Easy to talk to. And there had been a palpable chemistry between them that she'd never felt with another man. Not even Patrick.

But Livi couldn't find the words to explain any of

that, so she said, "I had a *lot* to drink, don't forget. But he is attractive."

"You're just not attracted to him when you're sober?"

"It isn't that, either."

"So you *are* attracted to him, drunk or sober," Lindie concluded.

She and Jani exchanged a knowing smile. Apparently both were satisfied with that information because they went back to their earlier position.

"Don't you think that it's the responsible thing to do— tell him he's going to be a father?" Lindie said.

"Isn't my biggest responsibility now to the baby?" Livi countered. "This guy is already on overload. He's a self-proclaimed neglector of relationships. Is it really what's best for him or me or the baby to push him into another relationship he's not equipped to handle? Wouldn't I just be setting up the baby for hurt when Callan neglects him or her, too?"

She was thinking out loud, not making any kind of decision yet, but she could tell that she'd made some valid points, because neither her sister nor her cousin said anything for a moment.

Then Lindie said, "I vote that you tell him."

"Me, too," Jani added.

But Livi thought that they were both picturing some kind of fairy tale—her telling Callan, Callan immediately dropping to one knee to propose and everyone living-happily-ever-after. And Livi couldn't picture that herself. She didn't even want to.

"Callan isn't Patrick," she warned them. "Patrick was all about our marriage and the family we wanted to build. Whenever I needed him, he was there for me, one hundred percent. He wouldn't have ever done what Callan did with his ex-wife—pushing off anything to do with her onto some paid assistant. Callan had the guy stand in as a proxy for him so often, his wife ended up leaving him for the assistant."

"He delegated being a husband?" Jani asked.

"He did. And now he's delegating taking care of the older couple to the wife's nurse, and I was just on my own with Greta for the last two days because he was nowhere around."

"Yeah, that's not good..." Lindie admitted.

"But he's new to all this," Jani reminded them, though clearly some of her enthusiasm had waned.

"Sure," Livi agreed. "But he didn't figure out how to be present as a husband, even though he was married for eight years. And even if he gets the hang of looking after Greta and the Tellers, how good will he be at it? And how far can I expect him to be stretched?"

Neither woman had any answers to those questions and their expressions conceded the possibility that she might be right.

"Well, whatever way you handle this, we're behind you," Lindie said.

"All the way," Jani confirmed. Then, with a beaming smile, she said, "And we'll have another *baby*!"

"And if you end up doing it on your own, we'll be there for you every step of the way—you know that."

Livi *had* known that. But it was still a huge relief to hear for herself that they weren't judging what she'd done, that they would rally round her and that the consequences—her baby—would be as welcome as if it *was* hers and Patrick's.

But relieved or not on that count, she found it didn't change the situation she was in.

And she had no idea what to do about Callan.

The visit from her sister and cousin slowed Livi down and she ended up texting Callan to tell him that she would meet him and Greta at the private school later that day. When they arrived, kids and parents were bustling around, decorating and setting up for what they learned was to be a school sleepover that night.

During the principal's tour and basic orientation for Greta, he introduced her to several little girls who would be her classmates.

Livi was glad to see that the other nine-year-olds greeted Greta warmly. They loved her long blond hair, telling her that she looked just like an animated character they all adored.

Greta was not at all shy and responded without reservation, making what appeared to be fast friends with two of the girls. She even begged to be allowed to attend the sleepover that night when they asked her to.

Callan, appearing awkward and uncomfortable, seemed perplexed by the request and looked to Livi.

She laughed and said, "I think if she wants to go, you can probably let her. They said the school would be locked up tight, and parents will be here to supervise, so it seems safe. And someone can always call you to come and pick her up in the middle of the night if it doesn't work out."

"Can I? Can I? *Please*…" Greta begged, with beseeching doe eyes thrown in for good measure.

"Well, yeah, I guess…" Callan said uncertainly.

One of the other little girls ran to a woman helping

set up and then ran back with a sheet of paper. "This is what she'll need," the other girl announced helpfully.

Callan took the paper, staring at it and frowning.

Livi peered at the list from beside him and asked Greta if she had a sleeping bag. When she said no, Livi suggested they finish the tour, do some shopping and then stop at home for her to pack, making it back for the six o'clock lockdown.

"Yes! Yes! Yes!" Greta exclaimed, and Callan, still seeming out of his element, agreed.

"Is there really a chance that she'll call me to pick her up in the middle of the night?" Callan asked Livi after they'd walked Greta into the school again—this time for her to spend the night there.

Livi laughed. "Anything is possible. With the ten of us there were plenty of middle-of-the-night trips to pick up one or the other of us from sleepovers because we got sick or scared or couldn't sleep or whatever. That's part of being a parent."

"But for now I have the night off…" he said, as if he'd just realized that on the way to Livi's car.

Because she'd met Callan and Greta at the school, Livi had driven, too. They'd left her sedan in the school parking lot to shop and get Greta's things, but now Livi headed for it.

"You do still have the Tellers at your place," she reminded him.

"Yeah, but they already thought that Greta and I wouldn't be there for dinner. I was going to see if I could take the two of you to eat and then find an arcade, or maybe go to that fright-night thing that's running all month at the amusement park."

"Really? You planned a kid thing?"

"I did," he said, as if he was proud of himself for it. "And since I told the Tellers not to expect us tonight, they decided to have a marathon of some crime show they like. So how about I treat you to dinner—to say thanks for all you did for Greta this last week, and for coming today?"

"But no arcade or fright-night?" she joked, as if she was disappointed.

"Well, we *could* do either one of those. But it seems like a nice dinner says thank-you better..."

A thank-you dinner, not a date.

Once Livi convinced herself that that distinction existed, she considered the invitation. It didn't take long.

"I don't have any other plans," she said. "But nothing fancy." Because fancy would seem like a date.

"Sushi?"

The obstetrician had said no raw fish.

"I like sushi, but I'm not in the mood..."

"There's a good Mexican food place in LoDo?"

Not living far from there, Livi was familiar with the lower downtown historic district referred to as LoDo. "I'm a fan of Mexican food."

"Then Tamayo it is. Why don't I follow you to your place to leave your car?"

Callan was in tan slacks and a red-and-cream-colored sport shirt that were nice enough for the restaurant. Indian summer temperatures had allowed for black pants and a lightweight white sweater set for Livi—and she knew that was dressy enough for that particular restaurant, too. Which meant she didn't need to change, either, and could have offered to just meet him there.

But the thought of not fighting traffic or parking was appealing, and she ended up agreeing to his suggestion.

It was nearly seven by the time they got to the restaurant. It was packed, but the hostess recognized Callan and they were seated at a secluded corner table right away.

Livi refused wine or any other liquor—again on obstetrician's orders—and insisted sparkling water was all she wanted, so Callan didn't drink, either. Then they studied the menu, made their choices and were left to share guacamole and tortilla chips.

"You must come here a lot for the hostess to know you," Livi said then.

"I do. But I also went out with her—twice, I think."

Livi couldn't help taking a second look at the other woman. She was taller than Livi, model-skinny, with coal-black hair, pale skin and dramatic makeup. Pretty but severe.

And as with Kinsey, Livi didn't like the idea of Callan with someone else, even though she knew it shouldn't matter to her.

"She doesn't seem to have any hard feelings," she observed.

"She turned me down for what would have been the third date. Or maybe the fourth, I'm not really sure. It was right after my divorce, but there were weeks in between our dates—"

"Because you were working," Livi guessed.

"Yep. And even those dates never happened when they were supposed to. They were rescheduled a couple times each because I got busy. So the last time I had my secretary call her—"

"Your secretary makes your dates for you?"

"She didn't make the first one—that happened one night when I came in here late and Dray just sort of joined me."

"So, like your ex-wife who scheduled herself into your free time, this one did the pursuing, too?"

"There wasn't much pursuit. I think she was just bored and I was alone and sitting at the table nearest to the hostess station, so she struck up a conversation and it went from there. But it didn't go very far. When my secretary called her again, she said no. There had been too much time between dates and she'd met someone else."

And he didn't seem to care about that. Which made Livi feel better on the one hand. But on the other hand, it was another relationship—however brief—that he'd let fizzle through neglect, and she couldn't help noting that.

"Greta surprised me today," Callan said then. "I thought she'd be afraid or worried about starting a new school, so she'd hang back. But she jumped right in, didn't she?"

"She did. But she's outgoing and that's good for her. Believe me. I was just the opposite and it was miserable."

"You were shy and withdrawn?" he asked, sounding surprised.

Which of course he would be, she realized. Not only because of Hawaii, but because she did feel comfortable enough with him for her shy side not to show.

"I was *horribly* shy and withdrawn as a kid," she said, omitting how often that was still the case. "When I was Greta's age, if I'd had to change schools, I would have been a mess. I wouldn't have even been able to think of something to say to those two girls Greta made instant friends with, and I would *not* have had the courage to go to that sleepover tonight. I was a mouse."

"No kidding?"

"No kidding. In fact, that's what some mean kids used

to call me—Mouse—because I was so timid. I was actually miserable in school until the sixth grade."

"What happened in the sixth grade?" Callan asked.

He seemed genuinely interested. The way he always did when they were together. His attentiveness didn't seem in keeping with someone who often disregarded relationships.

But in spite of seeing that, appreciating it, she had a bigger issue on her mind—telling him about Patrick.

There wasn't a reason not to, though. So she said, "In sixth grade, I met my husband."

Callan laughed. "Was it some kind of arranged thing? A joining of two powerful families through the marriage of their kids?"

Their tortilla soups arrived and after the waiter had left again, Livi said, "No, Patrick just moved here from North Carolina with his family and joined the class."

"And changed your world?" Callan said, still with some doubt in his voice.

"Kind of. I'd been in school with the same kids since preschool—a private school that was also near GiGi, so that didn't change when we went to live with her. My siblings and my cousins were my only friends, and everyone else in school either overlooked me altogether because I was so quiet, or teased me unmercifully. Then Patrick came in—"

"That's your husband's name—Patrick?"

"It was."

Callan paused in eating his soup and looked at her. "It *was* his name? He changed it? I mean, I've been assuming you're divorced..."

Livi shook her head. "I said I wasn't married anymore, I didn't say I was divorced. Patrick passed away."

And while her voice cracked just slightly when she said that, for the first time she managed to get the words out without tearing up.

Callan's surprise showed in his expression. "I didn't think that... At our age you just automatically go to divorce. Car accident?"

Livi shook her head again. "Four years ago—a month after our fifth anniversary—Patrick was playing basketball with my brothers and cousins. And then he just dropped—died on the spot of an undiagnosed brain aneurysm."

Callan's eyebrows shot up. "Seriously?"

"Seriously."

She hadn't had to tell this story in a long while and was pleasantly surprised to discover herself able to do it less emotionally than she ever had before.

Whether because Callan was easy to talk to or because of that comfort level she'd realized she had with him, it was a relief not to have to relive the agony the way she had in the past.

Not that she didn't still feel the sadness, the underlying grief, but to be able to talk about it without breaking down was a big step for her.

"Geez, Livi, I'm sorry. That must have been a shock," Callan said gently.

"Oh, yeah," she answered with a small, mirthless laugh. "To say the least. We'd been together almost since the first day he walked into my sixth-grade classroom. There was never any sign that he wasn't healthy as a horse and—" she took a deep breath "—I never doubted that we'd be together forever, that we'd grow old together."

There was a moment of silence—some of it taken up by their waiter replenishing their water. Then Cal-

Ian backed the conversation up. "So Patrick came into your sixth-grade class and everything changed for you?"

"Patrick was..." She shook her head and chuckled briefly. "Even as a kid he was personable. He was a cutup who made everyone laugh. Everybody loved him. He fit in everywhere he went. I never met anyone who *didn't* like him—"

"And he liked the quiet little girl in the corner."

That was a nice way to put it. "He did. Don't ask me why he even noticed me, but he did."

"And tell me he beat up the mean kids who called you Mouse, so they left you alone."

That made her laugh again. "He defended me, but he was a little guy—shorter than I was in sixth grade and not tall or bulky even after puberty—so he didn't get into fights. He actually would just head off the mean teasing by joking around with the bullies. What he did for me was more along the lines of drawing me *out* of the corner by bolstering my confidence and getting me to participate. Eventually I lived down the nickname."

"He showed everyone that you were smart and funny and amazing yourself, even if you were hiding it?"

Was that what Callan thought of her?

It felt good to think he might.

"Patrick just helped bring me out of my shell and that changed things."

"So you married him—when? Seventh? Eighth grade?" Callan joked as his chipotle-rubbed pork chops and her carnitas were served.

"I might as well have."

"Come on... Really?" he said, as if he thought she had to be exaggerating.

"Really. Puppy love through sixth and into seventh

grade. After that, when our friends were starting to have boyfriends or girlfriends, we officially became that—a couple. And we were a couple to the end."

Callan's eyebrows rose again.

"I know, it sounds kind of weird," Livi said, seeing his astonishment. "But once we were together that was just *it* for us. It sounds corny, but we really were two halves that made a whole, and even though we discovered each other as kids, we both believed it was just meant to be."

"The soul-mate thing?" He sounded skeptical.

But Livi said definitively, "Yes. I felt it. Patrick felt it. He was my one-and-only, and I was his."

"And that's all she wrote? You were *together* from the sixth grade on? There wasn't even any on-again, off-again?"

"None. Through grade school and college."

"You went to the same one?"

"Oh, yeah, so we could stay together. There was never a question about that. We got married the week after we graduated, and Patrick went to law school at Denver University while I took my place at Camden Incorporated."

"He was a lawyer?"

"He passed the bar the first time," she said with pride.

Callan was looking at her as if seeing something he hadn't witnessed before. "So it was a real love story," he marveled.

"Kind of like your friendship with Greta's mom and dad. Or their relationship with each other."

He laughed. "I never thought of a friendship as a love story, but I guess I can see the similarities. But when it comes to Mandy and J.J., they didn't get together until after they'd both done the kind of dating around that everyone did. It wasn't love from the sixth grade on. And that two-halves-of-a-whole thing? That one-and-only stuff? I'm not sure even Mandy or J.J. thought of each other that way. I mean, they were great together, but…" He shook his head. "I don't know about *that*."

The waiter came to take their plates and Callan enticed Livi into sharing a dessert.

Once they were alone again, he said, "Since Mandy and J.J. died I've felt kind of like I've lost my safety net or something. But you…you must have felt like you lost a limb."

"I think I kind of felt like I lost all four," she said. "I don't remember much of the first year—I was just a zombie so it's a blur. And it's been a slow climb since then."

"But you're okay now?"

"I think I am. It's been a long road and grief still dances me around the room every once in a while, but that's pretty rare. All in all, I'm back to myself."

"And dating and…" He frowned as something seemed to occur to him. "Hawaii wasn't your first…*date*…since your husband?" he said, as if it couldn't possibly be true.

Their dessert came before she had to answer him.

It was a flourless brownie topped with chocolate ice cream and a layer of salted caramel, glazed with white chocolate before a blood-orange reduction was drizzled over it all. And remembering that he hadn't opted for a chocolate doughnut the night before, she appreciated that he'd recalled her love for chocolate and ordered with that in mind.

Livi took a spoonful from her side of the confection and oohed and aahed over it while he continued watching her.

She was afraid he was waiting to have his question

answered, and encouraged him to dig in, hoping to distract him.

It failed.

"Come on," he said. "Was Hawaii a first for you?"

"I thought we were forgetting about Hawaii?" she hedged, uncomfortable talking about it.

"So that's a yes—it was," he answered, as if he'd read it on her face.

"Patrick was a very tough act to follow," she said quietly.

And yet Callan had...

For some reason, that was the first time she'd attributed what had happened in Hawaii to him and not to the liquor or the setting or the anniversary insanity.

But she didn't want to think too much about that, so she didn't.

She merely said, "You don't go from what Patrick and I had, from what he was to me, and just dive in to...well, to just anything. I didn't know if I'd ever be able to... *date*. Then Hawaii—" she shrugged "—just happened."

So naturally...

Livi took refuge in her second bite of chocolate.

"I don't know whether to be honored or...not," Callan said, frowning again.

He finally tried their dessert. Livi had the impression that he was using it to buy himself a little time to think. To consider if he did or didn't like the position he'd now found himself in.

Then, as if he'd decided to put a positive spin on it, he said, "So I brought out a little something in you, too?"

Him and her anniversary and a lot of booze.

But now that she was adding him to the list, she couldn't

deny that—like Patrick—Callan *had* brought something out in her.

"I guess so," she admitted, more under her breath than not, because realizing it was slightly unnerving. Callan and Patrick were *not* alike. So why did she respond to Callan in some of the same ways? Especially when there was so much about him that didn't recommend him?

"So can I assume—considering Hawaii—that you at least aren't some long-suffering widow who's thrown herself on her late husband's pyre?" he asked then.

"I'm not exactly sure what I am these days."

Pregnant—that's what she was.

"Because who could compete with a guy like you lost," Callan guessed. "Let alone some stranger you just met on a beach. But you ended up in my hotel room anyway, and that doesn't fit."

He was perceptive. And right.

But at that moment she didn't like the sense that he could see into her head.

"I didn't think anyone could compete with Patrick, no," she said.

"Past tense? You've changed your mind?"

Sometimes it seemed it was changing on its own.

But she didn't want to admit that, so she only said, "I'm still in flux in some ways. I thought…" Livi shrugged again. "I just thought I'd settled in to the way things would be from here on."

"Being a widow? Alone? You didn't think you'd ever find anyone else or *be with* anyone else?"

"It just didn't seem…likely," she admitted.

"Ever?"

"I couldn't picture it ever happening, no. But Hawaii… confused things."

"Because you found out that you're still alive and well and kicking."

She shrugged once again, thinking—reluctantly—that in four years that *had* happened only with him. And that just made it more confusing.

Too confusing for her to want to keep exploring right then.

They'd finished their dessert and Callan had paid the check, so Livi pointed out that with a crowd of people still waiting for a table, they should probably go.

Their conversation seemed to have left Callan with a lot on his mind, too, because he was less talkative than usual as he drove his SUV back to her house. They chatted a little about Greta and if she would make it through the night at the sleepover, but not much else.

Then they reached Livi's two-story, white, Cape Cod style house.

Callan walked her to her door and along the way she fretted.

She was inclined to ask him in. But she was also worried about what it would be like if he accepted. How would she feel if she brought a man into the house she and Patrick had designed and built and lived in together?

But before she'd resolved her dilemma, Callan said, "I suppose I'd better get home. Even though Greta is gone for the night, I still have the Tellers there. And since I was in trouble last night for not going home..."

Livi seized that excuse and agreed that it was probably best for him to limit his time away.

Then she said, "My family has a big Sunday dinner every week at my grandmother's house. GiGi asked me to invite you and Greta and the Tellers tomorrow. It's a whole lot of Camdens, but there's always other people, too. And good food. GiGi thought it might be a way for the Tellers to get out a little, to meet some folks their own age. Kinsey is included in the invitation, so she could still look after Maeve, and there's plenty of room for the wheelchair. I just didn't know if there was any chance you might risk consorting with even more of us…"

And why did she sound—and feel—so hopeful that there was a chance?

"I think I can take the risk," Callan said facetiously. "But I'll have to run it by the troops. Can I text you when I know where everyone stands?"

Not an immediate acceptance, but not a no, either.

"Sure."

She should have said good-night then, but there she was, lingering, gazing up at him in the glow of her porch light, wondering why he had to be so great-looking with all those chiseled angles of his face and those dark eyes and that hair…

He was studying her just as intently when a small smile appeared. "So…" he said, his voice lower and more confidential. "I'll try not to let it go to my head."

"You'll try not to let *what* go to your head?"

"You know—I might not be *the* one-and-only, but I am the one-and-only guy in the last four years to wake up Sleeping Beauty. I mean, look at you—there have to be a lot of single guys lined up hoping for a shot with you."

"Not that I'm aware of."

"Because you were Sleeping Beauty and were focused on dealing with your own stuff. But trust me, they've been there waiting for a chance and you just haven't noticed."

It was nice that he thought so, but she didn't agree. Instead of arguing, though, she goaded, "You've decided you're one in a million, but you're trying not to let it go to your head."

His smile turned into a grin that wasn't even slightly humble. "Hey, don't take away the little bit of one-and-only status I have. I'm playing out of my league, up against the memory of the greatest guy who ever lived."

He said that as if it was a fact, without any sarcasm, and since it was the way Livi knew she'd portrayed Patrick, she didn't take offense.

She also didn't tell Callan that in some ways Patrick wasn't in *his* league...

She'd worn her hair loose, the way she usually did, and he raised a hand to the side of her face, smoothing back a strand. Then his hands ended up on her shoulders, squeezing firmly, comfortingly, consolingly. But there was more than that to the touch, too—a sensuality. Or maybe she was imagining things.

But she wasn't imagining how good it felt to have those big, capable hands on her.

"I'm sorry for the tragedies and losses that hurt you," Callan said in a quiet voice. "But I can't say I'm sorry that it landed us here..."

Here, where his big hands steadied her as he leaned forward and kissed her.

He pulled her to him once his mouth was on hers, wrapping her in his arms as his lips parted and the kiss deepened.

It was such a powerhouse of a kiss that it actually washed away all that they'd talked about tonight. And everything else that had brought them there, leaving Livi with her eyes closed and her mind adrift, lost to everything but the feel of his lips urging hers to part, too.

She was aware only of his arms around her, holding

her tight, bolstering her when that kiss weakened her knees. Of the intoxicating scent of his cologne. Of how very good he was at kissing—so good that she didn't think twice about welcoming his tongue when it came to greet hers. About accepting and reciprocating that added intimacy.

Her hands went from his chest around to his back, and that allowed him to bring her in closer still, holding her against him, showing her suddenly how sensitive her breasts were. And how nice it felt to have them burrowing into him.

For a while she even forgot that they were standing on her front porch, out in the open, under the spotlight of the lanterns on either side of her door where any of her neighbors could see. There was only his mouth on hers, his muscular arms holding her, their bodies pressed together as their tongues toyed with each other.

Until the sound of a car driving down her street made her remember with just enough of a jolt for Callan to register it.

Still, his tongue didn't bid hers a hasty farewell. Instead it was a reluctant one, retreating and letting that kiss become softer and sweeter before he brought it to a conclusion. Then returned to kiss her again. And again.

And even after that he didn't let go of her. He kept holding her while he looked down into her eyes and she looked up into his.

After another moment he took a long pull of air that raised his shoulders, and then dropped them with his exhale. Clearly, he wasn't happy accepting the fact that the night had to end. "Isn't there supposed to be some kind of appeal to having people to go home to?" he joked.

"There is," Livi confirmed, even though the last thing she wanted at that moment was for him to leave.

"So...I should do it."

"You should."

He kissed her again, a long, deep kiss that caused her to think about stepping into the shadows of her porch, where they wouldn't be so much on display and could keep kissing awhile longer.

But then he ended that kiss, too, and took his arms from around her. "I'll text you about tomorrow," he promised.

Livi nodded and opened her door. But even with one hand on the knob she didn't go in. She stood there and watched Callan return to his car, drinking in the sight of him, before she closed the door between them.

Then she stood in her entryway, looking around at the house she alone occupied, and imagining what it would have been like if Callan *had* come in.

But while she expected that image to have a negative impact on her, for it not to feel right, she discovered something entirely different.

She found she *could* picture Callan there.

And more than that, she was wishing he was...

Chapter Eight

"Oh. Hey. Morning," Callan said when he came out of his at-home office on Sunday for his second cup of coffee. He was surprised to find John Sr. sitting on one of the bar stools at the island counter in the kitchen.

"You up before me again?" the older man grumbled, as if it was a competition he resented losing.

"Work to do," Callan answered tersely, leaving out the part where he was having trouble sleeping because Livi was occupying his mind.

After that kiss on her porch last night he'd been even more stirred up and wide-awake and restless than every other night since they'd reconnected in Northbridge. Finally, he'd just given up the fight and decided to get something accomplished rather than go on trying to sleep, wrestling with thoughts he knew he shouldn't be having.

"Guess you didn't get all you got layin' 'round in bed," the older man concluded.

There *was* a scenario in which Callan would have liked to be lying around in bed. But it included Livi. Without Livi and alone there, thinking about her, wanting to repeat Hawaii so bad it was nearly driving him crazy, he found his bed was like a torture chamber these days.

But while that was something he would have said to J.J., it certainly wasn't something he would say to John Sr. So instead he asked, "How come you're up so early without cows to milk and animals to feed?"

"Habit. Don't even need an alarm clock anymore."

Callan nodded toward the mug on the counter in front of John Sr. "Got your coffee okay?"

"Yep."

"I just came out for my second."

The elderly man made no comment and Callan went around the island to the coffeemaker while silence hung in the air.

Instantly, Livi was on his mind again.

But this time he wasn't thinking about how shiny her hair was or how blue her eyes were. About how much he liked the sound of her voice, her laugh, how soft her skin was or how much he wanted to get his hands on her. He wasn't thinking that he had no business thinking any of that, given that he was fresh out of a marriage he'd tanked, and had his hands full with the Tellers and Greta. He wasn't even thinking that Livi was a Camden and he should be trying for distance from her rather than the opposite.

This time he was thinking about the things she'd said to him on Friday night. And he knew that if she saw what was going on between him and John Sr. at that moment, she'd blame Callan for dropping the ball, missing a chance to break some ice.

And he knew she would be right.

So once his coffee was ready, rather than taking it back to his office, he turned to drink it standing at the island facing John Sr.

Who scowled and stared at him through narrowed eyes as if he was up to something.

Callan ignored the suspicious glare. But seeing it and knowing the man, he also paused a moment to consider what he was going to say before he said it. Because he knew that if he didn't handle this conversation delicately he could aggravate him, injure that pride Livi had talked about and do more harm than good.

So Callan considered carefully before he said, "I'm thinking that I could use help with some things."

"That so?"

"It is. Greta needs to be taken to school in the mornings and picked up in the afternoons. And I'm guessing there will be supplies she'll have to have for projects that come up, and times she wants to go to friends' houses or after-school things and will need rides. She'll probably have to be taken to a doctor or the dentist now and then—all of it during my work hours. And there's Maeve—I know how she likes to cook and I'm looking forward to coming home to that when she gets well. But I also know she'll need trips to the grocery store and what not."

"There can be a lot of running around, that's for sure," John Sr. agreed.

"So I was wondering if you would, uh, consider taking care of stuff like that if we got you a car and I showed you around, got you familiar with streets and routes to everywhere?"

Even though it didn't seem possible, John Sr.'s eyes narrowed even more and bored through him assessingly.

Callan expected the worst. A tirade about how the elderly man didn't need anyone buying him a car and wasn't taking any charity. About how he didn't need to be shown how to drive anywhere as if he was a punk kid with a new driver's license. About how Callan was asking him to do his own job as guardian, because Callan was a lazy, no-good something or other.

But instead, after a moment, John Sr.'s bushy gray eyebrows arched a little and he said, "I could probably do that."

Feeling as if a door had opened a crack, Callan nudged it a bit wider. "I'm sure there's a branch around here of that lodge you used to go to in Northbridge—wheels would get you there, too. You might find yourself a poker game."

"Need to keep up my membership in the Cattlemen's Association, too," he said.

"Sure. I guess there are meetings and whatever. Maybe they could use a man like you during the Stock Show…"

"Happy to lend a hand," the elderly man said, in a way that didn't make it clear whether he was happy to lend a hand to Callan or the Cattlemen's Association.

Callan thought it was more likely the latter, but what *he* was happy about was that John Sr. was so willingly— in his own way—accepting Livi's idea of getting him driving again here.

"Think about what kind of car you'd like to have," Callan said then. "Something heavy and able to get you around even in the winter snow. I have a car guy we can go see…maybe tomorrow night?"

"Got nothin' else planned."

But the elderly man did seem to have a new attitude. He almost looked chipper. At least as chipper as Callan had ever seen him.

"Great," Callan said with some relief. "I figure we're all family now and whatever it takes to get things done, we'll get them done—together."

"Makes sense."

"Good then..." Callan was stumped for anything else to say. He'd already talked to the Tellers about Sunday dinner at the Camdens when he'd come home last night, and they wanted to go. Livi hadn't given him a game plan for more than talking to John Sr. about a car, so he was at a loss. And certainly John Sr. didn't seem to have any more to say.

So Callan decided to take his win and go. "I should probably get back to work."

The elderly man didn't speak. He merely raised his chin in acknowledgment.

Without another word between them, Callan took his coffee and headed to his office.

But he still counted what had just happened as a step forward. Maybe only a small one, but still a step.

And it was thanks to Livi.

Who was on his mind again by the time he closed his office door behind him.

"I don't know, Mandy," he said to the memory of his friend. "She might be a Camden, but she's great with Greta and your in-laws—not to mention she's doing me some good. So far I can't find much to fault her."

He knew what his friend would say if she were there to answer him—that the Camdens started out looking good and then pulled the rug out from under the people who trusted them when it suited them.

But the more he got to know Livi, the more he thought he might have to argue that with Mandy—even though she'd have argued back that his opinion was colored by the fact that he had the hots for Livi something fierce.

And that would be where he'd lose the argument.

Because he couldn't deny it.

But still, he knew he needed to find a way to curb what was going on in him when it came to the lovely Livi Camden.

He had enough to deal with trying to figure out how to be a surrogate dad to Greta and a surrogate son to Maeve, and even to John Sr.

And they had to come first.

Livi thought that Sunday dinner at her grandmother's house with Callan, Greta, the Tellers and Kinsey went well.

Greta had had a great time at her school sleepover and was full of stories of her new friends to share with Livi, before she went off to play with Livi's nephew Carter.

Kinsey mainly stayed by Maeve's side to look after her, but even in the course of that, the nurse still chatted a little with everyone and seemed to enjoy herself.

Maeve, John Sr., GiGi and GiGi's new husband, Jonah—who was also originally from Northbridge—reminisced about growing up in the small town. GiGi persuaded Maeve to join the book club she and Margaret belonged to, and even gave her a copy of the book being read currently so Maeve could catch up.

And John Sr. connected with Louie over talk of Louie's garden and yard, and what Louie preferred in a vehicle for getting around the city during the winter months.

For Livi, the evening was a mixed bag.

Jani and Lindie had promised they wouldn't tell the rest of their family about Livi's pregnancy. But Livi had no doubt that Jani had told her husband, Gideon, and that Lindie had told Sawyer, her fiancé. And with Callan also at the dinner, Livi worried that someone would make a slip, that the news might get out and Callan might hear it.

Running interference just in case, she stayed close to him throughout the evening as he met everyone and hit it off with her brothers and male cousins over the Broncos and football.

She told herself that maintaining her position by Callan's side while she suffered through the football talk really was purely a safety measure. But in all honesty… she didn't want to be anywhere else.

Especially when she discovered that being at Sunday dinner with someone for the first time in four years wasn't awkward or uncomfortable, the way she'd thought it would be.

Instead, she actually enjoyed being there with Callan and sort of being part of a twosome again—although she certainly didn't consider them a *couple*. And as much as she liked Sunday dinner ordinarily, having him there with her to share it all somehow made it even better.

But it was still a weight off her shoulders to walk out GiGi's front door, certain that her secret had been kept. And as nice as the evening was, she was glad when it was over.

Livi had driven Greta and Kinsey to the dinner so Maeve could have the backseat of Callan's SUV to herself to accommodate her broken leg. And when they returned to the condo, Greta wanted Livi's help choosing an outfit to wear for her first day of school, so she didn't merely drop off the nine-year-old and the nurse when she got them home. She went up to Callan's condo with everyone else.

Once she and Greta were in Greta's bedroom, not only did the little girl want advice on her clothes and shoes, she wanted to discuss hairstyles, too. And her backpack. And what to do at lunch. And she lamented that she didn't have pierced ears when *everyone* else did, and wanted Livi to draw earrings on her with a marker—an idea Livi nixed. To compensate, she lent the girl two of the beaded bracelets she was wearing.

Although it was clear that the sleepover had gone well and Greta was excited about starting school, Livi could see that she was also nervous. So even after all the fashion decisions had been made she stayed with Greta, urging her to put on her pajamas and brush her teeth. Then she read to her to get her mind off the day to come, not leaving her until Greta was dozing off.

Then Livi quietly slipped out of the room, closing the door behind her.

The condo was so quiet that she wondered if everyone had forgotten she was there and had gone to bed.

But when she got to the open-concept living space and kitchen, Callan was there. Waiting, it seemed, because he was standing at the bank of windows in the living room area, looking out over Denver.

She'd been so careful about not making any noise to disturb Greta that he didn't hear her coming. So for a moment Livi stopped and did what she'd wanted to do all night and hadn't out of fear that someone might notice—she just took in the sight of him. There, in the quiet of his condominium, with no one else around and him unaware she was doing it, she feasted a little, getting the front view of his reflection in the glass, along with the rear view, too. From the back she got to look at broad shoulders that tapered down to a narrow waist and a derriere that those pants loved.

There was no denying that the man was male-model gorgeous, with a body any designer would die to dress. And even though she tried not to, Livi couldn't help wishing once again that she hadn't been such a stickler about having the hotel room in Hawaii so dark that she hadn't had a real look at him in the buff...

He turned from the window and she went the rest of the way into the room, as if she hadn't paused to stare.

"That took a while," he observed, apparently none the wiser.

"We girls can't go out in just anything," she joked.

"The Tellers crashed—looks like we wore them out— and Kinsey left. But it isn't that late... Sit a minute?"

"Okay," she agreed, before she'd even had the time to ponder it, rationalize it, justify it. Following only the impulse to have some time alone with him.

"Wine?" he offered.

Under other circumstances, yes.

"No, thanks. I'm at my limit tonight for food and drink."

"Then just come and sit."

She did, going to the big leather sofa, where he joined her, both of them near the center, angled toward each other. Callan relaxed with an arm along the top of the cushions, an ankle resting atop the opposite knee.

"Was dinner too much for Maeve?" Livi asked as they settled in.

"I don't think so. They were both glad they went— they said so on the drive home. And they're looking forward to getting out again and doing stuff with people their own age—you were right about that. Maeve couldn't wait to dive into that book, and John Sr. offered to help Louie winterize the yard and garden. He's thrilled with the idea of getting his hands dirty."

"Once a farmer always a farmer?"

"I think so," Callan confirmed, before he changed the subject. "Louie and Margaret—they're the people who started out as staff and then helped raise you, right?"

"Right. They're my grandmother's best friends."

"And Jonah—he's her husband and he grew up in Northbridge, too?"

"He and GiGi were high school sweethearts who went their separate ways and then reconnected just recently here in Denver. They've only been married since June."

"Well, the Tellers said they felt at home with your grandmother and her husband, and with Margaret and Louie, too. So doing this tonight was a great idea. Thanks."

"I can't take the credit. It wasn't my idea…" And it wasn't something she would have suggested on her own, because she'd been worried about being there with a man who wasn't Patrick, and about someone spilling the beans about the baby. "It was GiGi who extended the invitation. I was just the messenger. But I'm glad it worked out." She paused and then said, "And what's this I overheard about John Sr. getting a car?"

Callan smiled, pleased with himself. "We talked early this morning. I used the same angle on him that you used on me."

"Angle?" Livi repeated, pretending to take offense at the word.

"You know, that stuff about how if John Sr. had wheels it would help me out?"

"That wasn't an angle," she insisted, even though it had been. "It was the truth."

"Yeah, but it was an angle, too. To make me see your point. But I *did* see your point and I thought it was a good approach to take to protect the old man's pride—also what you said needed to be done."

"Is this you giving me—a *Camden*—credit for something?" she challenged.

"It is. And also I'm giving you a hard time," he said, again pleased with himself.

"But you and John Sr. actually had a conversation?"

Callan nodded. "I think you could call it that. Enough to get the job done, anyway."

"You know it's only a start, though, right? I mean, you need to keep up a dialogue to actually *build* a relationship. One conversation doesn't do it."

"Yeah, yeah, yeah. But this *was* a beginning and I think I made a little headway—how about you give *me* some credit?"

Livi laughed. "Good job!" she praised, the way she might have praised a puppy in training.

But Callan didn't seem to care. He merely smiled, bowed his head as if humbly accepting an award and said, "Thank you."

She laughed at him.

He raised his head again and for some reason that simple movement caused her to hone in on his neck. Exposed to just below his Adam's apple, it was thick and strong, and from out of nowhere she suddenly thought that it was very sexy. And she had the oddest inclination to kiss it...

Shying away from her own wandering thoughts, she said, "What about you? Did you have a good time tonight?"

He looked very pointedly at her. "I did have a good time," he said, as if she was the reason for it.

"Did it convince you that we aren't evildoers and villains?"

He smiled again. "What would Sunday dinner with evildoers and villains be like? Surely they wouldn't want to give themselves away as evildoers and villains, would they?"

"You just think we were on our best behavior?"

"Well, it *was* Sunday dinner—how much evildoing and villainy would go on there?"

Livi rolled her eyes and shook her head. Obviously, he was feeling ornery tonight. But she didn't mind. She was enjoying it. Him. As usual...

"So if you still believe we're treacherous," she said then, "are you going to chaperone the book club and the yard winterizing to make sure Maeve and John Sr. are safe from Camden duplicity, too?"

Callan sighed dramatically. "Maybe I'll just have to hire bodyguards," he said, with a Cheshire cat smile that let her know he was kidding.

Even so, Livi reached across him to pinch his biceps.

"Hey!" he protested.

"Do you really still think we're horrible people you have to be careful of?" she demanded.

"The story of Mandy's dad is pretty compelling stuff," he reminded her.

"That you aren't going to ever let me live down?"

Callan smiled crookedly and a sparkle came into his dark eyes. "The jury is still out, but it's leaning in your favor. You might not want complete exoneration, though," he said enticingly. "I have to admit that to the old troublemaker in me, there's some appeal in flirting with danger."

"That's me, all right—pure danger," she said wryly.

"With your family background? You might not be *pure* danger, but there's an element there," he said, his voice slightly quieter, as if even a small element of it intrigued him.

Livi didn't think she'd ever before felt as if she was intriguing to anyone. Patrick and she had been close even before they'd reached puberty, so there was nothing unknown between them. And it pleased her that with Callan there was some mystery about her. It actually inspired her to be a little bolder. The way she had been in Hawaii.

"So I guess you'd better watch yourself," she warned.

His smile grew wicked. "I'd rather watch *you*," he muttered, just as he leaned forward to kiss her.

And deep down Livi recognized that this was really why she'd been so willing to come in tonight. Really why she'd stayed. Since the moment Callan had left her porch last night all she'd wanted was to kiss him again. And now she had her wish.

It was a simple kiss at first. Chaste and sweet—like on Friday night in the courtyard, except tonight he wasn't touching her at all.

But it stayed that way only for a moment before lips parted and tongues took to frolicking the way they had the previous evening. First with delirious happiness at meeting again, before their dance slowed to something more languorous, more mature and sumptuous and erotic.

Was this what Callan had been aiming for tonight, too? she wondered, somehow having the sense that it was.

He moved his left hand from the sofa cushion, sneaking under her hair to her nape. Then up to cradle her head as mouths opened more and that kiss dived to new depths.

The arm she'd pinched came around her, pulling her up against him—closer tonight. Close enough for her to register even more strongly how incredibly sensitive pregnancy had made her breasts.

Her nipples turned into knots within the confines of her lacy bra and it was as if they were demanding not to be neglected.

And suddenly Livi was nothing but a jumble of demands being made by a body that had taken over her brain, canceling every thought and leaving her a mass of sensations and needs and longings and cravings.

She couldn't get enough of Callan kissing her, of the feel of one of his hands in her hair, the other massaging her back.

Her own arms had gone around him and she couldn't get enough of the feel of his back beneath her palms, either. She wanted more, so she found the bottom of that sweater and finessed her way under it so flesh could meet flesh.

Every hill, every valley, every muscle and tendon of that oh-so-masculine and muscular back—she memorized it all with her hands. She couldn't press her fingers firmly enough into him, massaging and kneading, mimicking what she wanted him to be doing to her front.

Her front that ached with the driving need to feel his hands there as their mouths plundered each other, leaving her awash in a desire more intense than she could ever remember feeling.

Finally taking the hint, Callan dragged a palm to one of her breasts. Even through her blouse and bra, his cupping it sent a flash flood of even more longing through her, making her groan softly. After only a few caresses, he slipped his hand into the overlapping wrap blouse and down inside the cup of her bra.

Livi couldn't contain the gasp that came from her throat at that.

She hadn't found much to enjoy in pregnancy. So far, it had made her sick every morning, and tired and sluggish throughout the day. It had made her overly affected by simple smells and sometimes weepy when she least expected. But that was all before Callan's big hand formed the perfect mold for a breast that was so alive with sensation that she saw stars.

All on their own, her spine arched and her breasts expanded into his grip. And as he began to press firm fingers into her flesh, to knead and release, to tenderly pinch and twist her nipple and then let it nestle into his palm again, Livi felt the rise of even more demanding desires shouting to be satisfied.

But where?

They were at his place. They could go to his bedroom.

Like they'd gone to his hotel room in Hawaii...

And then what? Would they wake Greta or the Tellers? Would she cross paths with one of his housemates afterward? Would they somehow find out she was there, making love with Callan?

The thought quenched the desire in her just enough to clear her head.

She wanted him. More, Livi thought, than she had in Hawaii. More than she could remember wanting even Patrick.

But not here. Not worrying and sneaking around

Callan's new family. Not in any way that might leave her with another round of regrets and shame.

She yanked her head free of that kiss and covered his hand at her breast with her own. But despite intending to pull that away, too, she somehow ended up pressing it tighter to her.

Still she whispered, "We can't do this here."

"Like two teenage kids hoping not to get caught?" he said, as if he'd read her mind.

He kissed her again before she could answer, and Livi continued to hold his hand to her breast, wanting so badly not to let it go, not to end the contact.

But then he ended that kiss, too, and withdrew his hand from inside her blouse.

"I get it," he said with a resigned sigh. "But I gotta tell you it makes for a *really* big negative to having other people in my house..."

Livi was focused on trying to tame her own raging desires and didn't comment on that. Instead, after taking a deep breath to gain some control, she said, "I should go."

The look on Callan's handsome face told her how much he hated that idea, but he didn't say anything to stop her. He merely stood up and held out his hand for her to take.

She almost didn't want to, because touching him in any way at all seemed like an invitation back into what had been so difficult to end already.

But somehow her hand went to his.

As he walked her out of his condo, to the elevator and then through the parking garage, he kept her close to his side.

"Next Saturday night is a dinner-slash-silent-auction my company does for charity every year," he said as they approached her car. "My ex-wife used to plan it, but my new assistant and secretary have taken it over. I still have to attend, though, and I hate to go alone. Any chance that you'd keep me company? It's for a good cause—it goes to college scholarships for underprivileged kids, and we take the total raised by the auction and match it."

This definitely sounded like a date. After what had just happened—on top of what had happened in Hawaii—Livi's better judgment told her to say no.

But her hand was so snug in his and what had just happened had left her a little floaty—and she'd already exhausted all the willpower she had access to tonight when she'd first pulled away...

Livi heard herself say, "If it's for a good cause..." as if that mattered at the moment, when what she was really thinking was how much she didn't want him to let go of her, to send her on her way.

"Great," he said. "Now I can look forward to it."

They reached her car, and after she'd unlocked her door, he opened it.

But he still didn't release her hand. Instead he used it to swing her around into his arms, where he kissed her again so soundly that it left her slightly dazed.

"I'll get you the information about the auction," he said, his voice deep and clearly under the influence of the same emotions that were making her knees weak.

Livi nodded.

He took his arms from around her, and when he did, it was more disappointing than she'd anticipated. And her knees really were a little wobbly without him, so she got behind the wheel of her car, fighting against what everything in her was crying out for—to be back in his arms, kissing him...

"Drive safe," Callan commanded, before he closed her door.

She nodded, stealing one last glance at him, wondering how it was possible that she was feeling what she was and wanting what she was when he wasn't Patrick, and when there weren't any of the other factors or elements that had brought her to his hotel room that night in Hawaii.

Then Callan smiled at her in a way that made her think he was almost as confused by what was happening as she was, before he moved so she could back out of the parking spot.

But even as confused as she was, she still drove home thinking about how amazingly good it had felt to have his hands on her.

And how much she wanted to have them on her again...

Chapter Nine

After telling herself all week that she should, Livi did not cancel with Callan on Saturday night.

In hopes of getting some control over herself, she'd spent the week avoiding him. She'd seen Greta only in public places like the mall and the ice-cream shop, before delivering the little girl to the condo's front door and ducking out in a hurry.

But by Saturday Livi wanted to see Callan all the more and there was just no way she could give up that opportunity.

So she spent the entire day getting ready.

And thinking while she was waxed and manicured and pedicured. While she had her hair trimmed and styled so that it was curlier than she ordinarily wore it. While she had her eyebrows done. While she even had China—the makeup artist who was best friends with her brother Dylan's fiancée, Abby—do her makeup.

Thinking and thinking and thinking...

On Friday night Livi had gathered her entire family together to tell them she was pregnant.

Everyone had had the same reaction as Jani and Lindie: shock that quickly turned to support and vows to be there for her any time of the day or night.

But Livi had also been in line for some pressure from her cousin Beau and her other triplet, Lang.

They both had strong opinions about whether or not Livi should tell Callan she was pregnant. Lang hadn't known about his own son, Carter, until the boy was two, and it had shaken up his entire life.

Thanks to machinations by their great-grandfather H.J., Beau had been left in the dark about having gotten his teenage sweetheart pregnant, and learned about it only a few months ago, when the two of them had met again. The belated news had come as a terrible blow to him, compounded by the fact that the baby had been lost in a miscarriage that the mother had suffered alone.

Livi had made the same points against telling Callan that she'd made with Jani and Lindie. But her male cousin and her brother had been insistent.

"Do it anyway," Beau had commanded, discounting everything she'd said. "The longer you wait, the harder it'll be, and it has to be done."

Livi realized that her cousin was right about one thing—the longer she waited, the more difficult it was. Even now, she felt guilty over the fact that while it felt as if they were not only getting to know each other, but actually getting close, she was keeping this enormous secret from Callan. She was willing to be intimate with him in a way that she'd been with only one other man in her life, but she wasn't being honest with him.

But not even worrying and fretting and agonizing about that had gotten her any closer to a decision. Because whenever Livi tried to think about what she should say to Callan, her mind wandered instead to how much she wanted him.

She hadn't been able to eat, to sleep, to focus or concentrate on work, because no matter what she did, she kept finding herself remembering him kissing her, touching her, or making love to her once upon a time in Hawaii.

It was chemistry, she'd finally concluded. Chemistry at its most extreme. In Hawaii and again now. And that chemistry dominated everything else.

Maybe Livi just had to let nature run its course. To get wanting him out of her system before she would ever be able to think straight.

So no, she hadn't canceled with Callan for tonight. And she'd given herself a temporary pass on making her decision about telling him she was pregnant, too.

The only decision she'd made was to dedicate tonight to whatever it took to resolve their chemistry.

When her day of beautification was done late that afternoon, she went home to put on the dress she'd bought for the occasion—a little black, knee-length cocktail dress with a lace overlay on the V-neck bodice that topped a full faille skirt.

Sheer black, thigh-high hose, a pair of strappy three-inch-high heels and a small black satin clutch completed the outfit only minutes before her doorbell rang.

Anticipation of seeing Callan again erupted an almost overwhelming rush of excitement through her. But she forced herself to walk at a moderate speed to the door.

He looked so good that her first glimpse of him took her breath away.

He was wearing a black, slim-cut, shawl-collar tuxedo with a crisp white shirt, and rather than a bow tie, a solid black silk tie that matched the tuxedo to a T.

His hair was in its usual tidy disarray, his face was clean-shaven and he smelled of that cologne she liked so much. Livi wasn't sure whether he really did look even better than normal or if it was just that she was starving for the sight of him. But one way or another she was bowled over.

"Wow!" he said, after giving her the same kind of once-over she'd given him. "Aren't you...wow. I don't want to take you out and share you."

"You clean up pretty well yourself," she countered.

He didn't acknowledge that, continuing to stare at her for another moment before he jolted out of his reverie and said, "We should get going—they won't start anything until I get there."

Livi had her clutch bag in her hand and held it up. "I'm ready if you are."

Ready and too, too eager to be with him again.

But as the evening progressed Livi had her own regrets about the necessity of sharing Callan, because she had to do so much of it.

Although there was staff galore to run the event, as sponsor and host, he was in big demand by everyone attending the function. He couldn't be rude to the legion of guests who wanted to say hello and chat, who barely left them a moment for a few bites of food and who waylaid them every time they headed for the dance floor that they never managed to reach.

All through it Livi stood by his Callan's side and per-severed, chafing over not having him to herself.

It was eleven o'clock before the results of the auc-tion had been tallied and announcements were made by the emcee, along with instructions on how the winners could check out.

Livi won a bid on a mural painting service that she thought Greta would like to use to make her bedroom at Callan's condo more kid-like—having okayed it with him before placing the bid.

Callan won a limited-edition bottle of scotch, and once they'd paid and he had his scotch and Livi had the receipt and information about how to redeem her pur-chase, he asked if she wanted to stay or if they could begin their exit.

She voted for the latter, but it was still midnight be-fore they made it out the door and back into Callan's sleek silver sports car.

"Thanks for being my wingman—or is that wing-woman—tonight. It was nice not having to do all that on my own," he said as he headed for Livi's house.

"Sure."

"You're good at it, too—all the people and small talk…. I've never cared for that stuff."

"You and John Sr. have that in common," Livi ob-served. "But I couldn't tell that you don't like it—you hid it very well."

Callan cast her a mischievous smile. "All an act," he confided.

She watched him as he pulled off his tie, then unfas-tened the top button of his shirt and stretched his neck as if to get the kinks out. And she fought the inclination to reach over and rub those kinks out for him.

"I was hoping we might have a few minutes to ourselves—to dance or just to talk—and maybe I could make the event a little more fun for you," he said. "But there was no chance, was there? I'm sorry for that."

Me, too...

"It's okay. I'm not a newbie at things like this—we go to them or throw them ourselves all the time. I knew what I was in for," she assured him, keeping her thoughts to herself.

He gave her a sidelong glance. "And you came anyway...just for me?" he asked, wiggling his eyebrows comically.

Yes, for him. Because of him. But Livi wasn't going to tell him that, so she said, "For the cause."

He just grinned, as if he knew her real answer.

Then he said, "So where were you all week? I know you saw Greta almost every day, but you made yourself scarce otherwise."

"Busy week," she lied. "But I heard that you were home to have dinner with Greta and the Tellers every single night."

"Told you I'd make more of an effort, didn't I?"

"And you came through."

"You didn't think I would," he accused, as they reached her house.

"I hoped for the best," she said, just before he pulled into her driveway and turned off the engine.

He got out to come around to her side, and as he did, Livi took a deep breath.

Was she going to ask him in?

On the previous Saturday night, she'd wished she had. But it was a big step to actually invite that man into the home she'd shared with Patrick. Especially when she considered what could happen when she did.

Not that it *had* to…

She could stop it from getting to the bedroom if anything about that didn't feel right, she told herself.

And knowing that she had the option was enough to get her out of the car and to her house. Where Callan did accept her invitation.

"How was it—going home to a family, to dinner with everyone, every night?" she asked as she closed the door behind them and set her purse on a table nearby.

"I think things went pretty well," he answered, following her into the living room, where she kicked off her shoes.

As his hostess, she knew she should offer him something to drink, but she didn't want the wine issue she'd skirted around at the auction to come up again. She'd ordered only pomegranate juice with a twist of lime and explained it away by saying that she liked to keep her wits about her when there would be names to remember.

But now she wouldn't have that excuse, so she merely sat on the couch, tucking her legs under her.

If Callan noticed the lack of etiquette he didn't show it and instead made himself at home by removing his tuxedo jacket and tossing it across the back of an easy chair before joining her on the sofa.

He sat nearby, angled toward her, his elbow hooked atop the cushions behind them, relaxed but intimate.

And even though Patrick crossed Livi's mind, it was only in realizing that nothing about having Callan there like that alarmed her. She wasn't thinking that Callan was in Patrick's place. She was just somehow comfortable with the fact that she was there, like that, with Callan.

Who she was still drinking in the sight of…

"Did you and John Sr. talk over dinner or are the two of you still doing that thing you do—talking to Greta and Maeve and Kinsey and never really to each other?"

"We did a little better. Monday night we exchanged a few words about going car shopping, which we did on Tuesday. I got him an SUV that feels like a truck to him, he said. Then one night he said it ran well. Another night he told me he was picking up Louie so Louie could show him some shortcuts and easy routes to use around town. And after that I asked him how it went and he said fine."

Livi laughed. "Let me guess—none of that is a brief summary of longer conversations. They're the totality of the few words you said to each other before you both went back to not talking, or only talking to everyone else."

Callan laughed, too. "Well, yeah…" he admitted. "But John Sr. went all week without saying anything bad about me under his breath—that's something. And he even said it felt good to have a way to get out around here—I took that as a thank-you for the car. Oh, and Thursday night he told me he'd do some grocery shopping on Friday, and asked if I needed anything…"

"That's pretty big, actually," Livi commented.

"So I don't think we're doing too badly. We're not BFFs yet or anything, but we aren't at each other's throats, either."

She smiled at his BFF remark. She doubted that term had been in his vocabulary before taking in a nine-year-old girl. "And Greta has been talking your ear off?"

"I don't know how you know that, but yeah," he said, sounding somewhat worn-out by the little girl.

"That's the way she is with people she likes," Livi

explained. "It's great, though, that she's talking to you. That's how you build your relationship with her, too. You should enjoy it while it lasts, because in a few years she'll be a teenager and she'll clam up."

"How soon is that?" he asked hopefully, clearly teasing.

"And how about Maeve?" Livi asked. "Kinsey had her trying to stand on that leg when I brought Greta home yesterday."

"Yeah, Kinsey switched her over to a home health care service here. They sent a doctor to admit her and the new doc thought she could start doing that a little. Seemed to go okay. Kinsey's been great helping her through it, coming in even earlier, staying later."

Livi had a brief flash of that jealousy she'd felt thinking about Callan and the pretty nurse. But she reminded herself that there was nothing going on between them. Also, it was her own choice to make herself scarce this past week. Greta had tried to persuade her to stay for dinner every night and she'd declined, so if Callan had spent more time with the nurse than with her, it was Livi's own fault.

"So are we all caught up?" Callan asked then.

She laughed once more. "Why? Do you have something else you want to talk about?"

"You."

"Me? What's there to say about me?"

He straightened his arm along the back of the couch, catching a strand of her hair and letting it wind around his finger. "Now that I know more, there's something that's bothering me about Hawaii."

He paused, his frown making it clear that this was

troubling him. "Did I sort of take your virginity without knowing that's what I was doing?"

"My virginity? I was married, remember? You definitely didn't take my virginity."

"I don't know..." he mused, unconvinced. "It was a first—a couple of pretty big firsts, actually. The first time after you lost your husband. The first time ever with someone who *wasn't* Patrick. And I didn't know."

"Would it have changed anything if you had?" Livi asked.

He chuckled wryly. "Fair question. I don't know. I guess I would have been a lot more careful to make sure you knew what you were doing, and wouldn't hate yourself—and me—in the morning."

She smiled sheepishly. "I have to admit that there was some of that," she confessed.

"So I'm kind of worried about what it all means for you now. You were drinking in Hawaii, but since then I haven't seen you drink so much as a glass of wine. Did you swear off alcohol because of what it led to in Hawaii? Is that part of the 'keeping your wits about you' thing you said tonight?"

"No. After Hawaii it's probably not easy for you to believe, but I've never been a big drinker." Which was true.

"It isn't because you're afraid, and staying supersober to ward me off? I'm wondering if I've been pushing you, if I have a lot to apologize for—last Sunday night included. If maybe that's why you made yourself scarce this past week..."

Apparently he'd done a lot of thinking—and worrying—himself.

Livi shook her head firmly. "No, that's not true," she

said. "There's nothing for you to apologize for." Although she liked that he had enough conscience to be concerned.

"Yes, I was drinking in Hawaii," she said then. "And I'm not sure I would have done what we did if I hadn't been. But that isn't on you—it's on me. And last Sunday night…" She shook her head again and tried to repress the surge of desire at the memories.

But she wasn't sure how to finish that sentence now that she'd started it, and all she could come up with was, "It takes two."

"So you aren't looking at me and seeing a wolf in sheep's clothing who's been preying on you?"

Oh, she was looking at him all right. And seeing a hot hunk in well-tailored clothing. That she wanted to rip off him.

But she said, "No, I don't think you're a wolf in sheep's clothing. That's actually what you've been worried *I* am, isn't it?"

He laughed. "Yeah, I guess that does fit what I think Mandy would be worried about with you, doesn't it?" He paused again, then returned to what he'd been saying. "I just want to make sure that we're okay. That I can think back on Hawaii and not feel like some kind of slimebag who took advantage of you."

"Nothing about you makes me think for a minute that you're a slimebag," Livi said honestly. "I mean, I did, when I thought you'd just run out that night in Hawaii. But now I know what happened, and leaving the way you did is understandable. Anyone would have done the same thing."

"So is it okay if I do this?"

He kissed her, just a simple meeting of their mouths with gentle care. But soon his lips parted and drew hers along, and that kiss became potent enough to wipe her thoughts clean.

Then he stopped, and she said, "Oh, you're good at that…"

"Does that mean it's okay?"

She offered herself the option to say no. Knowing that he would accept that answer and that likely everything would halt between them—the times alone when they got to talk. The kissing. The touching. Everything. And they would become nothing but the passing acquaintances she kept telling herself they *should* be.

She could go back to just being Patrick's widow.

But in that moment, even in that house that had belonged to her and Patrick, even still loving Patrick and cherishing everything he'd been to her, Livi knew with sudden but absolute certainty that living in the past was no longer what she wanted.

But another night with Callan was.

And maybe if she allowed herself that, it *would* get it out of her system, so she could think more clearly about whether or not to tell him she was pregnant with his child.

"It is okay," she heard herself whisper, looking into those dark eyes of his. "I'm not really sure why it is, but it is."

He searched her face as if to read in her expression whether or not he could trust what she was saying.

Then he said, "I hope so. Because I don't think I've ever wanted anything as much as I want you, right now."

He brought his other hand to her cheek and guided her into a second kiss that was instantly more heated than the first, instantly more intimate. Lips parted, and tongues sought each other out with an all new fervor.

No more fiddling with her hair; Callan wrapped his arm around her instead. He pulled her closer while his kiss increased in power and passion, fueling every hunger and need she'd been fighting this past week. The kiss was so intense it wiped away all thoughts and left her awash in nothing but sensations and desires and excitement.

Her hands were in his hair, down his neck, across his broad shoulders and then splayed on his back, as she again imagined tearing off his clothes.

But now there was nothing to stop her.

So she brought her hands around to his front, where she began to unbutton his shirt, not pausing until she'd pulled the tails out of his tuxedo pants and had the whole thing laid open.

Then her palms traveled from impressively honed pectorals up and over his shoulders to push his shirt as far off as she could get it.

She felt him smile even as they kissed, and he let go of her so that she could take his shirt completely off.

When she'd done that, he reached around her to unzip her dress.

Livi was just as thrilled with the prospect of getting rid of her own clothes as she was with getting rid of his. But maybe not in her living room.

So before he got her zipper down too far she ended their kiss.

And Callan yanked his hands away and held them up and out to the side as if he was being arrested. "Changed your mind?"

She laughed. "Yes," she said out of pure orneriness, before she took one of those upraised hands and tugged him with her off the couch and to the stairs toward her bedroom.

"You're sure?" he asked, when they got there.

She was and she told him so, leaving him while she went to her nightstand and turned on the small lamp there so that a faint golden glow lit the room.

She'd wanted total darkness in Hawaii. She didn't want it tonight. And now that she could truly see Callan, shirtless in the lamplight, she realized what she'd missed.

And she had missed out, all right! Because it wasn't only his great hair and strikingly handsome face that were stare-worthy, so was his torso—sculpted and chiseled and buff.

When he bent over to take off his shoes and socks, she was hoping that his pants would be the next to go.

But all he did was unfasten his waistband, whetting her appetite, as he glanced around at the room she'd refurnished and redecorated a year ago to make it completely her own.

She didn't know if Callan was looking for ghosts, but that was the impression she had. He wouldn't find one, if he was. Packing away all Patrick's things had been one of the moving-on projects Jani and Lindie had talked her into. And although Livi kept several framed photographs of Patrick on her nightstand, she'd put them in the drawer earlier tonight when she'd been getting ready. Just in case this happened.

"Have *you* changed *your* mind?" she asked, when he continued scanning the room.

His espresso-colored eyes settled on her and he grinned. "Not on your life."

He closed the distance between them in three steps and pulled her to him with caveman force, claiming her mouth again in a kiss that was all primitive hunger while he found her zipper once more, wasting no time opening it.

He left her dress in place, though, only snaking his big hands inside, massaging her back and making her ever more pliable as his mouth plundered hers.

Her breasts had ached all week long for more of his touch, and the longer he denied them, the greater the ache became.

Livi raised her hands to his pecs and demonstrated what she wanted even as she reveled in the feel of him. She hadn't realized just how blurred and blunted by alcohol everything in Hawaii had been. Because now everything was sharper and clearer and so, so much better. So much more real. Now every sense, every awareness and response, every nerve ending seemed finely tuned and turned on.

Callan brought his hands up and over her shoulders, and down came her dress, to the beginning swell of her breasts.

But it was quite a swell. Her black lace demi-cup bra barely fit breasts that pregnancy had apparently increased a size.

He deserted her mouth to kiss the side of her neck, the tip of her shoulder and then those breasts where they spilled out of their confines.

He placed the lightest of kisses there, and still it felt so good that her breath caught in her throat.

And that was nothing compared to what followed.

He moved her dress down farther until it drifted to the floor around her ankles. And once it was gone he nuzzled one of the bra's cups below her breast and took that breast into his mouth.

Another breath caught, and as she sighed it out she heard herself moan, "Oh, you're good at that, too..." because, oh, he was! And coupled with the pregnancy benefit of heightened sensitivity that she'd discovered on Sunday night, it was almost enough to make her lose her mind. It was most certainly enough to give her the courage to reach for the zipper of his tuxedo pants, easing down those well-tailored trousers and the boxers he had on underneath.

He stepped free of them, ended the delights at her breast and scooped her up into his arms to swing her onto the bed, before returning to his slacks to extract a condom from his pocket.

But Livi barely noticed anything but him. Gloriously naked and magnificent and so clearly wanting her.

Then he came to the foot of the bed and with a devilish half smile began to slowly roll her thigh-high nylons off—first one, then the other—getting his own fill of studying her body before he crawled onto the mattress.

He again captured her mouth, ravishing it while his hand reached the breast that was still exposed above the bra's cup, tormenting her diamond-hard nipple for a while before he reached around and unfastened her bra, taking it off so both breasts were free.

His mouth went from hers to her breasts again, giving them both equal time while that big hand of his trailed down her stomach and dipped between her legs.

Oh. Things were more sensitive there, too. When he slipped a finger into her, Livi's back came up off the bed and a high-pitched little groan accompanied it.

She wasn't going to be able to contain herself. The pleasure was too keen already and building in her by the minute.

So she reached between *his* legs, encasing him, sliding from base to tip and back again, driving him as mad as he was driving her, bringing him to the same brink.

That was when he paused to make quick work of putting on the condom he didn't know they didn't need. Then he did what everything in her was screaming for—he repositioned himself over and above her and came into her in one lithe move.

Never had Livi felt quite what she did then, as he began to thrust slowly in and out, picking up speed as he went. She kept up, rising to meet him and then drawing just enough away to tempt him back again.

Her hands were again pressed flat to his back, her fingers digging into him, holding tight as he took her on a wild ride that just got faster and faster and more intense as it went.

Until bliss engulfed her and him at once, wrapping them in a whirlwind of primal, exquisite euphoria that suspended everything for that one endless moment, unmatched by anything that had come before.

When it passed, the sensations depleted her so totally that she nearly collapsed into Callan's waiting embrace, not having realized that somewhere along the way they'd come to their sides and were not only joined but entwined together. It was impossible to know where one of them began and the other left off.

There were a few moments of settling. Of calming. Of her pulse slowing back to normal, her breathing doing the same. Of wilting against the big, strong, muscular body wrapped around her.

"Amazing," Callan whispered in awe.

She couldn't refute or improve upon that, so merely murmured in response.

"Are you okay?" he asked.

"Ohh…yeah. Are you?"

He gave a throaty, replete laugh. "Ohh…yeah," he parroted back. Then, holding her a little tighter, he said, "Can I stay?"

It hadn't occurred to her that he might not. "I thought you would."

"Great," he said with an exhausted sigh, fully relaxing. He got up to dispose of the condom, and then settled back in beside her. She felt him tense as something else seemed to occur to him.

"The whole night," he added, as if he suddenly needed that specified. "I want to be here the whole night."

"I wasn't planning to kick you out as payback. Or disappear myself, to teach you a lesson," she said with a small laugh.

"I'd have it coming."

"The whole night," she confirmed sleepily.

Maybe he'd realized she was about to drift off, because he said, "Can I wake you up after we nap a little?"

She moaned, liking that idea a lot. "You can."

"Good," he said, resting his head atop hers as she nestled into his chest. He held her close as she felt him falling asleep.

And as she drew nearer and nearer to slumber herself, she suddenly had a moment of crystal clarity.

A moment in which she knew exactly what she had to do.

She had to tell him she was pregnant.

Chapter Ten

"Are you okay?"

This time Callan wasn't asking the question after a round of runaway lovemaking. He was asking it through Livi's bathroom door, after morning sickness had sent her running for the second time.

Sure, she'd decided to tell him she was pregnant, but she'd wanted to be able to choose the right moment, the right setting. Right now, just after he'd listened to her throwing up, really wasn't it. But she didn't seem to have much of a choice.

They'd had an incredible night together. But fearing what happened every morning, after their third round of lovemaking at nearly 5:00 a.m. on Sunday, Livi had tried to persuade Callan that he should go home before the Tellers or Greta got up and realized he'd been out all night.

He'd listened to and acted on all her other suggestions for this role he'd taken with his makeshift family. But not that one. And lying warmly, snugly, in his arms had felt so good she hadn't insisted.

Instead she'd fallen asleep, willing herself to wake up feeling fine. But just like every other day, at nearly the stroke of seven, nausea woke her up.

The everyday illness had settled into a pattern, though. After the second upchuck she knew she would be able to hold down a few soda crackers, and would be left with an upset stomach for only the next couple hours.

So she called back to Callan in answer, "I'm okay. I just need a minute."

Then she brushed her teeth, rinsed with mouthwash, pressed a cool cloth to her face, ran a brush through her hair and wrapped herself in her robe before going out.

To face the music.

"You don't look okay," Callan greeted her, frowning, sounding caring and compassionate.

Sick or not, Livi smiled weakly and wondered how he could look as good as he did right out of bed with his hair tousled and a scruff of beard shadowing his face. He'd pulled on his tuxedo pants and the shirt he'd worn the night before—left untucked and unbuttoned so a strip of his glorious chest and rock-hard abs peeked out, distracting her.

But right now she had to focus, to respond to his comment on her appearance. "Thanks," she said facetiously.

"You're beautiful, but you don't look well," he amended. "What's going on? Do you think you have the flu? This isn't some kind of extreme morning-after regret, is it?"

Livi laughed slightly. He'd clearly meant it as a joke,

but sounded a little worried that there might be a grain of truth to it.

She went to her nightstand and took a sleeve of crackers from the drawer. Turning back to Callan, she offered him one.

"Crackers? In here? Now?" he said, after he'd declined the offer.

Livi took a few for herself and returned the sleeve to her drawer. Apparently his ex-wife hadn't suffered morning sickness—or maybe Callan just hadn't been around enough during the pregnancy to know about the remedy that Livi's obstetrician had recommended.

"Keeping crackers in here and eating them first thing is not something I've done until lately," she said, thinking that waiting until now to tell him about the baby really did make it even harder to do.

But she knew she had to.

So she said, "The nausea *is* a morning-after thing, but not from last night." Taking her crackers, she went to sit on the end of her rumpled bed before she nibbled on one.

Callan came to stand in front of her, frowning down at her. "What does that mean?"

"I honestly didn't know whether to tell you this or not," she said with a sigh.

Then she took a steeling breath, shored up her courage, met his eyes with hers and said, "Remember that broken condom in Hawaii?"

She watched the color drain from his face. But he seemed at a loss for words as he just stood there, staring at her.

On the off chance that he might not have understood, she made it very clear. "I'm pregnant, Callan. A little over two months now."

"Pregnant…" he echoed, sounding thunderstruck.

Livi nodded. "I did a home test and then saw my doctor to confirm it." She told him her due date and saw him swallow.

The expression on his face wasn't merely a frown anymore. It had darkened into something more serious, something that reminded her of a gathering storm.

"Two and a half months," he repeated. "You've known for that long. You knew through this…" He pointed with a raise of his chin to the bed they'd shared all night.

"At first, I just couldn't face that it might be true. I've only *really* known and been able to accept it for a couple of weeks."

"A couple of weeks." More parroting, but with some outrage around the fringes. "The same couple of weeks we've been seeing each other, talking to each other… But again—we got all the way here last night without you telling me?"

He was definitely not happy.

But before Livi had the chance to say anything else, something seemed to dawn on him and make his ire grow. "Oh, my God, this is it, isn't it? This is really why you came around wanting contact with Greta! It wasn't to make up for what your family did to hers. That was just the cover story. You came to get to me. Mandy was right about you Camdens!"

Livi hadn't expected that.

"No! I was in Northbridge to see Greta. I knew she had a guardian, but I didn't have any idea it was you. I didn't even know your last name. And everything to do with Greta is completely separate from you or any of this—it was from the start, it is now and it will be from here on, regardless of what's going on between you and me. I was completely stunned to see you in Northbridge."

"Come on," he said skeptically. "Admit it—you realized you were pregnant and did something to figure out who the guy you'd spent the night with in Hawaii was, didn't you? You knew," he said accusingly. "You just put on a show when I walked into the Tellers' house that day. I'll bet your cousin Seth gave you the heads-up that the guy you were looking for was right there under his nose, and you all hatched some plot to get to me through Greta."

"That's not true," Livi insisted.

Callan huffed in disgust. "And just when I honestly thought the Camdens might be all right, after all. That Mandy would have been wrong to think of you in the same category with the Camdens who screwed over her dad. Just when I actually thought maybe you could be trusted…"

"There's no conspiracy, Callan. My family didn't even know until this past week—I told them Friday night, and Lang and Beau lectured me then, saying I needed to tell you. They were talking from your perspective, and I guess it sank in that you would *want* to know. But what you're saying now doesn't even make sense. Why would I need to use Greta to get to you? If I had known—or found out—who you are, what was there to keep me from just going where you live or work? What possible purpose could there be for doing it through Greta?"

Callan didn't have an answer for that, but he wasn't readily conceding to her reasoning, either. He still just stood there, his dark eyes boring into her suspiciously.

"Maybe I shouldn't have told you," she said then, thinking out loud.

But that just seemed to send him off onto a new path of anger. "I should have been the first to know—after you," he declared. "I sure as hell shouldn't have been the last. But then the end of the line does seem to be where I always am in these things."

Livi knew he was referring to his ex-wife's deception. "You aren't at the end of the line. My brother didn't know he was a father until Carter was two, and my cousin didn't find out that he'd gotten his high school girlfriend pregnant until just recently."

"Is that supposed to make this better?"

Livi's stomach lurched and she spent a moment waiting to see if she needed a third run for the bathroom, after all.

Only when she knew she was going to avoid throwing up again did she take a deep breath and say, "I know you already have your hands full with Greta and the Tellers. I wasn't sure you could handle more on top of it, especially when family is not really your thing. Not that you aren't trying, but still…" She took another small bite of the corner of a cracker to keep back the bile that seemed to be building again.

Then she said, "But Beau and Lang convinced me that you *could* handle it—that you *had* to know. So now you do. But if you want, you can just forget it."

"Forget it?" Callan shouted.

"I have a good support system," she went on, trying to reassure him. "I won't be alone in this. I don't need anything financially. If you don't want to see me again, then I can make that happen. We didn't see each other all last week. I can go on meeting with Greta the way I did, and you can go on about your business as if you were none the wiser. You can just concentrate on dealing with what you already have on your plate. It'll be fine. I'm giving you knowledge, not another obligation."

He released a huff filled with a combination of astonishment and fury and frustration and confusion—so many things that Livi went on to say, "I know this is huge. And believe me, it took me a *long* time to face it, to admit even to myself that it's happening. You need some time with it… I just want you to know up front that there are no expectations of you—"

He pressed all ten fingertips to his head as if to keep it from exploding, his eyes closed.

Livi had the sense that everything she was saying was making it worse—but she didn't know how to make things right.

Then he opened his eyes, took his hands away from his head and held them palms out. "I do have to wrap my head around this," he said, as if he didn't trust himself to say any more.

He started to button his shirt faster than she'd ever seen it done.

"Do you need me for anything right now?" he asked as he did. "Is there something I can do for the…sickness? Make you tea? Get you water? Something?"

It was the most irate offer to do something nice that she'd ever heard.

Livi shook her head. "I'm fine. I do this every morning. It passes."

And why on earth did she feel as if she was about to cry? Of course she hadn't fooled herself into believing that he would embrace this news and be thrilled with it the way Patrick would have been.

But rage and accusations, followed by Callan not being able to get away fast enough? Not only was it all a bad reaction, it was also an awful ending to the night they'd spent together. She wished they were still lying in bed, that she was wrapped in his arms, both of them just savoring the afterglow. But that couldn't happen now. Maybe it would never happen again. Instead she was sick and he was fuming.

They really didn't do the morning-after thing very well…

"You're sure there's nothing you need?" he asked.

"Positive," she said, struggling to keep her voice from cracking, to show him nothing but strength and proof that she could do this on her own.

"I need to think," he told her, as if he'd forgotten they'd already determined that.

She nodded and agreed. "You do."

She thought he would leave then. But for another moment he went on standing there, looking cross and confused and frustrated and helpless all at once. She didn't know why he didn't just go.

"It's okay," she assured him, sounding impatient in her attempt to conceal her own bewildering emotions. "Leave!"

She wasn't sure why that had come out so harsh, but it had.

Callan snatched up what remained of his discarded clothes and went to her bedroom door. But even once he reached it, with his hand on the knob, he didn't rush out.

Instead he paused there, looking back in her direction, but at the floor.

"You were right to tell me. But not to wait until now."

Livi didn't say anything. She couldn't. Not with a throat full of tears.

After a moment of only silence from her, Callan opened

the door and went out. Moments later, she heard her front door open and slam shut.

And that was when she recognized the feelings she was having.

Feelings she hadn't ever expected to have again.

The same feelings she'd had when it had sunk in that she'd lost Patrick.

Only this time they were all about Callan.

Chapter Eleven

"What am I doing?" Callan shouted, when he emerged from his fog and registered where he was—at his office building. But it was Sunday morning and when he'd stormed out of Livi's house it had been with the intention of going home.

Cursing, he hit his steering wheel with the heels of his hands as if the car was to blame for taking him to the wrong place. But the truth was he had so much on his mind that he'd driven without thinking.

Disgusted with himself, he slammed the gearshift into reverse and backed out of his parking spot to try again.

But his mind detoured once more, back to Livi and what she'd just told him.

She was pregnant.

Another rug pulled out from under him, with another pregnancy.

Maybe this baby wasn't his, either.

"You didn't even ask that, you idiot!" he said to himself.

Considering that he'd already had one woman try to pass off someone else's baby on him, that should have been his first question. But it had only just occurred to him.

Why was that? he wondered, as he pulled out of the parking garage and headed for his condominium.

Maybe it was because he didn't really doubt that he was the father.

The condom *had* broken, he reminded himself. Plus, everything he'd learned about Livi's past, about her and the kind of person she was, didn't leave him any doubts that he really had been the first man she'd been with since her husband's death.

"Yeah, but she could have come back from Hawaii and really cut loose," he argued with himself angrily.

But livid or not, he still knew that that wasn't Livi, either. She'd been so shocked that *anyone* had been able to shake her loyalty to her late soul mate. Spending the night with him in Hawaii had been way, way too monumental to her to have gone beyond that.

Until last night…

But he didn't want to think about last night. Last night had been mind-blowing, and remembering any part of it blunted the force of that bomb she'd dropped on him. And he didn't want it blunted. Not when he needed to see beyond the attraction between them to figure out how to deal with the fact that she was pregnant.

Pregnant, for God's sake.

And this time he was sure it was his.

Yet he somehow felt just as betrayed as he had when he'd found out his assistant had fathered his wife's baby.

How come? Callan asked himself. One baby was his, one wasn't, and those weren't the same…

But he'd still been left in the dark both times. He'd still felt played both times.

Played by Elly, who had been his wife and should have been loyal to him.

Played by Livi, who he'd just started to drop his guard with. Who he'd just started to trust. To let in the way he'd let in Mandy and J.J. And Elly. Just so he could be as blindsided by Livi as he had been by his ex-wife.

That was why the betrayal felt the same.

There was a part of him that wanted to push Livi away. To punish her. To protect himself. A part of him that wanted to just say to hell with her and everything to do with her! He didn't need another woman in his life who wasn't up-front with him!

But even as furious as he was, he couldn't forget that there was going to be a baby.

His baby.

And if that was the case, he couldn't say to hell with anything…

His condo was near his office, so it didn't take long to get home. This time when he parked, he turned off the engine and got out.

He was glad not to meet anyone as he stepped into the waiting elevator, then ferociously punched the button for his floor.

As the doors closed, he drew both hands through his hair, pulling hard on his scalp as if that might calm him down.

It didn't. And when he'd gotten off the elevator and

went across to his door, he jammed his key into the lock with a vengeance.

He was just so damn mad! He'd actually been thinking that Livi was something special. That things with her might have a chance of going somewhere.

Then she had to go and pull this!

He opened the door and went in, to find John Sr. already up and sitting at the island counter in his kitchen, drinking a cup of coffee.

Great.

"Morning," Callan grumbled to the elderly man, barely civil.

John Sr. gave him a once-over that took in the fact that he was wearing the same clothes he'd had on last night. But all his late best friend's father said was, "Morning."

Callan considered what to do in this situation.

What he wanted to do was just be alone.

But *that* wasn't going to happen.

On the other hand, he was an adult who sure as hell shouldn't have to feel embarrassed or ashamed of having spent a night with a woman.

And he wasn't going to slink off to his bedroom as if he was.

So he tried again to get some control over his temper, tossed his tuxedo coat and tie over the arm of the sofa, and joined the older man in the kitchen, where he poured himself a cup of coffee.

Unfortunately, there were still too many emotions running through him—running him—and when he went to stand at the island across from John Sr., the best Callan could do was set his cup down, lean on his elbows and hold his head.

"Your party didn't go well?" John Sr. asked.

"It went fine. Big success. Raised more money than ever before," he answered.

"Long night, though…" the elderly man said.

"Yeah."

"With Livi?"

Oh, the old man was pushing it.

But Callan wasn't a teenager under John Sr.'s roof now. He was a grown man, in his own home, and he was going to do whatever he damn well pleased without tiptoeing around it.

"Yeah," he said, intending to sound firm.

Instead it had come out with a mixture of the emotions cascading through him.

"I like that girl," John Sr. said.

"Yeah. Me, too." But there was still that edge of anger in the admission. He'd liked who he thought she was, yet he still wondered if she'd been playing him. It was true—there was no logical reason for her to try to get to him through Greta, but people weren't always logical when it came to getting what they wanted.

The other man ignored his tone. "She's a nice girl. Some in her family before her might have been bastards, but I don't think it's carried on in those folks now. Especially not in Livi. I think she only means well. She's been good for Greta. Good for Maeve and me, too—bendin' over backward for us same as Kinsey, only without any paycheck comin' her way."

The old man chose now *to get wordy?* Callan thought.

He nodded but didn't comment, loath to listen to anything at the moment.

"Wouldn't want to think the good in her is bein' overlooked," John Sr. said, as if finally making his point.

The point being, Callan thought, that John Sr. still

saw him as little more than a troublemaker who was doing Livi wrong.

But while his instinctive response was to get even more riled up, he also couldn't help thinking that in this situation Livi would tell him he had to have patience. That he had to resist the past roles, the past patterns. That he had to work on forging a new relationship with this man.

And somewhere in that, something else suddenly dawned on Callan.

Here, sitting in his kitchen, was someone who had been married to the same woman for decades. Someone who was committed to doing whatever it took to care for his ailing wife—even when it meant leaving the home and land he loved and had worked on his entire life, to live in the home of someone he'd never liked. And it crossed Callan's mind that maybe he should mine that a little.

So he pushed himself off the counter to stand up straight and look J.J.'s father in the eye.

"How do you do it?" he asked.

Bushy gray eyebrows arched over rheumy eyes. "How do I do what?"

"The whole marriage-relationship thing. How long have you and Maeve been together?"

"Oh, better 'n fifty years."

"So how does that work? Because…I don't know. I blew it once. I don't know what's going on now… Maybe I just don't get it. Every time I think things are good, I get knocked on my ass."

Once-strong shoulders shrugged. "No master plan I can give you. Knew from the minute I laid eyes on Maeve that I was a better man with her than without her. That

I was nothin' without her. Always loved her. Always wanted to be with her."

"And you'll do anything, go anywhere, swallow whatever you have to swallow to do it?"

"What do I have to swallow?"

Callan started to list all the enormous changes the man was accepting.

But as he got into it, John Sr. began to shake his head, and when Callan had finished, the elderly man said, "Means nothin' to me. Maeve's what means something. Greta. Whatever it takes to be with 'em is what it takes. Otherwise, no Maeve. No Greta. And that'd be worse than anything I can think of."

"Maeve never went about something the worst way she could have? Enough to piss you off no end?" Callan muttered.

The old man laughed. "Hell, yes, she has. So what? Pissed her off plenty, too. Means nothin' in the long run."

"No matter what? No matter how complicated it gets? No matter what might be in the way?"

"Guess it would depend how big what got in the way was. For us? Nothin' was ever too big, too complicated to where it meant more than keeping what we've got. Not even now, leavin' Northbridge."

Callan stared into his coffee cup, feeling John Sr.'s eyes on him, expecting this to turn at any moment, for the judgmental voice of his youth to sound again.

But instead, as John Sr. picked up his own cup and took it to the sink, the elderly man said, "Nothin' worth havin' comes easy, boy. Trick is figurin' out what's worth havin'—and what's not—before you know what you can *swallow* and what you can't."

Then he headed into the room he shared with Maeve and left Callan alone.

To stew.

Because he *was* still stewing. He couldn't move past how much he hated it that in all the time he and Livi had spent together—including the night they'd just had together—she'd known she was pregnant with his baby and he hadn't. That she'd kept something that big from him. That, for even one minute, she'd pulled the wool over his eyes.

He hated it!

He *hated* it!

He sighed.

But I don't hate her...

He leaned on the counter, held his head again and tried harder to cool off.

How much of what he was feeling was his own past haunting him? How much of his anger at Livi was really lingering outrage at being made a fool by Elly and Trent?

Some of it, Callan admitted.

And he also acknowledged that Livi had kept the news from him for only a couple weeks after a period of denial herself. That couldn't really compare to the six months his wife had let him believe that he was the father of her baby. At least there was no lie in what Livi had done; there was just a brief omission. And the first opportunity she'd had to tell him—that day at the Tellers' farm— she'd still been rightfully furious with him for abandoning her after their encounter. Would he really have expected her to trust him with news of her pregnancy right away after that?

So maybe calling it a betrayal was somewhat of an exaggeration...

He pushed up from the counter a second time and sighed away a large portion of his rage.

But that just made way for something else.

She'd said she was worried that he had too much on his plate for anything else—and she wasn't exactly wrong. There were so many elements that still made this whole thing overwhelming—work and Greta and the Tellers and learning how to be all he needed to be for so many people already. And now there would be another kid—his own kid—and Livi...

Livi...

Okay, yeah, just the thought of her now—without unreasonable irritation—had its way with him again.

So-o-o...what if there wasn't anything at stake here but *Livi?* he asked himself, thinking then of what John Sr. had said.

Is she my Maeve?

He and Livi were good together—there was no doubt about that. Great together, actually. In *and* out of bed. Their sexual chemistry was off the charts, but every other minute they were together was great, too. Talking to her seemed to put even the worst day right again. Just being with her was its own kind of refuge—like an island where chaos got sorted through and put in order. Where she helped guide him to better ways of handling problems that otherwise seemed insurmountable.

Like John Sr. had said about Maeve, Callan thought that he was a better man with Livi's help. And, yes, he wanted to be better *for* her, too—which was why he'd altered his work schedule last week to make sure that his job didn't get in the way of his relationships. His relationship with Livi included, because he'd expected to see her last week.

And when he hadn't? When night after night he'd gone home to dinner hoping she'd be there and she wasn't?

He'd felt a gaping hole where she should have been. Even surrounded by the Tellers and Greta and Kinsey, who all made for a much fuller house than he'd ever been used to. But still, without Livi, it had seemed empty to him. Drab and colorless. Lacking its most important part.

Because Livi *was* the most important part, he realized suddenly.

The way Maeve was for John Sr.

Livi was the first thing he thought about when he woke up in the morning. She was who he thought about in terms of everything—what he wore, what he ate, how he scheduled his day and—like this morning—even how he treated other people in his life.

She was who he wanted to be with every minute. Who he wanted to share every piece of news with.

Even today, when he'd been furious with her, he'd still found it hard to leave her.

So she *was* his Maeve...

But thinking that brought Callan back around to the rest—to having Maeve and John Sr. and Greta already in his life, already his responsibility in ways that demanded more of him than he'd thought they would.

It brought him back around to the struggles he was already having balancing work with commitments at home.

It brought him back around to the whole complicated mess that also included his lost friend, who would go ballistic at the idea of a Camden in the life of her daughter.

It brought him back around to the late husband Livi idolized.

And now there would be a baby, too?

Callan leaned over the counter yet again to put his head in his hands.

That was a lot.

But just as John Sr. had decided it was worth anything to him to have Maeve, Callan realized that it was worth anything to him to have Livi. Livi and their baby.

More work, more adjustments, more relationships for him to figure out. But it was still all worth it.

Because otherwise there was no Livi.

And John Sr. was right—nothing was as bad as that.

For a moment Callan felt the weight of everything on his shoulders. Of even more to come with a baby on the way. But somehow feeling that weight and thinking about having Livi to help him with it suddenly made it all seem workable.

"Here's how it is, Mandy," he whispered to the memory of his friend. "You're gonna have to trust me that Livi is different than the Camdens who sank your dad. You're gonna have to trust me that it's not only good to have her around Greta, but that Livi makes me better at being your daughter's guardian."

And in thinking about his late friends, he also suddenly knew that Livi gave him what Mandy and J.J. had had.

Elly hadn't—there had never been the kind of closeness that Mandy and J.J. shared, the bond, the connection.

But with Livi it was all there. That and so much more.

Feelings that were deeper and stronger.

He loved her. With a power and a passion that he'd never known was in him.

"And I walked out on her again…" he groaned when that occurred to him. "After accusing her of some pretty awful things." He wished now that he hadn't done that. And wondered how much damage it might have caused.

Especially when he recalled her telling him pretty bitterly to leave…

Yeah, that wasn't good, he thought.

But no matter how things had been left between them, he wanted her, loved her, too much to let anything get in their way.

And he wanted her too much to let any more time go by without telling her that.

Chapter Twelve

Weeks of morning sickness had taught Livi showers helped. So after an hour of crying and fretting about what had happened with Callan— and feeling even worse than usual—she called upon what little energy and strength she had, and went into the bathroom to shower and shampoo her hair.

The spray of water washed the tears away, but couldn't stop them from falling. The last thing she wanted to do was go to her grandmother's house that evening for Sunday dinner with red puffy eyes and a swollen face. So once she turned her shower off, she put every effort into turning off her own waterworks, too. But her sadness wasn't as easily stifled.

What would have happened if she'd told Callan as soon as they'd met again in Northbridge? She couldn't help wondering.

But *she* hadn't even been able to accept it then; she hadn't even bought the home pregnancy test until after that Sunday when they'd met again at the Tellers' and she hadn't taken it until after that. And she'd still thought that he'd ditched her in Hawaii. Even once he'd told her the truth, she'd needed time to adjust her thinking and accept what had happened.

Had she handled everything perfectly? No. But it wasn't as if any of this had been easy. It wasn't as if she had any experience with this.

So what if she'd bided her time a little?

So what if she'd taken a misstep by not telling him the second she'd stopped denying it herself?

It wasn't as if *that* much time had gone by before she *had* told him. It wasn't as if he'd found out some other way.

What had she done that was so wrong? she wondered, beginning to find some solace in getting a little angry herself.

The condom had broken—that wasn't the fault of either of them, and the pregnancy was as big a shock to her as it was to Callan. What gave him the right to get on his high horse and ride out of here the way he had? Much less accuse her of using Greta in such an underhanded way. Didn't he know her better than that?

"Jerk," she muttered, as she wrapped a towel around herself and tucked the corner in to keep it in place.

Anger felt better than hurt, so she hung on to that as she blow-dried her hair. But when she took a look at herself in the bathroom mirror, she saw plainly that neither anger nor her shower had erased the evidence of her crying.

Maybe lying down for a while with a cold washcloth on her face would help.

She wet a fresh one, then took it with her into the bedroom.

Where Callan was sitting on the end of her bed as if he'd never left. He was even dressed the same way he had been in his tuxedo pants and shirt.

And maybe she was a little angrier than she thought. Because after the initial shock of finding him there, Livi threw the washcloth at him.

It hit him smack in the center of that broad chest.

"You left!" she said heatedly. "What are you doing here now and how did you get in?"

He put the wet washcloth on the bed beside him.

"I did leave," he replied. "But I guess I didn't lock the door behind me. And apparently you didn't notice and lock it yourself, because when you didn't answer the bell, I tried the door and it was open. Not really safe…"

"Well, since it was you who didn't lock it on your way out, thanks," she said facetiously. "Try to do better on your way out now."

"I'm not going anywhere," he said flatly. "I shouldn't have left before. I'm sorry for that."

Livi only raised her chin, not offering instant forgiveness or acceptance or encouragement. But not *dis*couraging him, either, merely waiting to see what came next.

"You hit a hot button, Livi," he said then, not sounding completely calm himself. "You have to understand— after six months of Elly making a fool out of me, *no* amount of time being kept in the dark about another pregnancy can sit well. But…" He sighed and seemed to let whatever remained of his anger release on that breath. "I know a couple of weeks isn't the huge deal that I made it into. And I shouldn't have done that. I definitely shouldn't have accused you of using Greta—I know you'd never do that. It's just that when my trust in you was shaken, I didn't know what to believe, so I defaulted back to my old opinion of Camdens. That wasn't fair to you, or to your family, who were nothing but kind and welcoming to me and the others when we came to dinner."

Livi did understand how any delay in finding out he was going to be a father could trigger old issues for him. And she understood why Callan might assume the worst of any Camden. But she still wasn't going to cave that easily, so she just raised her chin a notch higher.

"And you gotta admit, it's a shock to find out there's a baby on the way," he said, his tone, arched eyebrows and crinkled forehead all conveying that fact.

"For me, too," she reminded him curtly.

"I'm sure." There was empathy in his tone that pushed some of her own anger away.

But she still wasn't sure why he'd come back.

So she went on standing there, wrapped in her towel, trying to be strong when she felt anything but.

Callan stood up and met her gaze.

"I don't know if you know it or not," he said, "but you're an amazing person, Livi Camden. You're gorgeous and smart and wise and kind and generous and funny and fun to be with and…well, a million other things that make you seem like some kind of hidden treasure to me. You open my eyes and widen my horizons and make me better than I am. Better than I ever have been."

Was this a lead-in to him saying "so it's not you, it's me"?

"A lot went through my head when I left here," he

continued. "First and foremost that I didn't ask you if the baby is mine—"

Livi stiffened.

"But then I realized," he went on, "that the reason it didn't even occur to me is *because* you are all the things you are and there's really no way that baby *isn't* mine."

"It is," she felt compelled to say.

"I know. And I also know that trusting you enough not to doubt it—after Elly—is a very, very big thing. Almost as big a thing as the way I feel about you."

But he didn't go on to tell her how he felt about her. Instead he laid out for her all the things he'd thought about between when he'd left and when he'd returned, and the conclusions he'd come to.

Then, when he seemed to have covered all the bases, he took a step closer, peering down at her solemnly. "I know I'm just beginning to get the hang of parenthood, and you're right, I'm in the deep end with just about everything right now. But there's still no way I'm not going to be involved in my own kid's life. And I want it to be hand in hand with you. I want dealing with all that stuff that I'm in over my head with to be hand in hand with you, too—even if it does seem a little unfair to ask that of you."

Another step toward her, close enough that he could have reached out and touched her. But he didn't. And despite everything, she still wanted him to.

"I know I'm up against that two-halves-of-a-whole business about Patrick," Callan said. "I know you've gone through the last four years convinced that there couldn't be anyone else for you. But I think that if you just consider how good we are together, what we have when we're together..." He stalled. Then said, "I think together we make two halves of a new whole. A whole of our own. And maybe I'll never measure up, but I'm willing to spend my life working on it. If you'll let me…"

He paused again, looked more deeply into her eyes and said, "I love you, Livi. Believe it or not, John Sr. actually helped me weed through things this morning to realize that. And even if there wasn't a baby on board, I'd still be here telling you this and asking you to give me another chance."

Apparently he was taking a turn at shocking her. And she didn't know whether it was that shock that sent a noticeable shiver through her or if it came from still standing there naked but for a damp towel.

"I need to put something on," she said. Which might have been true. But she also needed a moment to herself, a moment to think.

Callan nodded once, his expression making it clear that he feared the worst and was waiting for the hammer to drop. "I'm not leaving again," he informed her. "I came back to say what I've said and to take care of you while you're sick, and that's what I'm going to do no matter what. But I can wait downstairs while you get dressed if you want. Maybe fix you something for breakfast?"

"Crackers are all I can eat in the morning. But if you're hungry, then you could have something—coffee or whatever you find in the kitchen—and I'll be there in a minute."

"Okay," he agreed, but he didn't go anywhere, he just kept standing there, watching her as if he thought she might sneak out on him if he didn't.

So Livi turned and went into her closet, closing the door between them.

She was genuinely cold now, so she dropped the towel

and dressed in a hurry, opting for the comfort of gray sweatpants and a white T-shirt that fitted like a ballet top.

Still chilled, she also pulled on a black angora shrug, then grabbed fuzzy socks and sat on the upholstered bench to pull them on.

But the minute she was sitting she forgot about putting on the socks. Because she was facing Patrick's side of the closet.

His clothes were all gone, but in her mind's eye she still saw his shirts and jackets and slacks hanging just the way they used to be.

And as she stared at that empty space, she realized how distant Patrick felt now. She'd had not thought of him whatsoever in all the time she'd spent getting ready for the previous evening's auction, spending that evening—and then the night—with Callan. She realized that even this morning Patrick had been only a reference point, that his memory hadn't had the kind of presence it had had for her since his death.

Instead, everything had been Callan, Callan, Callan...

Callan, who was not Patrick.

But who, it seemed, loved her and wanted her.

That wasn't something she'd ever expected to hear again. And now that she had, she had to admit that the words had meant every bit as much coming from Callan as they had when Patrick had said them.

Maybe it was time that it was Callan alone she thought about...

"I'm sorry, Patrick," she said. "But I...think it's time for me to move on." Because it was Callan's baby she was having. Callan waiting for her downstairs. Callan, who had just told her he loved her.

And who she had to admit she loved, too.

Callan, who was warm and kind and sweet and caring and compassionate—even if that wasn't always visible on the surface, it slipped out from behind a protective barrier when he let down his guard.

But Livi understood that. Not only because her own shyness sometimes made her the same way, but because of how Callan had grown up. Of course he would have to feel comfortable with people before he let himself be vulnerable with them. And of course he wouldn't be family oriented; of course being in close relationships was difficult for him.

But look what he made of himself, Livi thought.

Yes, maybe he'd caused a little trouble as a kid, but he'd grown up to be an enormous success. And with that success, he'd chosen to give back with his charity auction, to provide generously for the Tellers and Greta, bringing them into his home and life.

It didn't matter that it wasn't coming easy to him. It mattered that he was willing to do it. That he was working hard now on those relationships.

That he had the kind of character all those things spoke of.

So while Callan thought he couldn't *measure up* to Patrick, the more Livi thought about him, the more she knew he genuinely did.

Patrick had taken her out of her shell when she was a little girl, and Callan had brought her out of the grieving haze that she'd been denying she was in.

Callan had lured her out of the limbo she'd been left in since Patrick's death, and helped her to see that she *was* still alive and well and kicking—what he'd said the night she'd told him about Patrick.

Being with Callan opened her up. It made her see the

world again as a brighter, more hopeful place. It gave her a dimension outside the cocoon of her own family that she'd crawled into, and put her in a place where she saw a future for herself that she hadn't seen since Patrick's death. Callan had shown her that there honestly could be a full life for her again. And he'd given her a baby to help that along.

A baby she believed—now that she'd seen how Callan had prioritized his relationships with Greta and the Tellers—he wouldn't neglect. A baby who instead would benefit from the work Callan was doing to be a dad to Greta.

And most of all, he'd shown her that she was capable of loving another man—him. That even though she'd loved Patrick with all her heart and soul, he wasn't the *only* man she could love.

"Oh, Patrick, it isn't that I don't love you, too. I do. It's just that..."

It was just that she loved Callan equally as much.

Somehow she didn't feel as guilty for that as she'd thought she would. Instead she felt something else—a sort of peace in it, a strong sense that loving Callan, too, was okay, almost as if Patrick was there with her and letting her know that.

Maybe he was. Or maybe it was just that she'd known Patrick so well that she knew he *would* be okay with this. That he would *want* her to be happy even without him.

"Callan is a good man, Patrick," she assured her late husband, as if he really was there with her. "And there's a baby..."

A baby and more life waiting for her that she knew now she needed to live.

Livi suffered a moment of sadness to think that Patrick hadn't had more life himself. But even in that sadness she didn't feel held back. She finally felt ready, willing and able to move on.

Still staring at Patrick's side of the closet, she kissed the air—the way she would have hurriedly kissed Patrick goodbye before leaving the house for work.

Then she left the closet, sat on the edge of the bed to put on the fuzzy socks and went downstairs.

Callan was in the kitchen, just turning from her counter with two slices of toast on a plate as Livi reached the doorway.

"Hi," he said tentatively when he spotted her. "I know you said you didn't want anything, but I was thinking maybe a little dry toast…"

Livi went the rest of the way into the kitchen, standing on the opposite side of the counter from him. "Actually, the nausea seems to be going away early this morning," she told him, only realizing then that it was true.

He offered her the plate, but it wasn't food she wanted. It was him. She just wasn't sure how to get their previous conversation back on track. So she took the plate and a bite of the toast to buy herself a moment.

"Coffee, too?" Callan asked.

She shook her head, set the plate on the counter between them and said, "I don't really want anything to eat or drink, but thanks for trying."

"Thanks for trying…" he repeated. "That isn't for more than the toast, is it? It isn't the start of a kiss-off?"

"It's only for the toast," she said, seeing that he was still fearing what she might say to him now that he'd opened up to her.

"I need to know something for sure," she said then.

"Anything."

"I need to know that what you said upstairs wasn't just what you thought you had to say. If you want a relationship with your child, then I'll support that completely. Our relationship doesn't have to be a part of it."

He shook his head. "I told you that I'd be here telling you that I love you even if there wasn't a baby on board."

"I know that's what you *said*, but…I'm not a teenage girl in trouble, Callan. I don't need to be made an honest woman. And we can raise a child together without being anything to each other."

He closed his eyes and took a breath, as if bracing himself. Then he opened them and said fatalistically, "You don't want anything with me. You won't even give me a chance—"

"No, that's not what I'm saying. You said you talked to John Sr. this morning, and if this is coming from him pressuring you to 'do the right thing'—"

"I didn't even tell him about the baby. All we talked about was how he feels about Maeve and Greta, and how it's nothing to him to have uprooted his whole life, because otherwise he wouldn't have Maeve. Or Greta. And I realized that I feel the same way about you."

"You'd uproot your life for me?" she joked.

"Yes," Callan said without hesitation.

"You're sure? You're already stretched pretty thin…" she said, persisting with the joke just to give him a hard time.

"I've never been more sure of anything in my life than that I want you. Sure enough to risk Mandy coming back to haunt me for bringing in a Camden to co-parent her daughter."

"So it *was* a proposal upstairs?" Livi asked, recalling that the exact words had not been spoken.

"What did you think it was?"

"Just making sure."

"Because you want to know what you're saying no to?" There was just enough cockiness in his tone to let her know he was feeling less vulnerable. But she liked that.

"I'm not saying no," she told him, going on to also tell him how wrong he was to think even for a minute that he didn't measure up to Patrick in her eyes, how great she thought he was.

"But I've had the real thing," she concluded. "And I don't want to go from that to someone being with me because there's a gun to his back."

Callan grinned and stepped around the counter. He took her arm and turned her to face him. "I was thinking that it might take a gun to *your* back to get you where I want you."

"You mean, as part of your family?" Livi said.

"Is that what we can all be?" he asked, testing the waters. "Is that what you'll let us be? Because I may be lousy at it, but it's what I want. With you. You and them and this baby."

"Families come in all shapes and sizes," she allowed.

"But will you—can you—come and be that with the rest of us?"

She knew what he was asking—if she could leave her past behind. If she would.

Livi didn't have to think any more about it before she told him what she'd realized while she was in the closet, even telling him that she believed they had Patrick's blessing.

"I don't know how it happened," she said. "I didn't

think it *could* happen. But I love you, Callan. Just as much as I loved Patrick."

Callan's eyebrows shot up as if that came as a surprise to him. "You're not just saying *that*, are you?"

"I'm not. I guess there really can be more than one love of my life."

"A two-and-only?" he said.

Livi laughed at the made-up phrase. "I don't think there is such a thing. Maybe we should just look at it as the second half for us both. And in this half, you'll be the one-and-only man I have a baby with, a family with..."

"Oh, I like that!" he said effusively, and if she wasn't mistaken, his eyes suddenly had a little extra moisture in them.

Then both his hands went to her arms, clamping them gently but firmly—as if to keep her from getting away. "So will you marry me, Livi?"

"I will," she said, surprised to ever be saying that again.

Callan smiled once more before he pulled her close enough to kiss her, so deeply that it laid bare all his feelings for her and chased away any last doubts.

When the kiss ended, he pressed her close, holding her head to his chest. "I don't know how this morning-sickness thing works. Is kissing a bad thing?"

She laughed again. "Not this morning."

But with her own arms around him, her hands grasping his strong back, and his arms wrapping her like a big, warm comforter, it all felt too good to disturb by raising her face even to have him kiss her again.

Instead she just stood there with him holding her, her holding him, and letting herself get used to the fact that this would be where she belonged from here on.

In the arms of a man who wasn't Patrick.

But who had given her her life back and now wanted to share it with her.

Epilogue

"Oh, Conor, finally!" Kinsey Madison said when she connected with her brother for a video chat.

It was six o'clock on Monday morning and she'd been waiting tensely for this since 5:00 a.m. to accommodate the time difference between Denver and Germany.

"Is Declan okay?" she asked.

"He came through the third surgery just fine," her oldest brother said. "He's in recovery. They were able to save the leg."

"Thank God," Kinsey said. "Is he awake?"

"Not completely or I'd let you talk to him—I'm in recovery with him. He's responsive, but he can only keep his eyes open for a few seconds before he drifts out again. That's normal. But what's important is that we'll have him back up and around before you know it."

"So he won't get a medical discharge," Kinsey concluded.

"He can apply for one, and at this point, get it if he wants it," Conor said.

"*If* he wants it. But you guys…" She shook her head in frustration. "You just won't ever do what I wish you would and come home for good."

"Actually," Conor said, as if he'd been waiting to surprise her, "I've filled out my discharge papers, Kins."

"Really?"

"Really. I haven't turned them in yet—and I won't right now, so I can stay with Declan until he's well again, to oversee his care. But after that…"

Kinsey sighed. "After that there will be some other reason for you not to turn in the papers, and the three of you still won't come home," she said dejectedly.

Raised by an ex-military stepfather, her brothers had had the military and service to country ingrained in them from earliest childhood.

"Things are different this time," Conor said, but not with enough conviction to convince her. "With the drawdown to reduce active-duty forces, the ranks are being trimmed. Could be I can do more stateside."

"In Denver?" Kinsey asked dubiously, knowing she shouldn't get her hopes up.

"I don't know, maybe. I know from here Declan will go to Bethesda, Maryland, and I'll go with him. Then we'll see. But once he's doing well in Maryland, I'll come home for a visit, anyway."

Visits were all that ever actually happened. Brief visits that were few and far, far between.

Without pinning too many hopes on anything, she said, "So I'll at least get to see you—and maybe Declan once he's on the mend. And how's Liam?"

"He's good. He made it to the base yesterday before

we left on transport. He's talking about the drawdown, too. Who knows, you might have all three of us back in the next year."

"I know what you guys are doing, Conor. You want to make me think there's that chance so I don't do anything about the Camdens."

"We know you're alone now that Mom's gone, Kins. None of us like that. We all feel bad about it—"

She cut him off to say, "I've met them—the Camdens— since I talked to you last…"

"Oh, no! You told them?" Conor moaned. "You said we could talk more about it before you would."

"I haven't *done* anything. I met them by happenstance. Remember the job I took with the Tellers? That I could start in Northbridge and then transition back to Denver? Well, it's a long story I won't go into now, but Livi Camden got involved with the Tellers' granddaughter, Greta, and I met Livi through that. Then I went to one of the Camden Sunday dinners and met the rest of them. I think it's a sign."

"It *isn't* a sign," Conor insisted. "It's a coincidence, Kinsey. And not a far-reaching one. We grew up in Northbridge and that's where the Camdens were from. You were there to take care of Mom, and then went to Denver, where the Camdens live. It's not like you went to the ends of the earth and bumped into one of them— *that* would be a sign."

"Mom told me the truth about our father so I could look up the Camdens. So I wouldn't be alone, since you guys keep going off halfway around the world," Kinsey said, taking a different tack.

"Mom told you to explain where all that money came from," Conor corrected. "Mom and Hugh Madison were our parents. They're who raised us. Our biological father doesn't matter. Just have some patience, Kinsey. I'm coming home. Declan may *need* to come home. And if we both do, maybe Liam will, too. Just let the other lay."

But Kinsey didn't know if she could do that.

Now that she knew she and her brothers were all half Camdens, she just wasn't sure she could keep it quiet.

* * * * *

Love the Camdens? Well, there are still some left to meet... Look for Kinsey and Sutter's story, coming in March 2017 only from Mills & Boon Cherish.

MILLS & BOON®

Cherish™

EXPERIENCE THE ULTIMATE RUSH OF FALLING IN LOVE

A sneak peek at next month's titles...

In stores from 8th September 2016:

- **A Mistletoe Kiss with the Boss** – Susan Meier *and*
  Maverick vs Maverick – Shirley Jump
- **A Countess for Christmas** – Christy McKellen *and*
  Ms Bravo and the Boss – Christine Rimmer

In stores from 6th October 2016:

- **Her Festive Baby Bombshell** – Jennifer Faye *and*
  Building the Perfect Daddy – Brenda Harlen
- **The Unexpected Holiday Gift** – Sophie Pembroke *and*
  The Man She Should Have Married – Patricia Kay

Just can't wait?
Buy our books online a month before they hit the shops!
www.millsandboon.co.uk

Also available as eBooks.

MILLS & BOON®

EXCLUSIVE EXCERPT

Emma Carmichael's world is turned upside-down
when she encounters Jack Westwood—her
secret husband of six years!

Read on for a sneak preview of
A COUNTESS FOR CHRISTMAS
the first book in the enchanting new Cherish quartet
MAIDS UNDER THE MISTLETOE

'You still have your ring,' Jack said.

'Of course.' Emma was frowning now and wouldn't
meet his eye.

'Why—?' He walked to where she was standing
with her hand gripping her handbag so hard her
knuckles were white.

'I'm not very good at letting go of the past,' she
said, shrugging and tilting up her chin to look him
straight in the eye, as if to dare him to challenge her
about it. 'I don't have a lot left from my old life and
I couldn't bear to get rid of this ring. It reminds me of
a happier time in my life. A simpler time, which I don't
want to forget about.'

She blinked hard and clenched her jaw together
and it suddenly occurred to him that she was struggling with being around him as much as he was with
her.

The atmosphere hung heavy and tense between them,

with only the sound of their breathing breaking the silence.

His throat felt tight with tension and his pulse had picked up so he felt the heavy beat of it in his chest.

Why was it so important to him that she hadn't completely eschewed their past?

He didn't know, but it was.

Taking a step towards her, he slid his fingers under the thin silver chain around her neck, feeling the heat of her soft skin as he brushed the backs of his fingers over it, and drew the ring out of her dress again to look at it.

He remembered picking this out with her. They'd been so happy then, so full of excitement and love for each other.

He heard her ragged intake of breath as the chain slid against the back of her neck and looked up to see confusion in her eyes, and something else. Regret, perhaps, or sorrow for what they'd lost.

Something seemed to be tugging hard inside him, drawing him closer to her.

Her lips parted and he found he couldn't drag his gaze away from her mouth. That beautiful, sensual mouth that used to haunt his dreams all those years ago.

A lifetime ago.